FAKE IT LIKE YOU MEAN IT

FAKE IT LIKE YOU MEAN IT

A Novel

MEGAN MURPHY

alcove
press

This is a work of fiction. All of the names, characters, organizations, places and events portrayed in this novel are either products of the author's imagination or are used fictitiously. Any resemblance to real or actual events, locales, or persons, living or dead, is entirely coincidental.

Copyright © 2025 by Megan Murphy

All rights reserved.

Published in the United States by Alcove Press, an imprint of The Quick Brown Fox & Company LLC.

Alcove Press and its logo are trademarks of The Quick Brown Fox & Company LLC.

Library of Congress Catalog-in-Publication data available upon request.

ISBN (paperback): 979-8-89242-064-8
ISBN (hardcover): 979-8-89242-229-1
ISBN (ebook): 979-8-89242-065-5

Cover design by Stephanie Singleton

Printed in the United States.

www.alcovepress.com

Alcove Press
34 West 27th St., 10th Floor
New York, NY 10001

First Edition: March 2025

10 9 8 7 6 5 4 3 2 1

For Michelle—I wrote Adam for Elle, but also for you.
You deserve a love so big it doesn't fit on the pages.
I tried my best.

And for Ethan, always—you are in every story I write.
All my best lines come from you, are for you, are about you.

AUTHOR'S NOTE

Dear Reader,

This book is an ode to the people and the places that have formed me, either directly or indirectly, into the person I am still becoming. It explores the phenomenon whereby even if we don't have a specific memory of somewhere, something, someone, the feelings elicited can be lasting and true. Elle and Lovie's story was inspired largely by my grandfather's own battle with Alzheimer's and my family's decision on how best to handle his care.

While AngelCare is fictional, the Alzheimer's Association is a very real charity and is doing the important, life-altering work Elle touches on in the book. If this story resonates with you in any way, if the struggles Elle, Adam, and Lovie face are ones you're familiar with, I encourage you to consider exploring their resources.

With so much love,
Megan

CHAPTER ONE

Redheads have more fun—and I would know. I've had every shade of hair under the sun. Platinum blonde with extensions, pink streaks, a purple moment in college with wash-in color that was not worth what I paid the girl down the hall to dye it.

Currently, my hair is the same shade of red as the face of the woman across from me, the conductor of the number five train, green line. The Chicago subway system is overrun and undersanitized, the workers who maintain it overworked and underpaid.

But this woman? This woman is a *gem*. I wouldn't have learned her name if it weren't for the badge peeking out of her uniform pocket, but in just a forty-minute interview, I've learned Rita's entire life story. She's been in this industry for ten years, starting as a custodian after her deadbeat boyfriend left when she got pregnant. Night school for engineering and solo parenting and sheer determination have landed her here, across from me.

The heat in her conductor's cab is busted, but the glow on her face is pride. The glow on *mine* is sweat. I wipe it from my brow, the plastic of my podcasting microphone threatening to slide right out of my hand.

"How long do repairs take?" I ask. "This has to be a health hazard."

Her cheeks turn rosier, and she ducks her head. *Interesting.* "Could be a month or two. But it's not anything to bother the maintenance crew with." The blush is creeping toward her neck now.

When you've been doing this job as long as I have—when you love it as much as I do—you learn exactly where opportunities lie, and you go after them. It's why I can't let go of Rita's blush. "Do you not get along with someone there?"

"Everyone's great." She adjusts in her seat, green eyes flitting to mine. Her thumbs spin around themselves, nails blurring in a vortex of red polish. "They're just so busy. I figure Isaac has more important things to do than fix the AC in my cabin."

"And Isaac's the maintenance tech?"

She blinks. "Oh, shit. I'm not supposed to name names, am I?"

I wave her off. The slight breeze feels too good on my sticky skin, but I ignore it. The subway tunnels rush past us outside the lone window, too-loud music of a passenger carrying from out in the main car. All things that can be fixed later in post-production. But I can't edit out the stale recycled air, even if it does smell of bug spray and, randomly, Funyuns. I switch to mouth breathing.

"*Elle on the L* is completely anonymous," I confirm, "but feel free to speak normally. I'll bleep out names, defining places or characteristics. Anything you want, really."

The twiddling stops. "Shit," she says. "I said 'shit' just now. And then I said it again."

"Don't worry." A smile stretches my face. "I keep all the curse words in."

The skin around her eyes crinkles with a small grin of her own, but she bites down on it. I dip my chin in encouragement. *I'm so close.*

"Isaac is the maintenance supervisor," she says on an exhale. "He, um. He's really nice to me." Her voice trails off, leaving me to fill in the gaps.

"You like him."

"It passed 'like' about four years ago." She sighs, her hands finally coming to rest in her lap. "I'm in love with him now."

The adoration on her face is contagious, and I lean into the butterflies raring up in my stomach. "What's your favorite thing about him?"

So far, I've led our conversation, but she takes the reins now. My podcast guests always tell their own story, for better or for worse.

They aren't always this lighthearted.

Rita tells me about her and Isaac's mutual disgust of the breakroom snack options. His kind attitude and how he's paid for her lunch a few times when she's forgotten her wallet or hasn't been able to justify the expense. Their rushed conversations out on the street corner over chili dogs that are cold by the time lunch is over because they're too busy laughing and talking to spare a single bite. How last Christmas he bought a model train for her son exactly like the one she drives, down to the serial number hand painted on the side.

If Isaac isn't in love with her too, I will lick the subway floor.

"So he's dependable," I summarize, steering us back on track. No pun intended, et cetera.

That same soft smile lightens her eyes. "The most dependable person I've ever met."

"And you didn't think he'd service the AC? Or, for that matter, service *you*?"

"You talk to your elders that way?" She chuckles. "Who raised you?"

A wave of nostalgia hits me directly in the chest; my elder *is* who raised me. I wink. "Where do you think I learned it? So. Isaac. Do you have his number?"

She narrows her gaze. "Yes . . . why?"

"Call him. Right now. Tell him how you feel."

She jolts forward. "I can't! He's working!"

"So are you. So am *I*."

She messes with a loose thread on the seam of her pants. "I don't know . . ."

I reach into my purse and produce a can of mints, holding it out for her. "Even if you don't confess your feelings," I say, "you still need to call him about the AC. I'm almost positive my thighs are melted onto the plastic."

Grumbling, she pulls her phone from her pocket. It takes very few clicks for her to find his number.

After another two seconds, she takes a mint.

"It's ring—"

A deep voice cuts off her comment. She swallows, then coughs. So much for icy-fresh breath. "Hey, you," he says. I can *hear* his smile. And she doesn't think her feelings are reciprocated?

"The air went out in my cab again."

I hear a muffled, "And you're running until eight tonight."

He knows your schedule, I mouth, bouncing my eyebrow. She waves me off, but the blush on her cheeks is turning into a permanent fixture. I am giddy for a complete stranger.

Isaac continues. "I'll be right there. I can ride this next loop with you while I fix it. If you'll have me."

I hold the microphone closer to my mouth, murmuring, "For everyone at home, the wedding speech is writing itself."

She freezes, eyes locking with mine. I give her a big thumbs-up and a nod so enthusiastic it hurts my neck.

"Do you . . . um." Rita's thumb rubs the seam of her pants. "Do you want to get dinner sometime? With me. If I can find a sitter."

My heartbeat suspends in my throat. I inhale deeply.

Well, as deeply as you can on a Chicago subway. In addition to the Funyuns and the bug spray, now it smells like piss.

"Yes," Isaac says immediately, loud and clear. She grins bright enough to light the whole city. "But I would still want to get dinner sometime if you couldn't find a sitter. Henry's a good kid."

After promising to talk more about their upcoming date in person, she clumsily hangs up the phone, and I can't help myself—I hug her, sweat and Funyuns and all.

When I pull back, she presses her palms to her cherry-red cheeks. "We've got to be running out of time."

"Thank you for talking with me today." I put every ounce of earnestness I can into my voice. "And to my listeners, wherever you are in the world, you are loved. You matter. You're important. Until next time, this is *Elle on the L*. Catch the train with me."

After packing up my equipment and nabbing an out-the-door promise from Rita to send me a wedding invitation, I step out of the conductor's car. A handsome middle-aged man carrying a tool bag passes me. I'd bet my last dollar his name is Isaac.

I've got my mind set on the café on the corner as I make my way up the stairs into early-fall sunlight. I'm reaching for the coffee shop door when my phone rings in my bag.

I bypass an errant floss pick, the pack of mints from earlier, and a pair of feather earrings—*there those are*—before I pull it free.

Angie from AngelCare scrolls across the screen in an endless loop. Angie is a senior nurse from the company I hired to manage my grandmother Lovie's Alzheimer's disease, and her case manager. She doesn't usually call with *good* news. Around me, commuters and tourists move in a blur, but my feet are stuck to the sidewalk and my heart is stuck in my throat.

Someone bumps my shoulder, and I move to the side as I answer before my phone rings out. "Hello?"

"Elle," Angie says. "How are you? You're not working, are you?"

"Just finished up." I lean against the café, taking care not to touch the questionable spots on the plaster that could be bird shit but could also be bodily fluids. "What's wrong?"

Her pause is weighted, significant.

"When do you think you'll be able to make it home next?" Her gentle tone slips into something more tentative. "Lovie's not doing too well these days."

My heart turns to stone inside my chest, settling down at the soles of my booties. "Define *not too well*."

The longer Angie stays silent, the more my lungs burn and the more my shoes turn to lead.

"She called one of our male nurses Bobby," Angie says. "We think she's moving into the next stage."

My grandfather Bobby passed away three years ago, right before Lovie's Alzheimer's diagnosis. She's been in the early stages since she took a tumble down her front steps and got a CT scan when she couldn't remember where she'd been going in the first place.

"We've talked before about how the best thing for her is constant care," Angie reminds me. While I mostly know Angie in a professional setting, life has a way of filling in the cracks through years of casual acquaintance and coffee chats. It's easy for her to slip into a mothering role with me, considering she has three boys who require constant vigilance.

"That's fine," I say, though it doesn't feel anything close to it. It's hard to breathe. Financially, it should be okay. I've been saving for this for a while now. "If you send me a list of places AngelCare recommends, I can—"

"None of them will take her insurance."

My brows pinch together. "I thought Medicare covered everything."

"Medicare does. But Lovie's not on Medicare. She's somehow still on your grandfather's insurance, and that doesn't cover hospice for spouses."

"Could I just pay out of pocket? How much would that be? A thousand dollars a month, maybe two? I can swing that."

She coughs. "A *week*." Another cough. "At least."

I wince. I . . . did not save that much.

"Besides," Angie continues, "the risk is too great. They need valid, legal insurance on file to consider her. And even then, there's a wait list."

"Can I add her to my plan?" I pay a pretty penny for private-market insurance. Might as well use it.

"If you claim her as a dependent, then yes, but that will take time too." Like with Rita on the train, I hear what she isn't saying almost as loudly as what she is: we don't *have* time.

I stare at the pastry display through the café window, my hunger quickly fading. "A few weeks?" I guess. The droning noises from the subway have followed me to the street, a buzz in my ears I can't clear out.

The sound Angie makes now is noncommittal.

"A few *months*?" I don't mean it to come out so harsh.

"It's not ideal." Angie is an actual angel—the company is aptly named—and overlooks my attitude. "If you got started right away with either getting her enrolled in Medicare or adding her as your dependent, I think a few months is manageable. Hopefully by Christmas."

"I'm on my way," I say, before I realize exactly what that means. My feet move of their own accord. "I think there's an Amtrak that leaves at one. It will be tight, but I'll make it work." I nod to myself. I can figure this out.

I have to.

"Elle," Angie says, more urgently now. "There's really no need to rush. I've already scheduled—"

"No, no. I'll be there as soon as I can."

And I end the call.

CHAPTER TWO

I collapse in my seat on the train idling in Union Station several hours later, after what will likely go down in history as the Most Annoying Day of My Life.

Earlier, after I hung up with Angie—okay, fine, hung up *on* Angie—I rushed back to my place to pack up clothes and podcast equipment and anything else I could perceivably need for the next few months.

By the time I made it to the station, I had exactly three minutes to buy a ticket and get to the platform on the other end of the hall. I may or may not have tweaked my ankle attempting the impossible. I bought myself a conciliatory coffee from the kiosk when I missed it, which I spilled all over my shirt.

I pull my headphones over my ears and hold my breath as the train pulls away from the station. With me on board, I'm fully expecting it to break down in the middle of nowhere.

The familiar sounds of my Queens playlist fill my ears as I tuck in for the two-hour ride to my hometown. Not Queen the band. Queens as in *queens*. Alanis and Janis, Whitney and Britney, Taylor and Adele and Beyoncé. You know. Queens.

And then my headphones die, and I'm forced to watch cornstalks and crop fields whiz by in the dark.

Despite being a large city by most standards, even having the crowning achievement of not one but *two* Walmarts, Elkhart, Indiana, has always felt like a small town to me. Lovie was never able to go grocery shopping without running into at least one person she knew.

The city's expanded since I last lived there over ten years ago. On a map, it sort of reminds me of a snowflake: the center dense with restaurants and shotgun houses and parks. The northern spindle stretches and bumps up against Michigan, the southern one leading the way to a prison, a golf course, and a seminary. The priorities of midwestern America, am I right?

Some people leave home and never come back, but I don't think that will ever be me. I've traveled lots of places. New York City for college. Road trips to Myrtle Beach and Philadelphia and Niagara Falls. Aruba, booked on my grandparents' credit card after one college midterm result that was poorly timed with a bad case of the Mondays and PMS. But nowhere I've ever been has felt more like home than home itself.

Except Chicago. That also feels like home.

I'm lucky this way—some people don't ever feel like they have a place they belong. I have two. I'd take either right now. I've never longed for a bed this much in my life.

I'm convinced the only reason I find my baggage and get a Lyft this late is because when I climb off the train and onto familiar Elkhart earth, the clock has rolled over to a brand-new day.

After such a long trip, I appreciate Lovie's house even more when it finally—*finally*—comes into view.

The two-bedroom Cape Cod is the same as ever: quaint, colorful, and outdated. The navy-colored vinyl shines black this time of night, and although I can't see the shutters, I know they're still painted a gaudy maroon. The stucco behind them is bubblegum pink. I picked that color when I was seven, and Lovie's kept it ever since.

As quietly as possible, I let myself in and lock the dead bolt before toeing off my shoes. It's one of Lovie's personal life rules, to take off your shoes at the door.

"You walk into public bathrooms with those shoes," she'd always say when I questioned her on it. "You are not going to bring someone else's business onto my brand-new carpet."

The carpet stopped being brand-new fifteen years ago. Then again, maybe making guests go barefoot is how she keeps it fresh.

Pit stopping at the bathroom to splash my face with warm water and slip into pajamas, I look at myself in the mirror, the pink of the walls and tiles making my dark circles and fatigue that much more apparent. This could quite possibly be the longest day of my life.

Moving down the hall, I poke my head in on Lovie's sleeping form. She's so frail there in the dark, a walker and cane at the ready by her nightstand. My eyes snag on the bedpan hanging off the edge of her bedside table. That's a harder pill to swallow.

Once I'm appeased, I haul my shit to the second bedroom, which has been mine for as long as I can remember. My bags find the floor. Unpacking can wait for daylight.

I just barely remember to set an alarm. Lovie probably wakes up at six or seven, so this will be more of a glorified nap than actual solid sleep, but I can do that. For one night, at least. For Lovie.

I think.

It takes three steps to get to the bed, and with every one sleep tugs at my body more and more, my limbs heavy with fatigue.

I fall down onto the mattress.

Or I would have, if there weren't a suspicious, human-shaped lump right where my body's supposed to go.

That's about the time I start screaming.

CHAPTER THREE

I'm dead.

Someone broke into Lovie's house and has a weird fetish for sleeping in guest bedrooms before pillaging old ladies. There was a *Criminal Minds* episode about this exact scenario, I'm pretty sure.

"Stop screaming," the probably-a-murderer hisses.

Oh God. What if I woke Lovie up and she comes running right into the middle of this shitstorm? If I don't know what the hell is going on, there's no way an eighty-one-year-old Alzheimer's patient will.

As my scream dies, my knees scrabble for purchase, connecting with something squishy. A heavy *oof* follows, then a muffled groan.

I think I just kneed a killer in the balls.

Oops . . . ?

For as fast as the contact was, it's over faster. In the pitch black I hear a violent squeak of the bed frame, a muttered "*Fuck*," and a subsequent loud thud.

The intruder has fallen out of bed. Now's my chance.

I scramble across the mattress, flip on the lamp, and come face to face with—

Oh.

Okay, hear me out. I know you can't judge a book by its cover, but this man certainly doesn't look like an intruder. Unless we're talking about Ted Bundy.

The man in front of me looks like he could wreck me in a very *different* kind of way. Make me scream, make the bed frame squeak . . . sort of how we were a few seconds ago. A shiver bolts up my spine, and I cross my arms over my tightening nipples, wishing I could force myself to sleep in a bra for once in my life.

There's something almost familiar about him. For a second I wonder if I'm the one with the memory problems, because there's no way I would have willingly forgotten this man.

In the glow of the bedside lamp, made sallow by the dusty yellow lampshade, his eyes are dark as midnight, two glowing onyx orbs. They're framed by bushy eyebrows, and shadows around the edges of his face and mouth clue me in to hints of dark stubble. That very mouth is pressed into a hard line.

His posture is a reflection of his face, harsh angles with no give. He rises to his feet, and when he crosses his arms over his chest, I can't tell whether it's because his nipples are also hard or because he's aggravated.

My eyes trace the rest of his body, clad in a soft-looking white T-shirt and plaid pajama pants. I snag on muscular arms and toned thighs before completing my perusal.

Cue the record scratch.

Socks. The psychopath is wearing socks. In bed.

My forehead scrunches as I find his onyx eyes again. "What the hell are you wearing?" Maybe—definitely—not the time, considering there is a literal stranger in my bedroom, but an important question nonetheless.

Fake It Like You Mean It

He leans against my dresser, crossing his ankles to match his arms. This entire man is cross. Beautifully, frustratingly cross. "They're called pajamas," he says, his voice deep and scratchy. "Most people wear them to sleep."

Smart ass. "I meant the socks. You sleep in those things?"

He studies me harshly, uncomfortably, the way I just studied him. One dark eyebrow tips upward. "You sleep in those?" he asks, staring at my Dalmatian sleep shorts.

Under his scrutiny, they don't seem long enough to classify as shorts. I tug down my oversized T-shirt. "I get hot at night."

Wait a minute. Why am I explaining myself to this man? This stranger who's infiltrated *my* Lovie's house and was sleeping in *my* bed and using *my* perfectly fluffed pillows. I reach for my phone, dropped during our scuffle.

"I'm calling the police."

"Don't," he says, and his insistent tone makes my thumb pause over my screen.

"You're a stranger. You could be a . . . a bad guy!"

Yes, okay, let's keep talking like we're in kindergarten. Great intimidation tactics we've got going for us tonight.

The man sighs like he's already had enough of my shit. I know I've had enough of his. Seriously, the *audacity*. He holds up his hands to show me they're empty and moves toward me slowly. Even still, my back is against the wall by the time he grabs the wallet on the nightstand and tosses it to me.

As I open it, he says, "Adam Wheeler. Home health nurse. I work for AngelCare."

The gears in my mind, which had started to shut down for the night, whir back to life. "Angie didn't say anything about this." Maybe she would have if I'd given her the chance. I was all gas, no brakes today.

I shake my head, intent to stay on track. Adam's wallet is thin, fraying at the edges, and contains only three cards. Driver's license, credit card, and some kind of credentials. They all match.

His license picture is a younger and less grizzly version of the man standing at my bedside. He probably got his toxic masculinity all over my sheets. I bet he smells like pine cones and . . . ugh, a bar or something.

Okay, so he is who he says he is. It still doesn't explain what he's doing here now. At—kill me, please—one thirteen in the morning.

"Your turn," he says, flipping his hand so his palm faces the ceiling.

"Elle. Annoyed granddaughter of this home's owner." I set his wallet back on the nightstand and look at him expectantly. I hope he's satisfied, because it's all he's getting.

He isn't. He just keeps holding out his hand.

It takes a second to catch his meaning. "You want me to *show you my ID*?" As attractive as he is, his attitude negates it all. Every time he speaks, his cockiness costs him.

His mouth pulls up in an arrogant smirk. "How do I know *you're* not the . . . what'd you call me? A '*bad guy*'?"

I could probably smack that shit-eating grin right off his face if I leaned forward far enough. "Yes, because all criminals wear polka-dotted pajama pants."

His bark of laughter is low, grumbly. It vibrates through me, even halfway across the room. "Those are *not* pants."

I fiddle with the hem of my shorts again, resisting the urge to tug. If I pull them down any farther, they'll slip over my ass.

Adam gestures with his hand again. "Come on, cough it up."

"If I show you my ID, can I go to sleep?"

"I'll consider it."

I worked my purse into my duffel earlier to have less to carry on the train, and I'm regretting that decision now. I'm not a big blusher, not like Rita from the train or my best friend Liss, but as I lean over my things and come up with my wallet a minute later, all the blood in my body has relocated to my face.

"You dropped something," he says, and somehow he's haughtier than he was a few seconds ago.

On the floor by my feet is my bright-blue vibrator.

I try to snatch it off the floor but fumble, and it seems to fall in slow motion, landing on the button and buzzing to life.

I get it now. I must have sleepwalked at some point last night, under about five ladders, twirling an umbrella inside my apartment. The umbrella hit a mirror or thirteen, and I've used up my entire bad-luck quota for the rest of eternity. That, or this is the most realistic nightmare I've ever had.

Since there's no more free real estate on my face for embarrassment, my flush crawls down my neck. Bending down to grab the offensive item—which, for the record, has never done me dirty *this* way—I catch a glimpse down my too-big T-shirt. It gapes wide enough that Adam probably got a free peep show. And yeah, I'm flushed all the way to my nipples.

My fingers aren't working, can't find the button to turn off the toy. Adam watches me wordlessly. It's both unsettling and infuriating. He could have pretended not to see my personal effects. That would have been the nice thing to do.

I'm beginning to think Adam Wheeler is not a nice man.

I give up and take out the battery, because the damn thing will not stop buzzing, and drop it inside my bag. Zip it shut for good measure. He's still waiting, hand outstretched and stifling a smile. I slap my ID into his palm as hard as I can.

Adam's body language is all chill as he glances at it. "What's your full name?"

Indignation steels my spine, and I have to unclench my jaw to answer. "Carolyn Michelle Monroe."

"When's your birthday?"

"You can't be serious. Give it back." I lunge for it, but he lifts his hand above his head.

"Ah-ah," he tsks. "Birthday?"

"This is ridiculous." I reach for it anyway, and my body presses against sharp hard lines even through two layers of fabric.

My ear is near his throat now, which is why I hear him swallow.

"Here," he says, bringing it within reach before our bodies connect more fully.

I nearly thank him. That would be stupid, considering I could have called the cops on him five times over by now. I'm still not sure why I haven't.

Adam's not smiling anymore. The look he's giving me isn't playful or teasing or flirty the way his grin was. This is deeper, more introspective. Vulnerable, almost.

"I still don't understand what you're doing here now," I say, crossing my arms like I'm cold, even as sweat threatens to break out along my hairline. I'd forgotten how toasty old ladies keep their houses. It's got to be eighty degrees in here. He's wearing socks despite this, which only further cements my psychopath theory.

He sighs, sitting on the edge of the bed. "You might as well get comfortable."

At this rate, I will never go to sleep. I eye the bed speculatively, not because I don't want to sit—that honestly sounds quite lovely—but because I don't get it. Adam has taken command of the room, and I've just . . . let him. This isn't a situation I find myself in often. Ever, if I can help it. Things usually go according to plan. My plan. And when they don't, I make a new plan as soon as possible.

Maybe it's his eyes that make me inch toward the bed. Now that mine have adjusted to the lighting, I can see they're not actually black but dark, dark blue. Lake Michigan in the heart of summer, and just as inviting.

Once I'm perched on the corner of the mattress, he tips his chin in a gesture that my sleep-deprived brain classifies as a nod.

"Like I said," he starts, "I work for AngelCare. We provide in-home health services for elderly patients who—"

"I know about the company." I *hired* the company. "But let's skip to the part where you're here in the middle of the night, sleeping in my bed." I narrow my eyes, but that's too close to sleep, and I can't do that right now. I force them open again. I already have a headache tomorrow.

"Lovie was recently upgraded from a daily check-in to a twenty-four/seven watch," he says, shifting under my gaze. Maybe I should try the narrow-and-widen thing more often; that's the first thing I've done that's affected him. "Angie wanted someone to start as soon as possible, and that someone ended up being me. There's not much more to it than that."

Sighing, I give him a half shrug as a concession. "Fine. But the bed thing?"

"Obviously, if I had known you were coming, I would have slept on the couch." His eyes spark brighter. "But Lovie insisted I have this room. She said her granddaughter never comes to stay anymore, that she lives all the way in *Chicago*." He studies me for a stretching second. "That's obviously you."

Pain and regret lance through me like swords, sharp and direct.

I wet my lips, picking a loose thread in the blanket to avoid looking at his face, which I fear is full of judgment. "Oh."

I don't know Adam from, well, Adam. But the idea of him thinking me an ungrateful city slicker who detests her hometown and only came home because she had nothing better to do feels an awful lot like guilt.

It's all too much. My eyes water, the burning a clear indication I've been awake far too long. I only cry when I'm mad and when I absolutely cannot help it. Most of the time, I'd really rather not.

"I didn't mean to upset you," he says, leaning forward, elbows on knees. My eyes dart up in time to see his mouth tip downward, his bottom lip between his teeth. Or maybe my tears are distorting things, the way funhouse mirrors do. "I'm sorry."

"You didn't upset me," I say, too quickly to be true. "I don't even know you."

If he notices my lie, he doesn't show it. He dips his chin once in acknowledgment, but the groove between his brows remains as I blink away moisture. At least I've found *something* in him to appreciate.

I stand, desperate to get as much distance from this situation as possible. "Can we sort the rest out in the morning? This day has been a hundred years long, and I'd really like to go to bed now."

For a second, he just watches me, that unreadable expression muddling his gaze. I resist the urge to give him a *hurry up* hand motion. Or do something especially stupid, like touch him.

"I bet," he drawls, straightening up.

"So . . ." I say. He's still not moving. "Do you think you could . . ." I look pointedly at the mattress. When he remains immobile, I gesture with both hands before they fall and slap my bare thighs. "Can I have my bed?"

"Finders keepers for tonight?" he says, one eyebrow arching. "And we can 'sort the rest out in the morning.'"

"Fuck you," I murmur, reaching for the pillow behind him and tugging it free. The quilt comes next. He can have the bed. He never claimed the *bedding*.

I only barely manage not to slam the door on the way out, and it takes additional restraint not to stomp down the hall to the living room.

This couch must be from the seventies. It's faded mauve, fabric pilling in the well-worn spots on the armrests and cushions. I can't make them out in the dark, but I know there are fuchsia flowers woven throughout. We used to trace them together, Lovie and me, when thunderstorms knocked out the power.

"Stupid fucking Adam Wheeler," I grumble. Because I'm flustered, it takes me a solid minute to get the quilt situated. This pillow isn't as fluffy as I remember.

I still don't plug in my phone. I'm sure it will be dead by the morning, but I'm dead now, and I don't care. I just want to sleep.

Along with the familiar scents of ginger, cinnamon, and lavender, there's something new that lulls me into dreams. It reminds me of childhood, summer days spent in parks until my skin was sticky with sweat and sunscreen.

It smells the way sunshine feels.

CHAPTER FOUR

I sleep like the dead. There were many mornings as a child (and as a teenager, if I'm being honest) when Lovie or Grandpa Bobby had to shake me awake. *Forcibly.* Liss thinks it's incredibly unhealthy, but I think it's great. I've never been awoken by upstairs neighbors screwing at three in the morning or an early-riser roommate banging pots and pans.

To be fair, I'm usually that early-riser roommate. Since I sleep so well, I don't mind getting up with the sun.

Unless I'm up late the night before, fighting and bed-wrestling with annoying men who wear socks to sleep and make me take the couch. Then I sleep until—I grab my phone—*nine thirty?* That can't be right.

I blink at the clock on the wall, but the hands don't change.

"Shit," I murmur, jackknifing up. I should have charged my phone after all.

Has Lovie eaten yet? I don't smell anything burning (which is good, because I've slept through a fire alarm more than once). What if she usually sits on the couch in the morning and I ruined her routine? Consistency is one of the most important factors for Alzheimer's patients, and it will already be enough of a shake-up to have me back home. Especially when she told Mr. Grumpy Socks that I never visit anymore.

Soft noises carry from across the front hall.

The kitchen is a hodgepodge of colors and patterns, Lovie's eclectic style clashing violently with Grandpa Bobby's practicality. The windows above the sink and behind the table feature green-and-pink valances, perpetually pinned open. Blinding morning sunlight refracts off the oak cabinets and makes me wince, so it takes a second for the rest of the details to come into view.

The vinyl floor, a checkerboard of tan and brown, is so well loved, the pattern is worn away in front of the stove and sink. Opposite that is the refrigerator, which is so small I can see every dusty inch of the top. The other, smaller appliances breaking up the U-shaped counter are also brown. The island, with a gap underneath that serves no discernible purpose, is free and clear of clutter aside from a bowl of fruit in the corner. That is also, perpetually, brown.

Adam turns toward me from the stove. He's changed out of his pajamas and into scrubs, a light-blue matching set. It reminds me of a tracksuit I used to wear in middle school. It was blue velour with a rhinestone butterfly on the left tit. Liss had a pink one with a heart, and we switched jackets every morning to let other girls know we were Hot Shit.

"Good morning," he says. His voice isn't rasped from sleep the way mine is. Honestly, how dare he be anything less than dead on his feet.

"Where's Lovie?" I ask instead. "Has she eaten?"

With another yawn, I'm forced to move toward the cabinet. I dig out my favorite mug from the back, a purple, butterfly-shaped plastic one I've used since I was old enough to be trusted without a lid. When I started drinking coffee in high school, Lovie always made sure it was washed and ready to use.

I wipe dust from the inside now. How long has it been since I've used it?

Adam's head tilts at the sight of my questionable drinkware. "She's up, in the bathroom. It takes her a while."

"You should have woken me. I could have helped."

He chuckles, a beat of laughter gone as quick as it came. "I tried, but you were completely unconscious. I did make sure you were breathing, though. It was touch-and-go for a minute."

"What, did you check my pulse?" The thought of his fingers on my neck sends a crawling sensation down my spine.

His dark brows dip toward each other, mouth tugging down. "I wouldn't do that unless I had to." His disgust is clear.

I shoulder past him to get to the only chance I have of making it through this morning—caffeine. I eye the ancient coffeepot with hesitation, mug in hand. It's no Breville, that's for sure. I pour a lukewarm mug anyway.

"Don't worry." I roll my eyes. "We'll get this straightened out, and you won't ever have to touch me again, since it was so traumatizing for you."

Adam lets out a scoff under his breath, and the hairs on the back of my neck stand up as if it were nails on a chalkboard. "Well, I was going to suggest starting over, but that's clearly not going to happen."

My hand would be tightening into a fist if I weren't holding the mug. Still, I think the plastic creaks. I turn toward him, less than impressed, and throw on a smile so fake and sweet it hurts my teeth.

"Hi!" My voice drips with sarcasm and just a sprinkle of fuck-you. "My name is Elle Monroe. Lovie is my grandmother," is what I say. *She raised me* is what I don't. "I hired AngelCare to handle her Alzheimer's. That's the company you work for." A reminder about who's in charge here shouldn't hurt. I hold out my hand. "It is so, so nice to meet you."

Adam straightens, adding another few inches to his already massive build, and shakes my hand. His fingers are warmer than my mug. "I'm Adam Wheeler. Lovie is my patient. You hired AngelCare to handle her Alzheimer's. That's the company I work for. Nice to meet you too."

I roll my eyes, pulling out of his grip. "Fine. Sure."

"You look so much like her," he murmurs. "Your grandmother. I'm sorry I didn't believe you last night."

That, for a change, sounds sincere.

I shrug, bringing my mug to my mouth. Without the caffeine fully in my bloodstream, I can only return the bare minimum of hospitality. "Then I'm sorry about your testicles. I guess."

"My—" He coughs, and a tinge of pink lights his cheekbones. Or maybe that's from the curtains. "Well, thank you. I guess."

I take another sip. "You know, for a second I thought you might apologize for being so rude last night."

Adam blinks at me, his mouth falling open. "*Me*, rude? You *threw* yourself at me—"

I scoff, taking a step toward him. "Because it was *my* bed."

He spears a hand through his hair, messing some of the strands near his forehead. "Who shows up somewhere in the middle of the night?"

"I missed the train!" I set my coffee down on the counter so harshly some of it sloshes onto my hand. And maybe his socks.

Good.

"And *then* you assaulted me with sex toys—" he continues over me, his volume rising just like the throbbing vein in his neck. Splashes of red crawl up from it to his jawbone.

"It slipped out of my bag!"

"And made me show you personal identification—"

I take another step. If we were animals, bucks or bulls or, I don't know, lions, our foreheads would be pressed together in our face-off. I could count his eyelashes. If I wanted. "You did the same thing."

"You did it first!" He matches my step with his own. The color covers almost his entire face now, bleeding from the five o'clock shadow and lighting the corners of his expressions that remained hidden last night. All the way up to his eyes.

With the natural light, they're brighter than before. More . . . peacocky.

It's fitting. Because he's a giant dick.

Giant is the operative word. I didn't get the full force of his build last night. At five foot ten I'm used to looking down at people or standing on even ground. But with Adam my gaze stretches *up*. It's just another thing about him that pisses me off, especially considering the catch in my neck from sleeping on the sofa.

"You . . ." Adam fills his lungs completely, taking several extra seconds to hold in the breath before letting it out in one strong gust. We're close enough that it blows some of my baby hairs. A frown transforms his face into more dark shadows, and the remaining flush on his face gives him a ruddy complexion. His voice drops an octave the next time he speaks.

"You are the most infuriating woman I've ever met."

"Joke's on you." I glare up at him. "I take that as a compliment."

Another muscle in his jaw tics, like he's about to say something else unsavory, but a door opening in the hall smooths his face into a neutral and unreadable expression. "Lovie's coming."

So much for starting over.

CHAPTER FIVE

I smile when my grandmother rounds the corner. She does not smile back.

This is the first time I've seen her since last night, and that hardly counts. If I wanted to search Lovie's face for markers of fatigue as she ambles toward her spot at the table, I wouldn't be able to.

It's not just the people that age—everything about them turns tired too. Her skin sags, around her mouth and chin especially, and it's so paper thin that if she sneezed too hard it would rip. I got her eyes—the color of dark chocolate and just as bitter. Her hair is cut short and pure white, and the wisps curl around her ears, but it used to be a shade of red close to my current one. For my sixteenth birthday, she dip-dyed her ends blue to match mine.

I round the island and give her a hug. I'd squeeze her tighter if she didn't seem so breakable. "Hi, Lovie. I missed you."

She pulls back first, grabbing for her chair. "Hi, dear."

"Did you sleep well?" I ask. Expectant. Hopeful. Cheery.

"Yes, I'm fine," she says breezily, gesturing to Adam, who's plating the food. She doesn't meet my eyes. "This young man made me a lovely breakfast."

I bite back a snort. I can't imagine Adam doing anything that's *lovely*. "Well. Let's dig in, then."

A few minutes later, Adam and my grandmother are situated at the round oak table, a full breakfast spread on each of their plates.

"Is there creamer?" I ask. I'm going to need something to help this black tar go down, and forgoing the coffee altogether is not an option after last night.

"In the door," Lovie says.

I bend, examining the contents of the refrigerator. There's every condiment known to man, a few old butter containers that haven't contained butter since 1987, lactose-free half-and-half, and what's left of the eggs. No creamer in sight.

My brows knit together as I glance over my shoulder. "Where'd you say?"

Adam stares at me. I can *feel* him restraining himself from looking at my butt.

"She's talking about the heavy cream. Which expired four months ago and is now in the garbage." His tone is nonchalant, unbothered.

A hot flash of annoyance licks up my spine. "You couldn't have said something before I spent the last two minutes bent over searching?" I grab the lactose-free half-and-half and shut the door with my hip.

"I don't know what you mean." He rounds out his eyes, the picture of innocence, but they darken a shade or two as he tears a chunk of toast with his teeth.

Two can play at that game. "If you wanted to look at my ass, Adam, all you had to do was ask." I turn so he can get a better view, look over my shoulder at it in appreciation. "It's a nice ass, don't you think? I do squats."

He chokes on his toast, sputters his way through recovery, and glances at Lovie to see if she's bothered by my statement.

She isn't.

After I pour the half-and-half into my butterfly mug, I move around the island and behind Adam to claim my seat and own plate. If I happen to bump his shoulder, well—oops.

And if he happens to choke on his toast again . . . I guess it's good he knows the Heimlich.

Across from me with her back to the kitchen, Lovie tucks a lock of hair behind her ear. These days she's good with a simple weekly set-and-style, and I know Angie's started doing it recently as opposed to taking her to the salon. For all the times my grandmother washed my hair, cut bubblegum out of it, helped me fix it for prom, it will be nice to return the favor.

Sipping my coffee, I peek at her plate. There are two slices of bacon and scrambled eggs, all untouched. "Are you not hungry?"

Lovie is not the kind to blush, so she just throws up a hand and waves off my concern. "You eat. I'm fine."

"Do you want me to make you a smoothie?"

"No." There's a hint of firmness behind her words now.

I'm hungry enough that anything I say would be in retaliation, so I choose to stay quiet, picking up my fork instead.

The three of us—Lovie, Grandpa Bobby, and me—ate almost all our meals at this nicks-and-scratches kitchen table. There's a nail-polish stain conveniently covered by the knitted doily in the center, which I flick up with my thumb, just to confirm it's still there. It settles some of the unease in my bones as I stare at my grandmother, waiting for recognition. A light in her eyes.

As stubborn as Lovie is, she would never admit to not knowing me, or anyone for that matter. If she ran into a stranger at the store, she'd come away with an invitation to their grandkid's birthday party. And she'd *go*.

"If you keep staring at me," Lovie says, "your food's going to get cold." As if she didn't just dismiss that exact claim from my mouth, about her.

It's such a mom thing to say.

Hell, Lovie *is* my mom. Lovie is *everyone's* mom. That's just the kind of person she is. She passed out Popsicles to neighborhood kids, gave cookies to the postal workers at Christmas, and wrote thank-you notes for my teachers on the last day of school. She held me together the first time a boy broke my heart and held back my hair the first time I had a hangover.

To appease her, I bite off a chunk of bacon. "What do you want to do today?"

"Gardening," she says simply.

I grimace. It's October now. "I'm not sure that will—"

"That sounds fine," Adam interrupts, and I wish there were a butter knife on the table so I could stab him with it. "I'll bring you your meds in half an hour, okay?"

Through gritted teeth, I say, "Just give them to her now. She won't remember later." In the beginning days of her diagnosis, she'd forget altogether if they weren't sitting next to her orange juice.

Adam stares at me, contempt making his eyes appear black again, the way they were last night. "I'll remember. They settle in her stomach better if she lets her food digest for a bit."

That might be believable if Lovie had bothered to pick up her fork in the last ten minutes.

He sips his coffee leisurely, like we are anywhere else, talking about anything else. "Anyway, I won't bother you with the drug names." His words are sharp, crisp. Like he's trying to remind me of something I would have already known, had I been paying attention.

"Oh, please do." I abandon my food, resting my elbows on the table and popping my chin into my palm. "Is she still on the cholinesterase inhibitor twice a day?"

Now is Adam's turn to grit his teeth, and he shifts in his chair, facing me more fully.

"It's three times," he corrects. "And a glutamate regulator." His left eyebrow raises in challenge.

I nod, *so* over this conversation. "For cognitive issues. And a low-dose antipsychotic for anger and aggression."

In my periphery, Lovie's eyes volley back and forth between us, merely a spectator in this conversation that wholly concerns her.

Adam swallows, gives an agreement in the form of a single, brief nod. "But none of those are DMTs. Not the fun kind you and your city friends take at music festivals. A DMT is a—"

"Disease-modifying therapy. And I know that because I was the one who signed off on it in the first place." I'll be damned if I let this man come in here and act like he knows my grandmother better than I do.

Lovie stares at me, her eyes catching on, of all things, my hair. I give her a halfhearted, closed-mouth smile before trying to focus on my food, although my verbal sparring with Adam has stolen what remained of my appetite.

When Lovie doesn't do the same with her own meal, I look up again.

She's glancing between Adam and me faster than before, hardly moving her head. A deep groove settles into the space between her thin eyebrows, mouth moving over unspoken words.

For as ignored as I've felt by her so far this morning, now I am itchy under her microscope. "Is something wrong?"

Lovie grins, the waxy yellow of her coffee-stained teeth appearing between her chapped lips. "I just remembered where I know you two from."

I'm done eating, I guess. There's no more room in my stomach with all the disappointment.

Lovie didn't remember me.

Doesn't remember me. Raising me, taking me to dance recitals or to get my braces off. I knew this day was coming, but reading about it online, hearing it from various doctors, does nothing to ease the pain once it arrives. It's been a possibility—an inevitability—since the beginning, and still, it's a direct hit to the heart. And knowing it's not her fault doesn't make this pill any easier to swallow. It might be going down harder. Maybe that's what's lodged in my throat.

"And where is that?" Adam asks, thumb dancing along the rim of his plate. There's a chip there from when I was twelve. I'd tried to wash the dishes to surprise Lovie but hadn't realized the china was so heavy. I chipped it on the counter and hid the broken piece in a flowerpot outside, convinced she'd never know.

She knew.

She always knew.

Lovie scoffs like the answer should be obvious. Like we're the crazy ones. "You're Lovie and Bobby, of course."

CHAPTER SIX

Wait a sec.

We're *what*?

It's so incredulous, so unbelievable, just plain wrong, I can't help coughing out, "I'm sorry?"

"Lovie and Bobby Monroe." Lovie blinks at each of us in turn, her wrinkled face hardening before she nods decisively. "You know who you are."

I swallow hard. "Actually, you're—"

"Exactly right," Adam cuts in. *Again.* His gaze hardens, sending a message. "Of course."

Lovie gives him a smug grin and turns her attention to her food.

I, on the other hand, have lost not only my appetite but every ounce of understanding I've ever held. "Wait, no, that's not—"

Something heavy connects with my shin under the table, and I stifle a yelp. Adam obviously wants me to play along, but I can't do that when I'm not sure what the game is.

"May I have a word with you?" Adam mumbles, pushing back so harshly I wouldn't be surprised to find scratches in the linoleum. Lovie's juice sloshes up the sides of her glass. "*Privately.*"

I clench my jaw. This is going to be good. Or very, very bad.

"Don't do anything I wouldn't do," Lovie says, the smirk in her voice apparent. Her advice is null and void—there isn't much she wouldn't do.

Adam walks into the laundry closet off the kitchen, tucked behind the alcove between the fridge and stove, and pulls the string for the overhead light. There's a door on both sides, the other opening to the hallway outside Lovie's room. When I was younger, I would run around the house in an unending counterclockwise loop: hallways, kitchen, laundry, hallways. It hardly contained one child; there's no hope it will hold both laundry machines and two oversized adults without things squeezing out at the seams.

I slide the door shut behind me calmly before whipping around. "Would you care to tell me what the fuck that was about?"

To his credit, Adam doesn't back up. Maybe he isn't afraid of me (he should be). Or maybe his back is already at the other door.

Taking a step toward him and drawing up to my full height, I poke his chest. "Fix it."

Anger lights up his shadows, stretches his jaw tight, but he stays silent.

I narrow my eyes and give him another jab in the pec. "Fix. It." Each word comes with another stab.

He rolls his eyes, grabbing my hand from his chest and lowering it back to my side. "How much do you know about Alzheimer's?"

"She's my grandmother. I know as much as I can."

"Okay, whatever," he spits, trying to keep his voice down. "But what about the day-to-day? You haven't been here, Elle."

That is more insulting than he intends, probably. "What's *that* supposed to mean?"

It is sweltering in this closet, quiet enough that whenever he shifts, I hear fabric brush his skin. "The connections between the different parts of her brain are dying. The part that stores information about space and time is separate from the part that memorizes routine."

"The creamer," I guess. "That's why she thought she had it. Because she has, for the last forty years."

Once again, he doesn't acknowledge that I've spoken, just barrels on with whatever point he's trying to make. "And the part where she recognizes faces is disconnected from the part that remembers family members."

I rest my hip on the washing machine, hold pressure to my pulsing temples with my thumb and middle finger. "Get to the point. Why can't we just tell her she's wrong?"

Adam sighs, shifting on his feet. "With Alzheimer's patients, it can do more harm than good to correct them. She could have a breakdown, go catatonic or revert to something childlike. Some of the worst tantrums I've ever seen have been from ninety-year-olds. There's no antipsychotic strong enough for what they can do when they get thrown off. You'd be telling her she's wrong. Broken. That everything she believes is a lie."

"I don't like this."

He lets out a sound that could have been a laugh if the situation were different. It raises the hair on my arms. "Trust me, I don't either. But for now, we'll just play along. Redirect whenever possible. Go along with whatever she says until she moves on to something else."

My heart drops into my stomach. "Even if she thinks I'm her? That we're . . ." Under no circumstances can I finish that sentence, so I let it lie.

"It won't do any good to tell her she's wrong, because her brain just isn't wired to believe it. The only thing fighting will do is get us all frustrated. And she likely won't remember in the morning. For now, it's my professional opinion that we should just let her believe the fantasy."

As much as I hate it, he may have a point. I peek at him through my fingers. "Just for today?"

Adam's tongue comes out to wet his top lip, and he takes the smallest step toward me. The doorknob must have been digging into his back. His chin dips in a soft nod. "Just for today. Half of that will be spent with her digging in the garden, and the other half will be spent watching TV."

The more I ponder his outlandish idea, the more I see where he's coming from, much as I hate to admit it. If what he says is true—if correcting her false assumption really is that damaging—I don't want to make the situation any worse. Lovie's who taught me how to hold grudges in the first place, and if we're both pissed?

Well.

Grandpa Bobby used to golf on those days.

Could there be that much harm in pretending? I always wanted to be just like Lovie when I grew up; I'm flattered she considers me worthy now. Maybe this is her subconscious way of fulfilling that for me. Her forgetting me doesn't hurt as bad when I think about it like that.

I can only hope Adam's right—that she'll move on from this wild idea with a good night's sleep. Who among us hasn't counted on one of those to act as a reset button? Hell, maybe I'll get lucky and she'll move on by lunch. Dinner at the latest.

And, hey. At least Adam will be just as miserable as I am. That's something.

"Sure, whatever," I say, reaching behind me for the handle.

Which thuds to the floor when I grab it.

"Damn," Adam says, right in my ear as he inspects the source of the noise.

I try to stick my pinkie in the minuscule hole left behind by the knob, but it's too small.

"Let me." He huffs, moving his large body beside mine to effectively shove me out of the way.

"*Excuse* you," I grumble.

I peek over his shoulder as he wedges a finger in the door gap. I wouldn't be mad if it pinched him.

"It's jammed," he says. "Help me push this."

I press my left hip into the door next to his right one.

The air is warmer near him, probably because our bodies are so close. The scent of sunshine, the one I fell asleep to last night, clings to his clothes and skin. It surrounds us like a bubble.

This is categorically unfair.

The last time I was sweaty in a closet with a man, it was going a lot better for me. Less swearing and more orgasms.

Adam turns to get better leverage on the door, and his other hip presses into my stomach. There must not be enough oxygen in this room, because I'm suddenly a little closer to "more orgasms" than before.

My breath snags somewhere behind my lips, and Adam's gaze jumps there. Stays there. He tries to shift away, but that only lifts the hem of my shirt, a flash of blazing heat on my bare stomach.

The grunt he lets out is half frustration, half torture. He twists again, his body aligning with mine. Hot, hard planes against all my softest places.

Before I have time to process us touching, the door spills open, coming off track at the bottom. I trip over someone's foot—I can't even tell if it's my own—and fall face first toward the hot stove before Adam grabs two handfuls of my hips, tugging me into him.

We're breathing tandemly hard, sharp, quick. His chest rises and falls at my back, more of his heat searing through my shirt.

"Are you okay?" We're close enough for his low timbre to rattle my rib cage.

I look at him over my shoulder, pressing my lips together for a second so my voice won't come out as shaky as the rest of me currently is. "Yeah."

He gives me another dip of his chin, his version of a nod.

It's only when his thumb slides across the still-exposed skin of my hip bone that I remember the laundry closet has two doors, and we could have just gone out the other one.

"I remember those days," Lovie says, and I startle, jumping away from him.

My grandmother is still seated at the table. She chuckles down at her plate. "Nothing like a stolen kiss in a closet to curl your toes. Right, kids?"

Wrong, kids.

I mean, okay, she's not wrong in theory. Just in practical application.

She stands, wobbly. "Now if you'll excuse me, I think I'm going to do my puzzles for a while." Her posture screams *try me.*

I don't. Instead, I wander over and pluck a piece of bacon off her plate. It's cold now, and a little floppy. "Does she need someone to go with her?"

On cue, the bathroom door slams shut. That answers my question.

Adam's still by the stove, the island separating us with its harsh line.

"She would have eaten more if it'd been turkey bacon," I tell him. I stack the dishes to clear the table. "And eggs over easy." There's a hint of mockery in my tone. I'm trying to get back to equal footing after whatever *that* was in the closet.

He pulls the pan off the burner, rolls his shoulders and his eyes at the same time. When he speaks again, he's also back to his arrogant self. "I asked her what she wanted. This was it."

His gaze is trained on the plates in my hand, still mostly full. "I guess she forgot what she likes."

"You should have asked me. I know her better than you." *Even if she doesn't know me anymore.*

He grits his teeth. "Yes, please tell me more about how to do my job."

The dishes rattle in my grip as I round the island and head toward the sink. "Do you have experience with other Alzheimer's patients?" I meant it as another teasing question, but the ending falls flat. Maybe I need the answer more than I realized.

"Just a bit in private settings like this, but I've done rotations in memory care facilities," he says. "I was fully briefed by the other nurses who were here, and Angie—she said you have her cell phone number—she writes incredibly detailed reports. I know what I'm getting into. But you're welcome to call her, have my references. I know this is a big deal, and I want you to be comfortable with everything." He's blocking the sink, but instead of moving out of my way, he holds his hands out in invitation.

I hand him the dirty dishes. My head throbs with a budding headache. It's some combination of poor sleep, lack of caffeine, and the tension within these walls pressing in on me from all angles.

The toilet flushes down the hall.

"All I need to know," I say softly, looking up at him, "is that you're prepared to take care of her how she needs. She's . . . she's important to me."

His eyes flash with something I don't know how to read. After the morning, I'm not even sure what book we're in. "Of course she is. And yes. I know there will be some"—his head tilts as he searches for the word he wants, and he winces—"growing pains, but my job is to keep her healthy first and happy second. If that's also what you want, I don't see any reason why we can't work together for her benefit."

I see an only-one-bed-shaped reason *and* an only-one-pink-bathroom reason.

But I think back to Adam, describing all the care Lovie receives daily. The routines she's built and perfected, here in her life without her husband or granddaughter to keep her company. The memories she's already lost, the one she's clinging to with everything.

I know her, but not the way I used to, and she doesn't know me at all anymore.

I know this disease on paper, through saved internet articles and clinical studies, but I don't know how to do this on my own.

Whether I admit it or not, I need Adam Wheeler.

"So, you're here to stay," I murmur.

One succinct dip of his chin. "I am here to stay." He pauses for a long time, long enough for me to finish clearing the table and slide the butter back into the fridge. "Except on the weekends, when I work my other job. I already cleared it with AngelCare."

"Are you two lovebirds still canoodling in here?" Lovie says, poking her head into the kitchen.

Can we really do this?

Do we have a choice?

It's just one day of acting like I love him, and only in Lovie's presence.

Only one day.

CHAPTER SEVEN

Once the kitchen is cleaned from breakfast and Lovie is settled in the living room with her beloved puzzle books, Adam with her, I make my way to my childhood bedroom. My bags still sit where I dropped them last night, the offensive toy right there on top. I push it to the side with a shudder, finding a fresh set of clothes and my toiletries.

There's another bag tucked in the corner. Adam's, if I had to guess. Classic black, all pockets zipped, a pair of shoes lined neatly next to it, soles up. He's so organized it offends me.

He even made the bed, as best as he could without the quilt and second pillow.

It pisses me off just looking at it.

Me having a shower will do us all some good.

I nearly trip over the plastic bath chair when I climb into the pink-tiled tub. How does Lovie maneuver this without assistance? I think she'd deny me if I offered my help, and part of me is glad. There are a lot of things you don't come back from, and seeing your grandmother naked is one of them.

Megan Murphy

My phone starts chiming with alerts halfway through applying my conditioner, and it speeds me up. I miss a few patches when shaving my legs.

Wrapping myself tightly in a well-worn pink towel, I step onto the bath mat and pick up my phone from the counter.

The latest episode of *Elle on the L* just went live about an hour ago, complete with an introduction I recorded hastily before catching the train yesterday that explains my coming to stay with Lovie. The diehards who drop everything and listen every Wednesday at ten in the morning should be finished by now.

I didn't always think I'd podcast full time. I went to school for marketing in New York and lived about thirty minutes away from campus. Bored out of my mind, I used my commute to chat with the people around me on the subway. Even after I moved back to Chicago, I could never escape that itch, getting to the heart of what makes people human.

My friend Liss was the one who suggested I start recording those conversations, and I did just that on nights and weekends, until that wasn't enough. You interview one very married state senator's very pregnant sidepiece, and suddenly your name is in the *New York Times*. I couldn't afford to keep the desk job very long after that, not when I was single-handedly producing a "compulsive, bingeable exposé on the human condition." Humble brag. I didn't need the desk job anyway when sponsors started breaking down my door. Not-so-humble brag.

What if people are cruel about me taking this time off? People can—and do—get nasty if things go different from what you've promised. It won't change anything about my plan to stay with Lovie, but I'd be more hesitant to share personal things with my listeners in the future.

My muscles relax as I view the comments section:

@jollyxholly527: so sweet!! take your time bb, we'll be here.
@Purrrsiankitty8: grandmas rock anyway, but I bet yours is badass AF

Fake It Like You Mean It

I reply to my favorite comments, liking all the others. When you do this long enough, you start to notice screen names and regulars.

Ugh, like *@thatguy3k00*, who always says something snarky and unwanted. Today's entry: *Stick to telling sob stories for other people. Nobody cares about your own.*

I'm petty, so I like that one extra hard. My eyes keep scanning, and I smile when I come across Dakota's screen name. He's been the third member of my trio with Liss since he started working at her bakery a few years ago.

@DMillsBakes: I LOVE LOVIE. Take care of her for us, Fanning #1!!!

That brings a goofy smile to my face. It's a play on our names—Dakota and Elle, like the famous Fanning sisters.

A knock on the door breaks my reverie, and I scramble for my underwear. "Yeah?"

"Sorry to interrupt your forty-minute shower." Adam sounds annoyed through the bathroom door, and since he can't see me, I indulge in a large eye roll and middle-finger flourish.

"I didn't realize my shower habits concerned you."

"Only because I'm running to the store," he says, and yeah, that's definite annoyance in his tone. "I wanted to make sure you could keep an eye on Lovie while I'm gone."

"Give me two seconds."

I finish dressing quickly, pulling on joggers and a tank top bralette. When I open the door, billows of steam greet Adam, who turns hazy for a second before the air clears.

I try to imagine what he sees: cherry-red hair hanging limp and wet alongside my face. Decent boobs (but not so decent I need anything more than the bralette), trim waist leading to wider hips leading to even wider thighs. I haven't had a thigh gap since I was born. Bright-blue toenails, which now that I'm thinking of it, sort of—

"You like that color," Adam says, staring at them, one eyebrow quirked. "You own a lot of things that particular shade of blue."

If all the eye rolling I'm doing doesn't give me a headache, the teeth grinding surely will.

"Careful," I warn. "Spend any more time staring at my feet and I might think you have a fetish."

I push past him to my bedroom, throwing my dirty clothes in the hamper and donning a gray cardigan atop my bralette. No need to traumatize Lovie any more than she must already be, having spent the last definitely-not-forty-minutes with Adam's undivided attention.

Judging by the hairs on the back of my neck, that's what I'm getting now. His gaze tracks me as I move my bag to the dresser and start unpacking.

"Trust me," he intones. "There are much more interesting parts of your body than your *toes*." He palms the top of the doorway with both hands, his shirt coming up to reveal a sliver of tanned stomach skin and the band of a popular brand of men's underwear. "Like your mouth, when it's shut."

If he's trying to push me, see how far I'm willing to take this, he's going to be surprised. Like Lovie, there's not much I wouldn't do.

"Oral fixation. Hot." I tug open the top left drawer and start shoving my shit in haphazardly. "My boobs aren't bad either." I look down at my cleavage, then at Adam.

His jaw is so tense it sticks out wider than normal, takes up more space. Red splotches are building near the hinge. He's going to crack a molar.

Oh darn.

I flutter my lashes at him. "Did you need something else, or did you want to just stand there and stare at me all day?"

"I—" He huffs, moving from annoyed to frustrated. He turns away. "Just watch her."

I throw a hand over my shoulder in acknowledgment, but I'm not worried, and he's already out of view. There are turtles that move faster than Lovie ever has, even in her younger days. She's never in a hurry to go anywhere. Maybe that's why I missed that first train yesterday: tardiness is hereditary.

My reflection stares back at me from the mirror on the bureau, the sides and drawer faces covered in stickers and boy band posters. Silver picture frames sit in one corner, photos yellowing with age. The more important family pictures hang in the hall and living room—my grandparents' wedding, my high school and college graduation—but there's not enough wall space to hold them all. The overflow must have come here. There are a few of my grandfather from his military days, dressed in Army blues after coming home from Vietnam, and nostalgia tugs sharply at my heart.

Still smiling at the picture, I begin unpacking in earnest. The top left drawer fills quickly; I may have brought too many pajamas. No big deal—there are plenty of other drawers. Except when I pull open the next one, I find it occupied.

By neatly folded scrubs.

Leaving the mess, I march into the hallway, ready to give whoever will listen an earful about how I simply *cannot* share living space with Adam Wheeler, let alone a dresser.

But judging by the absence of any unfamiliar cars in the driveway or on the street, Adam is already gone. Come to think of it, I don't remember seeing Lovie when I was on my rampage either.

No need to panic. She's probably in the bathroom.

I give a gentle rap on the door. "Lovie?" I whisper, then clear my throat and repeat. "Lovie, are you in there?"

She's not in the bathroom, but it's a small house. There aren't many places for her to wander off. I peek my head in the other rooms. First in her bedroom, thinking she lay down for a late-morning nap. The living room, in case she's recently taken to trashy midday soap operas.

The kitchen, because I'm running out of places to check.

The front porch, where she sat earlier to do her puzzles. There's synthetic grasslike material covering the concrete, an off-white metal rocking bench, and nothing else.

My heart beats harder in my ears. How did I lose my grandmother already? It's been less than a day. It's been less than *twelve fucking hours*. I lean around the side of the porch to the driveway. Her car is here, but she is not.

I have to call someone. Not the police yet, I don't think. AngelCare, maybe? Or Adam? Maybe he decided to take her to the grocery and forgot to tell me. Probably to get further under my skin. But I don't have his number. And calling the agency to ask for said number or tell them I lost my grandmother is a surefire way to screw us all.

I'm on the verge of tears, but I swallow them down. Is this like when a kid goes missing, where the first forty-eight hours are the most essential? If so, we only have forty-seven hours and fifty-six minutes left.

I run back inside, doing another sweep of the interior. "Lovie?" I call over and over, trying not to let my voice give any indication of just how worried I am.

After I've checked every room in the house two more times, I pull my phone from my pocket and dial a nine and a one. I'm not ready to pull the trigger on that last digit yet. In the kitchen, I search the note cards and appointment slips magnetized to the fridge. Adam's number has to be *somewhere*.

Through the window above the stove, I catch movement in the side yard.

Sliding open the patio door, I spot Lovie on her hands and knees by the flower bed. Relief crashes through me, making my limbs go light and heavy all at once, like I've been treading water and just got a chance to relax.

"Lovie! Are you okay?" I drop to my knees next to her, pulling her hands from the dirt and checking them over for cuts, scrapes, dislocations.

Her eyes go wide, then fill with disdain. "I'm *fine*," she says, snatching away her wrinkled, arthritic hands.

I sit back on my feet, glad she isn't hurt or bleeding. "What are you doing out here?"

"I'm gardening. I always garden on Mondays."

That's why I didn't think to check here in the first place. "Lovie, it's Wednesday."

She scoffs, returning her hands to the soil. "No it isn't, girl."

I may sleep like the dead, but I didn't sleep *that* long. I pull my phone out and flash her the screen. "No, see? It's Wednesday. October first."

Lovie squints at my screen, and I can tell she doesn't really see the numbers or the date there. "Your generation and those damn phones. Taking them for fact," she says sharply. Quieter, maybe just for herself, she repeats, "I *always* garden on Mondays."

The relief I felt seconds ago gives way to anxiety, and the contrast makes me a little light-headed. My knees are soaked through from the grass, not yet sun-dried. Is this what Adam meant about going along with whatever she believes?

Unpacking can wait an hour until he comes home. So can peeing, and blinking.

"Do you want some help?" I ask, both hesitant and eager.

Lovie doesn't bother looking up. "I can do it myself."

So that's where I learned that. "Company, then?" *I'm scared to let you out of my sight now. When the hell did you get so fast?*

"I'm fine by myself."

I don't think she means to be rude or sharp, but it cuts like she did. "Okay, I'll . . ." I head back into the kitchen, where if I stand on tiptoes, I can see the top of her head through the window. I don't think I look away for the next hour. Or breathe, for that matter.

I would never forgive myself if my inattention caused her to get hurt, turned around, or confused. My love for her, this strong, determined woman who raised me, takes up most of the real estate in my heart, and I don't like to imagine how I'd function without her. She is my most important person.

Lovie's still outside when the front door opens. I finally blink my burning eyes and pull them away from her hunched form.

Adam unloads the groceries on the island counter. His forearms are tiger-striped with red and pink.

"No, thanks," he grumbles, leveling me with a scathing glare as he rolls out his shoulders. "I've got it."

I'd be quicker to tease him and his weak muscles if I felt remotely playful right now.

"So, hey." I rest my hip against the counter as he unpacks the first bag. "Funny story. While you were gone, I sort of lost Lovie for a second, and when I found her, she thought it was Monday. Is that something—"

His hand freezes inside the bag. His eyes are living thunderstorms. "You *lost* her?"

"I also found her," I defend. "You interrupt me a lot, you know." That's not *the* point, but it is *a* point I've wanted to make since last night.

Adam scrubs his jaw. Hard. "I told you to keep an eye on her."

My hands shoot out to my sides. "It was five minutes!"

"It takes five seconds!" he shouts, his shoulders shaking.

It's the first time I've ever heard the full impact of his voice, loud and abrasive. Gruff, like maybe he's smoked a pack or two before. He's always got the right words picked out too, ones that make the most impact.

And these certainly did. Since I arrived last night, I'm the one who's been unaware of her surroundings, off-kilter and out of orbit. Me, not Lovie.

Adam's expression goes blurry. Am I—oh jeez, *crying*? I must be more sleep deprived than I thought.

I clear my throat. "Please forgive me if I'm not an expert at this the way you are. She's only my grandmother, after all. What do I know?"

"This isn't going to work." His sandpaper tone abrades my already frayed nerves.

"You think?" I bite my lip to stop it from trembling. A whimper slips through.

"Well, I don't—wait." His voice changes midway through. "Are you crying?"

I bite down harder. "Nope."

"Shit," he mumbles. He runs a hand over his face, the perpetual shadow of hair there. "Shit, okay. Just—let me just think for a second."

"Should I go home?" I ask, because it's the only option I see. I don't want to endanger Lovie's care, and if Adam and I continue to butt heads this way, I fear it's only a matter of time.

Sighing, Adam drops his hand. His gaze is pensive, too heavy, so I study my blue toenails again. They scream at me against the ugly beige floor. Maybe I'll take the polish off later.

"No, no." He braces on the island with palms flat, arms locked. His head must be heavy, hanging there between his shoulders. "We just need to be more careful. Call a truce." The way he watches me crawls under my skin, settles uncomfortably there. He sees more of me than I want him to. "Around Lovie, at least."

That's fair. And also probably as much as I can offer. "Fine." I chew my lip, motioning toward the groceries. "Is there a bell in one of these? She moves faster than I remember."

He crumples an empty bag between his oversized palms. "You're just not used to having to care for her yet, when it's been the other way around for most of your life."

I hate how sure Adam sounds, how confident he is of the direction things are going and how sure he is that we can do this together.

I'm starting to get the sinking suspicion we don't *need* to do this together.

Lovie doesn't seem to need me at all.

CHAPTER EIGHT

I figure the best way to go about the rest of my day is to say and do as little as possible. And to avoid Adam like my life depends on it.

He was right earlier: most of Lovie's day has been occupied with gardening, puzzle books, and early-afternoon local access television. I keep a watchful eye on her. She tries to dismiss me on four separate occasions. I'm having none of that.

Adam's always there too, on the fringes, plying my grandmother with snacks and unsweetened iced tea he must have made at some point. He hasn't offered me a glass.

After leaving Lovie on the couch with a(nother) word search book, I move toward the kitchen. During some downtime earlier, wherein Lovie continued to ignore my existence like she's not responsible for it, I researched foods that help fight Alzheimer's. Leafy greens, vegetables like broccoli, and certain spices are all good options.

Adam's already at the stove, though, a warm and earthy scent filling the air.

His exhale is so close to a chuckle, I want to clean my ears, just to make sure I'm hearing him right. "If you're looking to make dinner, you're too late."

He sounds . . . nice. Definite yes on the ear cleaning. I add Q-tips to my mental Walmart list.

"It's not even that late," I say. "It's only five."

"She goes to bed right at eight. After *Jeopardy!*" Adam says, shrugging. He pulls a few plates down from the cabinet and starts scooping food onto one: roasted chicken, leafy greens, chickpeas, and cauliflower. Most of it looks disgusting, but it smells amazing. And it's Alzheimer's friendly.

I cross my arms, then think better of it when sweat starts to build under the thick fabric. My sweater was more to cover up than fight the cold, and it's excessive in this tiny kitchen, especially with the stove on.

Adam slides past me, grabbing forks from the silverware drawer on his way to the table. The only made plate goes in front of Lovie's usual seat. He looks like he's done this a hundred times before. He doesn't second-guess himself as he pulls a glass from the drinkware cabinet. Even the way he lets his hip rest on the island as he pours another glass of tea screams familiarity with these surroundings.

My brows gather as I lose the fight, tugging off my cardigan. "And you just started yesterday?"

My question gives him pause, and his eyes go tight before he looks away. The line of his jaw hardens. "I've done a few rotations here, when she had her weekly check-ins, then the daily ones."

Lovie was the one who chose AngelCare a year and a half ago, when there were more good days than bad. It was around the time she gave me her power of attorney and the deed to the house. She wanted to make this "easy" on me, as if this were a thing that could ever be easy. As if, with all the boxes checked (minus the health insurance, apparently), it wouldn't carve out my heart to see her this way, to have her see me without *knowing* me.

"You can make your plate next if you want," Adam says, pulling my focus back to him.

I'm still full from lunch—he also cooked that—but I'm pretty sure this is a one-time offer, so I don't argue. I'm seated with my plate and a glass of water before Lovie makes it into the kitchen, Adam just behind her, arms extended. Waiting to catch her if she falls.

As she's nearly seated, she loses her balance and tips sideways.

I jump to action so quickly I nearly fall myself, but Adam is faster, calm and collected as he steadies her with a gentle hand to her elbow. Less intimate than the way he grabbed me earlier as we fell from the closet, but just as grounding.

I wait for Lovie to bless the food. It's been ingrained in me since I could talk. Instead of counting sheep when I can't fall asleep, I say our family mealtime prayer: *Dear God, thank You for all that You give us. Thank You for our food, family, and friends. Please let everyone we know be happy, healthy, and safe. Amen.*

But instead, she grabs her fork and starts in on her greens.

Adam settles next to me, his portion size almost identical to mine despite him weighing an estimated fifty pounds more. Did he not think I'd be joining them for dinner? Some guilt-like thing tugs at my stomach.

Or I'm extremely hungry and my stomach has started eating itself, and that just mimics guilt.

Throughout dinner, I glance at Adam to see whether we're going to be cordial, have a civil conversation of some sort, but he doesn't return any of them, his own eyes focused either on his plate or Lovie's. I'm not sure how to interact with him when we aren't jumping down each other's throats. The silence barrels past comfortable and straight into awkward, and

I reach my breaking point somewhere around my fifth mouthful of cauliflower. I don't even like cauliflower.

I clear my throat. "Lovie, would it be all right if I watched your shows with you after dinner?"

If the chicken weren't already dead, her glare would have done the trick. "Only if you don't yell the answers. It's no fun for everybody else."

I poke my tongue into my cheek to avoid frowning. I hate having the right answer and not saying it until it's too late. I'm always worried people won't believe me when I say I knew in my head.

Adam takes a hefty sip of water—in contrast to me, I think he's trying not to smile—and when he's finished, his glass is nearly empty. Not only is he a bed thief; he's a camel too.

The rest of the meal is eaten in awkward, stretching quiet. It's so warm that at one point I get up to make sure the oven's not on, and my last bite isn't completely chewed before I offer to do dishes.

"You don't need to do that," Adam says. He brings his plate over and sets it next to mine.

"You cooked," I say, muscling the plate from him. I need to do *something*. I didn't come here for a vacation, dammit, and today I've felt about as useless as an empty aluminum can.

A contented sigh pings my ears, and when I turn, Lovie's watching us with hearts in her eyes. "You should do them together. The load is lighter when you have someone to help carry it."

If that isn't one of Lovie's Hard Love Rules, it should be.

I must have been eleven or twelve the first time she said something so poignant, so revolutionary, I stopped what I was doing to write it down. I knew even then how lucky I was to be brought up by a person who understood the value of her life and her time and instilled those same values in me. She would only ever use my screw-ups as opportunities to remind me of something I would have already learned had I been listening to her in the first place. It took me too long to start listening, so I vowed to never stop.

On her seventieth birthday, I gave her a list of my most favorites, with fancy font at the top that read *Lovie's Hard Love Rules*. There was no way I could ever have captured them all, but I tried.

For the first time I came home after curfew: *If you want to take the scenic route, make sure your destination will still be open when you get there.*

After she and Grandpa Bobby found out about that Aruba vacation I booked on their card to avoid responsibilities that felt too much, too hard, too fast: *Sweeping something under the rug doesn't make it go away. It just puts your dirt in a different place.*

When I called and told her about my wild adventures my first month at college, because I told her everything, and because I missed her, and because I thought I was making too many mistakes too soon: *Wear the lipstick. Kiss the guy. Make the mistakes. Especially the fun ones.*

Some were sillier, more lighthearted: *Never keep a secret for someone who wouldn't keep one of yours. Always wear clean underwear.*

Some were . . . not. *Being treated like a queen sounds fun until you remember all the heads that have had to roll to make it happen.*

It was somewhere in all those rules, those little throwaways I thought nothing of at the time, that she taught me how to live. How to become my own version of the person I always emulated—her.

"Go ahead, Bobby," Lovie says now, gesturing to the waffle-knit dishrag hanging from the oven handle. I mentally add her latest Hard Love Rule to my list. "Get to drying."

There's something unfamiliar in Adam's gaze. His lips purse and flatten a few times. "I'll wash, if you want to dry." He turns on the faucet.

We're really pushing the limits of this truce. I'm not sure I can be this close to both Adam and running water without shoving his head under the stream.

I glance over my shoulder, where Lovie's trying to leave the room undetected. "What if she tries escaping Alcatraz again?"

"That would imply she tried escaping the first time." He tests the temperature and adjusts the knobs. "But she won't. She loves her shows too much."

So we settle into something . . . well, not relaxed, but easy. Without anything else to do, I study Adam's hands as he sudses the dirty dishes. His nails are blunt and neat, his knuckles prominent and wide, turning red under the hot water. Veins and tendons crisscross up toward his wrists and forearms.

Why is it *always* the forearms?

I shove the thought away as he hands me clean, wet dishes and I dry and put them away.

Everything is exactly as it's been for my whole life. Except that the woman in the other room inexplicably believes me in love with the man at my side.

That's new.

CHAPTER NINE

Also new?

When I enter the living room a few minutes later, Lovie is perched in a different spot from the one I've seen her in my entire life. Since I can remember, whenever we'd curl up, whether it be for movies or sports games or the Macy's Thanksgiving Day Parade, she'd sit directly in the middle of the couch. She claimed it has the coziest cushion. I can't verify, since I've never been allowed to sit there.

But she's on the left side now, and Adam is on the other end. I'm about to be an Elle sandwich.

"Lovie, why don't you scoot to the middle?" I say, giving her a wooden smile as I set my drink down on a coaster—always on a coaster. Lovie's Hard Love Rule Twenty-Two.

She rolls her eyes, waving me off as the theme song for *Wheel of Fortune* begins. "Why would I do that? He's not *my* husband."

The sound that flies from my lips is half choke, half laugh.

But Adam's foot shifts *just so*, connecting with my shin where it's already tender, and even though he's smiling up at me, I see the dare written behind those indigo eyes.

Adam pats the seat beside him before slinging his arm across the back of the couch. "Come here, honey." His chin cocks sideways, and it makes him look . . . younger. Playful. Someone who has a secret but is really bad at keeping it.

I guess that kind of is what we're doing.

And there's an energy to Lovie right now, one I haven't witnessed from her since her last visit to the city. She's the woman I remember, mercurial in the best ways and sharp as a tack. My forced smile turns genuine.

Because of the coffee table, I have to step over Adam's legs to reach the middle seat. His hand comes up to my hip when I tip sideways, but a quick glare has it falling away, his mouth pinching to fight a smirk. He is not very good at that either.

Sitting down gingerly, I try tucking in on myself so as not to touch any of my body parts to any of Adam's body parts. Even this middle cushion, which *is* noticeably more comfortable than the others, isn't enough to relax my defenses.

Adam's heat is a wall at my right as I get situated, and there is so much of him, it makes me wish I'd done the counterintuitive thing and put my sweater back on. Less surface area to touch him.

For his part, he's shifting too, trying to make the best of a bad situation. Unfortunately, every time he moves, I get a whiff of his scent. It's not as toxically masculine as I first feared, which makes me fear it all the more. It's warm, smoky—I think I described it as *summer* before. Warm skin and good memories.

I sit stoically through the first puzzle on *Wheel of Fortune*—solution: *night and day difference*—and straight through a commercial break.

At one point, Adam's hand dips down and the band of his watch brushes my shoulder. I shiver from the cold.

He swallows thickly. "Sorry."

"Sure," I grit out. It's all I can manage.

Fake It Like You Mean It

When Lovie comes back from a bathroom break, she snorts when she sees us. "And here I thought you two were in love. I've seen more chemistry from a pair of dead fish. You don't have to be polite on my account, Bobby. I'm not a prude."

Now it's Adam's turn to sound like he's dying. It's nice of him to join me here, between a rock and a hard place. I scoot an inch closer to him and clutch his knee. "You heard the lady, honey." I give him an exaggerated wink and move my hand a few inches higher, then drop my voice. "Fake it like you *mean it*."

My eyes reflect a challenge of my own, and Adam accepts.

His arm falls from the back of the couch to my shoulder, his fingers on my upper arm. His watch isn't as cold on my skin anymore. He hugs me closer, our sides aligning all the way down. There's no reason to be this close, but when I try to pull away, his hold tightens.

The show returns from commercial break, and I'm relieved to have something else to focus on aside from his warmth.

A soft breeze rustles the hairs around my face. "*Catcher in the Rye.*"

His murmur at my ear is just as disarming as his breath on my neck. A chill and heat lance through me at the same time, and, like my heart can't decide how it feels either, it skips a beat before thudding clumsily in my chest.

I blink. "What?"

Adam's chuckle is so close, it hums through me like one of my own. "*Catcher in the Rye.* The answer. Lovie said not to yell, but . . ." He shrugs, and that jostles me too.

On the screen, one of the contestants guesses *s*. The host dons a consolatory smile. No *s*'s.

I peek at Adam in my periphery, then the puzzle again. Damn it. He's right.

And, after two more letters, Mary from Albuquerque is right too.

"I knew that," Lovie says, crossing her arms.

For all her talk of "don't scream the answers," the biggest offender is Lovie herself. Through the rest of *Wheel of Fortune* and into *Jeopardy!* as soon as the answer becomes clear to her, she spits it out fast enough that if she had dentures, they'd fly across the room.

Adam continues to whisper his guesses along my temple. His lips never touch me, but other parts of him do. The hand on my shoulder travels up my neck, takes to playing with the short hair at my collarbone.

Because I don't handle losing well, I decide to return the favor.

My hand migrates to midthigh, firm and muscled under my touch.

His breath hitches in my ear, his body tensing as he blurts, "Nineteen seventy-six."

Whoops.

Lovie huffs. When the contestant on the screen confirms Adam was right, she huffs again. I have to swallow a laugh.

I'd play Adam's game if I knew any of the answers, but unsurprisingly, Ancient Greek architecture does not come up often on the subway. Nor the 1992 World's Fair.

During Double Jeopardy, when the host reveals a category called, simply, "Podcasts," I sit up a little straighter. The contestant starts at $800.

"My granddaughter has one of those podcast things," Lovie says, and pride flairs in my chest. She may not know I'm sitting right next to her, but I'm in there somewhere.

"This show features two best friends who discuss death and crime of all kinds, and listeners can submit their own stories, called 'Hometowns.'"

I know this. Hell, you'd have to live under a rock not to.

But Adam stays quiet, as do Lovie and the contestants.

Steeling myself to be met by either his penetrative gaze or intoxicating smell, I turn to Adam and place my mouth at his ear. "*My Favorite Murder*," I whisper.

None of the contestants take a guess. After the time runs out, Ken Jennings proves me right, and Adam hums in appreciation, his eyes sparkling.

The contestants move on to the next question, and once again, I know the answer immediately but stay quiet, per Lovie's instructions.

Adam tugs a lock of my hair. "Well?"

"*Stuff You Should Know.*" A smile comes to my face, rare in his presence.

His gaze drops to it. "*Stuff You Should Know*," he echoes. Probably he's unused to my mouth forming a shape as flattering as my smile.

For every unanswered *Dark History* and *Call Her Daddy*, Adam's murmurs of approval are more affirming than knowing if I were a contestant, I'd have $5,600 on my board. Cutting their losses, the contestants move to another category before deciding not knowing podcasts is less embarrassing than not knowing astrophysics. They switch back to finish out the category.

"This show follows the namesake as she travels the Chicago underground and interviews other public transport riders."

"Oh my God," I say, sitting forward. Adam's arm falls off my shoulders. My heart is suspended in my throat. "That's my show."

Adam hisses, prying my nails from his thigh.

I can't even begin to formulate an apology. My brain's still stuck. My podcast is on *Jeopardy!* I need to do something. Take a picture, start a live stream, something. "Why aren't they buzzing in? *Elle on the L.* Somebody say it."

Nobody does. The buzzer sounds, and it remains unanswered.

I throw up my hand, nearly hitting Adam in the face. "Oh, what the fuck."

Three things happen at once: Adam barks out a harsh laugh, Lovie harrumphs, and the host says, "The answer we wanted there was *Elle on the L*."

Eyes wide and mouth gaping, I jump to my feet and spin around.

"I was on *Jeopardy!*" I yell over the now-ambient noise of the game show.

Lovie seems confused; Adam is too, I think, his eyes darkening as he takes me in.

I shimmy on shaky legs, and in my socked feet, I probably look like a footballer warming up at the Super Bowl.

My phone starts dinging with notifications in my pocket. My listeners are more on top of my shit than I am. One of them reminded me to schedule a Pap smear this spring.

Lovie mutters something about getting more tea and disappears into the kitchen.

Adam moves as if to follow her, but I pull my phone out and toss it to him. "Take a Boomerang."

He catches it with one hand, flipping the screen right side up. "A *what?*"

"Okay," I say. "Go to Instagram." I want to make a joke about how he's young for a boomer, but nothing can kill my vibe right now. I was on fucking *Jeopardy!* The name of my show will go in, like, the *Jeopardy!* archives. And since they never, ever, ever recycle clues, it's not a far jump to say I made history.

"Dakota Fanning with two exclamations says to check your social media," he says, frowning at the screen. "And I'm on Instagram now. Should I check this little box with five hundred notifications, or keep going for the Boomerang thing?"

"Five *hundred*?"

His eyes widen. "Make that seven."

I do my little happy dance again. "I'm famous. You, sir, are in the presence of royalty."

He rolls his eyes. "Should I rewind the episode so you can do"—he waves a hand in the general direction of my feet—"whatever *that* is next to the clue?"

"Great idea."

His mouth drops. He must have been kidding.

Adam rewinds the show, and I peek through the wooden half wall topped with banisters and check on Lovie in the kitchen. She's mumbling to herself—probably about how I shouted the answer before she could—as she roots around in the dry-goods cabinet.

I pose for the picture when Adam says he's ready. "Scoot to the, er, left a bit?" His brows slash a near-straight line across his forehead. "Maybe turn to me more?"

He looks so focused, his eyes trained on my phone, dwarfed in his massive hands. I can probably use filters to hide my blush. "I'll make an Instagram husband out of you yet, Adam Wheeler."

It's his turn to blush now.

To my surprise, the first Boomerang turns out cute and usable. I'm not sure whether it's a testament to my pure joy or Adam's abilities.

I'm in such a good mood, I'm willing to share the credit.

CHAPTER TEN

I'm on the couch, liking and responding to comments long after Lovie has gone to sleep. Chamomile tea cools in my butterfly mug on the coffee table.

@jollyxholly527: I SCREAMED!
@ElleontheL ✅*:* ME TOO!!!
@SweetiesCakesChicago: so proud of you bestie!

That's Liss. I type out a response, even though we've been texting all night about my newfound fame. I'm half expecting her to FedEx me a congratulatory cake.

@ElleontheL ✅*:* aw, bestie! I'm blushin'

I keep scrolling until I come across one that sours my blood.

@thatguy3k00: Big deal. There have been 500,000+ clues in the history of @Jeopardy. Obviously they're running out of material.

Fake It Like You Mean It

Oh, wonderful. Even the trolls have come out to congratulate me. I like his comment and move on to Dakota's.

@DMillsBakes: *WHEN YOU RETURN FROM THE WAR, WE'RE TAKING YOU OUT TO CELEBRATE.*

This makes me smile like an idiot at my screen, and I'm so engrossed in trying to get through the thousands of other notifications, I hardly notice the couch dip next to me.

"More Boomeranging?" Adam says. He swipes the remote from the coffee table.

I snort. "You can't say that. Makes me think of banging."

"My apologies." He flicks through channels before deciding on a late-night sports recap. The heat of his gaze is thick on my skin. I can still feel him pressed to my side. His fingers dancing in my hair. His firm thigh beneath my hand.

"I'd tell you to take a picture," I say, "but since you only just learned what a Boomerang is an hour ago, my hope for that isn't high."

His laugh is raspy, like the day is catching up with him. Before my catapult to fame, I was tired too.

"What are you doing?" Adam asks, breaking through my mental gymnastics.

"Replying to comments."

"*Still*? Are you really that well known on Instagram?"

I shrug. "On everywhere."

"Where's everywhere?"

Although he's still wearing scrubs, he looks more relaxed now that Lovie's down for the night. His shoulders aren't tight, his arms loosely crossed over his stomach. Shadows on his jaw for the second night in a row tells me he probably shaves every morning.

I eye the empty spot between us; the middle cushion must be some sort of self-declared No-Man's-Land.

Thank God I'm a woman.

I slide over, propping my feet next to his, and angle my screen so he can see. "So, this is the internet."

"Good to know. And what's this contraption you're looking at it on?"

"A MacBook?" My eyes slice sideways, and I catch the tail end of his smile before he wipes it from his face. He's a bigger smartass than I thought. "Well, Adam, this is a laptop. See how it's in my *lap*?"

He nods solemnly. "Internet. Laptop. No Boomeranging. Got it." He points at my blue checkmark. "And that?"

"Just my verification. No big deal."

When he doesn't respond right away, I glance at him. His brows are slashed downward, as is his mouth.

"You don't know what it means to be verified?" As someone who makes a living through the internet, I consider this a crime. A damn shame. "Oh boy. So, when you have a well-known name or brand or . . . I don't know, business or something, you can request to be verified. Which basically confirms you are who you say you are."

"Okay, but why? Why is that necessary, I mean."

This is teaching Lovie how to text all over again. "Well, because of trolls."

"The little elf things with fluffy rainbow hair?" The concern in his gaze is so alarming, my heart skips another beat. That can't be healthy. "My nieces are big fans, but what do those have to do with anything?"

A laugh bursts from my lips unbidden. "You've got to be joking."

He lets out a soft chuckle of his own, shifting, and I tilt toward him as the couch dips under his weight. "That time, yes."

I scroll back up to @thatguy3k00's comment. "This guy is basically my archnemesis. I'm convinced he gets off on pointing out my flaws."

Adam mouths the words as he reads them, looking increasingly like he sucked a lemon. "Can't you block him or report him or something?"

"It doesn't bother me, really. Because for every one of his comments, there are dozens more like this."

> **@DFWMama6:** *How cool! I'm so proud of you and all you've accomplished. Love you like my own! The work you do matters.*

"This woman is a mom of six who lives in Dallas," I say, pointing at the different parts of her username. "Her daughter has juvenile rheumatoid arthritis, and every week while her daughter's doing infusions, she listens to my show. It's one of the only pieces of her life she has just for herself. I love giving that to people."

His chin dips. "So you do it for the Dallas mothers of six instead of *those guys*."

My head bobbles in a mix of a nod and a shake. "I do it for me, mostly. I love talking to people. Cutting through bullshit and getting to the heart of what makes us human. These comments are just a bonus."

He stretches his arm across the back of the couch, much the same as we were earlier. He doesn't touch me this time. "I was going to ask what the podcast is about, but I think they covered it on *Jeopardy!*"

I let out a little squeak, then clap a hand over my mouth. A nervous giggle escapes anyway, my knee pressing into his thigh. I inhale, and a piece of loose hair flies into my mouth.

His gaze catches mine, a sparkle in the deep-blue ocean there. Moonlight reflecting off the motion of the waves, only the same for that one millisecond in time. It feels special to have seen it, like I've witnessed something rare. It stretches from one second to several, our stares locked. There's a magnetic pulse thrumming under my skin, and I get the feeling he's learning me inside out with those eyes.

They're almost black by the time Adam lifts his hand and brushes away the lock of hair with the back of his index finger, light enough to send a chill through my limbs. It takes him a few tries to get it. He looks annoyed that it takes so long, his lip caught in his teeth, eyebrows scrunched together.

Even after all the hair is gone, he reaches up again, his thumb brushing the corner of my mouth. My pulse jumps against my skin everywhere we touch, and I don't breathe for fear of rupturing this moment we've created.

There's no need for us to keep up pretenses now. Lovie is asleep, her brain resetting as we speak—or stare. Our little love charade can be put to rest, and we can go back to killing each other in our heads again tomorrow.

But Adam, when he isn't dickish and rude and refusing me my bed, is almost nice to talk to. At least he knows who I am, which is more than I can say for Lovie.

This is one hell of a truce. I could easily get lost here, in the space of being known.

"You've had barbecue sauce on your face since lunch," he declares, his hand falling to his lap with a smack. "It's probably in your hair too."

That'll do it.

As I scoot to the other cushion, I surreptitiously wipe my mouth on my shoulder. Adam snickers, his fingertips rubbing back and forth across his pants.

Feet firmly in No-Man's-Land as a barrier between us, I swirl my finger around the drawstring of my joggers. "You said you have nieces. How many?" My voice is raspy, sounds unused. There's glass in my throat. And the corner of my mouth tingles where he touched me, like some of it cut me there.

That could just be the barbecue sauce, though.

Fake It Like You Mean It

Adam lets his knee fall sideways near my foot before thinking better of it. "Three." He lets out a fake yawn so big they can see it from space. "How do you want to do this sleeping thing? Take the bed every other night?"

I should be generous, full of midwestern hospitality. As it is, this couch could give a slab of concrete a run for its money on which sleeps worse. I stand, stretching my arms above my head. My bralette rides up my ribs. A little yawn of my own escapes as I tug the hem back down. "I'll take the bed, thanks."

He nods, not meeting my eyes. "For tonight, or . . ." His face falls. "Forever. You're taking the bed forever."

"I am." Tucking my laptop under my arm, I give him a dramatic bow. "I usually do a green smoothie at seven before my run. Be there or be square."

"Wait." His voice catches me when I'm at the mouth of the hallway, and through the banister slats, I see him stand.

Is he going to touch me again? Finish whatever the hell we started on the sofa? Or maybe even earlier, in the laundry closet. My heart beats everywhere. My skin is hot and sensitive.

He inhales as he brushes past me, avoiding my body as much as possible. "I need my things from your room."

How could I forget all the precious drawer space occupied by his many, *many* scrubs? And honestly, how many pairs does a person need? Can't you mix and match those things? I trail him down the hallway. "Do you have an apartment?"

"I have a place near Goshen." He flicks on the light in my room, and I follow him through the doorway. "That anxious to get rid of me?"

"Just wondering how far I'd have to kick this to have it land on your doorstep." I toe his duffel bag.

"If it starts to bother you in here, just let me know and I can put it in the hall closet or something." He reaches around me, just barely brushing my knee.

I jump, and the mattress catches my legs. I cross them like I meant to fall. "Yep!" I squeeze the mussed comforter into a ball beneath my head. "Perfect."

He straightens, towering over me. He takes a step back, then another. Adam takes me in one last time, lounging on the end of the bed as if I didn't literally *bolt* from his touch, before turning toward the dresser.

"You're being very cordial." Somehow, even staring at the back of his head, I know he's smiling as he rummages through the drawers. "I'll let you have tonight, considering your great personal achievement. But tomorrow, all bets are off. Tell me, Elle, do you like cayenne in those smoothies of yours?"

I gasp, sitting up fast enough to twinge a muscle. "You wouldn't."

"Probably not." He looks over his shoulder as he moves toward the door. "But I guess we'll see."

Yes, we will, Adam. Yes, we will.

CHAPTER ELEVEN

There will be no cayenne in my smoothie, because I wake up early enough to hide it in the back of the spice cabinet. It hurt my soul when I saw the five and two zeros on my phone, before I remembered why I'd set my alarm so early.

For good measure, I also hide the paprika, chili powder, and red pepper flakes.

I'm not sure what time Lovie gets up, but when I peek in on her and find her in a deep sleep, I'm comfortable leaving a note on the counter and slipping out for a run. My eyes snag on a sleeping Adam in the living room, his mouth relaxed and letting out an occasional soft snore. His feet are hanging off the edge of the couch, and I only feel slightly guilty about taking the bed, before spotting his beloved socks.

Elle's General Life Rule Number One: never show sympathy for psychopaths.

Three miles and a half hour later, the sun is still only thinking about rising, dew clinging to the grass in fat drops. I barrel through the front door, ready for that smoothie now more than ever.

And when I round the kitchen after slipping off my sneakers, it's surprisingly there: a perfectly normal-looking green smoothie, right in the center of the island. Adam's at the stove. I don't see the blender, so he either already washed and put it away or hid it somewhere to go rancid. Probably under my bed.

"Have a good run?" His voice is casual, as if conversations between us are always this easy. There's soft music playing from somewhere behind him, maybe on his phone, something old and croony Lovie is bound to recognize.

Stepping up to the island, I peer down into the smoothie. It doesn't smell like grass, which is hard to do with green drinks. I lift my eyes but not my chin, hoping my dark circles make me extra menacing. "Where's Lovie?"

Adam is stirring eggs in the jankiest skillet in existence. Lovie's had that thing for years; the handle is so loose, you have to use two hands to move it or risk dumping the contents on the floor when it inevitably falls off.

"Getting dressed," he says, sliding bread into the slats of the retro brown toaster. "If she's not back in a few minutes, would you go check on her? She's very fond of her privacy."

"I know the feeling." I pick up the smoothie and tilt it side to side. Probably there's no glue in it. Treating it like a grenade, I set it down gingerly and cross my ankles under the island, hollowed out in this spot only. The space is about as wide as a dishwasher, but this house is old enough that can't have been the intention. When I was little, I would run through the gap as part of my hallway-kitchen-laundry loop. I cried the day I became too tall to fit.

I nod at the green drink. "What's this?"

His jaw twitches in what I now recognize as amusement. "So, a smoothie is—"

"What are the *ingredients*, Adam?"

"Apple, banana, spinach, and almond milk. Oh, and some pineapple I found in the back of the freezer, so if it tastes off, that might be why." He relaxes against the counter, takes a sip from one of Grandpa Bobby's old fishing mugs. "Or it could be the laxatives."

My jaw unhinges. "I thought we were in a truce."

His eyes flash, his tongue catching a drop of coffee on the corner of his mouth. Right where he touched me last night. "I don't see Lovie, do you?"

Well, *someone* woke up on the wrong side of the couch this morning.

I take a tentative sip of the smoothie to call his bluff. His expression never wavers. He either has a degree in reverse psychology and I'm going to regret this for the next forty-eight hours, or he's the worst actor ever and is completely unbothered by my presence.

The smoothie doesn't taste poisoned—or laced with laxatives. It's honestly not bad. I miss my shredded coconut and protein powder from home, but this will do for now.

Adam pulls the skillet off the burner as I take a more generous gulp. "Not dying?"

I'm not dying, no. But I am transfixed on his hand, the pan still suspended from the firmly attached handle. I swallow hastily, licking off my green mustache. "How'd you do that?"

"Do what?" He sets the skillet on a waiting trivet.

"The . . . the handle is loose."

He shrugs. "I fixed it."

This guy is from another planet. My brain can't wrap itself around all the little things he does, seemingly for no reason other than to make things easier on others. Not me, of course, but Lovie.

My ex, Grady, wasn't necessarily a bad guy. I think that would require him pulling his head from his ass long enough to be anything other than self-absorbed. I can't count the number of times he made me a smoothie, because it literally never happened. Not once.

And here comes *this fucking guy*, who makes my grandmother what she thinks are her favorite foods and appeases her by watching her shows.

Today his scrubs match his eyes, a deep navy that brings out his lingering summer tan. It's a nice color on him. And that material looks soft too, washed the perfect amount of times. I bet the fabric would stretch to accommodate any hands that slipped underneath. His biceps would flex as he pulled it overhead.

Elle, he'd say, gritty and a little undone. Or maybe as a question, a request. *Elle, will you take that off for me?*

"Elle? Did you hear me?"

I snap back to reality with a harsh blink, and yeah, he just caught me staring at his traps. Because he has those too.

"What?" I say, dazed.

Adam fights a smile. "I asked if you would go check on Lovie."

I pivot on my socked feet, not bothering with a verbal response because I cannot believe I just eye-fucked Lovie's nurse. Me being here has nothing to do with me and everything to do with Lovie needing a nurse in the first place.

I knock twice on my grandmother's bedroom door.

A frustrated sound carries to me. I don't know if she meant it to grant entrance, but it does.

She's perched precariously on the side of her bed, trying to work her sock onto one of those shoe contraptions. The other sock is backward, the heel billowing near the bend in her ankle. Her yellow shirt is misbuttoned, her reading glasses are askew, and there might be an actual bird's nest in her hair.

There's so much going on, I don't know where to start. My breath is shallow, shaky. It still shocks me how bad she's gotten.

When I was in college, I called Lovie once every other day or so, just to check in.

Fake It Like You Mean It

"I'm fine, Ellie," she'd always say. "Just old."

Every time, I rushed to correct her. "You're not old, Lovie."

But she was then, and she is now. I didn't realize I was doing her a disservice at the time, denying her something she knew in her brittle bones. I viewed getting old as a *bad* thing, something that slows you down and steals time, when it's really just a *thing* we have to deal with and adjust to. People are born and grow up, then they get old and die. And so many don't even get to have that honor in the first place.

I don't know if this is helpful thinking, but it does unstick my feet. I move toward her, and both fear and anger flash in her eyes.

"What are you doing?" She sounds like she looks—a mess.

I place my hand atop hers as she fumbles with the guide tool. "Helping you."

She snatches her hand away, pulling the helper so fiercely it whacks me in the leg. *Hard.* "I don't need help."

My thigh throbs, but also my head and heart and stomach. My entire body is a bruise. This might be the most uncomfortable feeling in the world for someone like me: knowing you can help but being told you aren't allowed. My nose burns with the threat of tears, but I won't let them fall. I have a job to do, dammit.

Ready or not, Hurricane Elle just touched down.

I crouch in front of her, plucking the errant sock from the end of the helper before she notices it's gone.

When she does, she pulls her arm back like she might strike me with it, but I don't flinch. I can't afford to again.

Her toes are cold enough that the slight blue tinge is worrisome. The yellowing nails could use a trim too. The skin is so translucent that the spider veins around her ankles jump out at me like fireworks against a night sky. I guide her toes in gently, but her nails cause a snag or two. She's getting her *Wheel of Fortune* with a side of pedicure tonight.

Maybe her outburst used up all her energy, because she doesn't fight me this time. She's shaking a little. After I correct the other sock and rebutton her shirt, I find the thickest sweater I can in her closet, which smells like lavender and home. Like love.

Like Lovie.

"Do you want help putting this on?" I ask.

She crosses her arms low on her stomach.

Rolling my eyes, I pull one arm free, slipping my hand through the hole to guide her. Learned my lesson with the socks. Her next arm goes better, and it's only after her sweater's on and the shaking has subsided that I move for her hairbrush.

I don't bother asking this time, and she doesn't fight me. Instead, she takes to rubbing her knuckles. She spends the longest time on the fourth finger of her left hand. She still wears her wedding ring every single day. The gold is scuffed and scratched, a physical manifestation of sixty years well lived and well loved.

Clearing my throat, I get her on her feet. I nod my chin to the walker in the corner. "Do you want that?"

She scowls.

"Okay, then," I say. "Let's go. Breakfast's ready."

Neither of us is smiling when we make it to the kitchen. My thigh pulses with every heartbeat, and I rub at it absently as I swipe my smoothie from the counter and sit as far away from Lovie as possible. Which, at a table for four in a house this size, is not far enough.

I know better than to take Lovie's outbursts personally. In one single day, I've seen the damage this horrible disease has done to the person she used to be. She's *always* been stubborn—I learned it from her—but this is worse.

And maybe I'm a little mad at her. For hitting me with assistive clothing devices. For thinking I'm in love with Adam.

For forgetting who I am in the first place. So I sip my smoothie noisily, chomp too loud on toast because I know it bothers her to hear people chewing. Petty, yes, but it can't be helped.

Adam just watches us, and I choose to ignore the concern on his face. What he doesn't realize yet is he's currently cohabitating with both the Queen and Princess of Cold Shoulder Kingdom.

"What do you want to do today, Lovie?" he asks when forks scrape porcelain.

She snorts down at her plate. "Stay away from her."

"Her . . ." Adam trails off. I rub my thigh again, and his face twists. I continue to ignore his worried glances. He blinks hard. "Gardening, maybe?"

Lovie's head snaps up to bark at him too, but the hostility slips as she sees him for the first time this morning. Literally melts off her face, into something eerily similar to admiration. Her hands come together, and she thumbs her wedding ring again. "You don't garden, Bobby. Only Lovie does that." She tilts her head my way. "Maybe she can teach you a thing or two."

The cherry drops onto this already shitty sundae of a day. Sleep was supposed to fix it. A good night's sleep fixes everything.

But not this. She's still stuck in her delusions, in the belief that Adam and I are Lovie and Bobby.

Which means we're stuck right along with her.

CHAPTER TWELVE

After breakfast, once Lovie's in the living room, I jump up from the table. My leg aches with the movement. Damn, she got me good.

"You said she'd forget," I say. "Why isn't she forgetting?"

Adam's hands shoot in front of him, defensive as I close the gap between us. "I don't know! It's different for everyone."

I wield my now-empty smoothie glass at him. I want to throw it at his head. "There are no common threads? Why does someone normally forget someone versus remember someone else?"

He stares over me, probably at Lovie as she roots around in the living room for a new puzzle book. "It just . . . It really just . . . depends."

"On *what*, Adam? How well she knows you? Because I've known her all my life, and she's known you all of five minutes, and neither of those things is helping."

He scrubs over the rough stubble on his jaw. "On so many things. Her specific disease progression, the areas of her brain that are affected. It usually starts in the hippocampus, moves through the lateral and parietal lobes, then to the frontal and whatever's left. But that's just usually, what's most common. I'd have to view her latest scans to know for sure."

Now it's my turn to scrub my face. "So you really don't know."

"No." He sighs. "I wish I did. Memory is so fickle. Have you ever smelled something completely random and been taken back to when you were four? It's like that for the rest of our lives. We don't outgrow it. It could be *anything* making her think this. A scent. A certain color. Hell, the way you style your hair."

Something niggles in the back of my brain, Adam's words having triggered a nearly-there memory. Before I can place it, Lovie's soft chuckle floats over my shoulder as she steps back into the room. "A little dancing in the kitchen?"

I'm in the middle of hoping Lovie's mood swings aren't severe enough to give her whiplash when I realize Adam and I are standing far too close.

And before either of us can create distance, she speaks again. "Well, don't stop on my account."

The aptly named Adam's apple in front of my eyes bobs, and when my gaze tracks up to his face, his eyebrow arches. An unspoken question. *Are we confirming or redirecting?*

Lovie's stance is strong. Her words are not a request or a suggestion but a kindly worded order. She's pleased with herself. What really does it for me is the smug, winning grin, ripening her cheeks into something rosy and plump. She's the woman in all my best memories, the one who raised me. How can I say no, especially when there's no telling how many more of these days she'll have ahead of her?

I dip my chin in a reluctant nod. Our feet shuffle closer, and his hand finds my hip. To steady myself, I grab his shoulder, firm and unforgiving under my palm. He tenses under my touch, then relaxes into it. Settling in.

As we attempt to arrange ourselves, his littlest finger slips beneath the hem of my shirt, scraping my skin and turning it feverish.

Adam isn't faring much better, his neck and ears flushed. His scrub top is a V-neck, giving him plenty of space, but he pulls at the collar anyway, bringing it back and forth a few times.

And yeah, now that he mentioned it, it is a little warm in here. Would Lovie *really* notice if we turned the heat down a degree or ten?

He throws her a complaisant grin, speaking out of the corner of his mouth. "We don't have to do this."

"Clearly we do." I smile, more puppet than master.

Anything less than full participation is insulting to Lovie. That's Hard Love Rule Number Four: *Whatever you're doing—cursing, kissing, punching, screwing up—you better make it count.*

She has a lot of rules involving kissing.

If I'd ever stopped to imagine myself in this scenario, I would have thought it awkward, dancing with a virtual stranger under the guise of a matchmaking grandma who has no idea she *isn't* matchmaking.

But it's not awkward. Not exactly. We're finding a rhythm, though the music can hardly be heard over our clumsy steps. Adam's hands are tender on my hips but firm enough to let me know he's trying his hardest too.

My socked foot catches a slick spot on the linoleum, right at the edge of the island. His grip sures up, fingers digging into me even as a few more of them find their way to my bare skin.

The corner of his mouth lifts, saying without words *I've got you* or maybe *easy there*. He guides us back into movement.

And suddenly, we are in sync.

Until—

"You stepped on my foot!" I gawk. "I'm not wearing shoes!"

"I'm not either." His grip tightens, along with his jaw. "You can't tell me you think I did that on purpose."

"And you can't tell me you're a—wait, how old are you?" His birthday was on his license, but that was too much mental math after dark for my taste.

"Thirty-five."

"You can't tell me you're a thirty-five-year-old man who doesn't know how to slow-dance."

The tops of his cheekbones go pink.

"It's been a while," he grits. "*Honey.*"

Somewhere behind me, Lovie harrumphs, and a few seconds later the sofa squeaks.

I take back what I said earlier. She's the one giving *me* whiplash.

He starts to pull away, but I tighten my grip on his shoulders.

"We should probably go for a few more minutes," I murmur, in case her hearing is still as good as it was whenever I tried to sneak in past curfew. "Just in case she comes back."

"Right." He swallows. "Just in case."

The music playing from Adam's phone, now that our steps have quieted, is something melodic. Familiar. I let it wash over my fraying nerves, allow myself to relax in a way I haven't since I showed up here not two days ago. It's not the worst thing in the world to have to dance with an attractive man.

I give myself over to the moment, tucking my head so it lays tentatively on his shoulder. His heartbeat thuds under my cheek, slightly faster than the tempo of the music, and faster still when he pulls one of my hands into his and rests them on his chest.

I try not to think about it, what any of this means. This is what Lovie wants right now, and I'm giving it to her. It doesn't mean I have to like the way my hand fits in his or enjoy his thumb brushing over mine, all the way down to my wrist. It just means she's watching, probably.

"Since we've got each other's undivided attention," I murmur, "should we discuss what this means?"

He maneuvers us so my back is to the living room, giving himself a clear view over my head to Lovie's exact location. "You mean, the small problem of her still thinking we're in love."

I wince. "That'd be the one."

He's quiet for a bit, and in that time, I can't help but notice our dancing doesn't quite match the beat of the song that just started. Adam's not in a rush to correct it, though. "We still have the option for you to leave—"

This freezes me in place, and his foot skims mine again before he saves it. "*No*," I say. "Absolutely not."

"That's fine." His throat bobs, half of his mouth tilting up. "I knew you'd say that. I just thought I'd offer. Thought maybe seeing less of us together would give her brain more time to disconnect."

I still don't consider it. Going back home would mean giving up precious time with her I can't recover.

She wouldn't get to see how good she did with raising me. How strong I am, simply because she was strong first.

"I'm staying," I say.

Adam nods, and there's a glimmer in his eyes—it looks a bit like pride, but maybe it's just seasonal allergies. Mine always get worse when I come home.

"In that case . . ." He pauses, top teeth sunk into his full bottom lip as he switches the hold of our hands. Now our fingers are entwined. "We should set some boundaries."

I stare at them for a second. "Like touching."

"I don't think it's necessary to get more intimate than this." He squeezes my hand.

I squeeze his harder. "This, plus *Jeopardy!* cuddling. Washing dishes. You know. The usual fake-dating stuff."

"Sure," he says. He blows out a breathless laugh. "If any of this is usual."

That pulls a reluctant grin to my face. "We should probably keep it up, like—all the time, I guess?" I wrinkle my nose. "I mean, she is fast as *fuck*."

The scratch of Lovie's pen in her word search book and her morning talk show almost drown out the music. His face softens when he looks at her.

I can't imagine doing this for a living. I know how much my own heart hurts when I see my grandmother. Does his hurt as much as mine, or is it just bigger, with more capacity for the pain? How does he do this every single day, for so many people?

"It doesn't have to be all the time." Dark eyelashes dance along his cheek as he looks at me. "She goes to bed at eight, after all."

There's an undertone to his words I can't quite decipher, more mischievous than usual. What does he imagine we'll be doing after Lovie goes to sleep?

"So, when she's up and active. That's not too terrible."

"Thank you so much," he intones. "What a compliment. 'Not too terrible.'"

Another glaring problem presents itself. "Will this affect your, um—I mean, you sort of work for me."

Some of the color recedes from his cheeks, and he switches the hold of our hands back to how they were before. Takes a half step back. "I guess you'd be the one to decide that. If you want to hire someone else to replace me, I understand."

This particular complication hasn't been an issue with any of Lovie's previous nurses, and I've been over more than once while they've been here. Granted, that was temporary, not this permanent, around-the-clock care.

Lovie's comfortable with Adam, though. She trusts him, lets him dress, bathe, feed her. He listens to how she's feeling; she takes the medications he proffers in response. I'm no longer naïve enough to believe I could do this completely on my own, but I'm hesitant to move on to someone else quickly, especially when things are working okay-ish as is.

"I won't ask you to leave." With how close we are, it's impossible to miss the flash of relief on his features. "But if you wanted to—"

"I'd like to stay," he says. "We'll just figure out the rest later. But we should agree up front that if anything risks her health or safety, we drop the act. No matter how much it upsets her."

Something warm and bright blooms in my chest. "Agreed."

Our dance stretches another minute, to the end of the song. With one more infinitesimal squeeze, he drops my hand.

Maybe our rules should have been a bit more defined. Is it or is it not okay to stare at his ass as he walks away? The curve of those traps, which my hands rested on so nicely. His cute smile.

Wait. *Cute?*

I haven't thought a man was *cute* since the tenth grade. Handsome? Sure. Sexy? Daily. Fuckable? On occasion. But cute? I can't stop running my fingers over the sensation still lingering on my palm, where Adam's coarse hair tickled. And if you gave me a marker, I could still trace the imprint of his hand on my waist.

There may not have been cayenne in my smoothie, but there's definitely something in the water.

CHAPTER THIRTEEN

"Thank you so much, Elle," Liss gushes in my ear. "I don't pay you enough."

This morning, like yesterday, I slipped on my running shoes bright and early, up before the rest of the house, and when I came back there was another green smoothie waiting for me on the counter.

There was also a frantic voicemail/text message chain from Liss on my phone, asking if I remembered the password for her website software, because one of the links broke.

"You don't pay me at all," I remind her, draining the dregs of my smoothie. Adam sure can . . . blend them, I guess.

I'm still suspicious of the ingredients.

He left for his own run about thirty minutes ago, making sure I was good to check in on Lovie during her midmorning nap. I hardly looked up from my computer when I said I had it handled, waving him away while deep in the flow of HTML and user interface.

I didn't just fix the broken link. I updated the entire site, including a rotating live feed from the bakery's Instagram, a new graphic that shows average order turnaround times, and an updated "About Me," complete with Liss's most recent headshots.

"Oh. Well, I definitely should." She squeals again over the speakerphone, the sound echoing through the otherwise quiet house. I thought about wearing my headphones while I worked but wanted to hear in case something happened with Lovie. "This is amazing. Truly. I would be lost without you."

"We both know that's not true." I stretch my shoulders and neck after hunching over so long. "I never would have made it out of that corn maze in ninth grade if you hadn't come in and found me."

The front door opens on the other side of the dividing wall. The heavy footsteps clue me in that Adam has returned.

Liss snorts, and a mixer starts up somewhere in her kitchen. "You and I both know the reason you got 'lost' in the first place is so you could make out with Eli Kowalski."

"Hey, you leave Eli out of this. He's like a priest or something these days." I save the website one more time for good measure, then check as a guest to make sure the changes carried over correctly. "Aren't you supposed to be making wonderful, orgasmic cakes right now?"

"We've made at least four orgasmic cakes this morning already. Want me to ship you one?"

"I do love a good orgasm."

Someone coughs violently, and I startle. Adam is frozen in the front hall, exactly halfway between the living room and kitchen.

Well, not quite *frozen*. It's not hot outside, so I can only imagine how hard he had to work to get this result: toned calves, peeking out from the bottom of his athletic shorts. Sweat gleams on his arms and neck, and his hair is so weighed down it falls over his forehead. His faded gray T-shirt is soaked through around the collar, down to his sternum. His chest heaves. Hints of his scent waft to me from across the room, warm with sun and endorphins.

"What did you just say?" His voice must have gotten a workout also, because it sounds just as toned. Tense. It rasps across my skin, even with an entire room stretching between us. His eyes blaze trails across me, dipping from my face to my neck, where I pressed a hand after he startled me. Dips lower, to the neckline of my tank top. "I can come back if you need a few more minutes to . . ." He wets his lip slowly. "*Finish.*"

What was that about orgasmic? My own exercise was over hours ago, but my heart rate picks up again with no issue. "Finish what?" I breathe.

Adam's eyes drop again, to my phone on the table, still on speaker. "Your conversation." He shakes his head and turns for the hallway. "Why? What did you think I meant?"

My mouth falls open, a scoff escaping.

"Who was that?" Liss prompts. "Lovie's nurse?"

My head falls forward on a groan, slamming into the keys. I really hope I saved all that work. "My newest archnemesis."

* * *

Aside from my call with Liss—and related awkward encounter with Adam—the day is almost a perfect mirror of yesterday. Lovie avoids me like the plague and throws me dirty glances whenever Adam can't see. She does her puzzle books, I desperately try to keep her attention, and Adam is caught in the middle. He beats me to the kitchen for dinner again.

"Remember," he murmurs along my temple during a *Wheel of Fortune* commercial break. It immediately sensitizes my skin, sending cold chills skittering down my neck. "Starting tomorrow, I work another job. Angie is sending someone to cover me. They should be here at six in the morning."

"You have two jobs?"

Adam throws a weary half smile in my direction. "We can't all be *Jeopardy!* famous."

I have the distinct feeling he's never going to let me live that down. "Do you know who Angie's sending?"

He shrugs, jostling me. "Call her, if you're curious."

Accepting his help was one thing. Having another stranger come in and prove my incompetence for Lovie's care is something else. It doesn't sit well in my gut.

Or maybe Adam really did put laxatives in my smoothie. The delayed-release kind.

Adam's thigh pressed to mine loosens my burning thought, and his touch on my neck knocks it free: "I don't think I need extra help."

His fingers freeze on the base of my skull. He looks down his body, exaggerating the movement, and back up to me.

I—politely—jam my elbow into his ribs. "Any *more* extra help. I was never supposed to be here in the first place. This is a one-person job, right? I was just auxiliary."

Adam's eyes flare. "I wouldn't exactly say—"

"*The Rio Grande!*" Lovie shouts in my ear. I couldn't even tell you the clue.

"Logic would say that I can do this job as well as anyone else. And besides, I'm looking forward to getting some time with her," I continue, "without any grumpy, overbearing, bed-stealing nurses."

A frown pulls at his mouth. "You think I'm grumpy?"

He must *love* how my elbow fits in those ribs. "Seriously. I can do this."

He's quiet for a long moment. Lovie blurts two more incorrect answers. "Yeah, okay. I'll tell Angie. And we'll go over her meds schedule and dosages."

As if they haven't been taped to the fridge for days. I can spell all the medications in my sleep—their scientific names, even. "Adam, I've *got*—"

"For my peace of mind." He stands and extends a hand to me.

Like during our dance yesterday, I rest my palm in his, and am surprised at his warmth; his fingers curl around mine in something awfully close to an embrace. I could probably attribute the heat to the thermostat, which Lovie keeps at a brisk seventy-eight. Something, though, tells me his warmth is all self-made.

Lovie is engrossed in a commercial and hardly notices us leave. He goes over the instructions, and I confirm I've got a handle on it.

"And if I don't," I tell him in conclusion, "I will fake it till I make it."

He winces. "Please call AngelCare before it ever gets to that point."

Lovie is staring at us from the living room, if the hairs on the back of my neck are anything to go by. I entwine our fingers and swing them between us. Bat my lashes. "Don't you trust me?"

Adam's gaze turns teasing, his eyes narrowing into dark-blue slits. "With your grandmother? Yes." Accepting my challenge, he lifts our joined hands to his mouth and presses a slow kiss to my knuckles. "With absolutely anything else? No."

My stomach dips. We should have drawn clearer boundaries.

Then his words register. *"Hey!"* I choke on my disbelief, squeezing his hand until it hurts and poking him in the ribs with my other one. "Careful. I know where you sleep sometimes."

His eyebrow rises slowly, the same way his eyes search my face. Snag somewhere below my nose and above my chin before locking on mine, pinning me in place.

"If you're okay with the med list," he says, "I've got to get Lovie to bed soon so I can go myself. I'm due at work at seven."

Fatigue sags the skin under his eyes, pulling his mouth, his eyelashes, his shoulders down.

When did we get close enough for me to see those details?

"We'll be fine."

And Lovie and I are . . . something.

But it's more faking it than making it.

Lovie doesn't attack me with her shoe helper again as I guide her into hot-pink sweatpants and a Lake Michigan crew neck the next morning, but she does shove me away so forcefully my hip hits the dresser. It bruises almost instantly. And she makes so many comments about the way my body looks in my own clothes, I end up changing after breakfast.

To set things straight: I'm perfectly within American body standards (the societal ones, not the ones doctors made fifty years ago and perpetuated with magazine diets of cigarettes and wine). What extra pounds I do have, I carry it well. Boobs, ass, thighs. A lot in the thighs.

Which is why when Lovie's first jab at my cellulite, clearly visible in the day's choice of leggings, happens right before lunch, it hits a little harder than it might have otherwise. Hearing it from *her* makes it ten times worse.

The space I allow her after that is for both of us. I follow at a safe distance as she gardens (it's "Monday" again; it's always Monday), does her word searches and crosswords, and drinks enough caffeinated tea that if it were me, I'd be up until next century.

It's 8:01, promptly after *Jeopardy!* when all hell breaks loose.

CHAPTER FOURTEEN

It's not supposed to be a competition, but I wiped the floor with Lovie tonight. I even got Final Jeopardy correct. This time, the answer actually *was* the Rio Grande.

It was nice, not having to account for all of Adam's limbs. I got to stretch out, enjoy the silence without having to be *on* or play a part I was ill equipped for.

I push to my feet and hold out a hand to Lovie. "Let's get you ready for bed."

Her own hand trembles. Her skin is thin as paper, the translucent cream clearly showing her swollen veins and knuckles. "Where's Bobby?"

"I—what?" I've already dropped my defenses for the day. One of my many mistakes.

"Bobby." Her cloudy brown eyes dart toward the kitchen. "Where did he wander off to?"

I'm not sure whether she means Bobby or if it's Adam she's missing. Either way, the solution is the same. "He's at work. Don't you want to go to bed? It's getting late."

Lovie shakes her head violently, white hair flying out around her head. "I need Bobby."

"He's at work," I repeat softly, clasping her hand tighter. "But I'm here, and I bet by the time we get you settled—"

She pulls her hand free. "I'll wait for him." She scoops her puzzle book off the side table and flips it open upside down, patting the page. "I'll just wait." In this soft light, her wedding ring glows on her finger. She looks up at me, a wistful smile tugging the wrinkles taut around her mouth and producing extra at the corners of her eyes. "I don't like sleeping alone."

Squelching the panic in my chest, I return to my spot on the couch. "Well, who would? It gets cold at night." I give her a few more platitudes, eyeing the ticking clock. It's another ten minutes before I'm brave enough to ask again.

"I'm waiting for Bobby," she reiterates. She glances at the door. "He'll be home any minute. Maybe he'll bring me flowers. He does that sometimes, even when it's not payday."

And why would it be payday, when today is Monday? Always, always Monday, and always, always waiting for someone who will never come home.

"Are you sure you don't want to change into your pajamas? The blue ones? He loved—loves those," I correct myself hastily despite the pulse of hurt in my chest, then dance my eyebrows.

"I'm sure." Her voice breaks, and it does the same to my heart. "I'd wait for that man forever."

Part of me is glad she doesn't remember losing him, the pain and emptiness we pulled each other through. Then I'm sick to my stomach, as if that means I'm glad he's gone.

"You know what?" I force a waxy smile. "Let me just call Bobby and see where he is."

Lovie pats her puzzle book twice, then a third time. She clutches the corners. "Oh, that'd be great. Thank you so much, dear."

She won't go to bed. And she has to go to bed, because sleep is the reset. Sleep will fix this. But she won't get off the couch.

What else is a girl to do? She calls Bobby.

"Hello?" Adam's voice is distorted over the phone, like the distance between us isn't just physical. When we swapped numbers yesterday, I hoped to last a little longer before needing to contact him. Preferably forever.

"Hey, it's me. Elle," I tack on, just in case he has more than one "me" calling him at this hour.

"What's wrong?"

"Um, well—"

"Is that Bobby?" Lovie bellows, leaning over to speak into the microphone. "Bobby, when are you coming home? This girl's trying to take me to bed. She must not know I've only ever been with you."

I throw my gaze to the ceiling. I don't think I knew that. Didn't want or need to. "*That's* what's wrong."

"Oh," Bobby/Adam huffs.

"Are you—doing anything right now? I know you *just* got off." He's probably at his apartment already, drinking a beer with his feet on his own coffee table.

"But you want me to come back and help get her to bed. After I worked twelve hours today."

I can't read his emotions as easily without seeing his face, the little quirk of his eyebrow or the angles of his jaw. "If it's the money, don't worry. I'll make sure you're compensated."

"It's not the money, Elle, I—"

A woman's voice cuts through on his end of the phone. I guess there *is* another "me" at this time of night, probably petite and blonde and with a cutely upturned nose. Unease settles behind my belly button, a gnawing feeling I equate to not having had enough dinner.

"Don't worry," I backtrack. "I'll figure it out."

"Wait." More muffled conversation from Adam and his lady friend. My pulse thuds behind my eyes. Why am I holding my breath? I force it out as he says, "I can be there in half an hour."

* * *

You'd think Adam was Elvis, the way my grandmother lights up at the sight of him twenty-six minutes later.

"Bobby!" She shoots to her feet, as steady as I've seen her since she arrived. "I missed you."

She throws herself at him. *Bodily*. He staggers back before catching himself. Her arms wind around his waist, not questioning that he's in scrubs even though Grandpa Bobby worked for a farming company. Lovie buries her face in his chest.

Adam's wide eyes meet mine, and I bury my mouth against my shoulder to stifle a laugh. He pats her on the back, the movements slow but deliberate. "It's good to see you. I heard you were being stubborn."

She cranes her neck to look back at me, and I straighten my features, biting the inside of my cheek so my smile doesn't poke through. Adam hardens his gaze.

"Can we go to bed now?"

His eyes soften when he looks at her. I think I even see . . . is that a *smile*? Is he smiling at her and grimacing at me?

He takes over like he never left, like he didn't work a full shift somewhere else. His temper is nonexistent; he's patient and kind as she tells him about her day. I was none of those things to her. Maybe if I'd been nicer, engaged her better, she would have been more amenable.

I'm not needed here, once again. I excuse myself when Adam starts helping Lovie out of her day clothes. I'm at the kitchen table, head in my hands and tea cooling in front of me in my butterfly mug, when he clears his throat.

"So."

I groan. "Please don't. I already know."

The chair across from me scrapes the floorboards. "What is it you think you know?"

I look up, resting my chin in the crook of my palm. Adam leans back, and one hand comes up to adjust the band of his watch. The stubble is back, the shadows beneath his navy eyes more pronounced. There's a muscle in his neck that seems tight enough to snap.

"That I said I could do this. Obviously, I was wrong."

He wets his bottom lip. "Elle, look around. It's almost nine thirty." His hand falls to the table, the watch letting out a dull thud. "As far as I'm concerned, you *did* do this. All day."

That sounds a little too much like a compliment. "I know you had different plans for your weekend." Petite plans. Blonde plans.

He shrugs, taps a rhythm on the table with his index finger. "Well." The corner of his mouth tips up. "I did offer to have someone else come in."

"I don't think another nurse would fix anything." I move my hair away from my neck, which is sticky with cold sweat and panic. "It's not the scrubs, Adam. It's *you* she wants." That makes one of us. "You as Bobby."

His finger stills. We stare across the kitchen table at each other. If his watch weren't digital, I'd swear I could hear it ticking.

Adam's throat bobs. "That could be a problem."

I give him a Capital-L Look, like, *You think?*

"I could . . . I could stay?" he says. "Sleep here on the weekends. Act as a backup in case it goes like tonight did. Or worse."

I imagine what *worse* looks like. I don't want to go anywhere near *worse*.

"Would that cause any issues?" I ask. "With anyone. A roommate, or . . ." Or the woman on the phone.

This time, I actually do hear his watch buzz, and we both glance down. He mutes it. "No. I'll—" The watch buzzes again, and his jaw hardens. He leaves his hand over the screen. "I will make it work."

Is he really so spectacular that whoever's on the other end can't afford not to hear from him for even five minutes? Show me the evidence. I need receipts.

I wrap my fingers around the still-too-hot mug, bringing it up under my nose so the herbs have a chance at calming my frayed nerves. "Looks like you're staying, then."

Things just got interesting.

CHAPTER FIFTEEN

My brilliant idea deserves some credit.

Zero points for execution.

The day begins hot and grows hotter with the promise of an early-fall storm. By lunchtime it's sweltering, too hot for Lovie to even bother with her gardening. Sometimes when it's this warm and humid outside, you just have to accept your fate.

I'm still not very good at that.

It's been a week since Adam agreed to stay full-time. A week of awkwardly avoiding each other in the hallway every morning. He showers before me; the bathroom is steamy, enough warm water left for me to shave my legs. Any puddles mopped up to avoid hazards for Lovie.

A week of smoothies on the counter after my runs, the blender clean and put away, apple cores and banana peels in the trash. A week's worth of scrub colors: light blue, royal blue, light green, dark green, navy, black, and burgundy.

(And no, I'm not jealous of Petite Blonde getting to see his ass in scrubs. That would imply I care what others think about a man whose ass I have no claim to and haven't even thought about all that much.)

Adam's at his other job now, and I'm jealous, if only for the fact that it probably has functional air conditioning. Which makes me wonder if Rita the train conductor and Isaac the mechanic have gone on their date yet. That episode is scheduled for a few weeks from now.

I adjust the thermostat to seventy, then turn it off altogether when it just moves the sticky air around the house instead of cooling it. It's not broken; it's just that hot.

I throw open the windows instead.

That doesn't help either, and by the early afternoon Lovie and I are both grumpy and rude. At my wits' end, I offer the only thing I can think of, even if it's the last thing I want to do.

"How about we take a drive?" I'm willing to add more anxiety to my plate if it means getting out of this furnace, go somewhere the walls aren't closing in on me. "We can get something greasy for dinner and something cold and bubbly to drink."

We've earned our cheat meals today. Lovie's Hard Love Rule Number Fifteen: Calories don't count unless you count them.

To my chagrin, she picks Subway for dinner. It's not a Double Quarter Pounder, but it'll do, I guess.

She looks happier with a full belly, even as storm clouds roll in the distance. The working air conditioning in her car helps our moods some, but more so, I think, she appreciates the break from the monotony of her days, even if on a subconscious level.

My body is tense behind the wheel, the way it always is, but I take the long way home anyway, traveling backstreets to point out all our old haunts as we pass them. The civic center that hosted my first dance recital and my second cousin's second wedding. The library where I spent my entire fourth-grade spring break, earning reading points in the hopes of attending the end-of-year pizza party. The park where my grandfather proposed. The church where they got married.

She's lived an entire life in this town, and she's forgetting all the pieces of it.

With that heartbreaking thought in mind, I try to navigate us to my favorite park by memory, fingers clutching the steering wheel as the rain starts. My shoulders ache, my spine ramrod straight against the backrest. I won't claim this as a mistake. Yet.

Turns out I've been forgetting things too. Namely directions, and the parts of town that Public Works pretends don't exist. Before I realize it, I've driven over a pothole filled with— judging by the way the front driver's side tire is blown out— nails, screws, *and* spike strips. Maybe some Legos too.

Adam is the one to call me. Probably since it's seven thirty PM, he's home, and we aren't.

"Where are you?" he barks.

I wince as deluges of rain pound the exterior of the car. He's *mad* mad. "Funny you should ask," I say. There's an elephant sitting on my chest. Sweat gathers along my hairline. "Do you know what a wheel lock key is? Lovie's is missing, and I can't change the flat without it. I think it's in the workshop. Probably in Grandpa Bobby's red toolbox."

He completely ignores my question and asks one of his own. "Is she with you?"

"No," I deadpan, rolling my eyes at Lovie like she has any idea how much this man exasperates me. "Last I checked, she was heading toward the second strip club of the day, the one off the highway. That's her favorite. She gets the best tips there."

He barely manages to spit out, "Drop me your location," before he hangs up.

"Rude," I hiss anyway.

Lovie is, thankfully, content in the passenger seat, watching raindrops race down the window. At least this drive was a good idea for her. I cannot say the same for myself.

When Adam's car comes around the bend in the road behind us, headlights reflecting in the side- and rearview mirrors, I brace myself.

I throw open my door as Adam exits his own car, fists clenched. The cool droplets ease some of my nausea, relax the stiffness in my neck and shoulders.

The rain dampens today's green scrubs one Rorschach blot at a time. He seems taller, wider—or maybe that's his anger puffing his chest, inflating his ego into one giant ball of *I told you so*. He thrusts out his hand. "Here."

I grab the wheel lock key and move to the front driver wheel well, dropping down into a crouch. "Can you kill the engine? And have Lovie sit in your car. It's cooler now, but I don't want her without air conditioning."

The crunch of his jaw is louder than his feet on the rocks as he stomps around me. Louder, even, than the crack of thunder that echoes from a few miles away.

After Lovie is secure in the other car and the jack stand is in place, I attach the key to the lug nuts, twisting the way my grandfather taught me. One of the life skills I was required to have before leaving home, even if I never intended to use it.

But Grandpa Bobby didn't teach me how to do this with rain sliding into my eyes, drenching my top and making my hands slippery. With an angry hulk of a man watching my every movement.

"Let me do it," Adam yells. Demands, really, with his clipped voice leaving no room for argument. I don't particularly like his tone.

"I'm basically done." With the first nut. Sort of.

"We'll be here forever at this rate," Adam calls.

"Just take Lovie home," I argue, pulling the hem of my shirt up to wipe my forehead. It's instantly wet again. "It's getting late."

A pained noise gets mangled in the back of his throat. "Don't be ridiculous. I'm not going to leave you on the side of the road with a flat tire, after dark, when it's raining." It's still only dusk, but him placing me among the night creatures says a lot about his faith in me and how long this will take.

I call him on it. "Does that mean you'd leave me if it were daylight?" I look up in time to see him pinch the bridge of his nose, and I swallow a laugh. "I'll call roadside assistance."

He scoffs, throws a hand haphazardly to the cornfield at our left. "If you wanted to get murdered, all you had to do was ask. I will do it for free." His hand slides into the pocket of his pants. Is that the only way he can resist not taking over? Strangling me? The rain would wash away any evidence . . . decisions, decisions.

"Hurry up," he shouts. The fire in his eyes matches the acid under my skin. That might be steam coming off his head. "I'm getting soaked."

I drop the lug nut key, and it lands at my feet in a growing pile of mud. I grab it, sludge caking under my nails, and stand up to my entire height.

"*Dammit*, Adam!" My voice carries even over the downpour, across the empty stretch of highway, and disappears into the trees. I march onto the road, putting some distance between us. It's not far enough with how livid he makes me. "God, just leave me alone for two seconds! I can't fucking think straight with you—"

Tires squeal, a massive black pickup truck rounding the bend in the road not fifty feet from me. I am right in its path. The back end swings around as it loses traction, revealing dual-wheeled tires larger than my wingspan.

My lungs freeze. My legs too. The headlights shine into my eyes. Even if I wanted to move, I couldn't see where I was going.

I'm *plucked* off the road like an inconvenient afterthought, tugged into Adam's broad and sturdy chest as the truck whirs by, regaining purchase as its tires race through the exact spot I was just standing on.

"Are you okay?" Adam's brusqueness pulls me back to present. His hands span my rib cage, his eyebrows drawn into a single angry slash across his forehead.

"I . . ." My insides burn hot enough that the water should evaporate from my skin. Rain coats his face, and a single bead of water falls from his lashes to his nose, clinging to the tip. I flex my grip, surprised to find something soft under it.

I'm clutching his shirt, drenched green fabric peeking between my fingers.

He looks down at my hand, which has left a smear of mud behind. I go to apologize, but my throat won't open.

"Elle." He grips me around the ribs infinitesimally tighter. "Are. You. Okay." Each word comes with a shake, and it should be a question, but it's not. The words rearrange themselves in my head. *You. Are. Okay.*

It does just enough to turn my brain back on, and I manage a small nod. "Yes." Then, louder and firmer: "Yeah, I'm fine. Um." I blink water from my eyes and take in a shaky breath. "Thank you."

With one quick nod and a squaring of his jaw, he reaches up and not so tenderly removes my hand from where my nails bite into his chest. In our shuffling, I dropped the key, and Adam reaches down, saving it from another puddle. He holds it between us with his thumb and forefinger. "Why does it matter who the hell changes the tire?"

His voice is softer now, less abrasive after my near-death experience.

I grit my teeth. There is dirt in my mouth and water in places that should never be wet. The rain had already taken most of my defenses, and what just happened stole the rest. I have nothing left for him but the truth.

"This day with Lovie was not easy. None of her days are easy anymore, and there's nothing I can do about it. But this—I can do this." I close my hand around the key, his fingers. How is he still so warm when we're both soaking wet? "So I need you to let me. *Please.*" My voice breaks, and I'm glad my face is already wet. I clear my throat. "Go wait in the car or something."

He doesn't fight me when I take the key. Or as I refit it onto the lug nut and try to calm my racing pulse.

He makes himself scarce, but I still feel him, just over my shoulder. I'm not sure why we both need to be out here in the rain, but to each his own. He doesn't actively try to take tools from my hands or wring his shirt to soak me, which is more than I could say for myself if the situation were reversed. He lets me work in peace.

When I stand up to retrieve the spare from the trunk, he has it ready, so all I have to do is slide it on. I don't thank him, but I also don't kick him in the shin, so there is that. While I tighten the bolts, he throws the old one in the trunk.

My hair is sopping wet, hanging in clumps around my face. My light-colored shirt is translucent. I think there's grease on my forehead. But I did the damn thing, took something back into my hands when everything since coming home has seemed to spill out of them.

Adam's eyes are hard in the fast-fading light. Almost black, same as the night we met. They wander across me, my smirking mouth and trembling body, and shutter as he pivots to his car. His voice is hardly audible over the rain. "I'll take Lovie home with me. There's no need to make her move again."

I drive to Lovie's in silence, my muscles tight for so many reasons. I can't stop shivering. I pull in behind Adam but give myself a few minutes to peel my hands off the steering wheel.

The clock on the dashboard reads just after ten, but it's a few minutes ahead. Lovie has set it that way on purpose for my entire life to try to counteract her perpetual tardiness. But since she *knew* it was a few minutes ahead, she gave herself time she didn't actually have. I wonder if it works the other way too. If I set it backward, can I travel back in time before the horrible blowout with Adam on the side of the highway?

Through the rain-spotted windshield, I watch as he leads Lovie inside, shielding her body as much as possible. It will take hours to unwind after driving in this downpour, ease my shoulders away from my ears, get feeling back into my hands. I think my bones are soggy.

Inside, my shoes thud to the floor next to the two other wet pairs; there will be dirt to clean up tomorrow.

With Lovie taken care of, I go in search of a towel. There's a load in the dryer from this morning, and I pull a few out. It's too late to blow-dry my hair, and I'm too tired to hold up my arms that long anyway, so I wrap one around the sopping-wet red locks.

Adam finds me standing atop a towel in the kitchen, wringing my shirt and what I can of my shorts onto the terry cloth. "Interesting method."

"Thank you." I grab the last extra towel from the island and hold it out. "For earlier, I mean."

He looks like he might refuse, but I throw a pointed look at his hair, which drips water into his eyes at that very second, proving my point. He takes the pink towel with a shake of his head, flinging water in my direction. "You already thanked me." Adam's gaze is heavy, and something he sees makes his mouth tip up, fighting a grin.

I frown to compensate. "What?"

"You look absolutely ridiculous." He tilts his head in the direction of the window.

"Thank you," I say again, because I know it will get on his nerves, and check my reflection. My makeup, alongside my sanity, was ruined in the rain. Dark mascara rims my eyes and stripes my cheeks.

I'll give it to him this time—I *do* look absolutely ridiculous.

I let out a chuckle but slip quickly into hysterics. My jostling makes my hair towel flop into my face, and that's hilarious too.

Adam is also chuckling when he grabs my hair towel and uses it to straighten my head. My laugh gets trapped in my throat, a weird gurgle coming out as he pushes the towel out of my eyes with the utmost concentration.

He ignores me. "You want the bathroom first?"

"Sure," I murmur. "Thank you."

"Stop saying that." He drops his hands. "It's weird."

In the bathroom, I pull on sleep shorts and an oversized tee. Comb my hair away from my face and scrub the black streaks from my cheeks. I think some mindless furniture restoration videos while tucked under covers will work wonders on my psyche.

I'm pulling the blankets down on my bed, excited to have it all to myself after the weekend on the couch, when someone curses loudly in the living room.

I throw open the door, running toward the source of the sound.

Adam stands with his hands on his hips in the living room, still in his rain-darkened scrubs and gray socks. His mouth is pinched so tight his lips have no color. "Did you leave the window open?"

Shit. "Why do you assume I did it?"

He eyes the window behind the couch, still spitting rain deep into the fabric. "Because it wasn't me, and the only other person in this house has arthritis and a bad hip."

Okay. Fine. Maybe it was me. "The forecast didn't call for rain." I was so eager to get out of the house earlier, I didn't actually check.

His jaw clicks shut. He's going to break a tooth. "You should know better than to trust a midwestern weather forecast. I thought you grew up here." He presses a hand into the cushion, and it comes away soaking wet. He holds it up for me to see. "Or did the big-city girl forget what it's like after being away from home so long?"

An incredulous laugh slips free. The few seconds of tranquility we found in the kitchen are, apparently, long gone. "Chicago is still the Midwest! It's two fucking hours away!"

I try to find a dry spot he missed. My fingers also come away wet.

"Did you really not believe me?" he mutters.

I grab the back of my neck, hoping it will cool my blood. It's not that I didn't believe him. It's that I didn't want him to be right. Because— "Where the hell are you supposed to sleep tonight, Adam?"

Color leaches from his face. "Surely it's not that wet."

* * *

It is that wet.

Adam and I are up to our ankles in sopping towels, my clothes are grafting to my body, and we're no closer to a solution than when we started.

"I can sleep with Lovie," I offer, moving my hair dryer to a different part of the sofa. The joke was on me earlier—now I have no choice but to use it. An old dehumidifier hums in the corner, working overtime.

He huffs, flipping his cushion up to dry the underside. "No, you can't. Nobody takes kindly to waking up with a stranger in their bed." His eyes find mine, mouth relaxing from a near-permanent smirk. "No offense."

I brush aside my hurt at the word *stranger*. "What other option do we have?"

"I'll stay in a hotel." He lightly grabs my wrist, redirects the hair dryer. It's as if someone dumped buckets of water directly onto this couch. The windowsill, on the other hand, is hardly damp.

I scoff. "Don't be ridiculous."

"I can sleep in my car."

"It drops to the forties at night."

"So I'll leave it running." His cushion is soaked through, and he leaves it flipped up to try to dry the middle one.

There's no saving the one in front of me either. I let it fall to the side, turn off the blow dryer. My arms ache. The knots on my shoulders have knots of their own.

"Not with global warming, you won't." I thrust a hand toward his face as his mouth opens again. "Just—stop talking."

Because of my oversight, Adam and I are, for the night, at least, an *our*. A *we*. An *us*.

I pinch the bridge of my nose so hard I see stars. Maybe give myself a nosebleed. And then I say the thing I feared most: "Let's just sleep together."

CHAPTER SIXTEEN

I pace in my bedroom. There will be a rut in the carpet by the time Adam comes back from the shower.

One of us will probably decide to sleep on the floor. It will—should—be me, since I created this mess in the first place. If I'd stuck it out today, been more patient instead of taking matters into my own hands, I would have been here to shut the window when it started raining.

But the thing about taking matters into your own hands is sometimes your hands aren't big enough to hold all the problems.

I perch on the bed; there's no sense in getting comfortable. I don't even think it's possible. This is *firmly* my fault, and I know the second Adam comes through my bedroom door wearing pajamas and his stupid little sleepy-time socks, it's time to face the consequences.

There's a blanket draped over his arms, and he doesn't pay me any mind as he unfolds it. He fans it out over the floor, then grabs a single pillow from my bed and drops it on the ground.

Throwing me a nasty glare, he lowers himself.

"Wait." I stand before I'm sure my legs will support me. "I'll take the floor. You can have the bed."

"No." His voice is firm on the tiny word, but fatigue still seeps through. His shoulders sag. He worked a complete shift today, and since the second he clocked out, he's been dealing with my bullshit. I won't win this fight.

But I can pick a different one.

"We'll share," I say. "It's a big bed."

His jaw clenches. "Not big enough." The cords in his neck stand out in the dim light. "The hotel is still an option. The Elkhart Inn has two stars."

"And two cockroaches." I throw the covers back and crawl in. "Be an adult about it. It's only one night."

"Yeah," he says faintly. The floor creaks beneath him. "Because that worked out the first time we said it."

When I was fifteen, I pushed my bed against the wall to have more space in my room. What it means for sharing said bed, though, is that the person on the left-hand side is effectively trapped, forced to either climb over the other person or do acrobatics and crawl out at the bottom. I hope I don't have to pee tonight.

Adam shakes his head, giving in with a heavy sigh. Maybe he's out of energy to fight anything else today too. He sits on what is now, effectively, his side of the bed. There aren't a lot of extra inches to fiddle with.

Getting comfortable quickly proves impossible. Every time I shift, some part of me touches him, and whenever he adjusts in response, I fight to keep from rolling into the hard side of his body. Maybe it's time for a new mattress.

"You know," I say, scrolling mindlessly on my phone, "I thought you'd try to strangle me before you willingly got back into bed with me."

"Keep talking." Our legs brush under the covers, and I clench my teeth to keep from biting him. "I'm strongly considering it."

"Quit," I hiss when his foot nudges mine.

He scoffs. "I'm not even touching you."

I punch my pillow and pretend it's his face. "What are you, five?"

Every nerve ending is alive in my body, screaming *Danger!* His smell is too strong after his shower, clean clothes and spicy skin. I scratch my nose and am rewarded with a sharp exhale.

"Can you not—move so much?" he says through his teeth.

"Sorry for being itchy." I roll my eyes. "I'll try to do that less. Totally my fault."

"You have this amazing tendency to boil my blood," he murmurs.

"Thank you." I swear I hear a molar crack. No telling whether it's his or mine. "And you're welcome."

He huffs in answer, and I spare a glance in his direction. Moonlight comes through the gaps in the blinds and stripes his face. He's staring at the ceiling. His hands are clasped loosely over his abdomen, on top of the blankets. I try that, but I still can't settle. My skin is crawling.

I can see him in my periphery; maybe that's the problem. With a huff, I flip to face the wall and continue scrolling.

"Done now?" he asks smugly. His fake smile is burned onto my brain. It's on the wall in front of my face, behind my eyes when I shut them.

This will be the longest night of my life.

* * *

I'm surprised to wake a few hours later, considering I didn't think I'd fall asleep at all. There's no good reason for me to be up. The house isn't burning down and there aren't any earthquakes rattling the foundation or the mattress. Based on the twilight filtering through the window, dawn is still hours off.

I listen for Lovie, other noises in the house, but nothing. Everything is quiet, still. I yawn, nestling further into the bed to try to reclaim the sense of peace I just came from.

Something twitches low on my stomach, pressed possessively beneath my sweatshirt, and I arch into the movement. This is a waking dream, one of those nights where you toss and turn, convinced rest will never come, only to realize in the morning it did. Sleep fights to bring me back down, and I could let it, with how warm, how comfortable I am. I give in to the tug along my limbs, relaxing my sore muscles and slowly sinking into the feeling. Cotton fabric rubs my feet, and I rub back. That's nice. My feet were cold, but now they're not.

Stop moving, someone in my dream mumbles, a mouth close to my ear. A nose skims the skin beneath it. A butterfly's touch, soft enough that trusting yourself is the only way to know it was there for certain. *Can't sleep with you squirming all over me like this.* Another butterfly lands on my stomach, *in* my stomach, as a hand curls around my hip and tugs. I nestle further into it, scooting my hips back.

I must flex under that gentle yet greedy touch, because it flutters again, harder against my skin. A *don't move* sort of gesture.

Stay, someone says in my dream.

I hum a contented, "Fine."

A rough groan.

My eyes fly open, and those butterflies in my stomach turn to stones. I was not dreaming. Adam's hand flexes under my sweatshirt again, his nose buried in the hair at the crown of my head. And—yes. My ass is cradled in his lap.

"Adam." I grab his arm, shaking violently. "Wake up."

I look over my shoulder, and as his sleepy eyes find mine, the hold on my body tightens. Hips shift. Fabric rustles. My mouth falls open, a long exhale escaping. It dips up at the end, a moan.

He rips his hand away and untangles our feet—because those were entwined too. "Sorry."

I flop to my back and scoot over until my hip bumps the wall. "I'm pretty sure I was a willing participant." I'm talking louder than I need to, if only so he can't hear the way my heart thuds.

"Yeah. Well." He rolls over. A throat clears. "Good night."

"Night," I say, though I don't think I'll be able to sleep again. As Adam's breathing slows, I stare at the wall and wiggle my toes, trying to figure out why they're suddenly so cold.

CHAPTER SEVENTEEN

I wake up alone, my head foggy from a night of drifting in and out of sleep. I wasn't delusional enough to think Adam and I would wake up together and forget all our past animosities, pull the covers over our heads, and drown out everything but each other.

But a quick "Hey, that was miserable; let's never do it again" would have been nice.

When I pad into the kitchen, still in my pajamas, Adam's face is unreadable.

There is a smoothie waiting for me on the counter, though, no laxatives in sight.

"Hey," he says, his voice gruff. "Lovie's having a bad day, woke up with a headache. She went back to sleep. Can you stick around while I go take care of some things?"

His watch dings. What *things* does he have to take care of? The girl from the phone? And if so, what does that mean for what happened last night?

I brace my hands on the island, the only thing separating us a single yard of countertop. And one slow dance in the kitchen. And one shared bed. *Let's talk about this*, I scream in my mind. *Did you dream about it too, with hands that slide over stomachs and mouths that slide over skin? How did it feel, waking up like that, with me?*

"Yeah," I say instead. "Of course. Is everything okay?"

When he rounds the island on his way to the front door, his shoulder brushes mine.

Just before the front door closes, I swear I hear, "About as good as it ever is."

Lovie stays in bed for the morning, so I make breakfast for myself, place hers in the fridge in case she's hungry later, and scroll social media. Which turns into two hours on TikTok and nothing to show for it aside from a plethora of cat videos and a new way to fold my jeans.

After topping off my coffee, I grab my laptop and return to No-Man's-Land, intent to work on *Elle on the L*. I wiggle my butt into the cushions. Lovie was right; it really is the best spot.

The "Where Are They Now" episode from last week is set to outperform every episode for the last six months. I worked forever on it—some of the people I've interviewed remained anonymous even to me, and I had to depend on random chance to run into them again. Pride puffs in my chest as I switch over to Instagram, the channel with the most engagement by far.

@thatguy3k00 is back on his bullshit. Today's tactic is jumping down the throat of a nice person from Toronto, who commented that my vulnerability is a "shining light in a dark time."

@thatguy3k00: Only because she thinks the sun shines out of her ass.

I roll my eyes, preparing to brush it off like I have the dozen others, when a reply to his comment catches my eye.

@AdamWheeler082790ElkInd: *Elle could tell your life story better than you.*

Surely that can't be who I think it is. I search for the username and find more comments.

@AdamWheeler082790ElkInd: *Elle's great at what she does, and her 1.3 million followers clearly show that. How many do you have? Twelve?*
@AdamWheeler082790ElkInd: *That's a pretty big word for no good reason. Compensating for something?*
@AdamWheeler082790ElkInd: *That insult was cool twenty years ago. Now it's just lame.*

Adam, Adam, Adam. We'll have to talk about proper screen names and oversharing, but the sentiment is there, *right there* on the page, for the world to see.

When did he do this? During some downtime at his other job? One night before bed? This morning, maybe, after he woke up beside my angelic, sleeping face? My stomach ties itself in a knot. What would Petite Blonde think about this?

And did he stumble upon these comments while scrolling his normal feed, or did he seek them out? I hadn't even realized he follows me.

I scroll back up to the original comment, an idea catching like kindling in my mind.

Elle could tell your life story better than you.

This is what Adam finds me doing when he comes back from his mysterious errands: telling a life story. Lovie's lying on the couch. It was completely dry this morning, like the storm never happened.

When he clears his throat from the doorway, I jump five feet off my kitchen chair, knocking my knee into the edge of the table. My empty water glass tips over.

"Stop *doing* that! Heart attacks are real, Adam!" I clutch my chest, my heart thunderous beneath my ribs.

It's because he scared me. *Definitely* not because of the burgundy scrubs under his jacket or how he spins his keys around his index finger.

Adam pockets the keys and slides his jacket off. "I thought you would have heard the door open." His head tilts. "I guess I should've known better after last time."

Ignoring that completely, I drop my eyes to the screen, trying to recover the thought I had. Once again, he has completely derailed me.

"What are you working on?" he asks. "Podcast stuff?"

Closing my laptop, I clasp my hands on top of it. "Speaking of podcast stuff, we need to talk about your vigilante efforts all over my Instagram."

He takes in air through his teeth. "You saw that?" A hint of color peeks out from his collar.

My words come out as hot air. "Adam, it's the internet. Everyone saw that. You need to change your username."

His brows dip together. "Why?"

Throwing open my laptop again, I tab to the browser window. He rests a hand on the back of my chair, leaning over my shoulder. His breath is minty as it coasts over my neck. His other hand rests beside mine on the table, effectively caging me in.

I have enough typos in the next ten seconds that I'd be embarrassed if I could think about anything besides how close we are.

"Adam Wheeler of Elkhart, Indiana," I finally say. "Born August twenty-seventh, 1990." I calculate. "Virgo."

He winces. "It was one of the recommended username options."

Of course it was. Because all social media wants is information, and for others to have as much of it as you're willing to overlook. But that's not a hill I want to die on. Today, at least.

I click on his inciting comment and angle it at him. "This got me thinking."

After a quick check on Lovie, he slides into the chair next to me. "About what?"

I navigate back to my brainstorming document. "This."

His face is stoic as he reads my jumble of thoughts, scrolling when he needs to, drumming his thumb on the edge of the trackpad otherwise.

I search his expressions for any indication he thinks this is brilliant—or completely insane. Some things he reads makes him smile. Others make his mouth flatten.

He turns his stare my way, licking his top lip. "You want to start another podcast."

"About Lovie," I confirm, ripping my attention away from his pink mouth before I lose the plot. "Caring for her and her Alzheimer's, through my own eyes. I'll tell stories from when I was younger, how I witnessed her go from the badass woman who raised me to . . ." I search for a word to convey everything Lovie is without being offensive, but I can't find one.

"It will help me sort through my emotions," I try instead, raspy. His face tightens. "Provide an outlet for other people in this situation, whether it be in a caregiving capacity or just as a support system. This disease changes *everyone* it touches, not just the ones with the diagnosis, and if I have the platform to bring awareness to it, I think it's my duty to do that."

His eyes flick to the screen again. I don't need his support for this, but I would like it.

"And I mean," I continue, "it's not like I don't have the time. She goes to bed at *eight*, after all." I try to mimic the teasing dips of his tone when he said that.

Adam planted this seed in the first place by telling off the trolls. The more I talk through it out loud, the more the roots take hold. I snatch the computer back and return my fingers to the well-worn keys, saying the words as I type.

"All the sponsorship money and revenue will go to a charity that benefits Alzheimer's research. Or one that supports caregivers. Listeners can vote. And I'll personally match the donation. You can be a guest! You can talk through the medical stuff and explain it like you explained it to me. I'm no doctor, that's for sure. And we can talk about the health care system and how stuff like this falls through the cracks until it's too late and—"

"Elle," Adam says, laying his hand on mine. "Slow down for a second."

Ever stubborn, I keep typing, but I end up with a string of *fjdkaslfaeils* that, honestly, makes more sense than some of the ideas around it. I surrender, letting my fingers fall flat.

He gives me a small smile. I immediately don't like it. "This is a little . . . personal, don't you think?"

"What is? The podcast, or—" I drop my eyes to where he's still touching me, and he pulls back like I've shocked him.

He takes a second to gather his thoughts. When he meets my eyes again, some of his coloring has faded. Some, but not all. "Are you sure this is the best idea?"

"It's a great idea," I say without considering it. "I can make this something big, Adam. Something important."

"I don't doubt that. I'm just worried you think . . ." His head tips sideways, like he's not looking forward to whatever comes next. "That this might change the outcome somehow."

His words aren't intended to land a blow, but they do, right on my sternum. I lose all my air. "I'm not stupid."

"I don't think you are," he says, steady and sure. "But Lovie is not good, Elle, you know that. And this journey will be hard. For her and for you. Hard enough on its own without *those guys* having a front-row seat."

Even if Adam doesn't realize it, he's trying to protect me. Sort of ironic, considering the man is four digits away from being the victim of identity fraud.

"I appreciate your concern, really." I pat his log of a forearm. It tenses. "But haven't you ever just . . . haven't you ever just seen something so clearly in your head, wanted it so badly, that when you close your eyes, it's real?"

"Yes." It's one single word, but it comes out so thick and heavy, it forces my eyes to his.

Adam's eyes, however, are trained on my hand on his arm.

Then he looks up, and the lock of our gazes is just that, a lock. It's unmoving and unyielding and strong and forceful and unbreakable. His scrubs today make his irises almost purple, set deep into his face with the rest of his chiseled features. He's more distinguished in this color. More take-charge.

I can only imagine the things he'd *take charge* of in the bedroom. The quiet yet commanding tone he'd use. *Clothes off. Flip over. Let me see you.* The way the forearm I'm clutching would tense and twist with his hand's movements, hold me down so I couldn't squirm away when, inevitably, it became too much. How his jaw would lock right before he came.

I inhale sharply at the thought, and his pupils dilate as they drop to my mouth. *Yes,* I think. *This.* My pulse is in my throat before it drops lower, and lower still.

It's neither Adam nor I who makes the decision to pull apart. Lovie sounds off in pain from the living room, that universal old-person groan they make when they're getting to her feet, and Adam is on his faster than I've ever seen him move.

I start to stand. "Wait, I can—"

"I've got her," he says, glancing at the screen once more before flashing me a devastating smile. "Anyway, it sounds like you've got a lot of work to do."

CHAPTER EIGHTEEN

It takes a week and a half to get the podcast idea organized enough for me to even think about recording.

This will be a totally different style of episode. Whereas *Elle on the L* is unscripted and raw, I want this one to be more thought out. Especially since, as Adam so carefully pointed out, it's personal.

I've got episodes outlined, hooks cast to industry professionals, and a blurb for the show notes. I've vetted charities to partner with and toyed around with logo artwork. But the buck stops there, because I cannot for the life of me decide what to call it.

In all that time, Lovie hits me twice with her shoehorn and once with her fist. That's not counting when she "accidentally" swings at me with the cane Adam insisted she started using earlier this week after she lost her balance and nearly cracked her head on the countertop.

It nauseates me to see her so vulnerable. I don't know what the worst-case scenario is with her anymore—they're all the worst case. Every day I'm more and more thankful for Adam, that I'm not on my own in this.

My heart hurts for everyone who can't afford this service, and it makes me hopeful for all the good this podcast will do.

Adam's still wary of the whole thing, and he hasn't said one way or another if he'll appear on an episode.

He worked again this weekend. I haven't asked why he needs two jobs. Is AngelCare undercutting him? He puts up with far too much of Lovie's shit to be underpaid—literally. She had an accident this morning. It's not the first.

What is surprising, though, is when Adam presents me with a grocery list, adult diapers on top.

Before now, it was only theoretical that Lovie and I would switch roles. She bought and changed my diapers.

Now, it seems, I will buy hers.

I'm not opposed to going, mostly. Adam's been doing the shopping for the weeks I've been here, without fail, every Wednesday. It's my turn. The "mostly" comes into play when I consider driving to the store.

"I think my license expired," I say, handing the list back.

He pushes it to me again with a wide palm. "Not until May. You're good."

Of course he would remember from my license. "I don't like driving Lovie's car."

"Take mine," he says nonchalantly.

The one thing I didn't want him to offer. "You don't want me to do that."

"Are you"—Adam's eyes turn playful and pensive all at once—"Elle, are you *scared* of driving?"

I'm already turning for the door, away from him, sliding into my trainers. "Nope. Not at all."

"I don't think I believe you."

"See for yourself, then." I spin on my sock, my other foot jammed in my shoe. "Let's go on a field trip."

"Lovie shouldn't 'go on a field trip.'" He redirects his air quotes through his short hair, then scratches his ear. "You know how she is."

His eyes trail from mine to my shoulder, my hip, my thigh, my shin. All the places I've hidden bruises. His attention there makes the skin throb like the hits are fresh.

I squirm away from the feeling and wrestle with my other shoe. "When's the last time she left the house? Got fresh air. Stopped for a milkshake." All the things I used to do when I was little, with the grandmother who let me skip school and drove us an hour to Pullman Park in Michigan City. Who ignored calls from said school about where I was as we licked ice cream in freezing weather on the shore of the beach across the street. Who would give me five more minutes five times, even though my nose was a faucet and my fingers were blue.

His mouth opens. "She shouldn't—"

"Eat a ton of high fats or sweets, I know. So she'll skip the milkshake today." I make sure not to say "we'll" skip the milkshakes. I'm PMSing. I'm not skipping anything. "But I think it would be good for her. As long as it won't risk another bad day. I don't want company that desperately."

Adam purses his lips in contemplation, but before I can truly win him over, Lovie shuffles in, oversized purse in hand and slippers on the wrong feet.

"I hear we're getting milkshakes." She rattles her keys at me. I'm only slightly terrified. Those were supposed to be hidden.

It's something that, at its core, is so *Lovie*, for a moment I almost forget. Where I am and why. A smile stretches across my face before I can help it.

Lovie jingles the keys again, and I giggle.

Clearly outnumbered, Adam just groans.

Fake It Like You Mean It

It takes him approximately four minutes to regret this outing—or maybe it's my chauffeuring he's regretting. Between Lovie's complaining from the passenger seat that it's too cold, then too hot, then back to an icebox, and my jerky turns and rolling stops, he's a little green in the rearview mirror.

Considering it's only a seven-minute drive, he got off easy. I could have gone to the store across town. Nestled within those seven minutes are three questionable driving decisions, two of which include running yellow lights.

I approach a third light that also turns yellow, and I grit my teeth as I slam the brakes. Tires squeal behind us and I flinch, bracing for impact.

When none comes, Adam huffs. "*Seriously*? You choose *that* one to stop?"

"Never run the third yellow," Lovie and I say in sync. And while the look I give her is a happy one, full of unexpected connection and excitement, the one she gives me drips with contempt. It's Lovie's Hard Love Rule Number Three.

Our toe-stepping continues after Adam convinces Lovie to use a motorized scooter inside the grocery. She *accidentally* backs into me while getting herself situated.

The final straw is when Lovie comments on my speed. "It's all those extra pounds on your thighs that's slowing you down, girl."

For a second, all I do is blink. She'll snap out of it now, laugh, say she was teasing or kidding the way she did when we were younger.

But she never teased me about this back then, and I don't think she's kidding now.

Adam's expression is cloudy through my tears. He gives me a sympathetic frown. I'm not even sure he realizes he's doing it.

Embarrassment heats my cheeks. Beyond my mortification, something hot and acidic gurgles in my stomach, and to avoid tipping her scooter over or leaving her stranded, I head toward the personal care items. We're not strangers to prank wars; I can just embarrass her back, and we'll be even. I've got my arms full of adult diapers to do just that when she rounds the corner on her scooter.

Or she tries. She doesn't have the hang of steering and she bumps into the endcap. Dozens of shampoos and conditioners spill onto the floor, and three of them burst open, goop flying everywhere.

Adam places a hand on her shoulder as she bends to clean it up. He's squatting in front of her, the way I've seen him do so many times at home. They're too far away, his voice too low for me to hear what he says.

Lovie's wrinkled cheeks go pink, her hands coming together so she can twist at her wedding ring.

I don't need to embarrass her after all. She just embarrassed herself. My limbs are heavy, my insides going slimy with shame.

I still have an armful of adult diapers when Adam looks up.

Though I haven't seen this particular expression of his, I know instantly what pulls his eyebrows into one angry jagged line: disappointment. In me. He saw straight to my intentions and found them lacking. It's unnerving and uncomfortable.

Unraveling.

A worker scurries past me toward the commotion, and it knocks air back into my lungs. I set the packages back on the shelf and move to help, but Adam's glare stops me in my tracks.

There's an entire aisle stretching between us, but I feel cornered. I swing around so he can't see my eyes water.

And since I'm already going this direction, I make sure to grab some heavy-duty tampons. This period is going to be a doozy.

When Adam and Lovie still haven't found me after I've decided I need new razor heads, extra deodorant, and dry shampoo, I swing back by the adult diapers and grab one package of overnights.

Fake It Like You Mean It

". . . happens all the time," the worker is saying to Adam, who, judging by having his wallet out, is trying to pay for the two shampoos and one conditioner currently being scooped into the garbage. "Corporate has space in the budget for it. I swear. You're good, man."

Lovie's not next to him. I spot her down the main aisle, near the gardening supplies. From his position, Adam has full view of her. Which is more than I can say for myself.

Humiliation and guilt seem to be my only two states of being these days.

I don't meet Adam's eyes, just move past him and the WET FLOOR sign, heading in her direction. I'm not sure what I'm going to say when I reach her. I'd run me over if I were her. I cautiously lower my items into her basket.

She's perusing a carousel of seeds. It's far too late in the year to plant anything, but try telling that to a woman whose weeks consist only of Mondays. She's probably already in 2042.

"Hand me those," she says, pointing with a trembling hand at a packet of seeds with blue flowers on the label. She drops them in the cart, already reversing away from me.

I back up so she can't roll over my feet. "Do you want anything else while we're out, Lovie?"

She grunts a soft, "Milkshake."

She can't remember my name but can remember a malted chocolate drink.

Girl after my own heart.

* * *

We make it home by the skin of our teeth. Lovie's car has a guardian angel pinned to the sun visor, and it must have had to call in reinforcements.

"Isn't home that way?" Adam said as I turned in a different direction than how we came to the store. I'd thought I might drive better with Lovie in the back seat and Adam riding passenger, so I could be farther away from the woman who makes me so nervous. Turns out it's not them. It is firmly on me.

I said, "We're getting milkshakes," squeezing the leather steering wheel so hard my knuckles popped as I merged into traffic. I was taking back control, dammit.

Adam didn't comment again until I passed two McDonald's, a Burger King, and a frozen yogurt shop painted bright pink and blue. "Where are we getting milkshakes, Cleveland?"

"It's an Elkhart staple," I insisted, and Adam shut up.

Until he looked at the speedometer. "The speed limit is forty-five."

"That's just a suggestion," I insisted again.

The sound he made was equal parts shock and defeat. "I'm going to die today."

Spine tingling, I slowed down. I was expecting the worst from Adam when we pulled up to the aforementioned Elkhart staple.

"It's a Dairy Queen," he said.

"The *best* Dairy Queen," I corrected as I got in the drive-through. "In the world."

"Two for two," Lovie said. She was almost smiling in the rearview.

I got her a kid's size chocolate shake, ordered a large peanut butter, chocolate, and banana for myself, then turned to Adam.

"I'm good," he said.

I got him a Dilly bar.

All I'm saying is, for a man who said he was good, that DQ Dilly bar disappeared PDQ.

By the time we made it home, me avoiding routes that would have driven us past two Dairy Queens closer to Lovie's, she was overdue for her afternoon nap, and Adam was back to a weird mixture of gray and green.

I thought he was going to kiss the ground when we got out of the car. "From now on—"

"You're driving," I agreed, two steps ahead of him.

Now, while Adam gets Lovie settled for a nap, I put away the cold stuff from the grocery bags and try to remind my muscles I'm not behind the wheel anymore. When I come to the diapers, I pause. I don't know whether they'd do better in the bathroom or Lovie's room. Maybe some in each location?

That's a Nurse Adam question. I leave it for him.

I grab my recording equipment from my room, desperate to get out some of these big feelings after the Walmart fiasco. This idea is burning so bright in my head, I can already hear how the episode will sound.

But Lovie's tone, her hateful words, ricochet in my heart and drown out the noise, and I'm tearing up by the time I've got everything arranged on the table.

Adam enters the kitchen, scrubbing a hand over his face. When he sees me wiping my own, he pauses midstep. "Are you okay?"

I can't seem to get my emotions in check today. "Just—" I wave a hand in the direction of Lovie's bedroom. "That."

When he sees that I've already put away the cold things, he frowns at the empty bags, then me.

"Exactly," I say at his expression. "I feel exactly like that inside."

Adam's face softens, and he comes around the island, leaning against it. "I'm sorry."

A laugh of disbelief flies past my lips as I hook a hand over the back of my chair, resting my chin on it so I can look at him. "I don't think you're the one who owes me an apology. And something tells me I shouldn't hold my breath waiting for the person who does." More tears burn behind my eyes, up in my nose. But before I can brush them away again, he shifts.

Indecision flashes across his face before he reaches out, rests his hand on mine. "I don't like the way she talks to you."

"That," I say, "makes two of us."

His hand flexes like he might squeeze mine. Tangle our fingers together. "I just—" He shakes his head violently, pulls his hand away and shakes that out too before knotting it into a fist. "I don't think that's who she really is. Or who you are."

His words, the worry on his face, send honey through my veins, warm and slow.

"Adam, are you . . . are you being *kind* to me right now?"

He scoffs, breaking eye contact as he turns to the counter. "You wish."

Sometimes I do.

Although it's not the first time I've let my mind wander down this path, the frequency is becoming cause for concern.

I need to focus my thoughts on something beneficial— something that will help more than just myself. Exploring this weird tension with Adam . . . that won't get me anywhere.

I turn back to my computer, getting everything set up while Adam continues to put away groceries.

"Hey, everyone," I say into the microphone. "This is Elle, host of beloved *Elle on the L*." I press pause and turn around. "Can you call something you made beloved? Or is that too pretentious?"

He reaches for the last bag of dry goods. "I don't think it's cocky if it's true. People love your show, and for good reason."

The ancient chair creaks under the weight of me (*yes, Lovie, and my thighs*). "You listened?" I knew he made an Instagram account to troll the trolls, but I thought that was the extent of his involvement.

"To a few," he says, continuing to root in the bags. There can't be much left for how long he's been putting things away. "I started with the "Where Are They Now," but then I wanted to listen to the original episodes, so I went and found them. It was helpful that you put the episode numbers in the show notes. That was a good idea."

I clamp down on my smile. "Did you listen to any others?"

He pulls out my tampons like they are literally anything else in the world. They may as well be loaves of bread.

Adam nods. "Yeah, so after those, I went back to the beginning. I'm on episode . . ." He looks at the ceiling, calculating. "Twelve, I think?"

"Ew, no. They were so rough back then. The production quality is horrible." Much like this new podcast is about to be, with the subpar acoustics and Lovie coughing every five minutes.

"I disagree. The meat of them was there. Your personality still shines through, even with cruddy equipment." He lifts a shoulder, holding my gaze. "You're really good at what you do, Elle." His deep, strong voice resounds off the cabinetry, hitting my entire body at once.

It's not the first direct compliment he's paid me, but my heart doesn't recognize that. It grows wings, sinking a few inches and nudging the walls of my stomach. When's the last time a guy gave me *butterflies*? Grady sure as shit didn't.

"When did you listen?" I ask.

Although that wasn't what I was going to say originally, I want to know that too. While we've been around each other long enough for me to know how he takes his coffee—exactly one tablespoon of milk, one-half teaspoon of sugar—his personal opinions are still a mystery to me.

"On my way to work last weekend, and a few hours on shift when things were slow."

"What do you do?"

He chuckles, waving a hand down his body to gesture at his scrubs. A playful gleam shines as he rests on his forearms, stretching over the island in my direction. "Really?" His laugh is lighter, but somehow it makes the butterflies in my stomach get stronger, ramming against the sides like hippos. There's a whole zoo in there. "I'm a nurse, Elle. I work in a long-term acute care hospital."

I dissect through each of the words. "So, rehab?"

"Yes and no. It's long-term care for patients who can't afford to stay in a regular hospital for as long as their treatment takes. Or for patients who need specialized care. Burn victims, dialysis or intensive respiratory therapy. Chemo patients, sometimes, if they have a rigorous treatment plan."

Oh, so AngelCare really *does* employ bona fide angels. "That sounds . . . tough."

"Sure. But it gives me a chance to bond with the patients, which is the best part of what I do."

I chew my lip. "Isn't it easier to just see them for a day or two and send them on their merry way? How do you avoid getting attached?"

"I don't." A dry laugh. "That's the whole point."

I love, love, *love* my job, but I don't think I'd love it as much if I had to emotionally invest in every person I talked to. If their lives were in my hands—if it truly were life or death—it would make it exponentially more difficult.

"Why do you have two jobs?" I ask instead, unable to stop myself. Sugar makes me kind of blurty, and after the milkshake I've got enough to make, like, a dozen of Liss's orgasmic cakes.

Adam's eyes shutter, a hard wall coming down and snuffing out the shine there, and he gathers the miscellaneous paper products into his hands. There's a line, and I've unknowingly crossed it. "Do you need me to go somewhere else while you record?"

"Um." I shake my head to snap out of the trance he's clearly snagged me in. "No. I think it will sound lived in. I'm not hiding this arrangement. Listeners can deal. Just try not to start any hair metal bands and I think we'll be good."

He suppresses a smile. Not as bright as before but just as impactful on my pulse, which acts like it's in one of those hair metal bands. Adam holds up the tampons. "You want these in the bathroom?"

"Um," I say again. "Under the sink. Thanks."

It's oddly domestic, us in the kitchen, working separately but together.

Pretending, but not.

"Lovie got flower seeds," he notes.

I wave my hand dismissively. "It's too late to plant anything. It frosted last night."

"It can't—" His voice catches at the end like he choked on it.

"What?" By the time I turn back to him, he's already holding up the packet for me to see. To read.

Forget-me-nots.

He tugs the corner of his lip with his teeth. "Did you know," he says, his eyes wide, "that forget-me-nots are the Alzheimer's awareness flower?"

My heart races so fast it might explode. "Adam," I breathe. I stumble out of the chair, bracing on the island.

"I know." He runs a hand through his hair, lets off a light chuckle of disbelief.

"No." I grip his shoulders as he clutches the two packets of flower seeds, dwarfed in his hand, but that's not enough either. I grab his face. The stubble tickles my palms, his eyes searching mine for something.

"You don't understand," I say. A quick inhale floods my brain with his summer-sunshine scent and—maybe I don't understand everything either.

He lists toward me as his gaze drops to my mouth. "Elle, I think—"

I force the words out, cut off whatever he's about to say. "I think Lovie just named her own damn podcast."

CHAPTER NINETEEN

All I can say is—all I want to say—is thank you to Whoever is listening upstairs, whether that be Jesus, Buddha, or maybe Gandhi, for the absolute *glory* that is Amazon Prime.

After how horrible our last few outings have gone, delicious milkshakes notwithstanding, I've decided I am never driving again. It took the rest of the evening for my heart rate to calm. Again, though, might have been the sugar.

I'll just order everything I could possibly need online. For the rest of my life.

Speaking of sugar, I rip into lush, brightly colored bags of it like a kid on Christmas morning. Like *myself* on Christmas morning in this living room. One of the bags splits down the side, and individually wrapped chocolate bars and gummy candies spill across the kitchen table with plastic plinks and dull thuds.

It's midafternoon, but Adam is already cooking. Soup, I think, or spaghetti sauce. Whatever it is has been simmering for a few hours, and the entire house smells of roasted meat and vegetables, fresh herbs and spices. There's a loaf of bread on the island, waiting to be sliced and toasted. We're in a cold snap, something that didn't deter Lovie from gardening this morning until her fingers were blue.

She planted the forget-me-nots, and the irony wasn't lost on me that she probably wouldn't remember by morning.

Adam looks at me over his shoulder. How he manages not to splash any of the simmering liquid onto his hands, even as he takes his eyes off the pot, is beyond me. "I thought the chocolate cravings were over."

Which means he also knows my period is over. "You think there's a scheduled time for chocolate? Screw diamonds. *Chocolate* is forever."

"I guess I don't have much of a sweet tooth."

My hand freezes deep within the bag. My eyebrows almost touch from how hard I'm wincing. "This isn't going to work."

His jaw twitches.

"What?" I say. "I'm serious."

"Oh, I know." He shrugs. Still doesn't spill a drop of soup. He loses the battle with his smile, and his face softens with it. "This is just the first time I've ever been fake dumped."

I close my hand around the candy I'd been searching for and pull it out. "What about real dumped?"

The smile slips off his face. "Yeah, of course." A cord in his neck jumps. "Hasn't everyone?"

I tear the end flap off a box of Dots so hard it splits down the middle.

Grady James and I go way back, if *way back* is five years ago, when I was twenty-six, the podcast was just taking off, and I was juggling a job I didn't care about with a passion I loved but didn't have time for.

You might be wondering how Grady fit into this cozy little dreamscape. Like a square peg in a round hole, that's how. But I tried. Embarrassingly hard, for much longer than I care to admit now.

Lovie's in the other room, out of earshot. It only needs to *look* like I'm in love with this man, and I don't have to share my life story to do that.

"Of course," I repeat, robotic.

Adam runs a hand over his hair and hooks it on the back of his neck. Maybe there's something in my face he doesn't like either, because he returns his focus to the stove.

"Have you ever dumped anyone?" I ask.

His ears go pink. "Does kindergarten count?"

I picture kindergarten Adam, all knobby knees and wild hair. "Tell me everything," I beg. "Immediately."

He chuckles. "Her name was Jessie, and we were tablemates." I rest my head in my hands, shooting playful googly eyes at his back. Without turning around, he says, "Quit looking at me like that."

I grin wider. "What did Jessie do that was so horrible?"

"She," he mutters under his breath, with unexpected animosity, "stole my pizza pencil."

A laugh slips from my mouth. "Your *what*?"

"It's stupid."

"I don't care." His shoulders are still tense beneath his scrub top. "Adam. I promise I won't laugh." *Laugh again.* "If it's important to you, it's not stupid."

He rolls his shoulders, a quick dip of his head the only sign he's heard me. Sensitive subject, his pizza pencil.

A knock on the front door startles us. I squeal. Adam curses softly, swiping the dish towel from the oven handle to wipe hot soup from his wrist. So he's not impenetrable after all.

I grab two large handfuls of candy on my way to the door. "It's time!"

"Time for—"

He's drowned out by three children screaming, "*TRICK-OR-TREAT!*"

Fake It Like You Mean It

"Honey," I call to Adam, putting enough inflection in my voice so he knows I hate the title as much as he does. "Did you call the fire department without telling me?"

The three-foot-tall firefighter in front of me giggles beneath her helmet. It tips sideways as she holds out her bucket.

I'm giving a generous handful to the last of the trio, one of the fearless leaders from *PAW Patrol*, when Adam appears at my side. The children crane their necks to see all of him. One of them gasps.

Fine. Same.

After they run back to their parents waiting on the sidewalk, I study my partner in crime. "This isn't going to work either. Where's your workbag? The duffel you take with you."

His head tilts. "Why?" He stretches the word over several beats.

"Because you need a costume, and we're running out of time." I tap an imaginary watch.

"And why exactly do I need a costume?" He leans into the open doorframe, crossing his arms. The porch light is on, and it illuminates a teasing gleam in his eyes that the waxy fluorescents inside always cover up.

On the street, two preteen girls start up the driveway, but they see Adam's hulking figure and share a look, giggling.

I grab his forearm, toting him fully onto the porch as I wave them forward. When they approach, I slide my arm around his waist. I drop my voice. "This is why. I told you before—with your general form, you could be a *bad guy*."

The girls, dressed as fairies, approach. I pinch Adam's hip. His gaze jumps to me, but when he sees we have company, it changes. Goes softer. Much like our nightly *Jeopardy!* escapades, he slings his arm across my shoulders. "If I'm a bad guy, what does that make you?"

"I am very"—I lick my lip, sugar bursting across my tongue; Adam's eyes flash dark—"*very* good."

He presses a thumb into the deep groove between his eyebrows. It shows up whenever I get on his nerves or under his skin. I see it once a day. Hell, once an *hour*. A new vein pops out in his neck.

Once the girls collect their candy, I drop my arm and shrug his off my shoulder. A crisp breeze rustles through the tree in the yard, and we step back through the door. "So. Your bag."

Adam stares at me through his lashes.

I throw him a blinding, you-won't-win-this smile.

He breaks. Sighs. "In the bedroom."

Lovie doesn't look up as I pass the living room. Luckily, her favorite movie is on television tonight. *Beetlejuice. Beetlejuice.* I won't say it the third time. That, at least, is something we still have in common: you don't have to have lost your memories to want to keep coming back to what brings you comfort. Some things can just be *good*, deep in your bones.

Once I've retrieved Adam's bag, I sling it onto the table. "Can I?"

He's back at the stove. "Something tells me you're going to anyway." I wait, though, and he sighs in resignation, throwing a nasty glare at the vent hood in front of him. "Yes, Elle. Let's get it over with."

I tug the zipper, anxious to see what's inside. It already smells like him—warm skin and bad decisions—but it's amplified here, in this fabric. I'm not sure what I'm searching for, but I'll know it when I find it.

There's an old pair of trainers, the same brand as the ones I wear to run, and a clean pair of athletic shorts to go with them. A phone charger, bundled neatly and tied in a self-sustaining knot. A smaller version of the toiletry bag he keeps in the bathroom: a stick of deodorant, toothbrush, toothpaste, some acetaminophen. The interior pockets are empty; maybe where he stores his keys and wallet. No old food containers or moldy coffee thermoses. The last time I cleaned out my workbag, I found an uncooked macaroni noodle.

Aha! I pull out my object of desire and unclip his work badge from the handle before rounding the island in his direction.

"Find anything good?" he says over his shoulder.

I tap him there, and when he turns, we're closer than I was expecting. The tips of our toes are touching. He flexes his, and mine do the same involuntarily.

"Hold still," I say, even though, aside from his toes, he's a statue now. Is he breathing? We're close enough that I'd feel it, his chest brushing mine.

I sling the stethoscope over his neck, but it gets twisted in his collar. His eyes dart around my face as I fix it, from my ears to my chin to the tip of my nose. When the stethoscope gets snagged on his tag, I groan in frustration, and his gaze drops.

The soup is bubbling to my left, Lovie's too-loud movie to my right. And in front of me, always, is Adam. With his uniform, with those eyes, with this unreadable expression.

It's just a black stethoscope, no fuss or frills, but it changes his entire look. I swallow hard as I hook a nail in his chest pocket, clipping the badge on.

"There," I murmur. I move my hand to his sternum and give him a pat. He is warm and firm there even through the fabric. I'm starting to think he's warm and firm *everywhere* I could touch him. I pull away with a sharp inhale, rub my fingertips over my burning palm. "Now you're dressed for the part."

His gaze tracks down the length of my body. I feel every inch of it, like it's his hands dragging over me instead.

Or something sharper, like his teeth.

His voice rumbles through my bones, dropped low so Lovie doesn't overhear. "And what are you supposed to be?"

It bites into soft parts of me—definitely his teeth.

"I, um—" What am I wearing again? I look down. I'm just in my normal clothes, but I—unlike *someone*—planned for this.

"It's the twenty-first century, Adam." I step back, toes touching laminate instead of Adam's socks. I hold my hands out to the side, palms up, showing off my leggings and zip-up jacket with *Elle on the L*'s logo on the front pocket. "I'm a podcaster."

My skin grows itchy under his undivided attention. While his gaze traces the line of my leggings, the podcast logo, I eye the soup on the stove. My stomach flips inside out—it really does smell amazing.

While he's distracted, I inch my hand toward the spoon.

Adam frowns at me, my hand freezing with mere inches to go. I've started to notice he frowns at me quite often. Displeasure again, the expression I see enough to draw with my eyes closed. "You look like a hoodlum."

I widen my eyes, move my hand another half inch. "Well, it won't win any costume contests, but—"

He pushes my hand away before I can grab the ladle. "Nice try."

"*Rude*," I say, but he does that thing where he palms my shoulders to move past me without knocking me off-balance.

It doesn't matter. I'm less and less *balanced* every day.

How much of that has to do with the man who's swiping my editing headphones from where they sit on the kitchen table? The same man who scared children off the driveway approaches me now, his face drawn tight in focus as he gently hangs the headphones around my neck. Takes care to move some of my hair over my shoulder. His fingertip brushes my skin, and I shiver.

"There. Now you're dressed for the part too."

CHAPTER TWENTY

I drop my head to the back of the couch. I gave myself permission to sit in No-Man's-Land for a minute, and it is splendid. I'm *exhausted*.

I had no idea there were so many children in this neighborhood; there weren't when I was growing up. I usually chose to trick-or-treat with Liss anyway, as the candy haul on her side of town was significantly better than here.

There were so many knocks tonight, I didn't even get to watch *Jeopardy!* Lovie was frustrated with all the interruptions, so after a quick conversation with Adam, I sat on the front porch instead, intercepting potential doorbell ringers and passing out candy.

I recognized a few people. *Went to school with them*, as Lovie would have said. Some have children of their own now, which is a whole other thing I'm too tired to touch. But it was nice to catch up, the way you never can master via social media. A few of them listen to the show. One guy asked for a picture together. Adam was getting Lovie ready for bed when I came back in, the bowl of candy mostly depleted.

A husky laugh makes me jump awake. "It was the last little tiger that did you in, wasn't it?" Adam leans in the threshold, stethoscope still around his neck.

"It was terrifying. Took ten years off my life." I'm about to fall asleep staring at him.

He's quiet for a few minutes, so I let my eyes close. When he speaks, it's soft enough not to startle me again. "You didn't eat dinner."

I yawn, rubbing my cheek against the back of the couch. "Not to be dramatic, but I'd rather starve than get up right now."

He harrumphs but doesn't say anything else, and I think I've won the battle.

I force myself to sit up anyway. Falling asleep like that would give me the worst crick in my neck. I swipe the remote from the coffee table.

I've just found *Hocus Pocus* on television when Adam reappears, carrying a precariously balanced plate with a bowl stacked on top, two slices of crisp bread hugging its curves.

"Dinner is served," he says, bending at the waist in a sketch of a bow.

There is an explosion in my chest.

I extinguish it quickly by looking more closely at the food. The soup, from what I've seen and smelled of it, is thick, tomato based. Stain inducing. I never would have been allowed to eat this in the living room, even at this age. "Lovie will be scandalized," I hedge.

A small smile lifts his mouth. "It's a good thing she's not here, then." He sets the plate on the coffee table, his grin slipping off just as fast as it came. "Seriously. You need to eat."

To appease him—and my grumbling stomach—I slide to the floor and tug the table my way. He sits in his normal spot, on the right side of the couch, over my shoulder.

"What movie is this?" he asks. I'm already stuffing my mouth, too busy moaning to answer. His foot nudges my hip as he shifts. After I've inhaled several bites, I finally come up for air.

"*Hocus Pocus.* Have you seen it?" I click the volume a few notches higher, nibbling on a corner of buttery French bread.

"Maybe when I was younger."

I rest my chin on my shoulder to look at him. "Have you ever taken your nieces trick-or-treating?"

"I usually do," he admits. He absently scratches through the dark shadow on his jaw. "But I'm working this year."

"You can ask for a day off whenever you want, Adam. I'm sure your girlfriend would appreciate it."

"I'm sure she would." Guilt sluices through my middle and down to my legs, which now feel like they're made of rubber. "If I had one."

I nearly knock over the soup with my jolt of shock. "You do have one," I protest. "She's a petite blonde."

Confusion fills his face, and I flounder. "But—you were with a woman when I asked you to come back that first weekend. I heard her on the phone."

"Sister." Adam tilts his chin, mouth smoothing into a straight line. "Exactly how much of that conversation did you hear?"

"And then," I continue, bowling over his question, "you left the other day to take care of something. You said things were 'about as good as it ever is.'"

Oops. I didn't mean to reveal how often that particular interaction plays on loop in my mind.

His eyes tighten. "Same sister. One of the girls was sick. I . . . made a house call."

I bite my lip. "Is she okay now? Your niece."

"Yeah. She's much better." This brings some levity back to his expression, the edges of his face softening. It does the opposite when he looks at me.

His dark eyebrow tips toward his hairline, an easy smile dancing along his mouth. "Elle?"

I'm still not used to the way he says my name. Like he thought about each of its four letters carefully and decided there was simply no other way. He can't *not* say it.

"Adam?" I question, my lips parting. Waiting to see why, this time, he felt the need to use it at all. We are the only two people in this room. The only two people awake in this house.

His knee knocks into the back of my shoulder. I could kiss it if I wanted.

"Eat your soup, please," he says, "and watch the damn movie."

That statement—or maybe his touch—does what he intended. I grab the remote and start over from the beginning.

After a few minutes, my soup and bread are gone, and with nothing to fill my mouth, my most burning thought makes its way out. I've said it before: sugar makes me sort of blurty.

"Never in my wildest dreams did I imagine I'd be sitting here with Adam 'Wears Socks to Sleep' Wheeler, watching a children's Halloween movie." Eyes on the screen, I haul myself up to the couch.

"In your *wildest* dreams?" Adam murmurs, closer than I'm expecting. I've somehow ended up in No-Man's-Land again, his thigh skimming mine. His heat scalds me more than the soup did. "Does that mean you've fantasized about me?"

The rasp of his voice vibrates through all my sensitive places. I press back, either in challenge or invitation, I can't tell. With no Petite Blondes in the picture, things look a little different. "You wish."

Lovie is asleep. Our arrangement should be paused right now. We're not acting that way, though. Part of me wonders if we're acting at all.

This isn't just playing with fire—this is touching live wires.

A deliberate choice to do something dangerous, just because we can.

In the beginning, we're side by side. Not quite to the level of a middle school first date, but close. I don't move from the middle sofa cushion. Our feet are arranged *just so* on the coffee table, in a way that has us bumping toes and ankles whenever we shift or talk. Footsie Lite.

About fifteen minutes in, Adam pauses the movie and comes back with the candy bucket from earlier, the graveyard of wrappers from what I've already ingested. I can't tell whether the unsettled feeling within my ribs is a stomachache or butterflies. I wonder if it isn't both.

He sets the bucket between us, one half on each of our legs, and we pick through it as we talk about the plot.

"My first movie crush was on Max," I offer.

"Weak. The kid's a virgin."

"Does that matter?"

Adam snorts, ripping open a Milky Way. "It's the entire point of the movie, Elle."

"Firstly, you're so incredibly wrong I'm not going to waste my time explaining why. And secondly"—I snatch the Milky Way from his fingers and pop it in my mouth before he can stop me—"virginity is a social construct that means absolutely *nothing*."

I smile at him, full stop, with chocolate smeared on my teeth and across my mouth.

He blinks in slow motion, his lips separated by just a sliver of space. I stick my tongue out at him. With an eye roll, he places two fingers under my chin to push my jaw closed. "Didn't anyone ever teach you not to chew with your mouth open?" It's a whisper of a touch, but the ghost of it is still there, stinging. Burning.

I shake my head, licking at the chocolate. "Never. I was raised in a barn. It's behind the fence. You can see it from Lovie's room if you know where to look."

He slings his arm across the back of the couch. He doesn't touch me like during *Jeopardy!* but he's close enough that he could. His warmth ghosts across my neck, my shoulders. So many ghosts tonight.

He grabs another mini candy bar from the bowl. No sweet tooth, my ass. I steal that one too.

Adam stares at me so long, I miss my favorite scene in the movie because I'm so distracted. There must still be chocolate on my face.

I poke his thigh. "Focus. The love of my life is speaking."

Some growl-type noise brews in his throat. The shift of his weight has my body listing toward him. "I thought we weren't allowed to talk about your fantasies."

"Watch the movie," I say.

I don't know if it's the spices from dinner, warm in my belly, or the heat from the man next to me. Maybe the fatigue of talking to approximately ten thousand kids under ten. Or that I've been home an entire month and we're no closer to a permanent solution for Lovie than when I got here.

But something tells me, about halfway through the movie, it would be a *fabulous* idea to rest my head on Adam's shoulder, let my eyes close for a few blissful seconds.

Sleep tugs at my body harder and harder, and I burrow deeper into my makeshift pillow.

"Shit," someone says faintly. Hardly audible above the movie.

More ghosts, probably.

After all, it is Halloween.

* * *

I wake up when Adam shifts.

Fake It Like You Mean It

I blink back into reality, becoming increasingly aware of our positioning. My head on Adam's chest, his arm that was on the back of the sofa draped across me, hand resting on my hip with his thumb on my bare skin. Confusion draws the corners of his eyes tight.

The movie is paused not far past where I remember. I swallow, trying to add moisture to my suddenly parched mouth. "I'm sorry. I didn't—"

He nods, that single, succinct dip of his chin. "I know." I go to sit up, but he tightens his hold on my hip. Reaches for my face. "Wait." Determination sets his jaw with hard, harsh lines.

There's no question: when this man wants something, he gets it.

Right now, I think he might want me.

And then Adam tugs at a lock of my short red hair wrapped around his stethoscope. "We're tangled."

We're something, that's for sure. "Tangled like, your hand on my hip?"

His nails scrape my skin as he pulls away, and a lightning bolt of heat shoots up my spine. I grind my back molars to prevent letting out a sound that betrays how good that felt. A whimper escapes anyway.

Lines from Adam's scrub top are indented in my cheek, and I rub tingling fingers over them as he stands. He swipes my dirty dishes off the coffee table. I follow behind with the candy bowl.

We're quiet now, which in some weird way is overstimulating. The only sounds are my breathing. His footsteps. My own heartbeat, drumming in my ears. I drop the bowl on the island; he sets the plates in the sink.

He's *right there*, not three feet away. An emotion I don't have access to yet crosses his gaze.

Do I want access? To know what he's thinking, the fantasies *he* has?

Adam takes another step forward, and *yes*. Right now I want that very much.

"You make . . ." He chews his lip. "You make me want to make mistakes."

Something flashes in his face, and my brain wants to register it as regret, a half-formed apology.

But I don't get the chance, because that's when he kisses me.

CHAPTER TWENTY-ONE

It's one second, maybe two. It shouldn't be long enough to feel. To taste.

Shouldn't be.

But is. I do.

Adam's mouth is warm against mine, sweet from chocolate and spicy from dinner. It sends those same sensations rippling through my body. Sweet, aching pleasure blooms in my chest, fuzzes out my mind into a haze of only him. And heat—his hand on my hip, the other on my face, a thumb dipping into the creases from where I fell asleep on his shoulder. The liquid fire unfurling deep in my gut. How can one man taste like so many different things and still be my new favorite flavor?

He jerks back, shock widening his eyes. "I'm—"

"No." I shake my head violently, capturing his mouth again. Our teeth clack together. He doesn't get to be sorry. Not when it's this good.

Adam groans deep in his throat, and my mouth catches the sound, keeps it somewhere below my belly button. His hand wraps more firmly around my skull, fingers entangling with the hair at my nape as he slants my head for better access. I stretch on the balls of my feet, desperate to be closer. As close as possible.

The hand on my face slides languidly over my neck, my shoulder, the edge of my bra and back around my ribs, and with another deep-throated grunt, Adam lifts me with one arm, towing my body into his so our mouths can fit together again and again.

I reach with my tongue first, because I need more of him. I wish my feet were still on the ground, so I could move for us, have him press me into the counter, slot between my legs and have whatever's digging into my stomach go lower. Groaning, his tongue meets mine, nails scraping my scalp. He holds me tighter. Kisses me harder.

"That's what I'm talking about," Lovie says, letting out a whoop that turns into a cough.

Adam pulls back, all his features painted with surprise. He flexes his hand on my waist, and the shock grows louder, like he didn't give it permission to move there in the first place.

He slides me down his body slowly. I'm too numb to appreciate all the hard planes I have to pass to find the floor again.

"Don't stop on my account," Lovie says, purple pajamas disheveled.

Bitter cold flashes up my spine as his hand falls away from my body once I'm on solid ground. If you could call it that. My eyes water with the ice in the air, how fast the temperature dropped after his hands left me, and a sound of disbelief gets lodged in my throat alongside the last Snickers bar I stole from him.

Is the only reason Adam kissed me because he heard my grandmother coming?

I thought—

Well.

It doesn't matter.

"I—" He steps back, his hands fisted at his side. Manages to get out the apology I stopped before. "I'm sorry," he says, knives to my ears and still-stinging lips. He pivots on his socked feet. "Did you need something, Lovie?"

She goes on to say something about how thirsty she is, or a headache, or something else I can't hear over the torrent of blood in my ears.

I slip through the laundry closet and lock myself in the bathroom. In this light, with the rosy curtains and hand soap and toilet paper (October is breast cancer awareness month, after all), my face has taken on some of that coloring. Bright-pink splotches on my cheeks that trail down my neck like ivy.

Was it the flirting? The kiss? Adam himself? I wipe the back of my hand across my mouth but leave it there, like I can keep his kiss longer that way.

If I'm going to be kissed, I want to be *kissed*. Make it count, the way Lovie always told me it should. Not have it followed up with an apology or halfhearted excuse.

I guess he didn't read that line in his employee contract—

Oh.

Of course.

He's working. He is my *employee*. Not directly—I pay the agency, and the agency pays him—but it still crossed one line too many. This is strictly a professional situation for him. And regardless of what Lovie believes, it doesn't give us express permission to go around lip-locking, no matter how much our toes touch during movies or *Jeopardy!* or when he pours me coffee.

No matter how much I'm starting to suspect I want those very things.

CHAPTER TWENTY-TWO

Adam's weekend job rotation begins the next day, and I'm happy to put some distance between us. I lay awake for hours on the sofa last night, staring at the marijuana-leaf ceiling with the last remnants of our candy binge pumping through my veins, my brain.

Or maybe that was our kiss.

Our *fake* kiss. Since we're *fake* in love.

Ugh. This is why I don't eat sugar.

It's a bad day for more than one reason. Lovie woke up angry, and even giving her a mood stabilizer didn't help the way it should. She hit me hard enough on the shoulder that it's still tender, already bruising. And it really pissed me off.

Frustration simmers beneath my skin, at a lot of different things. At my grandmother's disease, how it makes her feel like all she can do to stand up for herself is lash out with whatever weapons are at her disposal. At my grandmother herself, for not giving us more time together. And maybe at Adam, who can be so hot one second, when he's teasing me in the glow of my laptop screen and leaving me all the chocolate candy, and cold the next. He didn't say good-night last night, the way he'd started to.

But that was before he kissed me.

Lovie is napping, and I have half a mind to lock the bedroom door, just to put some extra space between us.

This house used to be my safe place. It was *home.*

At one point, though, it started feeling more like a vacation: somewhere I came when city life was too overwhelming, too loud. I'd return to my childhood bedroom, to the grandparents who raised me, and be able to breathe again.

Now I'm suffocating.

I don't lock Lovie in her room (because yes, it's still elder abuse even if you're related), but I do confirm she hasn't crawled through a window to escape me. I settle onto the couch with my laptop instead, intent on distracting myself by bingeing my favorite guilty pleasure—*Jersey Shore.*

Snooki and JWoww are constructing the infamous *Ron is cheating on you* note to Sammi when a text pops up in the corner of my screen.

> **Liss Kessinger:** *We miss you!!! Call me when you can. Give Lovie kisses.*

I shoot her a response:

> *Lovie's more "punch first, kiss second" these days. Calling now!!!*

When she picks up, I jump the gun to avoid her prying questions about Lovie. "Did you miss me?"

Liss laughs, and my heart reinflates. It's been too long since I've heard that sound. "More than a kidney. And you know how much I pee already."

Hearing her voice is nice, but it only scratches the surface. A sharp tug of nostalgia and, surprisingly, homesickness, lances through my middle. I need to see her. "I'm switching to FaceTime. Get decent."

She squeals, because she hates unplanned video calls more than I hate driving.

The call connects and her pixelated face beams back at me. Her frizzy blonde hair is tucked in a high, messy bun, her blue eyes a watered-down version of the ones that looked so regretful after kissing me last night. Whereas Adam's are a deep, middle-of-the-ocean blue, hers are the water as it meets the shore.

Those exact eyes narrow on-screen. "Why do you look like that?"

"I missed you. And I think you have some flour freckles on your nose. It's a good—"

"No," she cuts in. "That's not it. You look . . . you look like you did something bad."

This is definitely Soul Sister Shit.

It's a blessing and a curse to have someone know you so completely. I'm not sure I believe in soul mates, but if I did, I think mine would be Liss. No one has ever known me as inside out as she does, known what I need before I realize it myself.

It'd just be nice if I could sleep with her.

Wait, no.

That sounded wrong.

I very firmly like penis.

It would just be nice to have the whole package. Someone who can knock my socks off in bed and also knows how I like them folded.

"Let me see," a familiar voice says off-screen. Liss moves so Dakota is in frame. "Yeah," he muses. "I see it too."

I squint at myself in the preview window. What, exactly, does it look like when you've done something bad?

"Elle . . ." She draws my name out to last three entire beats. "What did you do?"

"Nothing," I say, too fast for her slow inquiry.

Her eyes narrow further, baby blue hardly visible, before blowing wide open. "You slept with someone!"

I said before how great it is to have someone know you inside out. I'll be retracting that statement now.

"I—what—*no I didn't!*" But despite it sort of, technically, being the truth, it's too insistent to be believable.

She gasps. "Was it that guy from high school? The mechanic. What was his name? James? Jack?"

"John," I mumble. "And if you must know, *Alissa*." I level her with a death stare I hope she feels the heat of through the screen. "No. It was Adam."

Liss's mouth quirks, a mannerism she picked up sometime in the college years we spent apart. She was baiting me, and I fell for it. "You've been gone a month."

"Which is why," I stress, "I'm not allowed to leave without you ever again. Clearly, I can't be trusted."

Dakota's head pops back into frame. "Adam is the nurse, right?" His blond hair also, somehow, has flour in it. How they get any work done is beyond me.

"The hot nurse," Liss corrects. "Who Elle is pretending to be in love with around Lovie."

"Why?" Dakota asks.

His question wraps a vise around my lungs. "Lovie's gotten . . . she's *mean* now. I have bruises, plural." I still haven't mentioned them to Adam. There would be no point. "She's called me fat multiple times, says I talk too much, doesn't want to spend any time with me. She . . . doesn't remember me."

Saying everything out loud is almost too much. It gives it more power than it deserves. That must be what pulls tears to the brim of my eyes, and gravity must be what pulls one down my cheek. A month here and I'm turning into someone who has *emotions*.

Gross.

"Oh, Elle." Liss frowns. "I'm so sorry."

I sniffle hard enough that if I hadn't already wiped it away, the tear would have been sucked back into my eye. "She needs to be in a full-time facility." I fill them in on the details of the past few weeks with Adam, our stilted dance in the kitchen, morning smoothies and *Jeopardy!* cuddle sessions. Last night with *Hocus Pocus*. The call I had this morning with the insurance company about some additional required documentation. "Until then, we're stuck in this impossible situation. She pops up unannounced all the time, so we have to stay *on*."

Liss's blonde eyebrows pinch together. "Wait. He's staying in Lovie's house too?"

"Scrubs in the dresser and toothbrush on the sink." I was pleased to discover Adam's toothbrush is in good shape, like he replaces it every three months exactly. I'm not even that diligent. "Lovie doesn't do well when he's not here. It was a whole thing."

"Isn't there only the one bed?"

She knows there is. When Liss and I were younger, we'd share that one bed for sleepovers. But it's a lot different for two preteen girls to share a double mattress than it is to share *anything* with the behemoth that is Adam Wheeler.

"We've been sharing."

Unfortunately, Liss doesn't know Adam's girth, so I recognize the second the words are out she's going to read them wrong.

Back up a second. *Girth?* I meant size. Stature. Build. But I'm sure Adam is proportional everywhere. His shoes are size *fourteen*—not that I checked.

"You *slept* with him?" they say together, pulling my thoughts back on course.

"Fuck. No. I misspoke." Well, except for the one time, but they don't need to know that.

"Since when does Elle Monroe misspeak?" That's Dakota, and nope, I didn't miss *him* one single bit.

Liss whispers, "She doesn't," and the two of them snicker at my expense. "Nurse Adam must be hot if you kissed him."

I pull my knee up and drop my chin to it. "Not my idea. Lovie thinks Adam and I are her and Grandpa Bobby. She thinks we're . . ." The words are lodged so deep in my throat I have to clear it three times to shake them loose. "In love or something."

"And?" she says.

"And what?"

"Are you?"

"Am I what?"

Liss groans. "Elle."

"Of course I'm not in love with him. I hardly know him. I *don't* know him." And it's the truth. But so is this: "It's just maybe, possibly, *slightly* terrifying how he's already so familiar."

Dakota voices his dissent. "Familiarity isn't necessarily a bad thing. Especially if you'll be living with this guy for the foreseeable future."

He doesn't understand.

"You don't understand," Liss echoes, shooting him a glare. She may have learned to smirk in college, from that elusive boyfriend I never met and who I'm forbidden to bring up, but she got that look from me.

"Can we go back to the bed-sharing thing?" she prompts. "Are you sleeping in shifts? Switching off nights? He gets one half and you get the other? And is the split vertical or horizontal? If you could mark up a photo, I'd—"

"Can we go back to Lovie?" I say, desperate not to talk about Adam or our sleeping arrangements anymore.

"Okay." She nods. "Are you holding up okay? Mentally?"

I shrug, picking at a loose thread unspooling one of the couch flowers. "It's getting better, and the podcasts are helping." I've still been posting weekly episodes of *Elle on the L*, pulling from my backlog and unaired archives, and putting my thoughts to paper about Lovie is therapeutic. I give an exaggerated pout. "But my best friends are all the way in Chicago."

Liss throws a smile so sweet it gives me a toothache. "Well, even if we're here, you can always call me—"

"Or me," Dakota chimes.

"And I know it's not the same, but you have millions of adoring fans who will support you no matter what you go through."

Dakota mumbles something I don't catch. Liss fills me in. "Hey, we need to run a delivery uptown. But call me if you need me, okay? Hoes before wedding cake."

I want to reach through the phone and pull her back with me for a hug. "I love you."

She accidentally hangs up in the middle of returning the words, and when the call ends, I'm lonelier than before.

CHAPTER TWENTY-THREE

To my credit, the smoke alarm goes off a lot later than I thought it would.

The chicken is unsalvageable, and Lovie is having a meltdown. I say this with all the love in the world, because I am also about to have a meltdown.

"Lovie, it's okay," I say, fumbling the broom tucked by the fridge. I jab it at the smoke detector, unsuccessful as my grandmother clutches at her ears and rocks back and forth.

I took it upon myself to handle dinner tonight, and I felt confident I could keep an eye on both the oven and my grandmother.

That was when the first thing went wrong: a package deliveryman knocked on the door. A few weeks ago, I'd ordered a NIGHT SHIFT WORKER LIVES HERE, PLEASE DO NOT KNOCK sign to hang by the doorbell. There was a surprising lack of UNEXPECTED VISITORS WILL SEND MY GRANDMOTHER INTO A TAILSPIN options. It's worked well.

Until today.

I have half a mind to return the air fryer on principle.

Lovie was already agitated at having her puzzle time interrupted. I thought she might be hangry; she hadn't eaten many carrots during her afternoon snack. I knew hanger. I could fix hanger.

I chopped vegetables for a thick leafy salad, prepped chicken to bake in the oven, diced potatoes to boil and mash. It wouldn't be anywhere near as delicious as the soup Adam made on Halloween, but it would still be good, dammit.

Then Lovie had an accident. She was too embarrassed to tell me, but I noticed the wet spot when she got up from the couch. Her briefs were soaking, too much to have been from just one use.

So I stuck her in the shower, made a mental note to flick off the oven on my way to the laundry room for stain remover. But then I heard a crash, and all was forgotten. It wasn't a bad fall—the shower chair caught her—but she was still upset, visibly shaking and naked and wet.

She slapped me across the face when I reached for her with a fresh towel. "Go *away*."

It still stings now, in so many more ways than one. The most heartbreaking part was I could see where her emotions were coming from. Lovie had never been one to need assistance; she was usually the one to offer it.

And I wouldn't want an audience for my worst days either.

All of Lovie's days are her worst ones now, and I have a front-row seat.

"Make it stop," Lovie whimpers, clutching her head. "It hurts."

I know. I know it hurts. It hurts everywhere, in all the places that matter.

I keep missing the hush button, my vision cloudy with unshed tears. Growling, head ringing and heart breaking, I stretch up—I mean, what good is being five foot ten if you can't even reach the tall things?

I'm still a few inches shy, so I climb onto a dining chair. But I forget the leg wobbles. My balance wavers, and my chest squeezes. Lovie is openly crying now, and I'm falling, and I am going to smash my face into the hot oven and die to the soundtrack of a smoke detector.

It's been a good life.

Strong hands catch me on the hips, stopping my descent with a firm grip and the faint scent of sunshine.

Adam.

It's the first time he's touched me since our kiss. We're in the same spot. He's wearing the same scrubs. My breath hitches like it did then, feet find the floor in the same way, a foal on new legs. He sets me to rights.

When his eyes lock on mine, I'm steadied, even though the kitchen could very well be burning around me. His chin dips as his eyebrows rise. *You okay?* he says with no words.

I lift one heavy shoulder. *I don't know.*

His hands tighten on my hips marginally. A squeeze, maybe. Or a muscle spasm. Adam's eyes flash to Lovie, cradling her head and devolving with every second that ticks by on the ancient clock near the patio door.

He lets go of my hips. Reaches up and hits the silence button on the smoke detector.

My eardrums echo with sirens and Lovie's cries. She's sniffling now, which I'll take over wailing any day of the week.

"What are you doing home?" I flash my teeth in a grimace, taking care to run my tongue along the sharpest ones. *"Honey."*

His grin, on the other hand, is sheepish. "I . . . I thought I would come home early and help with dinner."

"Did you get fired?"

"What?" He chokes on air, and I use his distraction to step away. "No, I didn't get fired."

"I won't pay you more to compensate," I warn. The exposed skin of my waist grazes the oven, and I jump back toward him. I can't tell which is worse.

"I didn't get fired, Elle." His jaw is hardening again. Good. "I just wanted to . . . *be here*. I thought I could help with dinner."

"I don't need your help." My sharpness now comes from many exposed wounds. The two biggest are how he kissed me with an ulterior motive, and how he could reach the smoke detector when I couldn't. I don't *want* to need his help.

He's quiet for a few seconds, but with the way my head pounds, it could be hours instead. Days. "No, you don't," he admits. Almost like he's heard what I didn't say and is answering that too. "But I still want to give it."

Lovie whimpers again, and I see it, then, in the tightening of Adam's eyes. Her hurt causes his own. Phantom pain.

We stare at each other long enough that someone's stomach growls, and since I can't tell if it's mine, it's a good indication I'm losing the fight.

Scrubbing a hand over my face, I sigh, defeated. "Fine. Whatever. But see if you can fix . . ." I grab a knitted potholder and throw open the oven, smoke billowing out. I drop the pan of burnt chicken on the stove. "This."

He blinks down at it. "Yeah, no." He pulls his phone from his back pocket.

I peek at his screen. "Are you calling the health department?"

"I," he says, biting his lip to stop the ever-present smirk there, "am calling the Italian restaurant down the street to see if they deliver."

* * *

Adam gets Lovie cleaned up properly after my rushed job from earlier, and I do my best to air the smoke from the house, throwing open the windows (no rain in the forecast, thank

God). The chicken goes in the garbage, and the vegetables and salad ingredients go back in the fridge to try again tomorrow.

With Adam's help, we've almost salvaged the night.

Until, in the commercial break between *Wheel* and *Jeopardy!* my grandmother looks me square in the face and says, "Lovie, will you tell me how you and Bobby met?"

When I was little, my grandparents' love was my favorite bedtime story. It would calm me after nightmares, ease me to sleep after too much sugar. Today must have been harder on her than I realized if she needs that same comfort now.

On my other side, Adam's body presses into mine, leaning into the words I haven't yet spoken. His arm is around my shoulder, and though it's hard to tell through the fabric of my Cubs sweatshirt, it feels like he squeezes me—an encouragement. It sends shock waves into my chest, which is why my arms are tucked tight across it. Another pulse of awareness, a reminder that he's here with me.

As if I could forget.

"I met Bobby when I was eighteen," I say, slipping into Lovie's perspective. "Fresh out of high school. He'd been taking a day trip to the beach with some of his military friends. I was working at the ice cream shack. He must have bought ten cones that day. Kept passing them off to his buddies. One of them got sick from eating all that dairy in the sun."

Adam chuckles.

Lovie's smile is soft, her eyes far away. I hope for her sake she can picture it, even if she doesn't have access to these parts of her memories anymore. Tentatively, I take my hand in hers, hold my breath to see if she'll snatch it away. Or lash out again, maybe get my other cheek to make things symmetrical.

"Bobby stays the whole weekend," I continue. "He doesn't have money for a motel in the area, so he drives an hour each way just to see me. Helps me put out chairs and umbrellas in the morning, walks me to the bus stop after my shift is over." I laugh. "He forgot to wear sunscreen. Got sun poisoning."

The *Jeopardy!* theme song plays, but she stays locked into my words. I've always told my podcast guests that if I'm the only person who ever hears their story, they still deserve to tell it. I didn't realize exactly how much power that held until now.

I raise my voice to be heard over the music, and it belies the tremor there.

"He makes that hour drive once a weekend for the next four months, until I tell him to save his money for a ring instead of spending it all on gas. 'What makes you think I don't already have one of those?' he said. The way we acted, it was . . . I always told people we'd met already, in a previous life. He was that familiar to me."

Adam clears his throat. "He goes overseas. The picture's on the dresser." His thumb continues its ministrations on my shoulder, traveling toward my neck and sliding along the stretched-tight tendon.

I relax into him, tucking my curves against his planes and angles. "He does go overseas. We get married before he leaves, a full white-gown affair our mothers *rush* to accomplish in a month. It's the best day of our lives."

A tear slides down my cheek, and I slip my hand out from Lovie's to wipe it away.

Strong fingers slide up the base of my skull and into my hair, kneading away the tension. "But he comes back."

"He comes back. We . . . *celebrate*. Nine months later, we have our first and only child. A boy. We name him Robert, after his dad. He's the light of our life. We want more kids, but it never happens. It's okay, though, because we're happy. We have love in abundance, a little house on a quiet street in a sleepy town. Room for Robert to grow. Bobby lets me tile the bathroom pink. It will never change.

"Robert grows up, goes to state school for college. Meets a girl of his own there. Her name is Carolyn." I pull a foot up underneath me, let my knee rest atop Adam's thigh.

"Your mother." Adam isn't asking a question, but I nod anyway, his fingers still cradling the base of my skull. Lovie's eyes are trained on the TV, but she hasn't moved a muscle. Maybe more telling, she hasn't blurted any answers.

"Keep going," Adam murmurs. When I glance at him, the blue in his eyes is dancing with emotion. "What happens next?"

The tears are coming too fast to wipe away, and my wry smile makes some of them dip into my mouth. "Robert and Carolyn take things slower, which is fine. Times are changing. They get married after graduation. A few years after that, along comes baby. They name her after her mother, but they call her Elle."

His mouth twists into a diagonal, one corner down, the other up. "I bet she was an absolute menace."

A racking laugh flies from my mouth, and I wet my lips. "A pure terror," I whisper, "and the light of my life."

He hears what I don't say. "She raised you." He's asking me as Elle.

I nod.

His teeth sink into his lip, toying with saying something he knows he shouldn't. "Where are your parents now?"

If this goes any further, it will tear me open. I'll be left raw and bleeding all over this ugly upholstered couch.

This time, I shake my head.

He opens his mouth, but the lines of his face shift into marble, his eyes blue steel. He catches my chin with two fingers and a thumb, the way he did on Halloween, and turns me tenderly so he can see the other side of my face. "What happened here?"

I jerk away from his touch, my pulse humming in that spot. "I think I just got a little overzealous in child's pose today. No big deal."

"You don't do yoga."

"You don't know what I do when you're not here."

"Elle." His tone is firmer now, like his jaw. "Look at me, please."

My reserves are depleted after such a long stroll down memory lane, and I just—I don't have any fight left. I turn back to him.

His thumb grazes the sensitive skin of my jaw where Lovie smacked me. I want it to hurt. I want a reason to be mad at him. I can't find one. Adam is gentle as he probes the welt in the shape of my grandmother's fingers.

"What happened?" he asks me again, still holding my chin. His eyes are like his touch—soft enough that it shouldn't hurt.

It hurts all the more for how gentle it is.

The concern in his gaze is a spark to my already frayed nerves. My electric fence is short-circuiting today, and if I give him more chances, he'll disarm it all together. And then what defense would I have against his eyes, his hands, his attention?

"I told you." It's hardly above a whisper, because I have nothing left to give. "It's carpet burn."

With one final graze of his thumb along my jawbone, he drops his hand. But he knows. I know he does, because he tugs me into his side, a hug. It is the exact thing I need. The perfect press of softness against all my jagged edges.

Because when my ear slots itself near the hollow of his throat, I hear his thick swallow as he works to hide the labor of his breathing. Because for a split second, his lips, tight and closed, rest on my hair.

Because for the rest of the evening, Adam doesn't let Lovie come anywhere near me.

CHAPTER TWENTY-FOUR

As I will later tell the police, I don't lose Lovie.

Technically, she loses me.

Like, *gives me the slip* loses me.

It started with her planting more damn forget-me-nots in the garden. Watching her plant something that was for all intents and purposes *meant* for her sparked an idea for the cover art of the new podcast, the last piece of the puzzle. After Lovie went to bed last night, I recorded the first episode and a new intro for *Elle on the L*, explaining the premise and assuring listeners the original show would continue as promised. And with the ideal photo in mind, I was one or two camera clicks away from being able to press "Make Live." I ran inside for *two seconds* to grab a picture from my dresser, one where I'm on Lovie's lap in front of that very garden.

But now, when I return with my phone and the picture, ready to snag a packet of seeds and set up the perfect shot, Lovie isn't in the garden anymore. The side gate is creaking, wide open.

Megan Murphy

I drop the picture frame, the glass cracking quick and rough like lightning on the cobblestone. The sharp pinch in my foot barely registers as I run around the side of the house.

"Lovie!" I yell. I wasn't gone that long, was I? Sure, I stopped to pee, but that takes two minutes max.

If I'm really not allowed to piss while watching my grandmother, we're going to need more adult diapers.

I bolt to the front walk, looking both ways down the sidewalk before running into the street, not even checking for cars. There are candy wrappers still littering the asphalt from Halloween a week ago, garbage cans from those who set out their bins a full day early. All of those things, and no Lovie.

I pull open the front door so hard the knob puts a hole in the stucco behind it. I run from room to room, shouting her name. No-Man's-Land is empty. The kitchen is empty, and the laundry room.

I get desperate and start checking random places. The shower, even though she just had her weekly one yesterday. The hall closet. My bedroom. The crawl space.

Everywhere she is supposed to be, she isn't.

She's nowhere.

Lovie is *gone*.

I clutch my phone in my trembling hand. I don't have to navigate far. My contacts are sorted by last name, but he's still under A. For *Nurse Adam*. His sister called him again, a conversation with hushed voices and tense tones. He ducked out shortly after to go "take care of something."

He answers on the third ring. "Elle?"

"Lovie's missing," I say. "She's gone. I can't find her."

His sigh is so heavy I feel the weight of it through the phone. "Call the police. I'm on my way."

"Please hurry," I say, right as he disconnects the call.

The police find my grandmother two blocks over trying to pet a dog, and she's returned to the safety of our home only seconds before Adam's car screeches into the driveway. Panic gives him a frantic energy, makes his jaw tight as he rounds his still-open car door.

"She's fine," I call over the policewoman's shoulder. "She's okay."

He stops there, in the driveway. I try to focus on what the officer is saying, but my eyes are locked on Adam, the way his chin drops to his chest as he sucks in a shuddering, relieved breath. As he nods once, then twice. Like both syllables of that word.

Okay. Okay.

"The elderly can be tricky," the officer says as she tucks her notepad in her belt. "If it happens again, give us another call. And try to keep a better eye on her."

My mouth gapes wide enough she can probably see my tonsils. She knows nothing. Nothing about how my grandmother hates me now for some unknown reason, how it's always *my* shin she finds with her cane, never Adam's. Why is it only me? Her face *lights up* when she sees him. When she sees me, she runs the other direction.

Literally.

The officers nod at Adam on the way back to the squad car on the street. I manage to hold it together until they pull away and we're left staring at each other from across the yard. A whimper escapes my trembling lips, and I sniffle. But the tears won't go back inside this time. They cloud my vision, slide down my cheeks and off the point of my chin.

This isn't fair. Lovie doesn't deserve this, to have forgotten all the memories that made her life worth remembering. Adam doesn't deserve to be working two jobs; he hasn't had a true day off in over a month. I don't deserve to have two police officers waltzing in like this is anything other than what it is: common and completely terrifying. And I know this shouldn't be about me, but I don't deserve to be abused by the woman who raised me or called fat every time I show a sliver of belly skin.

This disease has taken all the best parts of her and left us with the worst.

I'm crying so hard I don't hear him approach, but he's here. At first, I think he's got his hands on my shoulders to move me aside so he can go in the house. But then those hands slide around me and pull me to him, and he's hugging me. Just like that.

Adam Wheeler is hugging me.

It's as close as we've been since Halloween. Since he kissed me.

He fits me to his chest in a way that should feel like a cage but instead is more of a weighted blanket. His scrubs are soft against my cheek. He's stroking the back of my neck over my hair, while his other hand rubs small circles between my shoulder blades, and it's as calm as I've felt all day. Maybe since I came here. I sob onto his chest, grip the fabric on his back and let him hold me up.

And his *words*.

"It's not your fault, Elle," he murmurs. "It could have happened to me too. I'm here. I'm right here with you. She's okay now. I've got you, baby. We're okay."

Things he doesn't say: *Stop crying. You're being overdramatic. This is all your fault.*

It loosens something warm and buttery in my chest and gives me just enough of myself back that I'm able to pull away.

"I got your scrubs all wet." I lift a shaking hand to his collarbone and run the tip of my finger over the wet patch there.

"'S okay," he says, a little gruff. "They needed a wash anyway. And salt water helps get the stains out."

A wet laugh bubbles up my throat, and when I meet his eyes, they're fierce but not angry—at least, not at me. Maybe he's mad at the situation too. I don't want to let go, but Lovie has been alone inside for much longer than it took her to disappear the first time, and we can no longer afford to place bets on what she'll get into if left alone. There are gates to padlock and glass to clean up and—

"Are you *bleeding*?" Adam says in a panic, looking at my foot.

Ten minutes later, Lovie is down for an afternoon nap and I'm perched on the closed pink toilet lid.

Adam balances my foot in his lap while he sits on the tub rim across from me. He doesn't find any glass in it, but it doesn't stop him from digging around until I'm biting on a hand towel to avoid cursing his grandchildren. Or kicking him so hard he'll never have any in the first place.

There are blood spots all over the house from my search-and-rescue efforts, which resulted in a trickle of tears from my now-puffy eyes when I saw them setting into the carpet Lovie worked so hard to keep clean.

"Distract me?" I say, then hiss as Adam dabs more hydrogen peroxide on the cut.

He doesn't miss a beat. "Did you know goose bumps were an evolutionary response to help make us seem larger in the eyes of our predators? Since we had more body hair back then, it was incredibly effective."

I'm shocked and amazed and a little turned on, which is surprising but also not. Science is sexy. A loud laugh hiccups out of me, and I clap a hand over my mouth. "Sorry," I mumble through my fingers. "It's adrenaline, I think."

He smiles at my foot. His lashes are so long, they almost touch his eyebrows when his eyes are open, his cheeks when they're closed. "Don't apologize. I'd rather hear you laugh than see you cry."

There was a compliment in there somewhere. He's been paying me more of them lately. Did it start when we shared my bed? When he trolled my trolls?

When he kissed me?

He regretted kissing you, my conscience tells me. *He works for you.*

He is literally cleaning your wound, my heart weighs in. *He doesn't exactly hate you right now.*

It's got to be the air in here, warmed by more bodies than usual, that makes my neck heat.

Adam doesn't miss this either. "Humans are the only animals that blush. And it's believed we're the only ones who can be embarrassed."

"I'm not embarrassed." *It's just there's a sixty-nine-percent chance I'm undressing you with my eyes.* I'm having vivid nurse-patient fantasies. He doesn't even need to change. He's already dressed for the part. How considerate.

He looks down, but I've seen him try to hide his smile too many times now. He applies another round of antiseptic.

"You like science?" I ask.

"Oh, it's the first thing they ask on the nursing school application. It's a checkbox. The no's go straight to the recycling bin."

He's just trying to distract me, like I asked. It's not his fault he's good at that too. "What other things do you like?" I wince as he does something uncomfortable to the cut, jerking away involuntarily.

He gives me a few-second break, then grips my calf to guide me where he needs me, my foot back on his lap. The warmth from his hands counteracts the cold stinging along the heel. "Running. That's usually how I spend my lunches when I'm at work." Here, too, if he can swing a half hour to himself.

"When do you eat, if you run during lunch?"

"Whenever I can. That's the first rule of nursing."

"I thought the first rule of nursing was that you have to like science."

"No, that's the first application question." A grin wrinkles the skin around his eyes. It's a flash forward to how he will look in ten years' time, if life treats him well. He'll gray around the temples first, maybe grow a salt-and-pepper beard. "Come on, Elle, keep up. It's like you're distracted or something."

I toe him lightly in the shin with my other foot. "Keep going."

"I've also been into podcasts lately," he says, too casually to actually *be* casual. "There's this one I'm quite fond of. Maybe you've heard of it?"

What is he doing? What am *I* doing? And why can't we stop? "What's it called?"

He cocks his head. "Elle... Michelle..." His tongue rolls over his plump bottom lip. My heartbeat lives in places I didn't know it could. Inside my wrists. My ears. Deep in my stomach. He snaps his fingers. "*Hell in a Cell.*"

This time when my foot connects with his shin, it's a little more on purpose. "Tell me, Nurse Adam, will I survive?"

"Undoubtedly." He tosses dirty gauze in the trash can and grabs a fresh piece. "You'll live to be ninety-seven, have fourteen grandchildren, and a dog named Gigi."

I snort, his statement clearing away my lust. "The dog, maybe. But having grandchildren would first require having *children*, which sounds like a living nightmare."

He must think I'm joking when I shudder, because he laughs.

I'm not. Just the idea of children gives me stress hives.

The silence stretches a beat too long. His eyebrows rise. "You're serious. No kids?"

I shake my head. "No weddings either."

When his face flashes, I think I've revealed too much, and my blood pressure spikes. Why do I care whether Adam wants kids and a wedding? I've had my mind made up since the day I turned eighteen.

"Can I ask why?" he says.

"I love myself too much to ever risk getting lost in someone else."

He leans to swipe the bandage off the sink, and he's so close I smell those faint hints of summer I've come to expect around him. Citrus and sunshine. "I don't think you've loved the right people if you lost yourself because of them. Love is supposed to make you *more* yourself, not less."

I shrug and grip the toilet underneath me, locking my elbows. "That's great in theory, but I don't know if I'm that evolved yet."

He's tender as he applies the bandage to my foot. He smooths it down with the back of his finger, making sure none of the edges are loose or folded. It must be a big bandage, because it takes longer than I expect.

"The right person won't care that you don't want those things." He firms up his touch, effectively turning the gesture into a foot massage. "They'll just want you, in whatever capacity you're capable of giving."

It takes physical effort not to moan. I bite my lip. Besides a pedicure, when's the last time someone touched me this way? Awareness prickles to life on every inch of my skin.

"What about you?" I ask. "Do you want the wife-and-kids thing? Or partner-and-kids, I guess."

"It'd be a wife for me, yes, but I'm not going to rush into anything. Love . . ." His eyebrows draw together. "I think love should be about the person, not the title. And I don't have a burning desire for children, which I think means I'd be okay without them. My nieces are all the kids I can handle. Plus the world is, like, really shitty."

"Isn't it, though?"

We laugh together, and it echoes in such a confined space, bouncing off my skin and getting under it at the same time.

The sound dies, and the moment draws taut as we stare at each other. The space between us seems to shrink by a foot.

"You know what else goose bumps can show?" His eyes are near black. They captivate me—especially how they're on my mouth. "Reaction to strong emotion. Fear, excitement, euphoria . . ." His finger slips around my heel, massaging my Achilles tendon. "Arousal."

I grip the seat harder so I don't do something stupid, like reach out and touch him. Because as his touch wanders around my ankle, creeps up my calf, he's proving his point. Goose bumps erupt on my skin.

My eyes flutter as he reaches the area behind my knee, and I am in danger of melting into a puddle of pink goo right here on the tile floor. At least I'll match the aesthetic.

When his hand slips higher, to the back of my thigh, I moan, my knees turning to water even though I'm sitting. I've never been touched there so delicately. I've never been touched *anywhere* so delicately. I moan as his hands move higher. "I think the Band-Aid's on."

He jolts like I've electrocuted him, standing so swiftly my foot thuds to the floor and sends a spark of pain through my leg. "I'm sorry." Adam gathers the remnants of his first-aid efforts, tossing them to the garbage, not meeting my eyes.

What, exactly, is he apologizing for?

"No, don't," I say, but it's too late. He's already out the door.

I stay in the bathroom until my goose bumps fade.

* * *

"Hi everyone. This is Elle. I've already recorded an episode, but something happened this morning I couldn't quite shake. I think it's the perfect way to introduce this show, the why behind it. So we're starting over. My grandmother has mid- to late-stage Alzheimer's, and she doesn't remember me."

The cut on my foot throbs as a reminder.

"*This morning, my grandmother walked out the side gate of her garden and made it two blocks before she got distracted petting a dog. When the police found her, she didn't remember where she was or what she was doing. I can only imagine how terrifying that must have been for her. It was terrifying for me.*

"*But someone I've come to know recently told me something after we found her. Love is supposed to make you* more *yourself, not less. And I think that goes for all those we ever love, the people and the places and the memories that make us. I owe it to my Lovie's memory—her own, and the ones I have of her—to show all of her. The good parts and the bad. So that's what this podcast will be.*"

I clear my throat. Across the hall, Adam's got his eyes trained on the television, volume too low to carry, but something in the set of his shoulders, the way he's leaning into the open space between us, tells me he's listening.

"*I can't tell whether it's funny or sad—how we can get older and younger at the same time. So many things about Lovie remind me of a child, a baby, even. She needs help cutting her meat and bathing and has to be reminded to take medicine. She wears diapers to sleep, can't dress herself. There have been days where I haven't heard her say anything other than single words.* Hungry. Tired. Headache. No.

"*That's terrifying too, when you stop to think about it. How sometimes our best days really are behind us and we have absolutely no idea. And I don't know whether I should be mourning her now so it will hurt less later, or enjoying what's left of her and let myself hurt when the last pieces finally slip away. Hopefully this podcast will help me do both, and you, if you've ever found yourself in a similar position. This is* Forget Me Not.*"*

CHAPTER TWENTY-FIVE

Adam's avoiding me. Not rudely or dismissively, but enough to let me know spending time with me is the last thing he wants.

"Want to come garden with me?" I asked yesterday morning, giving my best convincing smile. I was planning to take pictures of Lovie's forget-me-nots for Instagram. I thought I'd post one each week with every episode. The dirt will only get more dry and gray as we slip further into winter. That's sort of the point.

He smiled back, and I thought I'd won. Until he said, "No, thanks. The last time a guy named Adam was in a garden, it didn't turn out too well for the general population."

And I was too busy appreciating his joke to protest. Or realize he'd dodged me.

This morning when I said I needed to get out of the house and invited him on another field trip, he didn't meet my eyes as he let me down gently.

"Lovie's having a bad day. She's not up to going anywhere."

"Oh, I can . . ." I trailed off. I didn't want to offer to stay, because I had Shit to Do. But was it rude if I didn't offer at all?

What I said instead was, "You haven't had a true day off in almost six weeks."

He shrugged from where he was wiping the counters. Lovie's pills used to sit there, but we can't leave them unattended anymore. A few days ago I caught her trying to peel off the labels. "I'm okay, Elle. I promise."

I hesitated in the doorway, waiting to see if he'd look at me. Do *something* other than keep his back turned. "Well, let me know if you want anything from Starbucks."

He didn't.

Of course.

When I get back from my failed attempt to find a sense of peace stocked on the shelves of Target (I'm considering calling someone; it concerns me too), Adam's got the entire kitchen table covered in gadgets.

It takes me a second to place them, but when I do, I have a moment of pride. He's making it through my episodes faster than I thought if he's already up to my partnership with SafeSpace Home Security.

I lean in the doorway. "What are you doing?"

He hardly looks up from where he frowns down at the sensors, dwarfed in his hands. "Installing a security system. I figure we can keep it on all the time. If Lovie gets out, we'll know instantly. There's an app you can use. I think it will give us both a better sense of—security." He grimaces. "Bad choice of words, but you know."

Something tells me if I push far enough, he'll start avoiding me again. I can't take that chance, especially since I've already been out of the house once today. Leaving if things get heated—or worse, awkward—would be cruel.

Taking a few steps into the kitchen, I spot the order slip and slide it from under the mess of packaging. The price doesn't look right. I rest my hip against the table. "You didn't use my code?"

He looks up. "What code?"

"Oh, Adam," I chide, laughing because I just can't help it when he gets that confused groove between his eyebrows. "You completely overpaid for this system. I have a sponsorship deal with them. You could have saved twenty percent."

"Well." He blinks. "Fuck."

I set down my half-gone coffee on the island, safely out of reach of the electronics. "Want some help?"

He looks me over, and the memory of his hands on my waist and in my hair, my mouth on his, settles between us. He's a puzzle I don't have all the pieces to yet, but maybe today I can put a few more in place.

"Seriously," I say. "You can hold the sensors, and I'll just grab what I need. I have this same one in my apartment. I'm familiar with it."

Finally, he nods, straightening his shoulders to take his job seriously. The way he always does.

We start in the kitchen with the window behind the table. Adam keeps frowning at the sensors that won't behave due to magnetic force, nudging them back in line.

The one above the sink proves to be more challenging. Most of the windows in the house open easily, but this one got painted shut about ten years ago and hasn't seen a fresh breeze since. Adam says we can leave it, but last night I had a dream Lovie climbed through the porthole in the bathroom that's designed not to open at all. I'm tempted to slap sensors on the dryer ventilation and the mail slot.

He reappears from the laundry room with a putty knife.

"How'd you get into nursing?" I ask, working the knife along the windowsill. "And is it your end goal to do home health care like this all the time, or is it just a stepping-stone? Oh, and where'd you grow up? It wasn't here, if you didn't know the Dairy Queen secret."

He blows out a breath. "I don't think I had enough caffeine this morning to withstand this line of questioning."

"I'm not surprised, considering that coffeepot is only capable of producing battery acid." I lift a shoulder. "I offered Starbucks."

He snorts. "Anything would taste like battery acid in that atrocious plastic butterfly you drink it out of. Can you imagine all the BPA you've ingested over the years?"

I pause, frowning at him. "Is that why my tummy hurts? I thought it was all the lead paint."

His eyebrows dip so low his eyelashes touch them, and I make sure to bat my own. "You're joking," he says.

"And you're deflecting," I say back. "I ask questions for a living. I'm nosy by nature."

"I'm starting to figure that out." His eyes are almost kind, though, and his jaw twitches the way it always does before he says something important and astute.

"You're right; I'm not from Indiana," he says, his eyes trained on the most recent unruly sensor. "I grew up in Toledo. But my little sister moved here for school. Purdue."

Purdue is basically a midwestern Ivy League. "That's amazing."

"It was. We were all so proud of her." His tone is guarded, though, not quite matching his words.

I flex my fingers around the putty knife and give the window another jiggle. It's barely loosened.

"And then she got pregnant when she was a freshman," Adam says.

My heart plummets for this woman I've never met. *Elle on the L* has given me the chance to hear the most amazing stories—and the most heartbreaking. I can't help wondering if Adam's sister is someone I've talked to.

"My parents were not a fan of her keeping the baby. They're big God-people, my parents, so they wanted Ruth—my sister—to give the baby up for adoption. Nothing else was on the table. She was a checklist to them. Have the baby, give it to a straight, rich, white couple who couldn't have one of their own, get back to school and pretend it never happened."

His earlier joke about Adam in the garden makes my heart hurt more.

"But then baby turned into *babies*," he says.

My eyes bug as I look at him over my shoulder. "Twins?"

He nods.

"Yikes."

He nods again. "You sure I can't try that?"

I shake my head and wedge the knife into the corner slowly, sinking it in another half inch. I may not have gone to an Ivy League, but I know seeing Adam's forearms in action will be counterproductive at best and detrimental at worst. "She didn't go through with the adoptions."

His stare is heavy on my skin, my hands. "No. But *when* she didn't, my parents refused to keep paying for her education." My insides twist. I think I know how this story ends. "I offered to help. She wanted to transfer to a community college, but I wouldn't let her. So she took out as many loans as she could, and I took out the rest. It—"

The putty knife sinks in.

"It what?" I say, unexpectedly breathless. I'm terrified he's going to leave me dangling off this cliff.

"It was fine," he says. "Until a year after she graduated, when she met Scott."

I let the putty knife rest in the crack and flex my fingers around the handle. I'll need to touch up the paint. "Based on your tone," I say, "he's not the favorite."

"He might have been. *Could* have been. The opportunity was his for the taking. But then they had Claire, the baby. Claire spent a lot of time in the hospital when she was born, in and out for the first year or so of her life. That was too much for him."

"For *him*?" The knife handle bites my palm; my knuckles are white. "What about *Ruth*? And Claire?"

Adam shakes his head. "What they needed didn't matter to him, which is why I think it's better this way, in the end. I'd rather my sister have no one than be stuck with someone who doesn't deserve her. You asked why I work so much. That's why. I support my sister and her three children. They're mine."

My head spins and my gut clenches. He cares so much, so selflessly. Every decision I've made since coming here has been self-serving in some way. Adam is the opposite.

It is both beautiful and heartbreaking. He lives his entire life for other people.

This doesn't feel like an interview, not like the ones for the podcast. Our back-and-forth is as easy as talking to Liss, or Lovie before her memory crapped out on her.

Is Adam my friend? When did that happen?

He clears his throat. "Your fingers are turning purple. Let me try to unstick the window. Please."

I don't have the capacity to push him away again. He steps into my space—takes it over for his own. I have to back up or risk our bodies touching in more places than one.

The window glides open fifteen seconds later. Show-off.

"How are your nieces now?" I ask, after he's installed the sensor on the patio door and we've moved to the living room. There are three windows in here—two side by side behind the couch and one on the other side of the room, by the bookshelf and television. Should be easy enough. We're practically done already. "And what are the twins' names? I don't know if you've ever mentioned them." I climb onto the couch, leaning over the back and pulling the curtain away from the sill.

Adam splutters, and I quickly realize why. He's stepped up, preparing to hand me the sensors. With the way I'm positioned, though, I'd fall over if I reached for them. Which leaves him to lean forward into me, putting his crotch right in line with my ass.

Being on my hands and knees near him does something to my bloodstream. Turns it hot and fizzy, like a Coke shaken and left in the sun. I also am likely to combust under pressure. I imagine the things Adam would do. Tug my hair. Make my back arch so I could look at him upside down.

He sucks his bottom lip into his mouth, dragging it with his teeth. My breath hitches.

"Cora," he coughs.

I chuckle, my laugh dipped in smoke and sex. "That's not my name." I want to tell him I know about five hundred ways to get him to say my name, but he heads me off.

"Cora is my *niece*." He places the sensors in my palm. "She and Chloe are nine. Claire just turned two in August."

My heart is a hummingbird in my throat. As I turn back to the window, the smaller of the two sensors slips from my hand and falls to the black hole between the couch and the wall.

The living room isn't big enough to move the furniture, so I push up to my feet and bend over the back.

A pained groan floats to me. "What are you doing?"

I'm thankful he can't see my face. I may be grinning now. After that very first morning wherein Adam was *maybe* looking at my butt, I upped my routine to include fifteen extra squats three times a day so he would *definitely* look at my butt. "I dropped the sensor."

My face smushes sideways and I lose sight of the little white rectangle. I also lose my balance and go tumbling head-first into the abyss of dust bunnies and hair balls.

Or I would, if hands didn't suddenly grip my hips in a vise. I clamp down on a moan, mostly because I can't tell whether it would be one of pleasure or embarrassment.

"Are you okay?" he calls.

"Yeah, just—" I close my fist tight around the sensor before I lose it again. "Wondering if this can get any more awkward. Hating how often you have to ask me that. The usual."

He works me free slowly, gentle tugs back and forth, side to side. When my head emerges from the shadows, my face is blazing hot and his hands have slipped under my shirt, lighting fire to my bare skin.

"You good?" he asks, except it doesn't sound like a question so much as a demand. *You're good, because I've got you.*

Any words I'd choose would come out obscene and vulgar, not safe for work, which is what this is. We're basically business partners. Nothing more, nothing less. And if this is truly, strictly, a business arrangement, I shouldn't care how he spends time with his nieces or how he takes his coffee or the color of his scrubs each day. I should be fine with the few offered details he gives me and leave it at that.

He doesn't let go of my hips until I nod, and even then, he's slow to release me.

I almost drop the sensor again when I put it on the window. The only reason I don't is because Adam's on the other side of the room now, far away from me and my hips. Which is for the best.

The front door is next, and Adam takes that one because he's taller. I, courteously, give him space. Getting close to him won't solve anything except the ache between my thighs.

His shoulders stretch as he reaches overhead, the cords in his neck disappearing and reappearing as he shifts. Same for the ones in his forearms, and on the backs of his hands.

When he clears his throat, I realize I've been staring, and based on the dryness in my mouth, it was open far enough to catch flies. "Sorry." I hold out the equipment, my heartbeat refusing to calm.

He gives me an amenable smile, and my gaze snags there, on the deep-pink color that matches the bathroom so perfectly. His fingers brush my palm as he picks up the sensor, and if I think about it hard enough, if I *force* it, that felt mostly platonic. Which is a step forward.

But my train of thought takes several leaps backward when Adam mutters, "You're staring at my mouth."

Fake It Like You Mean It

How are we playing this, Elle? Coy or straightforward?

"It's a nice mouth," I say. Straightforward it is.

This surprises him, if the laugh that splits his lips is any indication.

"You have a nice mouth too," he says. The same way he said *You make me want to make mistakes.* His eyes flash bright blue, the hottest flame in the fire.

Adam must be made of lightning, because the air between us turns staticky, electrified. If I touched the doorknob, I'd get shocked. The hairs on my arms are standing up.

"Goose bumps," he murmurs, running a lone fingertip down my betraying forearm.

I try to keep my wits about me. "Home security turns me on." *And watching you install it makes me so hot I can hardly hold myself up.*

"You," he murmurs, "are a terrible liar."

My wits have fled. The bastards.

His fingertips trail my arm, across my collarbones. I'm shaking. When they drag across my lips, I part them. He touches the tip of my tongue.

"If I kissed you right now . . ." His eyes are dark, the way they are first thing in the morning, and whenever I catch him looking at me. "Would you let me? Would you want that?"

The noise I make is feral. I moan like he's already doing it. "Only if you don't apologize after."

"I won't," he whispers, his hand curving along my cheek. A promise and a threat.

My response gets trapped between us, suspended and half given as he takes my mouth with his.

That first kiss *was* fake. Terribly, undeniably fake. Fake enough for my brain to get busy rewriting it as something other than a kiss. That was . . . a whisper, a slight breeze. A drop in the bucket. In the fucking *ocean*.

This kiss is a precipice. The knife's edge between deliciously tipsy and devastatingly drunk, the best decision and the worst. Adam kisses like he looks—hard around the edges but soft somewhere just below the surface. His hands clutch my face, wrap around the back of my head to hold me still. *Right here*, he's saying silently. *You belong right here, in my arms, with your mouth on me and my mouth on you. Got it?*

I do not got it. If this is how he's proving his point, it will take me a long damn time to get it.

Needing a taste of him, I plunge my tongue into the seam of his lips, rewarded when his hold tightens. Hot, soft velvet welcomes me. It's the last concession he gives me, and as his hand slides down and fits around my rib cage, he reminds me with a tug closer: *I kissed you.* He tells me again with a graze of his teeth to my lip, a hum in his throat when I return it. *I started this.* With a groan, his lips move to the junction of my jaw, and he shows me once more as his knee slips between my legs: *I own you right now.*

When my fingers find the hem of his shirt and slide underneath, scoring across his stomach, groan turns to growl, and my hands are pinned to the wall above my head.

His mouth returns to mine, trapping my tingling lips as he knots our fingers. I grip him tight, nails biting flesh.

Not to be dramatic, but this is the best kiss of my life. Grady who? Adam is a living paradox—the way his mouth is moving, pulling my skin between his teeth, grazing and sucking, is inconsistent with how the thumb of his other hand rubs lightly at the groove of exposed skin between my shirt and waistband. How his knee between mine offers a pressure that is both stable and insanity inducing.

He pulls away first. We're breathless. I'm sweating. My body is high and tight, and I won't be able to get off ever again without imagining his hold on me, his lips pressed against my neck. Whereas he's ripped me apart with his mouth—with clothes on, no less—he seems more put together than before.

I've been told I wreck men. Why isn't he wrecked? He should be wrecked. I want a refund.

Or another kiss.

His hand traces the line of my jaw and down my throat, and I swallow beneath his touch.

"Mmm," he rumbles, pressing two fingers to the pulse point in my neck. He almost did that my first night here. "Your heart's racing." His eyes trail his fingers, down my neck, across my low-cut collar. His pupils have devoured the blue color. "Can you feel it?" He spreads his fingers wide, the heel of his hand resting over my sternum, dangerously close to my breast. "Here."

What I feel is the burn of his stubble, fresh on my chin and jaw and throat. The millimeter of space between his thumb and the place that desperately wants his touch.

"I . . . I think you broke me," I rasp.

His mouth, reddened and swollen, morphs into his fullest grin yet. It's blinding, and, yes, Adam Wheeler is electricity incarnate. "We can't have that, can we?" Torturously slow, he pulls away, the nail of his index finger scraping fabric and sending a shiver down my spine. "You can put your arms down now if you want."

"What—"

By the time I realize my hands are still pressed to the wall above my head, his laugh is far away, floating to me from down the hall.

CHAPTER TWENTY-SIX

When my phone rings with a FaceTime call from Liss a few days later, I'm half expecting it. Alissa and I have a special form of ESP where we know when the other has done something potentially damning.

Liss thinks it's limited by geography. I think we have different definitions of *damning*.

And that kiss with Adam was hot enough to convince me I'd somehow skipped purgatory and gone straight to hell. There's no way you're this lustful in heaven.

He doesn't avoid me after the kiss, not like last time. If anything, he's around *more*. He finds unsuspecting ways to touch me—moves around me in the hall by grabbing my waist and rotating my body with his, even though there's plenty of space to squeeze by. Asks me to grab a sock that falls between the washer and dryer and holds my hips as I retrieve it. "We don't want a repeat of the living room, do we?" he said. But I did! I do! For television hour last night, the sides of our bodies were fused together, and his lips buzzed against my temple so much my nose tickled with the constant threat of a sneeze. The *Wheel of*

Fortune phrase *Can you keep a secret?* took on new meaning as Adam crossed his socked feet at the ankles, bumping intentionally into mine, and I'd never heard the name "Thomas Gage" muttered so sexily. Certainly not by the guy on *Jeopardy!*

One thing I've never understood about romance novels is how characters ever think doing it once—kissing, oral, insert other sex act here—will get it out of their system. Oxytocin, nature's love drug, increases during things like hugging and orgasms. If you want someone out of your system, touching them more is *not* the way to do it. And getting over someone by getting under someone else doesn't work either. Oxytocin's a greedy bitch, but she's not picky. You'll just end up having more love drugs in your veins, not less.

Adam is in my veins now.

"Elle!" Liss shouts before her face is completely pixelated, snapping me out of my head and into the present. "Guess what!"

She's in her shop. The kitchen lights (ideal for social media shots, thanks to my guidance) illuminate her bright-red cheeks and frizzy blonde hair. She is wild and happy.

Lovie and Adam are on the front porch, Lovie working through one of her puzzle books while Adam scrolls on his phone.

All I can think about is him mauling me in the doorway.

I try to turn my attention fully to Liss, but most of my brain cells are stuck on Adam in profile. I shrug. "Just tell me, babe."

"I got the Cubs guy!" she says excitedly, her body vibrating enough to shake her phone.

"What?" I sit up straighter. I don't have the slightest idea what she's talking about; Chicago doesn't have as many socialites as New York or Los Angeles, but there are a few, most of them tied to sports. "Is this a dating app match? Did you tell me about him already?"

She groans. "Brody Boswell! The third baseman for the Cubs? I texted you about him last week. His fiancée decided that my cake is the best—"

"Obviously."

"—and they booked me for their wedding next September! It's the biggest order I've ever had, Elle. And the most famous client. Well, besides you, Queen of *Jeopardy!*"

I think of Adam and me curled up on the couch last night. He'd dropped his lips to the skin behind my ear, didn't say anything, just left his mouth there for a beat too long to be misconstrued as anything other than what it was.

Liss gasps. "You kissed Nurse Adam!"

Her words jolt me back to the present, and as much as I want to avoid it, my face heats. "I told you that already," I try.

"No, this is different. Like an on-purpose one. Was it good? Where was it? Was there tongue? Can you rate it one to ten for me, please?"

Dakota's head pops up beside her. "Look into my eyes, Fanning Number One. Tongue is guaranteed on a man like that. But was there *biting*?" His eyebrows dance.

"There was . . ." I close my eyes. There was *everything*.

The front door alarm chimes, and I nearly drop my phone in my attempt to end the call. "You're breaking up and the alarm's going off and the mailman's here and I havetogobye!"

* * *

@ElleontheL ✓: *Episode three of* Forget Me Not *is live! This week I talk about Lovie's diet and routine now versus when I was a kid. Spoiler: we both still love milkshakes. What's your guilty pleasure food?*

@jollyxholly527: honestly it's @OliveGarden

@DFWMama6: My nana's baked spaghetti! I use the same recipe with my littles and they LOVE it!

@Purrrsiankitty8: anything with msg and lots of sodium. so like, ramen noodles?

Fake It Like You Mean It

*@**Anchorsawaym8**: nothing beats my dad's Superbowl Sundaes*
*@**thatguy3k00**: Apparently all your followers are children, just like you.*

*@**NurseAdamIndy**: Comfort foods trigger dopamine, the happy chemical. Many people associate comfort foods with positive memories, social connection, and certainty and routine.*

*@**thatguy3k00**: Who the fuck are you anyway?*

*@**NurseAdamIndy**: A nurse. Named Adam. From Indiana. I thought it was obvious from the username.*

Show more replies

*@**SweetiesCakesChicago**: Chocolate cake* 😋
*@**DMillsBakes**: SECONDED!!*

*@**BroBoswell14** ✓: Thirded* 😋 *Can't wait to have @SweetiesCakesChicago at our wedding next year!*

Show 678 more comments

CHAPTER TWENTY-SEVEN

"There's a storm coming."

I look up at Adam from my spot on the couch.

"You're telling me," I say, rotating my laptop screen toward him. "Adam, you can*not* keep egging on my trolls like this. It will only make things worse."

We're well into November now, and there's still no progress with the insurance company. I couldn't find the original documents they needed, so I had to order new ones. Who knows when they'll come in, especially with the upcoming holidays.

And, apparently, the ever-present threat of winter weather.

I'm still sitting on a nice backlog of episodes for *Elle on the L*, but for every week that passes with no forward movement with insurance, my anxiety ticks up a notch. I haven't had good pizza in over a month, and I'm going through Liss withdrawal.

"It's nice you noticed, but that's not what I was talking about." Adam's voice is dull and sarcastic. "There's winter weather coming in." He holds out his phone, the local weather forecast pulled up. "Some models say eight inches or more."

Don't go there, Elle. Don't take the bait. Don't—
"I can handle eight inches."

Oops. I love when I don't listen to my own voice of reason.

Adam's ears redden as he clears his throat. "I was hoping one of us could run to the store, grab bread and toilet paper before they're all out. Why people don't go for batteries and thermal blankets and ice melt first, I'm not sure."

"That would make too much sense." I'm smiling at him. I can't stop. It won't turn off.

The corner of his mouth twitches, but he has a much better poker face than I do. "So, do you want to go or do you want me to?"

"Yes," I say, a little too winded for such an innocent conversation, especially when there's so much distance between us.

His forehead creases. "What?"

I put the brakes on my lust to dissect his actual question. My pulse is already pounding at the thought of being behind the wheel. "Can we go together? A field trip?"

He scratches his jaw, and my focus narrows there. "That didn't work out well last time."

I lean forward, elbows on knees, to clasp my hands under my chin. "Please, Nurse Adam from Indy? I promise to stand up for myself with the trolls and make you a green smoothie tomorrow." I flutter my lashes, pop out my bottom lip, and go in for the kill. "I'll give you the bed for a week if you drive."

A warm smile flashes across his face, and I have the sudden, distinct feeling I just got played. "Lovie's car or mine?"

* * *

Adam was right: the stores are crazy. There are shopping carts scattered across the parking lot, not a worker in sight to wrangle them. Finding a motorized scooter for Lovie turns out to be so challenging we leave without anything on our list.

But we did get pretzels from the kiosk, so it wasn't a complete waste.

He has to circle the lot at the next store a few times to find a handicapped spot. There are so many people here. It's eleven AM on a Tuesday. Do these people not have jobs? We can't all be podcasters.

We follow a soccer mom through most of the grocery aisles. I've named her Karen in my head. She will *definitely* call the manager on you.

Karen will also grab ten loaves of bread. *Ten.*

When she steps out of the way, Adam grabs one. We don't eat bread often enough to get more than that. Judging by Karen's legs, she doesn't either.

When she grabs five packages of bottled water, Adam helps her load them on her cart, then grabs one for us.

After the third aisle, I realize he's making it into a game, just for me. In the toilet paper aisle, Adam throws me a wink and starts loading Karen's cart *full* of toilet paper.

She balks. "What are you *doing*?" She reaches for the pack he's placing, but he dodges her and gets it in anyway.

Adam's face turns innocent so fast I think I imagined the mischievousness there before. "I just thought you had seven kids with all the bread. You must need this much toilet paper."

"I have two children," Karen snaps, pulling out packs as Adam continues to place them in.

"Then do you have four spouses? Because otherwise there's no possible way you can go through all that bread before it spoils."

Karen's cheeks are the color of cherries. "I was going to freeze it." She pulls her cart away as Adam continues loading it up, and his last pack falls to the ground.

He scoops it up effortlessly and tosses it in the basket on Lovie's scooter. "My mistake. Have a great day, ma'am, and you stay safe." He waves down the aisle at her, smiling like a lunatic. She keeps glancing back over her shoulder. Any second, I expect her to abandon the cart and start running.

I'm in tears, my abs aching. I haven't laughed this hard in . . . I can't remember how long.

Even Lovie's smiling. "He's a good one, you know," she says, watching me. "Don't let him go." Something flashes in her eyes, so bright and familiar it halts my laughter in its tracks.

She isn't talking to Lovie about Bobby. She's talking to Elle about Adam.

The rush of relief is dizzying, and the guilt that follows is nauseating. If I were at peace with Lovie's mental state, I wouldn't be so happy she's looking at me, *Elle*. I understand these breakthroughs are rare. It could last for minutes or a week. I'm scared to move in fear of disturbing whatever aligned in her brain.

"Lovie?" I say, almost too soft for my own ears.

Adam turns to us before she responds. The recognition on her face dims but doesn't extinguish. He points down the aisle. "Let's swing by the outdoor section and see if we can grab some ice melt and another shovel."

Lovie reverses her scooter before I can say *wait*.

* * *

Forget Me Not

Transcript, Episode 03

Hi, everyone. Elle here. We were going to talk about the science behind Alzheimer's this week, but we had what is known in the Midwest as a Snow Scare. A false start to winter, if you will. We're talking DEFCON-level blizzard preparedness, buying kerosene heaters and ten loaves of bread—I witnessed that last one with my own eyes.

Megan Murphy

Here at Lovie's house, we gathered all the spare blankets we could find, premade a few meals that taste good hot or cold, and made sure we had candles and flashlights in every room. Salted the sidewalk and driveway and tuned in to the weather instead of our usual Jeopardy.

But there wasn't a blizzard. It didn't even snow.

We spent days preparing, listening to experts, and nothing happened. But last week, there was a tornado outbreak in the South that took ten lives. There are so many variables that it's almost impossible to predict what will happen, with chronic disease or storms or something as simple as traffic.

I think it's a great metaphor for Alzheimer's. I've used up a lot of unnecessary energy trying to predict the future, change the outcome. It's how I am, and how I've always been. I need to be in control of my situation. I hate asking for help and I hate taking advice from others on something I consider myself an expert on.

My grandmother, for example.

But while I may be an expert on who she was, *she's different now. Alzheimer's is changing her makeup, her physical and mental and emotional self. I'm not an expert on her any more than I am an expert on the weather.*

So I encourage you along with myself, to give up what doesn't belong to you. Quit wasting your energy on things you can't control and try and enjoy exactly what you have in this moment. What's that quote about holding sand with an open hand versus closed fist?

Yeah, I second that.

CHAPTER TWENTY-EIGHT

I kneel in the middle of a blizzard. It's cold here, so cold the flowers at my feet are iced over. Not dead, but dipped in water and flash frozen. Everything is encased in frost. My body is numb where it touches the snow.

In front of me, Lovie squats down, hands and knees on the white ground as she tends to a small bunch of blue flowers.

"Lovie, wake up."

Lovie looks up at me, but she shakes her head, and I do too. Not me, she's saying. *You.*

That floating voice is talking to me?

"Come on, love. Wake up for me."

An earthquake shakes the ground, and I grab at the ground to hold steady. The voice is getting louder, the shocks more apparent.

"Damn it, Elle. Wake up. Your friends are here."

Wait a minute. I think I know that voice.

"Adam?" I croak. I raise my head and encounter the pillow I must have burrowed under. It's a little early in the winter for hibernation, even for me.

"Thank God," he breathes. "Your friends are here."

I peek at him through one slitted eye. He stands next to the bed in dark-green scrubs, beautiful as ever. I'm not sure I'm wearing pants.

I try to make his words make sense, blink myself into a more conscious state. "What friends?"

Adam grabs my phone from the nightstand. "These friends, I'm pretty sure."

Behind a dozen notifications each from Liss and Dakota is a picture of the three of us last summer. Dakota's boyfriend Sam took it at their apartment-warming party. I was already buzzed by that point. My arms are around Liss and Dakota's are around me, and the three of us are singing a song I can't remember to save my life.

"That's sweet," I say, handing my phone back to Adam and returning my head to the pillow.

Then his words register.

"They're *here*?! Literally here, in this house?" I throw off the covers—I was right, no pants—and run down the hall. If Lovie has something to say about my thighs today, it's going to have to wait until I squeeze my friends to death.

Dakota's voice reaches me first ("I think she's coming!"), but Liss physically touches me first, rounding the corner the same time I do. It's been far too long.

Liss Kessinger is five feet five inches of pure sugar (and coffee). I have all the spice in this friendship.

"What the hell are you doing here?" I mumble into her hair, ever frizzy and the color of sunshine, even in the winter.

She kisses my cheek. "You seemed off the last time we spoke."

Dakota hip-checks her out of the way to pull me into a bone-crushing hug of his own. Dakota is softer, rounder, but just as giggly. He rests his hands on my bare shoulders. "She looks like Elle, she sounds like Elle, but it's been so long I can't quite remember."

I laugh. "Point taken."

"Seriously, though. We haven't seen you in too long," Liss says, her bottom lip trembling ever so slightly.

Dakota elbows her. "We said we wouldn't cry at the beginning."

She wipes her eyes. "Right. Sorry, you're right." And then I'm squished between them and two-thirds of us are crying anyway.

"Why are you almost naked?" Liss whispers. My tank top feels especially scandalous under such a heavy gaze. She gasps, her cheeks going bright again. "Did you share the bed?"

I hope Adam goes the long way around, through the laundry room. Maybe he'll start a load of towels or something.

But a throat clears behind me, and I know I won't be that lucky today or ever.

Adam steps up to our little huddle, holding out a pair of sweatpants and a jacket. "Here."

In my periphery, Dakota's mouth falls open, and Liss's clamps shut.

I scramble for the clothes, moving my hopes and dreams onto greener pastures. Like that maybe, just maybe, my friends will keep their comments about Adam's . . . *Adamness* private until he's out of earshot.

"If I wasn't already happily partnered, I would ask if you had a brother." *Dammit, Dakota.*

Liss nods vigorously as I pull on the sweats. "*Do* you have a brother?"

"He only has a sister," I bark, shoving each of them in the shoulder. I haven't even put on the jacket yet. But I have to separate my friends from Adam before they can ask any more embarrassing questions. Like whether he's worked through his childhood trauma and his opinion on family portraits for Christmas cards. "Out."

"But—" Dakota protests, pouting.

"It was nice to meet you, Nurse Adam!" Liss gasps, then covers her mouth as I lead her toward the kitchen. "Was that nickname supposed to be a secret?"

"We brought pizza?" Dakota tries, which, I'll admit, does make me falter for a second before I catch sight of a clock.

"Bullshit. It's only ten."

"I did bring doughnuts," Liss says over her shoulder, still resisting me. "And a cold brew, ice on the side so it didn't get watered down."

Now that gets me. "The good kind of doughnuts?"

She frowns. "Is there a *bad* kind of doughnut?"

Adam follows us down the hall. He's probably going to remind us to keep it down so we don't disturb Lovie's routine.

Instead, a tentative smile turns up the edge of his mouth. "Lovie's reading on the back porch. I've got the gas heater out there, but if she gets restless, I'll take her out for a drive or something. Enjoy yourself, okay? They really love you."

My hands drop to my sides. "Thank you. I'm sorry I slept so late. I must have forgotten my alarm. If you want, tomorrow I can take the early shift with Lovie."

He studies me. "You have sleep lines." His finger ghosts across my right cheek, and sweet heat curls around my spine.

Liss and Dakota swoon in tandem.

Adam heads toward the back patio, and Dakota literally gasps at the sight of him walking away.

Okay, fine. *Same.*

Liss starts three sentences before the door is fully shut, and I shush her each time, eventually resorting to physically holding her mouth closed. Once there's no possible way Adam can overhear us, I drop my hand.

She takes a big breath. "Oh my God. Elle."

"Did you see his traps?" Dakota says.

My head pounds from the disorientation. I'm dizzy from the tables turning so swiftly. "Can we please pause this conversation until I have that cold brew I was promised?"

* * *

"We have not slept together," I say for the fifth time. I thought I needed caffeine, but my friends are the ones not comprehending information properly right now.

Dakota's bushy blond eyebrows slash a straight line across his forehead. "Third base?"

"No."

"Second, surely."

I reflect on my doorway kiss with Adam, where his hands wandered. Teased, but never quite touched. Unfortunately, Liss and Dakota read my hesitation as confirmation and start fangirling again.

"No, no, nonononono." I set my cup too harshly on the table, and precious cold brew sloshes over the side. "Listen, both of you. I have *only* kissed him. And *only* a few times." Gushing about kisses, squealing over cute boys, blushing at the thought of him. "I didn't realize we were thirty going on thirteen."

"I'm only twenty-eight," Dakota says. "And you're never too old to have a crush on a boy. My nana has three boyfriends at the retirement home."

Okay, Dakota's nana. You go, girl.

"Adam is *not* a boy," I say under my breath.

Liss grins. "So you've got yourself a *man*."

I didn't expect any less of them, to be honest. I knew they wouldn't sweep this under the rug, especially once they laid eyes on Adam. I didn't show them his picture for this reason. And Adam is largely antitechnology, anyway. His Instagram picture is still a gray silhouette.

But they get it. They saw us together for two seconds and deduced something I've been trying to ignore for weeks.

"Is he a good person?" Liss asks, more serious now as she grabs my coffee and takes a heavy swallow.

"The best." My hands fall limply into my lap. "I think I'm screwed."

Dakota takes the cold brew next. Who'd they bring that for, anyway? Clearly not me. "Would that be a bad thing? The traps, Elle. Think about the traps."

Liss leans into his shoulder. "Dakota, you're thinking with the wrong head. We need to know if he's grumpy to the world but nice to her. If he likes baseball over hockey. If he eats a second lunch just because she's hungry and makes self-deprecating jokes." I think those are the exact criteria she has for her future husband. "We've seen him troll *that guy* on Instagram."

I'm split down the middle. I want to share everything good about Adam and somehow keep it all to myself. How he gets my favorite creamer at the grocery, makes sure my butterfly mug is set by the coffeepot each morning even though he'll inevitably comment about BPA poisoning, and has a green smoothie waiting when I return from frigid morning runs. The way he holds me during *Jeopardy!* even when Lovie's in the bathroom.

How he kisses me like he needs me.

A small, warm hand covers mine. Liss's face pinches. "You can keep it all to yourself if you want, but I've never seen you look like that when all you're doing is *thinking* about a guy. Never, ever. Not Grady, not that one guy from the band. Not even Miles Teller."

Has my infatuation with Adam surpassed that of my greatest celebrity crush? Oh shit. I really am screwed.

Dropping my head in my hands, I start from the beginning. It takes me so long to go through every detail, every lingering touch and glance, that by the time I'm finished, the cold brew is gone, the ice has melted, and I'm convinced Adam and Lovie have gone through two units of propane trying to keep warm outside.

Dakota knocks his knuckles against the table. "I just decided your love story is going to be called 'Adam and Elle's Guide to Gardening.'"

Then, and only then, do I remember there isn't supposed to be an *Adam and Elle*. The last thing I want to do is get him in trouble with his superiors, or somehow disqualify Lovie from AngelCare's assistance.

My head finds the nearest surface, which happens to be Liss's shoulder. "Why did I do this to myself?"

She pats my head. "I don't think you did it to yourself. I think this is a thing that happened to you. I think what you're *doing* to yourself is fighting something inevitable."

"Remind me why fighting it is bad?"

Liss hums, her pink bottom lip plumping out. "Remember when we went to Sydney Mattingly's pool party in the fourth grade and made that whirlpool? You tried to fight the current and almost drowned."

"Did not," I say, even though I truly did. Sydney's dad had to slap my back so hard, it left a welt in the shape of his palm.

Adam's eyes sort of remind me of a whirlpool, darker around the edges, lighter toward the middle. I've found myself lost in them a few times.

Annoyed at Liss's all-too-fitting anecdote, I boop her on the nose. "Can we talk about something else? How's business? Is your website doing okay?"

Liss's eyes light up, the way they always do when you discuss her pride and joy. "It's amazing. Since Brody Boswell commented on your post, I've been working nonstop. I answered emails last night until two in the morning."

"The official Cubs page follows us," Dakota added. "Our engagement is up like two thousand percent."

My heart warms. "You're going to need more space."

Liss nods, mouth as close to a frown as it can get. "Please don't remind me. It's on the list."

I quirk an eyebrow. "Just at the very bottom of the last page."

"How's *Forget Me Not* doing?" Dakota asks. "Have you convinced Adam to sit down with you?"

My eyes flit to the patio door. "Not yet. But I'm close, I think."

"Speaking of close . . ." Dakota's eyes sparkle as he clasps his hands primly on the table. "Can we please loop back to the sharing-a-bed situation?"

CHAPTER TWENTY-NINE

My friends wear out their welcome quickly, especially when Adam and Lovie come in from the porch and Dakota makes no effort to hide his thoughts on the one-bed issue.

"It's arguably *the* fan-favorite trope, Fanning, and you're misusing the privilege. It's a disservice to romance lovers everywhere."

I usher them out the door after that, promising to update them in the group chat *the literal second* any additional kissing and/or base running occurs. I try to point out that if I were able to text while Adam was running the bases, it wouldn't be very noteworthy. They don't agree.

Their unexpected visit coupled with my rude awakening throws off the rest of my day, and I end up showering right after dinner, forgoing the usual *Wheel of Fortune*.

I'm keyed up in a bad way, so when I grab my clothes before my shower, I also grab my vibrator. What Adam and Lovie don't know can't hurt them. I manage to keep it down, but it's a challenge.

I think I'm free and clear until I throw open the bathroom door afterward.

Adam does his casual lean on the opposite wall, his eyes trained on my bundle of dirty clothes. And the vibe, clearly visible among them. "Whatcha got there?"

"Clothes," I say. I don't try to hide it.

He raises an eyebrow, and I know he won't let this slide. "Is that so?"

Despite my flaming cheeks, I am the picture of cool, calm, and collected. You can Urban Dictionary that phrase and my picture will pop up. "That *is* so, yes."

Adam points at the bundle, where my fingers now have a death grip on my vibrator. "Where do you wear that?"

I arch an eyebrow of my own, calling his bluff. "Wouldn't you like to know."

"Maybe." His teeth snag on his lip, but it's not enough to hide his wicked grin. "But I can probably . . . fill in the gaps for myself." His voice is drenched in honey. "I have a pretty active imagination."

"Yeah?" I pout my bottom lip, make my eyes the slightest bit wider, joining in his little game. "Active enough to call them fantasies?" I move my hair off my neck, but a drop of water slides down and disappears into my cleavage. Adam tracks it the whole way.

His eyes snap to mine, pupils blown. "Wouldn't you like to know," he echoes.

Then he utters what is potentially the most sexually charged question I've ever heard in my life.

"Did you think about me?"

I must have taken my shower too hot, and my skin is having some delayed reaction to the scalding water. It's why I break out in goose bumps. "I—what?" I'm *squeaking*. Since when do I *squeak*?

Adam steps closer, his gaze steady but unreadable as he tucks a wet lock of my hair behind my ear. "In the shower." Another drop slides down my chest, and he watches that one too. "You touched yourself."

As his mouth nears mine, I draw a breath, his sunshine scent mixing with that of my soap. "Is that . . . is that a question?" And if it is, why is he asking when he already knows the answer?

His grin takes shape against my neck, and he inhales deeply enough that it moves my heavy hair. "My question is . . ." His voice is so low I strain to hear him. "Did you think about *me*? Did you pretend I was the one touching you?"

"None of your business," I try to say, except it comes out as a gasp, because one of his hands has slipped to the front of my sweats, pressed firmly to my stomach and hovering above the waistband.

"Can I show you what I think you did?" He is so, so casual, when I'm so, so close to falling apart.

I don't trust myself not to moan, so I keep my lips pursed tight. But I nod.

His lips descend on mine. He's gentler now than he was last time. That day, he kissed me like he needed my air in his lungs to live. Now he kisses me like he knows I'm not going anywhere. A lazy cherishing of my mouth, experimenting to see the ways our lips fit together. We won't discover them all right now, but we can certainly try.

And I hate him for it, because he's right. I have no intention of ever *not* kissing him.

I drop my clothes to grab at his chest, his neck, his *anything*, to pull him closer. He pulls back just long enough to realign our mouths, an even better fit with nothing between us now. A sound rumbles from his throat that I memorize instantly, a grumble-groan of want. His hands explore me, the curves of my waist and spine and ass. Everywhere. The heat of him throws me headfirst into a singularity. There is nothing but this.

My eyes flutter open when he breaks away, our foreheads resting against each other. Waiting. He's near panting. So am I.

This, yes, now, I tell him again with the tilt of my hips, the nod of my head, an open invitation. He accepts it, teeth dragging from jaw to ear to jugular. His breath is hot on my throat as his hand slides an inch lower.

Over his shoulder, a picture on the wall catches my eye, and I gasp as his fingers disappear beneath the waistband of my joggers.

"Wait," I moan, unable to hold it in any longer. "Stop, wait."

He removes himself from my body all at once. I'm left shivering in his sudden absence. "I'm sorry," he rasps, but I'm too struck by what I see to placate him right now.

"No, Adam . . ." I swallow the rocks in my throat. "Look."

He turns to see what I do.

My grandparents' wedding picture, taken in 1964. Lovie's hair was red, chopped off at her shoulders like mine. Her eyes are my eyes. I have her jaw, her cheekbones. Even her nose.

And my grandfather, Bobby. Dark hair, pomaded perfectly, aside from one piece near his crown that refused to follow direction. He's clean-shaven, but there's still a shadow around the edges; his face is chiseled and perfectly imperfect.

His eyes are navy blue.

"No wonder she gets us confused," he says, gaze jumping between the picture and my face.

"No kidding." With the light from the bathroom and the hallway, the reflections of our own faces become ghosts next to my grandparents'.

My grandmother thinks Adam and I are her and her husband, because sixty years ago, we might as well have been, minus one glaring difference.

"They're married. We're not. It's different." I step around Adam, resting my finger on the dusty glass atop their gold wedding bands.

Adam chuckles, grabbing my outstretched hand and knotting our fingers together. "You don't have to try and convince me, Elle. It's just a picture."

"This doesn't bother you?"

His hands messed up my hair earlier, and he fixes it now, clearing it from my face with concentration and care. "It's just a picture," he says again, tilting his head to capture my gaze.

There are a thousand emotions warring in me right now, and I can't name any of them. From down the hall, the *Jeopardy!* theme song starts playing.

Adam straightens. "I should get back."

"Right," I say, bending to pick up the things I dropped when Adam and I collided.

"Elle," he says from the bend in the hallway, cautiously optimistic. "I'll save you a seat?"

He doesn't say kissing me again was a mistake, that whatever we just did shouldn't or can't or won't happen again. He says nothing of being weirded out by being my grandparents' doppelgängers. And for as long as I've known him, Adam has said exactly what he thinks. He's never held back to spare my feelings.

Before I realize it, I'm nodding. "Absolutely. Your ass is mine tonight." Mostly I'm talking about the game show.

Adam disappears around the corner with a smile, and I'm more worked up now than I was before my shower. Before I head out to the living room, I fire off a text to the group chat.

Elle Monroe: Which one is second base again?

CHAPTER THIRTY

If Lovie notices anything different between us when I come into the living room, she doesn't speak on it. And honestly, what would she say? *Young man, did you have your hand down my granddaughter's pants outside my bathroom?* She has spunk, but not that much.

Between questions, Lovie snorts. "You two look awfully cozy tonight. Finally get laid?"

I stand horribly, painfully corrected.

"*Lovie*," I splutter, but it doesn't matter. She'll read me how she wants. And Adam's not hiding that smug grin of his very well, is he? That's not helpful. He hides it behind a fist to his mouth, but there's no hope.

My grandmother thinks I'm a floozy.

Fabulous.

Part of me is jealous of Adam's ability to separate personal feelings from professional ones. He can flip the switch so easily between flirting and caregiving, sparring and gentling.

I should be able to do that too. I've done hard episodes before. I've talked to people considered by modern society to be lowlifes, bums, *dangerous*. And while I am emotional, I'm usually able to distinguish my feelings from those of my guest, or the listener. Since starting *Forget Me Not*, digging up memories of my childhood in this house, in the brown kitchen and pink bathroom, on the flower sofa and in the garden outside, things have only become more tangled.

My growing attraction to Adam isn't helping. Maybe *that's* why I wanted to stay away from him at first. I don't need another tether to get tangled in.

Adam offers to get Lovie ready for bed. Which is just as well, because I need time to prepare for the conversation I sense coming.

Why didn't I notice the similarities between Adam and my grandfather? Now that I see it, it can't be unseen. It's like Jesus in the toast. Maybe it wasn't something I *wanted* to see. But that's not quite right either, because that would mean my brain assigned significance to it, enough to notice and then ignore.

After Adam confirms the security system is set for the night, he reclaims his spot on the couch and pats No-Man's-Land.

"Just a second," I say. I need a few more mind-numbing minutes to corral the thoughts ambling through my mind like sheep out to pasture.

He appeases me, flipping through TV channels while I proceed to dust the blinds and the ceiling fan.

Swiffer in hand, I cross the room, heading for the wooden slats cordoning the living room from the hallway, but he catches my wrist. "Elle."

"Adam," I parrot.

"What's wrong?" he asks. "Because something is."

"And you know me so well after six weeks?"

His brows slant downward. With just a few more degrees of slope, he'd be the physical embodiment of the angry emoji. "Don't I?"

There's so much emotion on his face, it unfurls something in my chest. I can't tell whether it's a good feeling or a bad one. I give in, laying the duster at the bottom of the television and reclaiming my seat on the couch.

Adam turns to me, sideways as I remain straight. "You want me to prove it? How well I know you?" He reaches for my hand, fingers wrapping around my wrist tenderly. He makes a loop, his thumb over his middle finger in some mindless, unconscious gesture. "For starters, you sleep like an actual dead person. This morning when I was trying to wake you up, I actually did check your pulse." He squeezes my wrist, mimicking just that. "I worry for your safety not only in the face of house fires but also earthquakes and zombies."

I grind my teeth to stop my grin. And he waits.

And waits.

With a groan and a poke to his rib cage, I turn to face him and tuck my leg under me. My other hand is in my lap, clenched into a fist, because if it isn't, I don't know what I'll do. Touch him, probably, just as affectionately as he's touching me. "Everyone knows that," I say. "Get deeper. Get real with me, Adam." It's a challenge to see how much he's been paying attention.

He's quiet for a long time, focused on how his hand wraps around my wrist. I am focused on the glide of his skin on mine, the electric pulses that radiate out. He relaxes his shoulder to the back of the couch and draws his knee up too, brushing mine, plus my thigh—he's never expressed disgust with them the way Lovie has.

He'll come up blank. I keep the real stuff deep down, locked away. It's a challenge for people to get close because I create hoops for them to jump through.

And I set those hoops on fire.

I am fire, and anyone worthy of me should risk burning up to get closer.

"When you're anxious," he says, interrupting my thoughts, "especially about a new episode of either *Elle on the L* or *Forget Me Not*—especially *Forget Me Not*—you do laundry. That, along with tonight's events, leads me to believe you're a stress cleaner. But you also have respect for others' belongings, so you only ever clean the communal spaces. Kitchen, bathroom, living room."

My heart careens into my throat.

"The scar on your left knee is from when you were little, three or four." He taps it through the fabric of my sweatpants. His hand stays there, curls around the bend of my leg, and my blood thickens to molasses, slow and thick. My pulse is sluggish. "I don't know how you got it yet, but you picked and pulled at the stitches. That's why it's such an irregular shape. You were too young to know better.

"And I know you thought Lovie remembered you the last time we went to the grocery store, the day of the snow scare. You're *hoping* she remembers." He scrubs his jaw and licks his lips as he chooses his next words. Whatever he's about to say must taste bitter. "You're counting on it, I think. But this isn't some *50 First Dates* situation, Elle. Her remembering will only make *you* feel better, and only for a little while."

Hot, indignant tears swell in my eyes, and my jaw loosens. "Fuck you."

Adam does something completely unexpected. He smiles. *Smiles*, and my stomach does a free fall into a feeling I'm not ready to name.

"And," he continues, "I know something happened with your parents that you don't like to talk about. I know someone hurt you, and now you'd rather not bother with feelings in the first place. That when someone gets too close without your permission, you push them away, shut it down. You like to be in control. And I make you feel completely out of it."

A single tear betrays me and slips down my cheek. "I don't like it."

He brushes the wetness away, the same way he traced the sleep lines on my face this morning. "I know that too."

Even through the sting in my nose, the cloudiness of my eyes, I see how soft his face is. Now, and whenever he looks at me. He knows exactly where I've drawn boundaries, which ones are safe to cross and which aren't worth the effort.

It's all too much.

I bolt to my feet. I just remembered the open carton of milk expires tomorrow, and Lovie hates to waste money more than she hates my legs. I'll just go drink a glass or four.

I try to ignore the part of my brain that tells me Adam is following, but it doesn't listen. I know he's right behind me, the way he always is. Close enough to reach over my shoulder and open the cupboard for me.

I grab a glass and spin the long way around to the fridge so I don't rub against him. *You are not a cat in heat, Elle.*

I pull out the milk. "You can leave now."

"I'm waiting for you to realize you don't want me to."

The carton falls from my grasp, splashing bright-white milk across our socks and the vinyl.

No.

No, no, no.

Messes make everything worse.

I'm a mess. I'm *the* mess.

Whipping the dishrag off the stove, I drop to my knees, attempting to sop up the liquid still gushing from the milk carton. It was fuller than I remember. Emotion clutches the base of my throat. I don't want to break down right now, surrounded by a mess of my own making.

But the milk keeps spilling, slipping, gushing from the carton.

"It was almost empty," I whisper. I don't trust myself to speak louder.

Adam clears his throat and crouches beside me. His knees go straight into the spill. "I finished that carton yesterday. This was the new one."

I just wasted a brand-new carton of milk, and now I'm crying over it. I can't even appreciate the cliché come to life.

This is what pushes me over the edge, hot tears spilling out onto my already flaming cheeks.

"It's just milk. I don't even know why I'm crying." I sob again, louder and harder, and it takes so much out of me I fall onto my butt, legs falling limply at my side. "It's just *milk*."

He pries the sopping rag from my clutches, throwing it aside. "It's not just milk, Elle."

And when he says it, I believe it.

This is more than wasting fresh dairy.

It's *everything*.

My frustration with Lovie, how I can't stand up for myself with her because it won't make any difference. *I* don't feel like I'm making a difference here. Seeing Liss and Dakota this morning made me realize how much of my regular life I'm missing out on, and not having an end date to this temporary situation makes it seem that much more permanent. Adam may do this for a living, but I don't.

Guilt, for agreeing to take on this project and growing to resent it. I loved my life in Chicago. Being within walking distance to coffee bars, having my wax girl squeeze me in five minutes before close. Having my best friends an L ride away instead of two hours and a hundred miles.

The wrongness of calling my grandmother a project in the first place. She isn't a project, but I've started seeing her that way. *Let's see if I can squeeze another episode out of this hurtful thing she said today. If I can't get her to remember me, at least I can get a few thousand downloads, right?*

With each thought, my tears flow heavier. They slide off my nose and chin and splash into the milk mess below me. I brace against the floor, nails biting into the linoleum until I'm sure I'll leave ten half-moons behind. My chest heaves, and I can't get enough oxygen. All the while, Adam is here. With me.

Adam, who looks like my grandfather, who has slipped past all my defenses. Who isn't running away.

"You're spiraling in there." Adam taps my temple, then swipes his thumb under my eye. "Think out loud for me."

"This is crazy. Everything is wrong. I'm not acting rationally. Definitely not"—I gasp for air, rest my cheek in his palm—"*thinking* rationally. I don't know what we are, but we look like my grandparents. I don't know what that means. And you said you know me, but . . . I don't know who I am if Lovie doesn't."

My voice breaks again, but Adam is still here. With me.

Even though I'm still sobbing, he arranges my limbs more comfortably, settles my butt in the cradle of his legs, and tucks my head under his chin. Rubs a path along my spine. It reaches in and realigns all my off-track pieces.

"I want to know these parts of you, Elle," he murmurs. "The messy ones and the crazy ones. I'm not asking for forever. I'm not even asking for next week. All I'm asking for is right now. But if that's too much, that's okay too. I only want whatever you're ready to give, even if it's nothing at all."

With one simple comment, he's taken a sledgehammer to my heart, already cracked and crumbling. In its place is something tender. More fragile. I don't know if it's a good thing, feeling this way, but I do.

"So, what? I just tell you exactly what I'm thinking?" I rub my nose on my shoulder and leave a glossy smear of snot behind. I am the epitome of attractive. "And you . . ."

"Tell you what I'm thinking about what you're thinking." He throws me a lazy wink as he rises to his feet, offering a hand.

I wobble up behind him. "You make it sound so simple." I move my foot, but it lands in some of the leftover milk and I slip.

Adam steadies me again.

All the time, he steadies me.

It's wonderfully terrifying to realize someone else can help hold you up. For the first time, I wonder if maybe it doesn't have to just be me.

"Come on." He nods his head toward the laundry closet. "Let's throw your socks in with my stuff."

CHAPTER THIRTY-ONE

"You know what's not simple?" I think out loud, as requested, as we step into the laundry room. My waterworks have slowed from a raging river to a gentle stream. "Doing laundry together. That's a serious commitment."

Adam chuckles. My pulse races at the sheer intimacy of this moment, the quiet, how his laugh bounces back at me from every corner of this closet. The only light filters in from the kitchen above the sink, and even that flickers. It gives the miniscule laundry room a dampened sense of warmth.

As do his hands on my hips, lifting me. By the time I gasp, I've already come to rest atop the dryer, my knees on either side of him. A fresh tear escapes from impact alone.

He closes the hallway door closest to Lovie's bedroom.

I've got a few inches on him now, and it feels indecent. So do his hands, which slide down the entirety of my legs, over the fabric of my sweatpants. It's like I'm not wearing anything at all. His index fingers hook into the heels of my socks and whip them off. Goose bumps appear on my arms. I'm cold and hot.

He opens the washer lid and my socks join whatever else is already inside, then he reaches for the hem of his scrub top. And lifts it.

"Oh my God," I whisper. The more skin he reveals, the wider my eyes get, the lower my mouth hangs.

He finishes peeling off the fabric and presents it to me. "Here."

I stare at him. "What am I supposed to do with that?" What am I supposed to do with anything, ever again, with him standing in front of me shirtless?

Adam's head tilts to the side, the jut of his chin more pronounced now that his face is off-center. It's like a rock formation, or a mountain range. *If you look out the window to your right, folks, you'll see Mount Nurse Adam.*

That even sounds dirty in my head.

"Dry your eyes. Blow your nose. Whatever. I'll throw it in after you're done."

My mind's still back on Mount Nurse Adam. It operates as two distinct parts of speech, which I appreciate. I could, technically, theoretically, mount Nurse Adam (verb and subject) *on* Mount Nurse Adam (proper noun).

Trust me, it's easier for me to focus on this than the issue at hand. Which is that he—nothing theoretical about it—gave me the shirt off his back so I could dry my tears.

I am unable to convert these thoughts into sounds that make sense, and Adam chuckles. He reaches up, thumb wrapped in the cotton sleeve, and wipes gently at my face. I wonder what he sees: the captain of the Hot Mess Express, or the strong persona I give off to the rest of the world, the Elle who likes troll comments and doesn't let anyone behind the curtain.

He brings the fabric to my nose. "Blow."

I'm back to Obscenity Overlook. The detour was nice while it lasted.

As instructed, I blow my nose on his scrub top, and he manages to hold in his laughter even though I sound like an elephant.

"Good?"

I nod. "You have a tattoo," I note. My eyes are drawn to the patch of dark ink among the weeds of his chest hair. He's toned but not flashy, cut but not chiseled. Call me Goldilocks. He is *just right*.

"Do you have any?" Adam drops his shirt into the washer and hooks his fingers in the waistband of his matching bottoms.

I shake my head. "Always wanted one, though. Just can't decide what."

Then he just—shoves his pants down. Is he *stripping* for me? This isn't the first time a guy's tried to cheer me up by getting naked, but it's the first time it's going to work. My eyes aren't wet anymore, but other parts of me are picking up the slack. He does a great job of pretending like I'm not ogling him as his pants descend his thighs, revealing more dark hair and navy boxer briefs.

A tsk pulls my focus upward. He's smirking at me. "Take a guy to dinner first."

"Sure thing." I nod fervently. "Do you like McDonald's? There's one five minutes away."

After the pants join the top—because "It's annoying if the set gets separated in the wash"—he adds detergent, and I'm riveted like I've never seen anyone do laundry before. He closes the lid softly, cognizant of our proximity to Lovie, and I enjoy the silence for a change.

"So." He leans an elbow next to my thigh on the machine, which brings him even farther into my vicinity. "How are you feeling? Freaked out yet?" His thumb touches the side of my leg, and if it was an accident, he owns it well.

"Slightly, maybe." I chew my lip. "How did you know I like to stress clean?"

Adam runs his palm down to my calf and up again. "The days the episodes go live, the house smells like lavender and lemons. Fresh towels in the bathroom. You don't respond to comments until later that night, after the floors are swept and the toilet is scrubbed. But Lovie's things, *my* things, are exactly where we left them." He grins, leaning closer conspiratorially. "Plus you mentioned it on an old Instagram post."

I let out a husky laugh and lean into him, his hand, which is now back on my knee, tracing that scar through my pants. "Are you admitting to stalking me on social media?"

His nose bumps my cheek. "What if I was? What would you say?"

I can smell him more now than when his shirt was under my nose. "Keep your friends close and your enemies closer?"

He surprises me when he picks up my hand and rests it atop his tattoo. It tickles my palm. His heart races fast and wild beneath me. "I don't feel this way about my enemies, Elle."

"What way?" My eyes flutter.

A soft groan floats from his lips, and he shakes his head in disbelief. "Like I'll go crazy if I'm not near them. If I don't kiss them, touch them."

"Kiss me," I say. "Touch me."

Instead of kissing my mouth, his lips land on the hinge of my jaw with a sharp inhale, where just a few days ago a red handprint lingered. It's the lightest pressure, a butterfly's kiss. Those butterflies migrate to my chest, my gut, as I run my thumb across the raised patch of ink on his chest.

His mouth takes a leisurely exploration of me. The curve of my neck, the space behind my ear, the point of my chin and the hollow of my throat. His teeth scrape and his tongue drags. His hands do the same to my knees, my thighs, my waist. I thought substantial friction was required to start a fire, but it turns out light touches do the same.

"Adam." The noise that escapes with his name doesn't sound like it comes from me. It's heavier, begging and wanton. I don't know how I managed to squeeze so much emotion into so few syllables.

His lips come over mine like a crash of waves on rock—you can prepare all you want, but the impact will still be hard and fast. His hands cup my face, wrap around the back of my head to give him a better angle for plundering. And plunder he does. His tongue meets mine in persistent, steady strokes that leave me content to die from lack of oxygen. Breathing's not necessary.

I pull him between my legs, his arm winding around my back to scoot me to the edge of the dryer. Even when I'm where he wants me, it's not close enough. I gasp when his hand closes in a fist around my mess of unbrushed hair.

My hips move of their own accord, seeking relief for the pressure his mouth has brought on so suddenly. I'm *desperate* for him, for more. For everything.

"Adam," I rasp again, into his mouth. I cant my hips into the growing hardness.

He separates with a groan, resting his forehead on mine. "Can I make you come?"

I manage to wrangle my squeal of excitement into a dry half laugh. "I sure hope so."

He captures my mouth in another passionate kiss; it lasts nowhere near long enough before he backs off with one last tug of my bottom lip with his teeth. It pops away. "That won't be a problem. I know I *can*. And I *will*, right now, if that's what you want."

The current list of things I want more than Adam is very short. I don't even know if world peace is on there, which makes me a horrible human and feminist and about a dozen other things.

I know I just got done crying over spilled milk. I know some people might not want to be touched right now, especially not by a person who saw them at their most vulnerable. That's where I'm different. Adam saw me that way and reacted exactly how I'd want someone to. He listened to what I had to say, didn't make me feel silly or tell me to stop crying. He saw me instead of my open wounds.

I nod. "I want."

His face stretches in a grin, and my pants get ripped down my legs. My underwear is next, and it doesn't need to be well lit in this closet for me to see the way Adam's eyes brighten at the sight of me. It's been over six weeks since my last wax, and for all my discomfort, Adam doesn't seem to mind one bit.

"Elle," he chokes, lowering to his knees in front of the dryer. "Thank you."

"For wh—"

The rest of my words are lost to my pleasure.

He moves surely, confident enough in his movements that I don't doubt what he said. He can and will get this done. As his mouth works, his hands caress me. He has a way of making each touch and stroke and taste deliberate. When he strokes my thigh, it's an intentional thing. *I see this piece of you*, he says. *I see this and I want this.*

My head falls back and bangs on the overhead cabinet, but I'm too far surrendered to care. The only pain I feel is pleasured zings from Adam, the fine line between too much and not enough as he teases and coaxes me.

He brings my leg around his shoulder, and my heel digs into his back. My butt's hanging off the edge. One jerk too far and I'll fall on top of him. How's that for mounting Nurse Adam?

The washer cycle starts abruptly, and my hips breach the lip of the dryer. He catches me, his grip focused on the place where my thighs meet my butt. He makes the save smooth, natural. Like all he wanted was to hold my ass in the first place. Purposeful. Direct.

Adam.

The flicks of his tongue pick up speed, severity. "Yes," I breathe, clutching his hair with one hand and the dryer's edge with the other.

He's not in a hurry to set me down, even though he's got most of my weight. That thought alone, what we must look like in aerial view, has my legs quivering.

"Come here," he gruffs. "I've got you."

As promised, he has me. He holds me better now, has access to more of me. He abuses the privilege in the best way. Every inch of me is sparking and electric, to the point I'm half convinced the dryer has short-circuited at my back. A loud moan escapes my lips, and my eyes fly to the hallway door, where Lovie sleeps between thin layers of drywall.

Adam's laugh hums against me, adding to my pleasure tenfold. "Shh," he murmurs, takes a light nip at my thighs, then starts again. Doubles down. He groans.

I bite down on my bottom lip hard to try and calm my noises, the racing of my heart, but it's no use. I'm a goner. It's hard to say who or what makes the noises in this closet, whether the vibration is from the washer or my throat or Adam's. It's definitely me who murmurs *yes* and *more* and *harder*. And it's Adam who contributes *that's right* and *come for me*. Maybe it's the stern tone he uses that makes me so apt to comply. Not that it matters.

"Good girl," he says, using his entire mouth to enunciate so he doesn't have to pull away when I'm already starting to tumble.

And tumble I do. The fall is long but weightless. Adam holds me the whole way down, guides me through the descent by lightening his pressure, slowing his pace.

He pulls away with parting kisses to my center, the insides of my thighs, and I didn't know it was possible to sigh so heavily. He places my feet on the floor but doesn't let go until I have my knees under me. Which, admittedly, takes a minute.

Speaking of long and heavy . . .

"Do you want me to return the favor now or later?"

Adam grabs my pants, holding them out for me like he did earlier today. Was it really only this morning when Dakota and Liss were here? "Orgasms aren't favors. They're gifts."

I stare at him, each of us holding a leg of my pants. "What planet are you from?"

He arches a brow, a challenge. "What men have you been with?"

"None, apparently."

There's no hiding his smile now, even in the dim light. "Will you tell me about them?"

He can't be serious. I busy myself with righting my underwear and stepping into them. "You want me to tell you about my exes?"

"I told you." He shrugs. "I want your messy parts too."

My brain is too sated to fully comprehend this conversation. It could use a spin in the dryer with a few ice cubes. I must've glitched the matrix somewhere. Maybe I'll wake up tomorrow and be in some weird *Groundhog Day* time loop. Adam will be shaking me awake and telling me Liss and Dakota are here, seeing me pantsless again. I'll have to remember to hide my vibrator when I leave the bathroom after dinner.

Or maybe not.

"Well then, Nurse Adam, would you like to have a sleepover?"

CHAPTER THIRTY-TWO

Things that take place during a double-bed sleepover with Adam Wheeler:
Discussions of my ex-boyfriends. Laughter. Secret-sharing.
Things that don't take place during a sleepover with Adam Wheeler:
Sex.
Our backs against the headboard and his arms around me, we talk about The Rockstar (real name Ryan), how he used his music connections to sneak us backstage at House of Blues and scored Liss and I free passes to Lollapalooza. How she took too much of an edible and slept through the only band she was interested in seeing. How I found The Rockstar in bed with his manager, the woman he swore six ways from Sunday was "strictly business." How, on the way out, I dumped my coffee into the body of his favorite guitar.
Adam has to wipe tears of laughter from his eyes as I tell him about my college flings. I call them the J Boys: Josh, Jeff, Jackson, and Jermaine. They were frat brothers who had a penchant for drinking Natty Ice out of a beer funnel and were late

more often than me. If I'd gotten a hundred bucks for every time I heard "It's not working out, but I think you'd hit it off with my friend," I might not have had to charge the infamous Aruba trip to Lovie's credit card. I tell Adam about that too.

I rest my chin on his chest, right over his tattoo. "In the spirit of honesty," I say on a sigh, "I should probably also tell you about Grady."

Adam's hand pauses on my back. "I already hate him."

"You don't even *know* him."

He studies my face. "I know how I'm supposed to feel about someone based on the way you say their name."

And then I tell Adam things I've never told anyone, not even Liss or Dakota. How when I was with Grady, I only felt like myself when I was physically *with* him. I'd check my phone four times in one minute waiting to see if he'd texted me. If he called and I missed it, he wasn't happy. How sometimes I'd go through his phone, like I knew he went through mine.

My voice grows scratchy in my throat, and I swallow a few times before I continue. Adam maneuvers me so my back is to his chest, as if sensing I need physical support in addition to emotional. I never did put my pants back on, but he doesn't seem to care. He just holds me, his legs bracketing mine, as his fingertips draw shapes and letters on the skin of my upper thigh.

The safety of his embrace unlocks deeper memories, and before I question it, I tell him those too. "One day," I whisper to him in the dim lamplight, "I needed to call Lovie for something, and I had to scroll for months just to find her in my recent calls.

"I sat on the floor, right there in our kitchen, and counted. In one day, Grady and I had called each other thirty-five times. We *lived* together. I saw him that morning," I say, and Adam kisses my hair once, twice, again, leaves his lips there.

"That was the morning Lovie fell. Cracked her head. While I was busy worrying about whether or not my partner was the one, my grandmother was getting stitches, CT scans, a life-changing diagnosis. I should have been there."

Adam's pulse is a metronome on my cheek, keeping steady time. "You being here physically wouldn't have stopped Lovie from getting Alzheimer's." He pulls back, eyes searching mine. "Tell me you know that."

I shrug, chewing my lip. "I know that on an intellectual level. But . . . my brain conflated the two. Lovie's diagnosis, the fallout with Grady. It was the one time in my life I didn't run when I should have, and look what happened." I lift my shoulder again. "I had one person and lost the other."

"Lovie didn't leave you, Elle."

I blink back tears, not trusting myself to speak.

He fills in the gaps, the corner of his mouth dipping into a frown. "So you left Grady before he could do the same," he realizes.

"We were on the way out anyway." We worked out the logistics. He got to keep our apartment since it was close to his office, and I packed a bag and took the L across town to Liss's place at four in the morning. I was the girl in my every episode, duffel bags on the sticky subway floor and tear tracks on my cheeks.

In the weeks that followed, I threw myself into helping Lovie prepare for the next phase of her life. Only to find out she'd done the heavy lifting, with picking Angie and AngelCare. With paperwork. There was nothing left for me to do besides feel, besides *hurt*.

"I think that's the time I started throwing more effort into *Elle on the L*. Coming home less." Shame burns bright flags onto my cheeks. "Meanwhile, Lovie was slipping away more and more. And Grady cared fuck all about fixing anything."

I yawn, and Adam takes a moment to shift us down the mattress, my head on the pillow. When's the last time I stayed up this late with a man, just talking?

"I don't know Grady," Adam says, his lips against my hair. "But I know you, and I'm being completely honest when I say it's not you, it's him. He should have fought for you. Fought *with* you, at your side."

I chuckle, fatigue making it sound like I slid my laugh across sandpaper. "You're just sucking up so I'll suck you off."

One eyebrow rises slowly. "Go to sleep, Elle."

"No." I yawn again, despite curling further into the mattress and Adam's side. "Now it's your turn. You tell me all about your toxic exes and embarrassing high school stories."

"I don't have any."

"Be serious."

"I *am* serious. I didn't lose my virginity until I was nineteen or twenty."

Jealousy loosens a playful growl in my throat. It's garbled from leftover emotion. "Hey. We talked about that."

He chuckles. "Sorry, sorry. I didn't lose the social construct of my virginity until I was nineteen or twenty."

"What was her name?"

"Jenny," he says after a second. I search in his tone, his expression, for how she makes him feel, so far removed. "We met in nursing school. Studied together. That sort of thing."

"Did you love her?"

I hold my breath. All the while, his hands are on my body. I refuse to consider that as its own answer.

"As a person, sure. She was kind and funny. As a partner, we wouldn't have worked. I was always focused on school, then supporting Ruth. She wanted more than I was capable of giving at the time."

"That sounds so . . . mature." I crinkle my nose.

He smiles, an eyebrow tipping up. "You make that sound like a bad thing."

"Was she your 'one'?" I'm toeing a dangerous line here. I can't stop.

Adam shrugs. "She was my 'once in a while.' As in, once in a while, two people are right for each other at the right time.

It doesn't make what we shared any less real just because it ended." His eyes search my face. "It also doesn't mean that *this* . . . just because something *doesn't* have a name—*fuck*, what am I saying?"

I bite the inside of my cheek, my stomach upside down in suspense, waiting, *waiting*.

"This isn't . . ."

I let him sit in silence, find his own words. He's so good at that with me; maybe it's time I learned to do that with other people.

His thumb strokes my hip, the crease of my leg. "This sort of thing . . . it's not something I normally do."

I want to ask what *this sort of thing* is to him, but then I'd have to think about what it is to me. "How'd you get into nursing?" I ask instead, even though my heart is so loud in my ears I'm scared I won't hear his answer.

"It's sort of boring."

"Helping people isn't boring," I argue. A small kiss, right to the words on his heart.

He adjusts us, pulling more of me on top of him. Arms around my waist. One of his palms stretches over my ass. It's my new favorite way for him to touch me.

"It was an eighth-grade job fair. They had all the different career professionals come in, give a lecture about what it was like to work in that field." There's color high on his cheeks.

I poke it. "You're blushing. Is it really embarrassing?"

"It's—" He swallows. "I just really liked the idea of wearing glorified pajamas every day."

I burst out laughing. Beneath me, Adam chuckles too, and we devolve into gasping, rocks and squeaks of the bed frame filling the silence as we try to rein it in and keep quiet. I can't breathe. His joy slips down his cheeks, the tendons in his neck straining. The smile stretching his face is miles wide.

It fizzles out, our eyes locked as the moment shifts like quicksand, flippant one second and crucial the next. "If that's what I have to tell you for you to laugh like that..." His throat bobs, eyes leaning black. "I'll tell you anything you want to know."

"Tell me a secret," I whisper.

He's faster than I think he's going to be, for someone who has such a "boring" life.

"Do you remember that day I came home early from work and all the smoke detectors were going off?"

I nod into his chest, stifling a yawn. I don't want today to be over. I want to record it, replay it like I do my most favorite episodes of *Elle on the L*.

"I paid a guy a hundred bucks to cover the last two hours of my shift after I tried to put in an IV and missed three times. All I could think about was kissing you."

His words unlock a new chamber of my heart, and all the extra blood rushes to my face. *"Adam."*

I think he's going to flip me, kiss his way down my body. Undo me again, give me a run at undoing him. It's the next logical step. His eyes search my face, though I don't know what else could be hidden.

Instead, he leans over, flicks off the lamp, and plugs in his phone. I haven't checked mine in hours. I don't even know where it is. "That's enough for one night. We have a busy day tomorrow."

"No," I protest again, feebler than before. My eyes won't open. "Wanna talk. Tell me all the ways you watch me when I'm not looking."

"If you already know," he says, "why do I need to tell you?"

It's my turn now to say something cheeky, continue our flirting until he has no choice but to screw me senseless.

But as he pulls up the covers, I lose the fight fast. I tuck into his side because the size of the bed necessitates it.

I'm already dreaming when Adam says good-night. Except when he says it, it sounds like, "Go to sleep, love."

Megan Murphy

* * *

Forget Me Not

Transcript, Episode 04

Hello, everyone. This is Elle from Elle on the L—*say that five times fast—with another episode of* Forget Me Not*. This podcast is an inside look at life with Alzheimer's, from a caregiver's perspective.*

Before we dive into today's episode, I'm so excited to announce the listeners have chosen two charities for donations. Because I believe in transparency, financial statements and documentation will be up on my website, and you can always leave questions on my social media or whichever platform you listen on.

The Alzheimer's Association, based in Chicago, is the country's leading organization for research, early detection, and support networks. They have a fantastic 24/7 hotline, financial and legal planning for caregivers, and even special resources dedicated to those in the LGBTQIA+ community. I've personally used their website dozens of times to help point me in the right direction.

We'll also be supporting AngelCare, the caregiving organization that aids our very own Lovie. If the Alzheimer's Association is the support network, AngelCare is the boots on the ground. Every person I've met has so much compassion and respect, both for the patients and for their loved ones. They see the person, not the disease. Which, coming from someone in the throes of the disease daily, is maybe the most important part.

Okay. Now on to the episode. I've got a comprehensive list of those financial and logistical steps to take at the beginning of a diagnosis. What I did wrong. What I did right. How [EXPLICIT] long it takes for health insurance changes to go through. You know. The usual. [Laughs]

CHAPTER THIRTY-THREE

I'm in the middle of the same strange, flash-frozen world as last night. Everything dipped in ice. Lovie in the garden. Someone calling my name.

"Elle, love, please wake up."

Oh no. It *was* all a dream. Liss and Dakota. The hallway kiss—and then some. Doppelgängers. Laundry rooms. Shedding emotional baggage until I was light enough to slip into the best sleep I've had in years.

I shove my head under the pillow. "No."

"We're going on a field trip today." Something warm grazes my lower back, and I'd arch into it if I thought I could feasibly move.

Then his words register.

I peek my head out from under the pillow. "Really?"

Adam's sleepy gaze meets mine. He's on his side, propped on an elbow as he studies me. It has to be before dawn based on the light outside. "Really." He brushes a strand of hair back from my face. "Does it take you a long time to brush this?"

His voice is still raspy with sleep, like it takes a little longer to wake up than the rest of him.

I rest my cheek on the pillow, collecting this piece of him like I have all the others. Tuck it away for safekeeping. "Not usually. The dye does make it a little harder to work with, but I just deep-conditioned last night."

He plays with some of the ends, runs them along my neck, almost tickling. "What's your natural hair color?"

"Brown." A few shades lighter than his.

He hums. "Like your eyes. So warm."

Funny. I think the same thing about him.

Those very eyes flutter as his hand travels the length of my spine. It makes me shiver.

"Are you cold?" Adam says, and I'm enjoying this lazy morning so much, I don't bother answering. His hand finds my hip anyway, and he pulls me to him. The blanket is tugged up next. Our legs tangle, then our feet. My head comes to rest on his chest. "You wouldn't be so cold if you wore socks to sleep."

"I'm not a psychopath," I say. I burrow into him, and the arms around me tighten automatically, making up for the distance. "You are, like, so comfy." His soft chuckle rumbles beneath my cheek. "Can we just lay here for a while?"

"Of course." Adam's hand slips underneath my shirt, spreading his palm across my back. "But you can't fall asleep again. I don't think I'll be able to wake you up, and we really do have plans today."

"Keep talking, then." I might fall asleep anyway, but what he doesn't know won't hurt him.

He's quiet for a long beat, and the tugs of drowsiness start to pull me under before he speaks again.

"A pizza pencil," he says, "is something you buy at the elementary school book fair, or maybe at the public library."

I'm still so drowsy it takes me a minute to remember what he's talking about. Halloween. The only time he's ever broken up with a girl.

"In one of those gumball-for-a-quarter type machines. Fake jewelry, temporary tattoos. Our library had one for food-themed pencils. They came with giant, food-shaped erasers." Adam lets out a soft laugh. "So, naturally, I wanted the pizza one."

"Naturally," I allow.

"It took me almost two months to get it, just finding quarters on the street or in the sofa. So imagine my surprise when, after it went missing, my kindergarten girlfriend showed up to alphabet practice with that very pencil the next day."

I harrumph, although more mirth is shining through than I'd like. "No wonder you broke up with her. I would have broken her *face*."

"She would have been terrified of you."

"Most people are." I consider something. "Did the pizza have a smiley face on it?"

"Absolutely." He kisses my forehead, then shakes his head on an exhale. "Cutest shit I've ever seen."

* * *

The next time I wake, Adam *is* shaking me forcibly. He's already dressed, surprisingly not in scrubs. I'm a little disappointed. They were supposed to be burgundy today. Instead he's wearing jeans, for what I think is the first time since we met, and a well-worn long-sleeved tee. I admire his denim-clad butt. God bless America, and also Levi's jeans.

"Where are we going?" I ask through a yawn. It's light outside now. "You said we were going on a field trip?"

Adam nods, runs a hand over my disheveled hair. "Wherever you want. We have the whole day free."

That sounds amazing. No plans. No obligations. No Lovie.

My heart plummets through my butt. "Oh God, what about Lovie? Is she awake? Has she taken her meds yet?" I move past Adam toward the hallway, ready to rip open the door and find my way to her. "Does she need help with her—"

"She's fine," Adam says, catching me by the wrist before I grab the handle. "Angie is here."

"That's—*Angie*?" My tired eyes grow to saucers. "Why?" I gasp, dropping my voice. "Do you think she knows?"

Adam's half grin is fully sexy. "Knows we slept together? Probably not."

I slap my hand over his mouth. "First," I hiss, "we did not sleep together. You wouldn't allow it." I make a show of rolling my eyes. He kisses my palm. "Second, don't underestimate her. She's very perceptive."

He peels my hand away, entwines our fingers.

"I think," he says slowly, "the longer we stay in here whispering to each other, the more likely she is to *perceive* something incorrectly."

That gets me moving. Adam slips out to give me privacy, but it's unnecessary. I'm frozen, staring inside the depths of my overstuffed dresser. I have no idea what to wear. Jeans, probably, right? Adam's in jeans. But it's also November. I'll need to think strategically, no matter how risqué I want to be.

Fifteen minutes later, after I've decided on a loose-fitting band tee and dark skinny jeans—I missed a leg hole, fell over, it was a whole thing—I move to the bathroom. I clip back my hair, slap on some mascara, and thoroughly brush my teeth (and sink-shave my legs).

I can only hope Adam is as good as picking up on my brain waves as Liss. *Don't touch me*, I beg him in my brain. *Don't smile at me in that way you do, and don't you* dare *look at the laundry room.*

Angie Brockman is at the kitchen counter, watching the coffee drip slowly into the pot. Amid the dull browns of the appliances, her golden-brown skin glows in this room.

"Elle!" she says brightly, rounding the island and pulling me into a tight hug. Her body is soft in all the right spots and makes this embrace *so* comfortable. She hugs like a *mom*. It's been a while since I've had a mom hug. She holds me closer, like she knows I need this right now.

"It's been so long." She pulls back and rests her hands on my shoulders. "How are you? You look good."

"It's been . . . we're adjusting," I say. "You know how it is."

She raises a dark eyebrow, threaded to perfection. "How *she* is, you mean."

"That too." I grin. I can tell why Lovie picked her. Angie listens to my concerns completely and uninterrupted. She hears me when I say something isn't working with medication or treatment. And she's always been honest with me, about what to expect timeline wise. How much time I have left. This whole mess with insurance.

I break eye contact when I remember I'm actively keeping something from her now. Someone.

That someone leans against the archway. I don't let myself look at him, even though it's all I want.

"What are you doing here?" I slide into my seat at the table. Lying goes straight to my knees.

Angie's gaze flickers. "Adam requested someone to cover his shift today. He politely reminded me that neither of you have had a full day off in nearly two months."

That's not true in the slightest. Adam gives me more days off than I deserve, and he goes to visit his sister and the kids when he can swing it, usually after his Sunday shifts or if Lovie stays in bed. I'm opening my mouth to refute her when she continues.

"And besides, it will be good for me to see how Lovie is progressing with my own eyes. Adam, your reports are impeccable, of course, but it's still nice to see firsthand. I want to do everything we can to make this a smooth transition." She pours coffee into a mug and dips her chin. It's her business face. "I hate to say this—"

"No you don't," I interrupt.

She smiles. "—but I have to. You don't have to go home, but you can't stay here. Just get out of the house for a few hours, half the day. I'd love to say I don't want to see you until dinnertime, but I know you both better than that."

She grabs the milk from the fridge, frowning as she jiggles the near-empty carton. I force my face not to flush. "I bet Elle has some great breakfast recommendations, Adam. She grew up in this town, you know. This very house."

"Is that right?" Adam says. I don't have to look at him to know how smug he is—his voice is doing that all on its own.

She nods out the window. "Her prom date picked her up on that front porch."

I regret ever telling her that.

Adam isn't even trying to hide his smirk anymore. "Did he now." The end of his sentence falls flat.

She nods. "Where'd you all go out to eat, Elle? Maybe you can take Adam there, show him around a bit."

"Angie." I close my eyes. "Under no circumstances am I taking Adam to *Hot Dog Eddy's*."

Needless to say, that date scored *no* bases. He struck out rather quickly.

"That actually sounds pretty good," Adam offers, sharing a complicit smile with Angie.

I want to slam my head on the table until I concuss myself. Start this time loop over again. I just won't get out of bed in the first place. Take that, universe.

Fake It Like You Mean It

She won't give up, though, and even if I have to take Adam to Hot Dog Eddy's after all, she is going to kick us out of this house.

When I have nowhere else to go, where do I want to be? More important, what places in my life do I want Adam to know too? I showed him so many parts of myself last night, and I'm still raw from the overexposure. So where do I feel safest?

"I know a place."

CHAPTER THIRTY-FOUR

"Where to?" Adam asks. We're both eager, so after the windshield is defrosted to a manageable level, he reverses onto the street. He's wearing a thick winter coat with the collar popped against the cold. All the air vents are pointed in my direction.

"May I direct you to the interstate, Nurse Adam? You said we were field tripping, after all."

He grins, the morning light reflecting off his teeth. "Want to listen to music?"

When I nod, Adam turns on the radio and connects his phone via an aux cord. "Sparks" by Coldplay starts filtering through the speakers.

"This song is depressing," I grumble, skipping to the next.

Which turns out to be "Wisconsin" by Bon Iver.

It's such a rare song, so unexpected from him, yet somehow not at all, that a laugh flies from my lips before I can choke it down.

His brow furrows as he fumbles for the knob.

"No, don't." I reach for his hand. "I love this song." My fingers twine with his.

The moment, like so many others between us, stretches taut. He's warm, despite the frigid cold outside and in the rest of the cab. I stare at him in profile, trying to collect as many details as I can, making note of the ones I can't. What he was like when he was younger; whether he has any scars of his own, like the one I have on my knee.

His tongue darts out to lick his bottom lip as he glances at me. When he looks at the road again, he has to jerk the wheel in correction.

He doesn't release me, though. Just rests our joined hands on my leg. "I like the heavy stuff."

"I can tell," I say as Justin Vernon's haunting voice fills the car. "How'd you get this song digitally? You can't stream it."

Adam is sheepish, a blush creeping up his jaw. "I ripped it. It's their best song. It deserves to be heard, often and by anyone with ears. My tattoo is one of these lyrics."

I fall in love with him a little bit then. Just a stumble, like when you're almost asleep and suddenly feel like you missed a stair. Enough to jolt your heart but not enough to make you question everything. No lasting damage.

"What's it say?"

"This." He nods his head toward the dash, and quiet descends as we listen to the music. He sings softly along with the line, off-key and scratchy. Adam has a Bon Iver tattoo about love over his heart and mine hurts just thinking about it.

Something is stealing my breath. The cold, probably. "That's beautiful. What does it mean to you?"

As we come to a stop sign, he studies our hands. I didn't have time to search for gloves, so my fingers are cold and raw. He moves deliberately, tucking them against my palm and wrapping them with his own.

"That for as messy as love can make life, love in itself is enough. All kinds of love—friendly, familial, romantic. Love can leave a lot of wounds, but it can also heal them." He stares over the center console at me. My lips. "If we let it."

I miss another step on the staircase. "Do you let it?"

As we resume our drive through the slow, quiet streets of my hometown, his thumb traces the crease of my wrist, my red knuckles. "I'd like to let it more often. I think you, more than most people, know what it means to get wrapped up in obligation to others and forget about the obligations we have to ourselves."

He's talking about Lovie. All the details I revealed to him last night. The growing resentment I have for a situation I can't change but desperately want out of.

But he said *we*.

"Who are you obligated to?" I ask softly. The music has faded to background noise. I focus instead on Adam's breathing, his fingers creating friction with mine as he warms me in the frigid November air. The road rumbles beneath us, and I hate it, but I get lighter the closer we come to the highway.

"Sometimes . . . sometimes I wish my sister was more self-sufficient." He scoffs, rolling his reddening eyes. "God, I feel guilty for even saying that. I *love* my sister."

"Of course you do, Adam, but love and obligation aren't mutually exclusive. You can feel both together, at any time. I love Lovie, but I still want to throttle her six days a week."

Adam chuckles absently, flexing the hand on the wheel. My face flushes when I remember how that hand dipped between my legs outside the bathroom. Gripped my thighs while his mouth explored my most intimate place. "I guess sometimes I fear that Ruth is growing dependent on my help," he says. "That if I continue to offer it, she'll continue to take it, and she won't ever see a need to do anything different."

"Do *you* want things to be different?"

His smile is almost sad. "I don't think it's sustainable in the long term—I'll put it that way."

"And in the short term?" I ask. "Maybe you could take steps to draw healthier boundaries, one thing at a time."

"It's just—" Adam's chest collapses with a deep sigh. "I could do that, I guess. I don't know what about the situation bothers me."

I switch hands, holding his with my right and resting my left against the back of his neck. "Can I give you my opinion even though you didn't ask for it?"

He throws me a wink. Nestles into my hand. "I was waiting for that."

I consider everything he's told me, and some things he hasn't. "I think you're an introvert, and you spend so much time being *on* that you never get to turn *off*. All of your free time is spent working—which, gross, by the way—or taking care of your family. What do you have for you? Adam time."

He looks over. "I've got things just for me."

I use the hand on his neck to turn his head back toward the road. "Good. So protect the time for them. You could tell Ruth your work hours, for starters. Maybe make a shared calendar so she doesn't have to keep asking if you're free? And block out days when you're burnt out."

"That seems . . ." He shifts in the driver's seat. "Sensible."

I beam. "I am the queen of sensibility. And she could add the girls' events to it too. That way you know in advance what days will be taken up by them. I know things pop up, that Claire gets sick often, but you'll just have to set the expectation that you might not always make it. I think talking to her would be a great place to start."

The corners of his face sharpen, still somewhat hazy beneath his morning stubble. I imagine if he'd had that last night, I'd be more raw this morning. "Have *you* talked to Lovie about how you feel?" He's redirecting, but I'll allow it.

"That's different," I say. "There's no point."

"Angie, then. I'm sure she'd find a different solution if you wanted one. A temporary care facility until something permanent opens up. One of the LTAC hospitals might have an opening. I could ask around."

My chest cracks open and honesty spills out. "I don't know what I want anymore." I throw my head back to the seat.

"I do." He tightens his grip. "Or do you doubt me again after I proved how perceptive *I* am last night?"

A warm flush creeps up my neck. Images flash behind my eyes: Adam's head between my thighs. His mouth on my skin, name on my lips, body in my sheets. If I let him, he'd be under my skin too.

In my heart.

I reach for his phone in the cupholder, coming back to reality. I need caffeine and bacon before I can make any big choices like that. This is a slight alteration of Lovie's Hard Love Rule Number Six, commonly referred to as HHALT: Never make any important life decisions when you're Hungry, Horny, Angry, Lonely, or Tired. I think she added the horny part. I asked once if horny and lonely were all that different. She said they were.

It's time to steer this ship back to calmer waters. "Can I play something I think you'd like?"

After he tells me his passcode, I navigate to Spotify. *Elle on the L* is in the queue. I find the song I'm searching for.

He listens to the piano notes for a few seconds, a little groove appearing between his eyebrows. "Who is this?"

"Taylor Swift and Bon Iver."

The groove turns to a chasm. "This . . . does not sound like Taylor Swift."

"That would be because your musical tastes are stuck in 2009." I make a sympathetic hum. "I bet you still think she's country, don't you?"

His brows gather. "She's not?"

I pat his thigh, just above his knee. "Oh, honey." I'm mostly teasing. I miss one more step on the staircase.

And when he grins, a few more.

After a drive-through breakfast without so much as a vegetable in sight (Adam said potatoes don't count normally, but especially not when fried with butter *and* lard), we continue toward the city, my excitement amping up with every mile.

I end up swapping out his music for mine and take him through the choices behind my Queens playlist. The two-hour drive may as well be twenty minutes, and I'm not even upset when we hit morning rush hour traffic, because it means our conversation will last longer. Our fingers tangle and untangle in a dozen different patterns; our thumbs battle lazy wars and our laughs are just for each other.

When we reach the city, I direct him toward Liss's shoebox-sized bakery.

"Do you come to Chicago often?" I ask as Adam parallel parks on the first try. My question sort of answers itself.

"Sometimes, for work. AngelCare is based out of a hospital here, so I come for that, if there's ever an issue with payroll, for performance reviews, things like that. The girls really love the pizza."

I smile. "Maybe we can take them some on the way back."

"I think we'll have to survive Liss first, won't we?"

"*You'll* have to survive her," I correct, unbuckling my seatbelt. "*I'll* be too busy eating chocolate cake to do anything else."

On the sidewalk, bitterly cold wind whips at our coats, bites our skin. I duck my chin as Adam absorbs Liss's shop, the dilapidated front sidewalk and dirty concrete siding. I call this color Corporate America Gray. Perfectly neutral and inoffensive, and yet, someone somewhere is *always* offended.

I point to the Sweetie's Cakes logo in the window. "I hung that."

"I'm impressed," Adam says, holding the door open for me. His knuckles are bright red. Maybe I'll get him gloves for Christmas. "Was that before or after you sanded the floors and installed the electrical?"

"After." Aromas of sugar, warm spice, and fresh whipped cream fill the humid air. "And you forgot rerouting the plumbing and leveling the foundation."

The door that leads to the kitchen bursts open, and Liss appears. Her hair is frizzed from the ovens, and there's a spot of flour on her cheekbone. "Oh my God, hi!" She practically vaults around the counter to hug me. Her smile is wide. Even wider when she notices Adam. "To what do I owe this pleasure?"

"We were in the area," Adam offers at the same time I say, "Angie kicked us out of our house."

Our house? Dreaming of Christmas gifts? The sugar's already going straight to my brain.

"Gave us the morning off," he amends to appease me. We're still holding hands.

Liss begins loading my favorite treat into a bakery box—two pieces of her should-be-world-famous chocolate cake. "How's Lovie?"

Ever the medical professional, Adam gives Liss updates on Lovie's care and treatment. I curse the American health care system for taking so long to approve dependents.

But my words stick in my throat, coated with guilt. Despite being called colorful names and hit with shoehorns and made inferior, I have enjoyed my time with my grandmother. Doing the podcast has allowed me to revisit old memories I otherwise would have forgotten, and I'm not sure who I should thank for that.

For some reason, part of me thinks it's Adam.

Speaking of, I hadn't realized until now I forgot to update Liss and Dakota on last night's base running.

Fake It Like You Mean It

I send her a telepathic message, but all she does in response is add a plastic container of fresh raspberry puree to the box. Not my intention, but I'll take it.

Liss wipes her hands on her apron, already dusted with a plethora of colors. "See anything you want, Adam?"

"The little red one." He pauses for a beat too long, and only when Liss's eyes grow wide and my cheeks flush does he point at the case. "Red velvet, right?"

As Liss reaches for the cupcake, her eyes dart to me, still wide. They say *Did something happen?*

I return a look that says *You have no idea.*

Pink splotches blossom on her face, and she clears her throat. "While you're here, Adam, can I get your help moving some flour? I don't know why I continue to order the fifty-pound bags when I can barely lift twenty."

"Of course. Just show me where you want it." As a parting gift, his hand brushes my lower back.

When Liss and Adam disappear into the kitchen, I sneak around the counter and grab another piece of cake for my box. I don't know what the secret ingredient is, but I'm pretty sure it's crack.

The doors swing open, and Liss starts talking immediately, mostly with her hands. "Did you have sex?" she whisper-hisses. "Did you *share the bed*? What's the score?"

Used to Liss's ramblings, I keep track easily. "No, third base. Yes, to snuggle and sleep. Nine—I subtracted a point because of the *no* for the first question."

"Details," she whispers, excitement making her eyes sparkle.

In as hushed a tone as I can manage, I tell her, "I may have sat on Adam's face in the laundry room last night."

The end of my sentence is drowned out by the kitchen doors swinging open, Adam emerging.

One thing to note about Liss: she has no poker face. None. We never had a chance to do any sort of debauchery in high school, because as soon as an adult with a semifunctioning brain saw her, they'd know she was lying through her teeth.

So when she pastes on a mechanic, saccharine smile, her eyes a touch too crazy, I think I'm had. Done for.

Adam only says, "You have a beautiful kitchen," which, to Liss, is equivalent to *here's one million dollars* or *you have a rare genetic condition where you have to eat cake to stay alive* or *I got you box seats for the Chicago Cubs.*

My best friend turns into a pile of mush. She braces against the counter, and her irises morph into hearts before my eyes. I'd be jealous if Adam's pinkie didn't brush mine in the same instance.

"What, um . . ." Liss blinks, dazed. I cough, and her eyes clear. "What else are you two doing today?"

"We're going to pick up some pizza for Adam's nieces. Otherwise, I'm not sure—"

"We're stopping by Elle's apartment," he interrupts in a tone gentle enough that I don't take offense. "She needs to grab some more clothes."

I stare at him. Did I tell him that? And if so, *when*? Sure, I've been doing more laundry than usual, but that's just because I packed for fall. Not for the house to feel like summer and outside to feel like a snowstorm could appear out of nowhere.

(And okay, *fine*, if I had known Nurse Adam was going to see—and subsequently take off—my undergarments, I would've packed nicer options than the Pick Five ones from Target.)

"That's fun," Liss says. A large boom sounds from the kitchen, where I can only imagine Dakota is up to his elbows in fondant filigree. She winces. "I should get back. It was good to see you both." She blows me a kiss and turns it into a wave for Adam. "Stay warm."

I may have left out the revelation of step-stumbling into love, but based on the way Liss beams at me as we turn to go, I'd imagine her eyes aren't the only ones that look like hearts.

CHAPTER THIRTY-FIVE

"So this is your place," Adam says three hours later.

We're chilled to the bone. After we left Liss's bakery, we made our way to the riverfront, window shopped along Michigan Avenue. Browsed booths at the Christmas Market tucked along the borders of Millennium Park. The same way he had on the drive into the city, he kept my fingers tucked inside his palm, always more concerned about my warmth than his own.

We talked about anything and everything—our favorite movies, concerts, other random thoughts that popped into our heads and demanded attention.

"I got mugged for the first time on this corner," I noted.

That stopped him short. "The *first* time?"

"Relax." I patted his chest. "I got an interview out of it, at least."

"You interviewed your mugger."

"Don't be silly. I interviewed the policeman who took my statement. Made him stand down in the station so it still counted."

We were at a crosswalk then, and he turned his entire body toward mine. "I'm both unsurprised and completely surprised by how your brain works."

"I take that as a compliment," I said, flashing back to that first morning. If I was infuriating then, I can't imagine what he thinks of me now.

He licked his reddened, wind-burnt lips. "Maybe I meant it as one."

The light changed, and we entered the street.

"What's next for you?" he said. "With your podcast. After *Forget Me Not* is over, I mean. Do you want to expand your network?"

"I think so. Chicago is amazing, but I'd love to do miniseries in different places. London, definitely."

He grinned. *"Elle on the Underground."*

"Exactly." I grinned back.

"You can do all the major cities with underground transportation."

"New York, DC . . ." I quirked my chin. "Are there that many more?"

"No," he admitted. Leaned in to kiss the tip of my nose. "You could do the bullet train in Japan."

"Those would be short episodes." I pecked his jaw in return, and his eyes flashed black.

We ducked into a café, got lattes to warm our bellies and fingers, and headed back toward his car. I'd lost track of how many blocks we'd walked. My feet ached in the best way.

"What about you?" I said. A drop of coffee slipped from his lip, and he caught it with his tongue. Oh, that talented tongue. "Do you always want to work for AngelCare? Is it your forever job?"

"I don't think so," he said slowly. "I love what I do, don't get me wrong. But it's . . ."

"What is 'boring'? 'Repetitive'? 'Mind-numbing'?"

"I'm sorry," he said, throwing on a Ken Jennings impression. "The phrase we were looking for there was 'emotionally taxing.'"

I pushed my shoulder into his and laughed unbidden, and he did too. I liked that feeling, one only we could understand.

Now we're standing in my apartment, dusty after so long undisturbed. The plant in my windowsill is yellowed and drooping.

It's home still, but it's different too. Things I've never noticed, I see with new eyes simply because Adam is seeing them too.

The mosaic contact paper I stuck to the kitchen window, casting rainbow fractals across the granite. The art prints in frames hanging above the gold velvet armchairs I wrestled upstairs the day I moved in, won in the furniture custody agreement with Grady. The geometric wallpaper behind the television. In the bathroom off the hall, a shower curtain with hand-drawn moons and stars. If we ventured into my bedroom, he'd see an unmade bed, rumpled pinstripe sheets underneath a purple duvet.

I didn't get to have a space like this with Grady, something so *me* I see myself in all directions. I didn't buy new artwork without asking him where we should hang it. Now I buy something simply because I love it and figure out later where it belongs.

Before I left to stay with Lovie, I'd been contemplating changing everything up, having grown sick of the visual noise. But this is me. A perfect mess. Bold. Unapologetic.

I nod, smiling. "This is my place."

Adam runs his fingers through the tassel of my favorite throw pillow. "It fits you perfectly."

"We won't stay long." I'm already moving toward my room. "Just let me grab a bag."

"Take your time." Adam lowers himself onto the royal-blue sofa, taking care not to disturb the pillows. Like they're living beings.

He's in almost the same position when I return with a tote bag stuffed full of lighter clothing, heavier socks, and silkier underthings.

He takes my bag while I arm the security system. Holds the door open for me again. Waits for me to be finished with the stairs before moving toward the street exit door. Swoon. Swoon. Swoon.

Our phones begin buzzing simultaneously, incessantly. I'm expecting an Amber Alert, but what greets me is an unfamiliar message.

"What the hell is a snow squall?" I ask, squinting at my phone.

Adam pushes open the door to the street, but howling wind rips it from his grasp. Frigid air rushes in, swirls my hair around me, pulls at my hood and steals my sight. He yells something, but the wind yells louder.

The hallway goes quiet, giving a vacuum effect. The silence is too loud.

"*That*," Adam says, both hands still on the door handle he tugged closed, "is a snow squall."

My heart thuds, and for a few seconds we're frozen as a thick wall of white falls outside. The general shape of his car is visible on the curb, but not the color.

"Can you drive in snow squalls?"

It's quiet enough that I hear him swallow. "In theory, yes, but it's not recommended. Me, personally? I wouldn't chance it. You? Never. No way."

This shouldn't be a big deal, but the mild sense of panic building in my lungs says otherwise.

"Just wait here," I say, determination straightening my spine. "I'm gonna see how slick it is."

"Elle, please don't—"

I open the door, and once again the wind wrenches it away, stealing my control. But still. This is the Windy City, after all. I've trained for this.

These boots have enough traction that I'm comfortable testing out the sidewalk. City Works is usually pretty good about salting. They really hate lawsuits for some reason.

I take a tentative step, then another. So far, so good.

"Adam," I call, "this is fine. We'll be—"

My feet slip out from under me, one going south while the other continues northeast. I land so hard on my butt my jaw snaps closed. I almost bite off the tip of my tongue.

Through the thick snow, I barely make out Adam shuffling his way to me. By the time he's close enough to extend a hand, I've gathered most of my dignity.

His mouth moves, but I can't hear anything over the wind. My cheeks burn, raw, and my eyelashes are sticking together. I couldn't unlock my jaw if I wanted to.

Instead of waiting for an answer, Adam scuffles his feet to the side door, and I follow suit, up four flights of stairs, back into my apartment. After turning off the alarm again, I point Adam toward the thermostat, and he cranks it up a few degrees.

Then come the adulting parts of an unexpected snowstorm. Checking the weather—it's supposed to remain unchanged for the next several hours. Calling Angie—she's worried for us, but we assure her we're safe and sound. Adam takes several minutes to talk her through where to find more detailed instructions. The list of all Lovie's medications, her usual schedule, the alarm code, and the other shit we've been inundated with for the last two months.

I slip off my boots by the couch, collapsing into a pile of throw pillows. "When should we talk about the irony that when we were expecting snow, it didn't snow, and when we weren't, it does this outside?"

Adam chuckles, slipping off his own shoes and lining them up next to mine. If my clutter bothers him, he doesn't let it show. "Maybe after we talk about what happens next."

What happens next?

I've always thought when you Define the Relationship, you're supposed to have an escape route in case things don't work out in your favor. I'm equal parts thrilled and terrified neither of us can run away if this gets too messy. But didn't Adam just say last night he wasn't asking for any long-term commitments? He wants my nows. Just my todays.

"I imagine we'll have to stay here tonight," I say, hoping my voice doesn't betray my delight. "The food situation might be a little dire, but I probably have a freezer-burnt pint of Ben & Jerry's we can fight over." A nice person might offer it to someone else without the threat of warfare. But it's Cinnamon Buns. It's hard to find.

"I'm sure we can find *something* to eat." His tone straddles the line between innocent and explicit.

A lot of his comments are like that. He waits for me to decide how I want to take them and rolls with it from there. If I want it to stay family friendly, he's happy to do that. And if I don't, he's happy to do that too.

Some of the butterflies in my stomach have migrated to my throat, and I have to speak around them. "Something to eat, yes. But I have no idea what we'll *do*. Thank God for Netflix, I guess."

His playful gaze warms my skin, the same way his hands do when he pulls my feet into his lap. "Are you suggesting we Netflix and chill?"

"I'm surprised you know a phrase as modern as that, Mr. What Does It Mean to Be Verified."

A laugh bursts from his pinkened lips. "I think the twins were conceived under the pretense of Netflix and chill."

Megan Murphy

"I'm sorry we won't get to visit them today." I sink farther into the cushions. My head falls to the armrest as Adam digs his thumb into my arch. It is obscenely delicious.

"I'll see them at Thanksgiving, and again at Christmas."

"Those *are* coming up soon, aren't they?" I close my eyes to his tender touch.

He chuckles. It vibrates up my leg to more private places. "Don't sound so excited."

"The holidays are a lot less exciting when you're a family of one." Before he can question that overly honest admission, I continue. "Do you still see your parents?" I force my eyes open, find his. They're on me again. Still. Whichever.

He nods. "Ruth and the kids and I go there on Christmas Eve for a formal dinner. And after the kids are told to sit still and be quiet for too long for kids to ever sit still or be quiet, Ruth and I make an excuse to leave and take the kids home. We make cookies and watch *The Polar Express*, and once the girls are knocked out from the sugar, Ruth and I drink wine and wrap presents."

Something warm unfolds in my chest, wrapping around my heart. I haven't met four out of five people in this story, but I can picture it. Adam, laughing, the good kind that shows the crinkles around his eyes. Giving his nieces secret smiles he doesn't use on anyone else. Putting bows and ribbons and tags that read *From Santa* on gifts he probably bought.

Adam's looking at me funny. "What?"

I pinch my lips between my teeth so they don't spread into a dopey smile. "I admire how much you care about your family."

"You care about yours too, even if it's smaller, less traditional." His brows slant down as he looks around the room at my lavish lifestyle. "You gave all of this up for Lovie."

My eyes burn, and I look at the ceiling. "She's given me everything. How could I *not*—"

Fake It Like You Mean It

As if sensing my oncoming waterworks, Adam shifts, drawing me closer to him. My cheek finds his chest, and I blink away tears to the beat of his heart.

"We should put up a tree," I say. "For Christmas. If we're both still . . ." *There.* The truth of our situation, the ominous end date of our arrangement, steals the words.

Adam's hand moves to my back, learning the shape of my spine for the umpteenth time. "I love that idea, but I'm not so sure that would work. Lovie still wakes up thinking every day is a Monday in May. If we tell her it's suddenly December, she won't take it well."

I remember when I tried to tell her it was too late to plant anything, confusion and anger fighting for dominance in her glare. "You're probably right."

"But—maybe you could come help us put up the one at Ruth's? We do it Thanksgiving night. And we can schedule another nurse to come in for Lovie again. Some of the young ones jump at the chance to work holidays because of the overtime."

This invitation feels very serious coupled with the revelation of the last few weeks. Hell, the last twenty-four hours. "I . . . I wouldn't want to leave Lovie with a stranger on a holiday."

"She won't know it's Thanksgiving either," he murmurs. He doesn't mean to be rude; it's just the truth.

I gnaw my lip. "You might be right."

His gentle laugh somehow still manages to shake my mainframe. "Two times in one minute? Could you say that again, but louder and into the microphone, please?" He mimes holding up a mic to my mouth.

I shove his hand away, reaching for the remote. "Adam, are you ready to Netflix and chill with me?"

CHAPTER THIRTY-SIX

Around five in the afternoon, my stomach grumbles loud enough for Adam to hear it over *Friends*. When I found out he'd never watched it, I hit play first and gawked second. "Watch the show, Elle," he said, but he was grinning. That crooked thing stayed on his face for *episodes*. I could see it in the corner of my vision.

I grimace as I head to the kitchen. "The time has come where you see how I truly live."

"And how is that?" He tails behind me, socked feet quiet on the tiled floors.

"Like a college freshman of the male variety." I throw open the cabinets and fridge for him to see. "I have three different kinds of Pop-Tarts, frozen chicken, bacon bits, and Velveeta. The end."

"And here I thought you just drank green smoothies and ate candy. Is this the part where you say *It's all about balance*, or does that come later?" Suddenly, Adam's breath is against my throat, sending a hot flush rippling out as his hands find my hips.

Fake It Like You Mean It

Come later. Seriously, he gives a girl one tiny orgasm and my mind permanently relocates to the gutter. I'll send out a change of address with my Christmas card, two birds and one stone and all that. It'll save on postage.

But yeah, I sure hope something is coming later. Someone. We'll need to cuddle to keep warm. Survival 101.

"I'm sure we can find something here to make." Adam's head disappears into my fridge, so purposeful, so *on a mission*, that I take a step back and let him have at it.

He pulls out a can of biscuit dough, shredded cheese, and the bacon bits. From the pantry, a jar of marinara I forgot I had—it's a little dusty. He stands, but when my stomach growls, he reaches back into the pantry and produces a silver foil package. "We can make pizza."

"With Pop-Tart crumble topping? I like the way you think."

Adam lays the ingredients down on the counter and turns on the oven to preheat. "The Pop-Tarts are an appetizer." He grabs my hips and lifts me onto the countertop. He presents the package to me, and I take it. And then I take a kiss.

He doesn't fight me on it, but when his stomach is the one to grumble this time, he pulls back with a parting peck. "As much as I'd love to stand here and kiss you all day, we need to get our strength up for later." His eyes flick down the length of me, lingering on the neckline of my shirt, the dip of my waist, where my thighs press together. Maybe I'm not the only one with a dirty mind. He looks back at the TV pointedly. "We're making it to season two tonight."

I nibble on my snack as Adam kneads the biscuit dough across a cookie sheet. It's not perfectly circular, but it will get the job done. I wonder if he came up with this on the spot or if this is something he's done with his nieces before.

I want to meet them, not only because they're important to him but because they *know* him. He's still somewhat of a puzzle, and they're holding pieces I need.

Megan Murphy

Once the dough is in the oven to prebake ("Otherwise it gets soggy"), Adam turns to me, stealing a bite of Pop-Tart that was on its way to my mouth. Karma is loyal as always, because half of it crumbles onto his chin and down his shirt. I help him brush it away, but my fingers snag on his collar, twisting in the fabric.

I see his intentions from a mile away when he glances at my mouth, a question in his eyes. But I want whatever he's planning, so I give him a tug.

This kiss from Adam is my favorite so far: melting, needy, with just a sprinkle of the desperation rising in my own body.

"You taste like cherries," he says, coming back for another sampling. His tongue is soft, hot, *talented*. How is it in a hundred different places at once?

My blood turns to champagne, and Adam makes my head spin like I drank a bottle of it too fast. Everything moves in flashes around us. I can't tell whether we're in slow motion or fast-forward. His hands sliding up my waist, around my back, down my legs, are slow like honey. But his kisses are gaining speed and severity, and my heart beats up-tempo in my ears.

Adam's shirt is on the floor before either of us realizes the pulsing in the air is the beeping of the timer. With a throaty groan, he pulls away, stepping out from the cradle of my legs to pull the baking sheet from the oven.

"That almost looks like pizza dough," I rasp. Have I always sounded like a phone sex operator?

He gives me a mollifying laugh, which is also crisp and jagged. When he shifts, reaches for the front of his pants, I see he's got a little problem on his hands. Maybe a big problem. His face stretches tight as he clamps his jaw shut. The strain in his jeans grows tighter the longer he stares at me.

We're alone. Actually, honest to goodness *alone*. We checked our obligations at the door, and we don't have anywhere to be, anyone to fix or take care of but ourselves.

Fake It Like You Mean It

Every word and phrase I've ever learned for moments like these escapes me, until all that's left is, "Oh."

His throat bobs with a swallow. It sounds physically painful. He winces as he turns back to the counter covered in makeshift pizza ingredients.

We don't talk and we don't touch. Not as he covers the dough in sauce and cheese and bacon crumbles. Not after he returns the tray to the oven. Eight minutes later, when he slides it onto the counter, I stay silent as I point to the drawer that houses the pizza cutter. And he watches with quiet contemplation as I pull plates from the cabinet over my shoulder. I eat sitting on my counter, him leaning beside me. Even our chewing is quieter than usual. No one chews quietly except when they're trying not to break a moment with unnecessary noise.

Our eyes stay locked the entire time.

The only problem is, his eye contact does me in worse than his mouth. I can't think of a single reason we shouldn't be horizontal right now. This moment is fragile enough that, if the wind were to rattle the windowpanes, it might shatter completely. I think of five different cheeky things to say but talk myself out of them before my mouth ever opens. We're terrified to misread each other, but it's about to come at the expense of missing the moment altogether.

He reaches for my plate, runs it under water. I slip off the counter and reach for a dish towel, the way we have countless times at Lovie's. Things are natural with Adam in a way they never were with Grady. Laughs come easier; smiles get brighter.

Adam's hand catches my wrist, thumb grazing my pulse point. His eyes are dark with want, and I know the time has come.

I lead him to my bedroom.

Maybe later Adam will take in these pieces of me laid bare before him. Mismatched artwork that just barely goes with my bedding. The cat tapestry Liss gave me for a housewarming gift hanging as a curtain, which is atrocious but reminds me of the months I spent living with my best friend. A shaggy Moroccan rug. A blue neon sign, which I flick on now, that reads *Good vibes only*. I've had it for a while, but Grady thought it was tacky to hang in the bedroom, since it matches my vibrator.

Adam smiles when he sees it.

And that's the last time I compare Adam Wheeler to Grady James.

We reach for each other in tandem. Our bodies are going fuzzy around the edges, begging to blur together. We fall to the bed, and it doesn't matter anymore that it's unmade. Adam kisses me soundly as I settle my weight over him, his hands tangling in my hair like he never wants his fingers to unknot. His tongue strokes mine in gentle—but commanding—waves.

My legs come to either side of his hips. His shirt is still on the kitchen floor, and I take this opportunity to learn his tattoo with my mouth. The hair on his chest is just soft enough to tickle. The noise that floats from him is half surprise, half content, and it hovers between the two as I trail my lips down Adam's chest, torso, and unbutton and pull down his jeans to reveal dark-gray boxer briefs. As I reach for their waistband, he flips me fast, my vision going hazy. But his hand cradles my head, lays it tenderly on the pillow, and I am once again shocked by the dichotomy of him. Hard and soft. Fast and slow. Naughty and nice.

His hand grips my ass, and—I whimper.

He pulls back.

"I fell earlier," I remind him. "It's still tender."

His gaze darkens. "Don't worry," he murmurs. "I'll kiss it better."

There's no awkward fumbling, no waiting so long for the other person to take your clothes off that you get frustrated enough to just do it yourself. I'm not questioning where I should put my hands or trying to remember the last time I put on deodorant. We move like we've done this before—practiced and sure. And let me say, Adam has *practiced* a lot, because I'm *sure* I've never been stripped so gracefully.

"Can I feel you?" He hooks a finger in the waistband of my underwear, lets it snap against my skin.

A whimper of "Please" later, his fingers dig beneath the fabric. We groan together at the contact, and it's just abrasive enough to pop our bubble of silence.

"Is this how you touch yourself?" His body is all hard lines, flush with mine.

I want to say something equally flirty, but the point of flirting is sex, and we're basically having it already. So I go for honesty instead. "You're better. Take them off."

His smile goes dark and splits his face in half as he tugs my underwear down.

"That first night," he says. His tone is casual though his words are not. "When you fell on top of me in bed. Do you remember what I said?"

I've only dreamt about it twenty times. "You told me to stop screaming."

"Yeah," he murmurs, running his fingers down the seam of me. "Forget I ever"—my loud gasp cuts him off momentarily as he slips in—"said that. Damn, that's so good."

I know I've used *obscene* to describe Adam a few times now, but it's the word that keeps coming back to me. I have this man—this incredibly rugged, dark, funny, considerate, gentleman-in-the-streets-freak-in-the-sheets man—in my bed, his lips on my breasts, his fingers exploring me, and it's all just too good to be true. He's my walking fantasy. If I wake up to find this was all a figment of my overactive and underlaid imagination, I'll be devastated.

"Condomsinthedrawer," I breathe, shoving at his briefs. When he's free from them, my mouth falls open. "Never mind. Get on your back. Or come up here. I don't care, just—let me—"

He grins, sliding off the bed to step out of them completely. "Cat got your tongue?" He hooks his hands under my arms and drags me to the edge of the mattress, right in line with him.

I'm staring at him upside down, and from this angle, his jawline is even more chiseled. "No," I say. "But it is busy."

And then I put my money where my mouth is—with my tongue, on him. He's warm, hard, and I'm eager, which only drives him further. This could be overwhelming, in this position, but he doesn't lose control.

"Elle," he groans, urgent, fingers tightening in my hair. His other hand rests on my throat. "*Please.* You're going to kill me."

I pull away, reaching for the nightstand as he climbs onto the bed. "Funny. That first night, I thought the same thing about you."

"Did you think we'd be here?" He grasps my waist, pulling me to straddle him. His grin turns wicked as he runs his hands up my chest, squeezing, pinching my nipples. "Here *again.*"

I take a second as he rolls on the condom to consider his question. The hard angles of his face, which soften around me. The hands he runs across my skin. The dark shadows backlighting his face, which I now know come from hard work and obligation and empathy, so much empathy.

I was kidding myself earlier, about falling in love. It wasn't just a few stairs I missed. It was the whole damn staircase. I am falling, hopelessly falling. *Have* fallen, past, and *am* falling, present, and will *keep* falling, future.

All the pieces of me love him.

"I hoped," I say. As I reach between us, he cups my cheek.

Despite the enormity of this situation, the flood of sensations and hormones ravaging my body, my eyes stay locked with Adam's as I take him in fully, slowly. His one hand doesn't stray from my face, his thumb brushing my cheekbone as his fingers caress the shell of my ear. When I brace against his chest, weeding my fingers through the dusting of hair, he holds my waist, my hip, my thigh, like he can't decide where to touch me first.

Like maybe he hoped for this too.

It's a slow, torturous rhythm I set, one that takes in every moan, brush of fingers or lips, and adds to it. Of all his expressions, this may be my favorite. Color striping his jaw, eyes half lidded, pupils fully blown. Hair mussed from my fingers. His lips strain to kiss my chest, and I lower, giving him easier access.

Without warning, he plants his feet, driving up, and it knocks me off-balance. My chest presses to his face.

Adam groans, deep in his throat, and captures my nipple in his mouth.

"Enough slow shit," he rasps, wrapping his arms around my back and flipping us. "I've wanted you too long."

He braces on the pillow under my head, hitching my leg over his hip, and begins to move.

Soft is good, but hard is good too, and I start to wonder if *everything* is good with Adam, just because it's him. I move my hand between us, because I'm growing more desperate with each drive, and Adam's moving faster, breathing harsher. My limbs are deliciously heavy, all the pleasure centers of my body screaming at me for release, for something more, *more more more please more*. I say these same words, tears in the corners of my eyes.

Adam's teeth close on my shoulder as his hand joins my own between my legs, and *here it is*, the beginning of my end.

I'm not sure who, technically, goes first. If it's his choked noises and hard pulses that pull me along, or if the feel of me, so gone for him, is what does him in. But we break, and it's together, and *we're* together.

And after, as we try to calm our racing hearts, as Adam's grip goes from possessive to gentling, fingers along my spine, I wonder how many stairs are in this staircase, if I will be falling forever.

CHAPTER THIRTY-SEVEN

Turns out it's really fun to have a secret sexual relationship with the guy your senile grandma thinks is your soul mate. We don't have to act anymore. The kisses we used to hide in hallways and laundry rooms are out in the open. Adam's arm around me during television hour is no longer pretend. There's no questioning who's getting the bed—now we share.

Adam and I stayed up late into the night in my Chicago apartment. We ate the rest of our makeshift pizza in bed and continued our *Friends* binge, and he was right, we did make it to season two. I'm not sure how much he remembers, considering my hands started to wander a bit toward the finale. But that was okay, because his mouth never strayed from some part of me—hand, hair, cheek, lips, neck—for more than a few seconds.

Our second time was much like our first, exploring with hands and mouths before we got too desperate to wait any longer. Resetting the clock with an agonizing speed, only to realize we hadn't reset it at all, just pressed pause. He managed to undo me twice that time, and once more from his knees in the shower the next morning. It was part of the reason we got back to Elkhart around lunch instead of first thing.

Also, the roads still sucked, and we were forced to take our time on the highway. Adam's hand sat on my thigh, claiming it again as we passed field after field, all of them blanketed in perfect white snow. It was in direct contrast to the chaos taking place in my heart. There, things were bright new colors and loud music.

They still are.

If Angie noticed anything different about us when we got back, she didn't say. What she *did* say, though, right before she left, was that there were still no insurance updates. I tried to be sympathetic. But waking up beside Adam is *quite* distracting.

A week later, I'm still in a daze, which I will need to snap out of soon if I have any hope of surviving the night. I'm prepping a vegetable tray, though Adam has warned me a few times it will go untouched.

"I'm telling you, Ruth orders fried chicken. We eat off paper plates. And I don't think Chloe has willingly touched a vegetable in her *life*."

He steals a cucumber slice, giving me a forehead kiss along the way.

My laugh is light, flirty, in a way I'm not used to. It's been that way a lot since coming back from the city. I talked to Liss for an hour on FaceTime yesterday, and my cheeks hurt when I was finished from all the smiling.

I sag into him, bury my face in the collar of his scrub top. Navy today. I close my teeth around his collar and give it a little tug.

His grin follows the curve of my temple, but before things get carried away, we hear Lovie moan as she stands, and Adam goes to help her.

I don't know how I would have done this without him these past few months. What if someone else had been assigned this job, had been in my bed the first night I came here? I know there's a lot to say about forced proximity, but part of me wonders if he wouldn't have found me anyway. If we wouldn't have bumped into each other on the L or in a coffee shop on one of his trips into the city. Adam is the kind of person who makes coincidence feel like fate.

Those are some big revelations for Thanksgiving— especially when I'm sober.

Something shifts in my peripheral vision: Adam, doing his cross-lean in the doorway. He's looking at me the way I was just looking at the carrots and celery.

We stare at each other, across the room, my heart swimming with sentiments too big to contain and too small to encompass everything.

"I'm glad you're coming today," he says. "You look... you're beautiful. I haven't said it before, and I should have."

I look down at my outfit. I'm wearing a fluffy red-orange sweater and black leather jeggings. My favorite winter coat— knee length, plaid—hangs over the kitchen chairs. I'll slip into booties before we leave. "It's nothing special."

His eyes narrow, but before he can refute me, a knock at the door cuts him off. "That will be Vivi, I think."

As Adam briefs the nurse, I make my way into the living room.

Lovie's on the couch, eyes trained on the television. "Hey, you," I say, perching on the edge of No-Man's-Land beside her. "Don't miss me too much while I'm gone."

She blinks at me. "Where are you going?" She takes in my makeup, the hair I've mussed and curled back from my face. I guess I meet her approval tonight, because a slow, sly grin appears on her mouth. "Is Bobby finally taking you out?"

Maybe on a different day, this would sting more. But I listen to Adam's deep timbre as I remember how that deep tone sounded in my bed, dipping along my lower back, *lower*, kissing the bruise from where I'd fallen on the sidewalk. Butterflies take up most of the space in my stomach. There's no room for sadness tonight.

"He is." I bump her shoulder with mine. "And it's about damn time, I'd say."

"Attagirl."

Adam clears his throat from the doorway. "You ready to go?" he says. The relief nurse beside him smiles widely.

Before we head out the door, I spare a parting glance at Lovie.

Her eyes are watery, but omniscient. I'm struck with that feeling again, the same one I got at the grocery. Even though her words don't match my suspicion, something deep in my gut knows. She's seeing me as *Elle* when she says, "Take the scenic route on the way back."

CHAPTER THIRTY-EIGHT

Adam's sister and nieces live in a rented house on the outskirts of Goshen, two towns to the southeast. It took exactly six turns and twenty-three minutes to get here. He pulls his car up beside a dirty green Corolla with a busted front fender and a crack spider-webbing through the windshield. The driveway is chipped and grimy, shriveled weeds poking through the cracks. The heel of my boot catches in one, and I start to say "Fuck" when the front door bursts wide open, two little girls spilling outside.

"Uncle Adam!"

These must be the twins, with matching eyes and cherub cheeks, but one is *tall*, the way I was tall at her age, and how Adam probably was. She's faster than the other, her legs carrying her to Adam sooner. She catapults herself at him, dark hair flapping in the late-November breeze. She's already up in his arms by the time the other one reaches the drive.

He gives them his full attention whenever they're speaking, even though they're both talking a mile a minute, their words tripping over each other's. Neither of them is wearing shoes, so he scoops them up. They're nine, he told me once, so it's not an insignificant load.

The shorter one has finally noticed me where I'm standing in the still-open car door. "Who's that?"

"Chloe," he says to her, then addresses the other. "Cora. This is my friend Elle."

Chloe giggles, pressing her reddening cheek into his shoulder. "She's so pretty."

"I *know*," Adam says emphatically, and my face is the one that's flaming now as he looks over. He talks to her, but he smiles at me. "Let's go inside before your toes freeze off," he says. And okay, I'm shivering too, but it's not from the cold.

The inside of the house is in much better shape than the outside. It's warm, for starters, but beyond that, it's lived-in in the best way. There are toys scattered and single shoes and socks posed as land mines on the floor. It smells faintly of sugar cookies and crayons. Adam sets the girls on their feet and shuts the door behind us.

"Hey, you made it," someone calls from deeper in the house.

Another child appears around the bend. She's the youngest, but it's not the only way she's different from her sisters. Her hair is lighter and more kinked, her eyes a different color.

I stoop down to her level, the veggie tray digging into my stomach. "Hi, Claire."

She studies me curiously, so I do the same. She's got juice or something else purple smeared along her chin and shirt. She's in diapers.

She runs to Adam, hiding behind his legs. He acts knocked off-balance, catches himself on the wall, and it makes her giggle.

Adam scoops her up and extends a hand to me. "Come on," he says softly. "Ruth's in here."

In here is the living room, where more toys and clothes lay scattered. I'm horrified to realize I'm still wearing my shoes, and pause. With a deep, just-for-me chuckle, Adam tugs me along, boots and all. His thumb runs along the ridges of my knuckles, centering me.

Even if I didn't know Ruth Wheeler was Adam's sister, there would be no denying it. They have the same dark-brown hair, and though the sharp angles on Adam's face are softer and more feminine on Ruth's, her cheeks rounded out and dusted with freckles, they are two sides of the same coin. Simply put, she is gorgeous.

And staring at me like I have two heads.

"You brought a *girl?*" She turns that crazed stare on Adam. I tug Adam's arm. "You didn't *ask* her?"

"Her name is Elle," Cora offers, collapsing onto a blue couch almost as threadbare as Lovie's. This one, though, probably doesn't sleep like a stack of bricks. It's well worn in the best ways. I could nap *so hard* on that couch.

Recognition flashes in Ruth's face at my name. Her eyes dart from my hair (yes, I know my roots need touching up) to my shoes. I don't remember feeling this scrutinized under Adam's stare the first time I met him, but I must have. Her gaze travels back up and snags somewhere near my waist.

Adam is still holding my hand.

It's a millennium before she meets my eyes again, and my body gravitates toward Adam's with anticipation. Our shoulders touch.

"Are you a vegan?" is what she says. She eyes the vegetables. "Because we do fried chicken on Thanksgiving, and I'll accommodate a lot, but not that."

"Oh," I say, relief blanketing me. "No. Not a vegan, thank God."

The corner of her mouth jerks toward a smile just like Adam's, familiarity crashing through me like a wave. "You can stay, then."

It only takes ten minutes to decide I love this family.

Cora is whip-smart, and every time Adam's hand so much as twitches in my direction in the hour we wait for the food delivery, she starts singing, "Elle and Adam, sittin' in a tree." Chloe loses it at this, whining about Adam's cooties. Which, as any self-respecting adult knows, is just an excuse to give that little kid as many kisses and raspberries as you can before they squirm off your lap. Adam is very good at this game. Claire is just happy to be here.

Same, girl.

Halfway through dinner, which we eat picnic-style around the coffee table in the living room, Ruth turns to me. "Does your family not celebrate Thanksgiving?"

"Ruth," Adam hisses, the warning in his tone crystalline. They have their own language the way Liss and I do.

"My parents passed away," I say, finding Adam's knee below the table. I've already caught his cooties, so there's nothing to worry about there. "And my grandmother has Alzheimer's. She's at home tonight."

"Oh God," Ruth says, standing so quickly it nearly topples the plastic gravy bowl. I get the feeling fine china wouldn't last in this house. "You need alcohol. Do you drink?"

"I'll take anything you've got."

I take a chance and lean into Adam's side, the tips of his ears a little red. "I like her."

"She likes you too," he murmurs. "She never shares her liquor."

"Not even with you?"

He chuckles. Leans in to kiss my temple. Press the words "Especially not with me" into the skin there.

Ruth comes back with a stack of plastic cups and a bottle of red wine tucked under her arm. "I don't have any fancier glasses," she says, handing the cups to her brother, "but I've always been under the impression that wine tastes good no matter what you drink it out of."

Fake It Like You Mean It

"Cheers to that," I say, accepting a cup. Ruth fills it a decent amount, then a cup for herself to match.

Despite Adam's claims, she brought a cup for him too. He accepts a small pour; we all clink. Cora and Chloe add their glasses of soda, and Claire thrusts her sippy cup into the mix with surprising force.

Claire smiles on my right. As I bring my glass to my lips to take a sip, she giggles, clanking her cup with mine again. "Fun," she says.

Red wine sloshes over the brim, spilling down my neck and dribbling onto my top.

"Oops," Claire says, her eyes still wide and excited.

"Claire," Ruth groans, hooking a finger into the back of Claire's diaper to pull her back from the table. Ruth frowns at my shirt. "I'm so sorry. If you want to borrow a T-shirt, I can pop some stain remover on that."

The littlest Wheeler is ready to cry, lip quivering and her brows gathering in a downward V that reminds me so much of Adam it *hurts*. Like I already love her too.

I wave Ruth away. "This shirt has a hole in the armpit anyway. No biggie." Adam's gaze is heavy on my profile. I scrunch my nose at a sniffling Claire, then draw a shape that traces the stain. "It's a flower. I love it. Thank you."

A quiet breath of surprise from my other side has my pulse jumping, but I hide my smile behind another sip of wine and reach for the spoon in the macaroni and cheese. Warm fingers find my leg beneath the table and make a home there.

Cora and Chloe talk through the rest of dinner about the Christmas decorations they'll put up tonight. Fight over which movie to watch first.

"What's your favorite Christmas movie, Elle?" Chloe says. She's sitting on her knees in a way my thighs haven't allowed in approximately fifteen years.

"I like *Elf*. What's yours?" My stomach is stuffed with a plethora of simple carbs, only ever good for your soul. Which is also full to bursting.

Chloe giggles. "That's my favorite too."

"Well, it's settled, isn't it?" Adam pulls his tree-trunk legs from under the coffee table and stands up. "That's what we're watching while we decorate."

I help Adam clean up, which consists of carrying the picked-over remains of dinner to the refrigerator, while Ruth herds the girls to the bathroom to wash their hands and faces. All the utensils and plates were disposable—my favorite kind of cleanup, but it means the garbage bag fills quickly.

"I'll take it out," I say to Adam, who's wiping the counters free from crumbs and lingering grease. "Just point me in the right direction."

He watches me pull the bag free from the can, draw the strings tight. "You don't have to. Just leave it by the side door and I'll get it before we leave. It's cold outside."

He doesn't have to worry. I'm never cold when I'm around him.

"What I just heard you say is that the can is by the side door." I throw him a playful grin. "Back in a second."

I'm reaching for the door handle on the way back when I catch movement through the glass pane. From where I'm standing, I've got a clear line of sight to the living room.

Adam is helping Ruth move the couch to the side to make room for the artificial Christmas tree. His smile stretches wide and open, a laugh I can see but not hear. Cora comes up to him, handing him a piece of paper, maybe a drawing or a school assignment. His mouths make words that could be *I love it*. Folds it, takes out his wallet, and slips it inside.

Ruth says something then, and it makes Adam dip his head, hang his hand on the back of it. He nods, smiles down at his feet. Glances out the side door to me.

Fake It Like You Mean It

Eyes locked from across the house, Adam nods again as his mouth moves over words I can't decipher. I wish I were better at reading lips, because I imagine my name among them.

A cold wind whips at my hair, my wine-stained shirt, and I reach for the handle again. It is *quite* chilly out here.

I want this, I think as we decorate the tree and unbox garlands and ribbon. I want to laugh uninhibited, have a place and people to call home.

Adam is pinning up a thinning tinsel garland to the living room archway, me helping him to hold it in place, when the giggles start.

He narrows his eyes at Cora and Chloe. I'm starting to suspect that conspiratorial laughter of theirs either gets them into or out of heaps of trouble, nothing in between. "What?"

"You're standing under the mistletoe," Cora says. Her round cheeks fill with color. "You have to kiss."

In sync, Adam and I look up. Nestled in the middle of the garland is a sprig of mistletoe so microscopic you'd only know it was there if you were the one who placed it.

"You didn't tell me they were evil," I say, loud enough for everyone to hear.

"I didn't know they were." He drops his arms, unpinned greenery falling around our shoulders.

My lungs freeze in my chest, though his gaze is bright enough to burn. How will he kiss me when there are people to see it? *His* people, who will all remember tomorrow. We've done many intimate things, but this might be the most important.

His pinkie hooks mine as he dips his head. "May I?" he murmurs, and I nod, eyes fluttering shut.

Adam's mouth touches the corner of my own, his other hand sweeping up my arm to cradle my face. It's soft, a promise of a kiss as opposed to an actual one, but it's appropriate for our current company.

It might be my favorite.

And the look he gives me after centers in my core all the same. I don't want to let him go.

"Whoever you're kissing, girls—" Adam's voice is gruff, stern, and he clears his throat, but it doesn't really help. "Make sure they always have your permission."

One of Adam's very own Hard Love Rules.

"In seventeen to twenty business years, please," Ruth adds. She chucks a red throw pillow at her brother like a football.

On the ride back to Lovie's house, I'm still not ready to go home. We were only a twenty-minute drive away, but it felt like I took a *vacation* tonight. Adam did this for me, brought me along on his plans. I am so thankful for him. Every day, but especially today.

I direct Adam to a spot I remember from high school, at the park down the road from Lovie's house. To the side gate, which I'm glad to find still rusty on the hinges and unlocked. To the corner of the lot, where the lightbulb is still burnt out on the utility pole.

Small towns are so good for hiding in plain sight.

I crawl over the center console and onto his lap and let him distract me not with nieces and Christmas trees but with mouths and hands and hips and whispers.

And every time I have a thought that scares me too much, that feels too big or too soon, I bite down on it until all that comes out is his name. *I love you*, I think. *I love my life, but I love it more with you in it. I don't know how I'm supposed to leave when this is all over.*

"Adam," I say instead.

"Adam," when his fingers dig into my waist.

"Adam," as he helps me over this burning ledge with his hand between my thighs.

"Adam," I gasp when he's there. *There.*

Fake It Like You Mean It

"Adam," I say. Over and over, I say his name tonight.

"Again," he says, on repeat until I'm shaking and sweating and blissfully numb.

And I wonder if maybe his words mean more than they should too.

CHAPTER THIRTY-NINE

We slip inside the front door. It's quiet, the lights dimmed.

Vivi gives a soft, sad smile when she appears from the living room. "I tried to get her to bed, but she wouldn't go. She kept saying she was waiting for Lovie to come back."

Adam and I share a look of alarm. I beat him to the living room.

Lovie fell asleep sitting up where I left her, head crooked at an unnatural angle as it searches for somewhere soft to rest. That will hurt in the morning.

"You did the right thing, Vivi. We've got it from here." Adam nods at her, and while the young nurse gathers her things and debriefs with him, I pad over to my grandmother.

I crouch in front of her, place a hand on her knobby knee. "Lovie. We're back."

She wakes with a start, hands coming up defensively. The Elle of two months ago would have shied away, especially knowing the damage she could do. I smile at her instead.

Her hand falls when she sees me. "Oh."

Fake It Like You Mean It

"You got her?" Adam asks from the doorway. His gaze is heavy on my back. It drips across my skin like candle wax, melting and languid.

"We're just fine," I whisper, more to myself, patting her cold and wrinkled hands. "Aren't we, Lovie? Let's get you to bed."

She is surprisingly amenable as I help her into pajamas and get her tucked in. Even under the blankets, she shivers, and her hands have a blue tinge I'm not a fan of.

"I'll grab another blanket from the closet," I offer. "Or some socks?"

She hums noncommittally, intent to sit there turning purple. Her ribs are practically clanking together.

I grit my teeth. Of all the things she gave me, all the lessons she passed down and bits of wisdom and DNA we share, did it have to be her stubbornness that's stuck around into this next chapter of her life? "A blanket it is."

I walk to her closet. She keeps chunky knit blankets at the top, alongside hatboxes stuffed with photo albums and mementos. First teeth, locks of hair, et cetera.

I pull a blanket from the shelf. Something heavy falls with it, toppling onto my foot. I stoop down to pick it up, but a loose paper hanging out the side catches my attention.

Hometown Heroine Goes Underground With Chicago Podcast Success

My eyes skim as quickly and thoroughly as they can in the dim light, but everything on this page is familiar. My name, my words. My story.

This article is about me.

Thumbing open the album, I bite the inside of my cheek. There are articles and interviews printed and preserved. Screenshots of my Buzzfeed and PopSugar features. They're all about me.

Megan Murphy

Catch the Train with Elle Monroe

Another Chart-Topping Year for Elkhart Native

15 Heartwarming Podcasts to Binge After You Finish Your Favorite

There's a photo of me on the next page. My hair is normal, mousy brown, pulled back from my face so as not to draw attention to it. Everything about me was that way back then: designed to fit squarely inside boxes never made for me. Lovie was the one who encouraged me to quit my desk job when the podcast started taking off.

I wrote my resignation email sitting by her side, and I sent her this photo exactly two weeks later, me pretending to throw my employee badge in the garbage. *Done*, I texted. *Officially self-employed!*

You can do this, she texted back. *You're doing this.*

I *did* this. And she saw the entire thing.

"What are you gawking at over there, girl?" Lovie says.

Will my voice still work if I try to use it? "My—your articles," I correct, holding up the book for her to see.

She struggles to push herself up, makes a surprising amount of progress for someone with so little muscle mass. "Bring them here, into the light. I haven't dug around up there in ages."

I shuffle across the room, draping the blanket over her lap and making sure her feet are covered. I point to the bed. "Can I?"

Lovie tilts her head. "Come on, then. Sit down."

With unusual sheepishness, I crawl up beside my grandmother. When I spread the book open between us, she sighs. "I used to love looking at this book."

"What made you stop?" I don't know what's changed tonight, why she's not at my throat. But I refuse to question things outside my control. I've learned so much since moving home, and, once again, I have her to thank.

Fake It Like You Mean It

She fiddles with her hands in her lap, forever spinning her wedding band, yellowing teeth catching wrinkled lips. "I think it—well, it makes me frustrated. Because I know they're important, but I can't remember why."

I shut my eyes to keep my tears at bay. She's reached directly into my chest and holds my heart in her hands. "I think she's your granddaughter. The girl in the articles."

"That would . . . that would make sense. I love them almost as much as I love her." Fatigue is making her voice droop like her jowls, the space between her words getting larger.

"Why not display these in the house somewhere?" A tear slips down my cheek, but I just let it splash onto my already ruined shirt.

Another tired sigh. "They're not for everyone else. They're just for me."

"I bet she'd like to see them when she visits, though." I press a fist to my mouth, trying to hold in the pain.

Lovie chuckles, and I open my tear-filled eyes in time to see her shake her head, smiling fondly down at the papers on her lap. "She's never needed anyone else to see how successful she was. Never lived for anyone else either." My emotion is invisible to her as she grins conspiratorially. "We have that in common. I needed to see it sometimes, though. To remind myself I did good with her."

I can't stop the whimper that comes out of my mouth, past my hand. I take her wrinkled one in mine, curling her cold fingers to her palm, the way Adam showed me. "Oh, you did, Lovie. You did so good with her. And she—she loves you very much."

"I raised her, you know." Her voice is distant, stuck somewhere in a barely there memory. "Her parents . . . they died when she was three. Car wreck. Drunk driver."

The defining moments stick with us longer than the rest, don't they?

Something moves beyond the open doorway, a form I now know as well as my own.

"She was in the car," I say, not for Lovie's benefit but for Adam's. I can't see his face, just his shadow leaning on the wall across from the door, but I know he's listening. In the same way I know what started as a trip home to my grandmother's has irreversibly changed my life. "Sleeping in the back seat. Her parents lost their lives, and the only thing she got was a scar on her knee."

I trace it now, the way Adam has so many times.

"She doesn't remember anything." I blow out a shaky breath. "She *was* three, after all." He was exactly right about that—that, and so many other things. "But she still doesn't like driving because of it. Has lived almost her entire adult life in cities where she doesn't need to."

In the hall, Adam is stock-still.

"But she's okay," Lovie says. Not a question. Maybe somewhere in her mind, she already knows the answer.

"She's okay," I confirm, wiping my cheek across my shoulder. I glance at the shadow in the hall again. "Every day, she is more and more okay."

I give myself a few more minutes to enjoy this, the comfort I have here, in this house. In the same bed I used to crawl into after nightmares, in the same arms that held me together in the midst of all my falling apart.

When Lovie succumbs to sleep, I pull the scrapbook off her lap, tuck pages into the album again. Place it back into the closet, for another time.

Maybe.

Maybe there will never be *another* time.

I shut her bedroom door and all but collapse into the arms waiting there for me, pain and bittersweet memories tearing my chest inside out. Adam leads me to the other bedroom. And like I did for Lovie, he holds me while I fall asleep.

CHAPTER FORTY

December arrives fully with little fanfare, the way all winter months bleed into one another in the Midwest. Today is as gray as yesterday, and just as gray as tomorrow.

"I need you to disappear for a few hours today," Adam says. I'm tucked into his arms early in the morning, tracing the lines of his tattoo over his heart as we come into consciousness for the day. "Can you do that for me?"

"Am I in trouble?" I add my lips beside my fingers.

His laugh tickles my cheek, and he presses a kiss to my crown. "Have you been bad?"

My hand starts to wander. "You tell me."

"Elle, love," he groans, stopping my hand's descent. "We have to get up."

How am I supposed to move now? His words stick in my brain, looping on that one single syllable.

Love, love, love.

He called me that the day Liss and Dakota showed up to ambush me. In my half-sleep haze, I'd thought I was being called Lovie in my dream.

When Adam speaks next, his voice is richer, grittier, like maybe the word surprised him too. What base number do I text Liss and Dakota for *that*? "I want to surprise you, okay? If you're okay with driving, that is. You can take my car. I did some research, and it's got a four-star rating. Plus I just got new winter tires last year, so those should—"

I shut him up with my mouth, letting my lips wander to try to distract myself with him. When he reaches for the top drawer of the nightstand and I catch a flash of bright-blue plastic, I don't have to try anymore.

We dress quietly, me in fleece-lined sweatpants and a sweatshirt from college. Liss doesn't know it yet, but I stole it from her four months ago. That's nothing, considering she stole it from me first six *years* ago. Adam pulls on scrubs. Beloved by all.

With nowhere specific to go, I swing by Starbucks and wind up in Michigan City. I drive myself all the way here. I don't even hit anything.

On autopilot, I drive to Pullman Park. It's one of my favorite places in the world. It's not barren yet, but it's close. The leaves are long gone from the trees, choosing instead to decorate the ground, benches, walkways like strips of confetti. On the playground equipment to my left, a woman pushes a child on the swing while another runs amok up and down the slide. Their cheeks are bright red, their noses dripping with snot. They're screaming with glee, the sound sharp and abrasive at my eardrums. I was like that once.

Maybe that's just what happens when you stick a child who can't be tamed with parental figures who thought they were done taming altogether. I caught Lovie smoking a cigarette one time and she offered me a puff. I was eleven. That could have been strategic on her part, though, because I haven't touched one since.

I had Liss's parents, who were wonderful and great but who were simply not mine. They got to ship me home when I started getting too rowdy. And I had myself for everything else, all the things I could never find in another person. I learned to be self-sufficient. I could always count on myself, and I would never let myself down.

I would never leave myself.

If I'd grown up in a household like Adam's nieces—Cora and Chloe and Claire, with their perfect matching names—and had their wonderful mother who maybe isn't perfect but who loves them and who is *there*, where would I be now? Would I have more space in my heart for something like that? Some days my friendship with *Liss* overwhelms me, and that's not even close to the same thing.

After a bit longer at the park, I decide I prefer to feel my toes and check on the podcasts from the warmth of Lovie's car.

Forget Me Not is on pace to outperform *Elle on the L* on nearly every platform. The growth is astronomical, honestly, and I don't quite know what to do with it. Ad revenue is through the roof; when I called the assistant at one of the charities my listeners chose, she almost hyperventilated when I told her the amount of the first donation. And then she asked me to tell her boss because she didn't think she would be able to repeat the number without passing out. I'm doing good work for good people who deserve good things. Giving to a community suffering from a disease that only ever *takes*.

Switching to Instagram, I scroll through a Thanksgiving weekend's worth of "thankful for you" captions. There are Dakota and his boyfriend Sam with their two dogs. Liss, her brother Alex and his wife, their mom.

An email banner appears, and the preview of the message has me fumbling my phone. I will sensation back into my fingers so they work faster.

Your Dependency Status Has Been Updated, the subject reads.

Megan Murphy

The email is rudimentary, the way all insurance matters are: they say the most by not saying anything at all. It takes reading between the lines to figure out what exactly this is saying.

Lovie is officially my dependent.

Relief is crushing. Sometimes you don't know how heavy your problems have become until you don't have to hold them anymore.

With this, Lovie will have access to state-of-the-art facilities, enrichment programs specifically designed for people with dementia and Alzheimer's. She'll be around people who understand her feelings more thoroughly than I ever have. And she will be safe, first and foremost.

And because of it, I will be able to breathe again, fully, for the first time in months.

I won't have to worry about whether I left the ibuprofen too close to her depression medicine, whether one more serving of dairy for the day will be the straw to break the camel's lactose-intolerant back. No more setting an alarm, locking windows, peeing with the door open.

And Adam.

Adam will get to move on to a new assignment, spend more time with his nieces.

If he's not keen on his parents' Christmas Eve dinner, maybe we could have the girls over to my apartment instead. Order deep-dish pizza and watch Christmas movies snuggled on my couch. I can help wrap presents. Supply the wine. I type out a text to Adam:

> Can I please come home now? I'll make it worth your while.

My heart grows wings in my chest, and I add:

> I have a surprise for you too.

Fake It Like You Mean It

Nurse Adam: Yes, come home. Is that a dinner hint? I don't think we have any eggplant, but if you grab some on your way home, I can make it for you tonight.
Me: Are you serious?
Nurse Adam: I take vegetables very seriously.
Me: That's not what that means.
Nurse Adam: No?
Me: I should have known 🍆 That is a metaphorical eggplant.
Nurse Adam: You'll have to come home and show me what it stands for, then. ♥

I see how it is. Sneaky. I also see, scrolling back through our recent conversations, usually ended by Adam sending a single red heart, that he's called Lovie's place home more than once lately.

It's funny, because when I think of that word now—*home*—I don't think of my apartment in Chicago. I don't think of this house, or even Liss and Dakota.

I think of Adam.

* * *

My eyes are trained when I walk through the door, searching for any sign of my surprise. I can usually figure them out with minimal context clues—Liss doesn't even give *hints* anymore after the Great Birthday Incident of 2019—but things seem normal as I slip off my shoes.

After our brief Thanksgiving reprieve, Lovie is back to her normal grouchy self, and Adam's still just as smug while he preps lunch at the kitchen island. Everything else looks . . . the same.

That's a shitty surprise.

I wind my arms around Adam's midsection, running my fingers flush against a chest I know from personal experience is as hard as it makes him when I touch it.

"Hey there," he rumbles.

I prod playfully at his stomach. "Is my surprise that your six-pack is now an eight-pack? I'm all for extra value, you know."

Without words, he grabs me by the waist and leads me through the laundry closet, toward the bedroom. He covers my eyes with a massive hand just before he pushes open the door.

It smells different in here than it did when I was little, or even my first night back. It's home, still, but there's a layer of newness that is only Adam. It's the warmth of his smile, the reverberation of his laugh through my chest whenever ours are pressed together. I want him like this. I just want him.

"So it *is* a sexy surprise," I muse. I can hardly hear my own voice through the pounding of my heart. "You shouldn't have. Also I'm lying."

"Easy, or you'll be disappointed." He situates me how he wants me, eyes still covered. "Ready?"

"Yes," I say, trying not to squirm like a little kid.

"Are you sure?"

"Yes." I bet I look like I have to pee.

Lips touch my temple. "Really sure?"

"Adam Nicholas Wheeler," I growl. "Get to the fucking point."

His mouth finds my neck next, the spot below my ear that lights me up. It's so distracting, I miss his hand coming away from my eyes.

I inhale sharply. Tears spring up in my vision. My nose burns. "*Oh.*"

"Do you like it?" He whispers the words to my throat but saves kissing me for when I start nodding furiously.

Adam got me a Christmas tree after all. My favorite shade of neon blue, no more than two feet tall. It fits right on the nightstand.

"I know you were disappointed we couldn't have a big one in the living room," he says. I reach out and run my fingertips along the bristles and lights. "So I improvised. We'll celebrate in here, deck *up to* the halls. I thought it would look nice in your bedroom in the city next year. It goes with your neon sign. And I just—" He cuts himself off. "Surprise."

He sounds a little winded and scratchy, like he chewed up dirt. He hangs his hand on the back of his neck. Waits.

"Adam, it's . . ." I swallow, and I think some of that dirt must have gotten in my mouth too. My throat itches; so do my eyes. "No one's ever—" But that's it. No one has *ever*. I don't even listen to myself this intently, and here comes this man who has figured me out, top to bottom and inside out, simply by paying attention.

I want to tell him. About the staircase and my stumbling down it, and how he is safe to me. How I still don't believe in fate, but maybe there *is* a reason we look like Lovie and Bobby. Maybe there's a reason this house has had it out for us this entire time, with smoke detectors and door handles that fall off and windows mysteriously left open.

Adam has wound his way through my heart and settled into parts of my soul I haven't shared with anyone else. I don't know exactly what to call us, this fragile infant *thing* we've started building here in this little magic pink house, but it's good. Good and terrifying.

"Will you think out loud for me?" he says.

The Christmas tree goes blurry.

Adam ducks into my line of vision, resting his hands on my shoulders. "Elle?" His brows create a confused V. "Why are you crying? I thought . . . You don't like it."

"I love it, Adam. I love—" A flash of emotion in his eyes halts my confession. "It's just that I'm so happy. And I think this tree will look good in my apartment *this* year."

His hold on me falters, just a bit. "What do you mean?"

I grin wide. "That was my surprise. The insurance came through. Lovie's on my plan now, which means she can get into a long-term facility. I can go home."

I think he must still be nervous about his gesture, because his hand, although it could never be unsteady, seems to tremble as he runs it across his jaw. "That . . . that is great news for Lovie."

He always wants me to think out loud for him. I owe him my honesty, and he asked for it, after all.

This is the loudest thought in my brain:

"Would you consider—" I cut myself off, start over again as the words flow from the aching place, right in the middle of my heart. The one that rips open whenever I think about that ambiguous *next*. "What if you worked in a hospital in the city or something? Maybe the one AngelCare is based out of?" This job is so hard on him, and I know he loves it, but I also know how draining it is, never having the chance to relax or turn off. He is always *on*, and he tries to hide it, but I know him better than that now.

Adam swallows thickly, gaze darting from the ceiling to the floor, everywhere but my face. Finally, his eyes land on me, serious. Maybe a little scared. "What are you asking?"

I love you almost spills out. Instead I say, "I want you to come home to me. Come home *with* me. I want to see your shoes in my doorway and have your green smoothies on my counter. I want your scrubs in my washer and I want your body in my bed."

The color drains from his face and enters mine. The longer he stares at me blankly, maybe even guiltily, the more I regret giving him my thoughts at all. Thinking out loud sounded so easy when Ed Sheeran did it. This shit is hard.

The last thread of my hope dies when he begins to speak. "But my family is *here*, Elle." His voice has been dragged through glass, and some of the shards jump out and touch me. "In Elkhart."

Two towns over, actually. Twenty minutes. Six turns. I counted every one of them on our drive, something in my heart pulling me closer and closer to where Adam's resided.

Fake It Like You Mean It

"It's not like you'd never see them again. You have a car, after all," I say, trying to tease him. It falls flat, like his face. "You have to find what's best for you. Because I hope I'm not alone when I say I did."

They're still not *the* words, but they're close, and maybe they're the ones he needs.

When he still doesn't concede, doesn't kiss me, doesn't do *anything*, I take a step toward him instead. "You said you wanted to pull back from them, didn't you? We talked about it. That you felt they were too dependent. This could be a good start to that. Just getting a little space."

His cheeks are striped pink; so is his neck. "A shared calendar is one thing. But leaving? I can't just—I couldn't do that to them. Move away completely, cut Ruth off like that? That's exactly what my parents did."

I should have been asking for his thoughts instead. One of us got off track somewhere. Has it been me this whole time? I nod, and it dislodges the almost ever-present tears in my eyes. I wipe them with the heels of my hand. I'm embarrassed to have misread this so greatly.

"Elle," he says, bridging the gap between our bodies, but there is still a chasm. "It's not that I don't . . . care for you. It's just so soon, and I—"

I hold up a hand to stop him, and it makes contact with his chest. Beneath my fingers, his heart jumps hard against his scrub top. His apology is writing itself across his features: eyes that seem to sink into his head, glazing over along the bottom rim. Skin stretching tight over his jaw. Throat bobbing repeatedly, breathing that grows increasingly ragged under my touch.

"I don't know who to make happy," he whispers, dropping his forehead to mine.

"Don't be silly." A tear tracks down my cheek. "It's not—not even a choice. You'll pick them. Of course. They're your family."

Because he has one. One that is *good* and that *matters* to him. We are so much of the people who make us.

"Maybe if I had more time," he offers weakly. "To get things sorted out."

I shake my head, eyes burning. "I don't know if more time will solve anything. Your family will still be here. And once a spot opens up, Lovie will have to take it immediately or lose it."

The thought of returning to Chicago was already overwhelming; to do it alone is unfathomable. Adam has become so enmeshed with my daily life that trying to go back to how it was before him physically hurts. I'm missing part of myself. And not just an appendix or wisdom tooth or something else extraneous, but a vital part. My heart? I already gave it to him anyway. Or maybe my lungs. That would explain why oxygen is hard to come by, why I'm underwater with grief for something that hasn't died yet.

How did I let this happen? Happen *again*. I told myself after Grady I wouldn't lose myself in another person, and I'm all but sobbing on Adam's shirt at the idea of saying goodbye. At the inevitability of going home to an empty bed. I won't be able to watch *Jeopardy!* again because I will miss his commentary. And how am I ever supposed to see this Christmas tree and not just *break* at the sight of it? I should have seen this coming. There was an expiration date on this arrangement from the beginning: just as long as it took for the insurance to come through. I'd started to become thankful it was taking its time.

I'd had that thought about Lovie, hadn't I? Choosing between saying goodbye now and saying goodbye later? There's no right answer. All goodbyes are hard.

We were always going to end, and I only realized it when we got here.

"I should go," I say. There's a small wet spot near his collar, and I hope he doesn't immediately change. That maybe, after

I walk out that door, he will stand with his own palm pressed there and come to the same realization.

"Wait, love," Adam says, but it's halfhearted and weak. And wrong.

All the warmth he's given me over the last few months leaches from my body, and I'm near shivering. I step out of his embrace. "What do you *want* from me, Adam?"

He throws his hands to his sides, but his jaw clenches as he works to stay in control. Even now, he's a fairer fighter than I will ever be. "I want to talk about this with you. Without you running away just because you're *scared*."

I stare at the spot where I dropped my bag that first night. The pictures atop the dresser, stuffed with his clothes. All the places Adam exists now where he didn't before. "If you were on my podcast, what would I say about you? Who would you be?"

"You know me," he says, his entire face tight. He is anguished. "You know the kind of person I am." His palm covers his heart like I wanted, where it beats against his tattooed skin.

It makes mine throb.

I swipe at the trail of wetness on my cheeks. My fingers come away smeared with black. "I know you're good at your job. That you love the people in your life with your entire heart, the way you have it written there. I just—I hate that you don't save any for yourself. That you would rather everyone else in the world achieve their dreams before you ever have to decide what yours are. I think you prefer it that way."

I'm pushing too far, I know, but I want him to push back. Push me away. It's easier if he does it.

"You said you wanted whatever I could give you. But this—this is me. This is all I can give you." I clear my throat, roll my eyes at the ceiling to try to stop my tears. "If I had to head back to the city, get things squared away with insurance, could you handle Lovie full-time? I know you work your other job on weekends, so I'll send someone to cover that. Looks like you got what you wanted after all."

"Elle."

"And don't worry about your contract—I know it was open ended, but I'll make sure they pay you through the end of the month, even after Lovie is moved. Christmas is coming up, after all. And you've got your girls to support." I force myself not to look at the tree on the nightstand.

His jaw ticks. "Elle," he says again.

"And besides, it's not like we were even that ser—"

"*Elle.*" His voice is sharp. His eyes sharper. Adam doesn't say anything else, doesn't finish his sentence, but I know what he's thinking. *We were. We were that serious.*

"If you can"—I clear my throat—"if you can handle Lovie . . . I'll have Angie touch base with you. Lovie likes her well enough, so maybe she can cover the weekend shifts. Otherwise, I—I really need some space."

My skin is too tight, his gaze too direct. I am lying through my teeth, and he knows it.

"Stay," he asks again. *Pleads.*

"I just—can't." I never could, could I? Not when love was on the line.

CHAPTER FORTY-ONE

I don't listen to music on the train ride back to Chicago, an hour later. Maybe the most telling thing of all.

It took twenty minutes to pack two and a half months' worth of belongings. The other forty is spent forcing myself to schedule a car. I could have just taken Lovie's, but if anyone could get a DUIH (driving under the influence of heartbreak), it would be me.

I only cry when I'm mad and when I absolutely cannot help it—and when I'm head over heels in love with the man I leave behind.

Chicago at Christmastime used to be my favorite, with holiday music spilling out of restaurants and department stores, red buckets with jingling bells on each corner. The hoard of tourists at Millennium Park, skating on artificially frozen ice. Friends shopping together for last-minute gifts, lovers stealing hot chocolate kisses beneath sprigs of mistletoe. Last year I got so excited for the holidays I decorated for Christmas the day after Halloween.

I won't decorate this year. Maybe because this hasn't been my home for a while.

I must be more heartsick than I thought, unable to stomach the idea of entering my apartment alone just because I shared it with Adam for twelve hours and some change.

By the time I get to my apartment, a familiar face greets me so I don't have to.

I fall into Dakota's waiting arms, and he tucks my head under his chin.

"I brought so much wine," he says. "And tequila. But I wouldn't recommend you mix them unless you're drinking to forget."

He takes most of my luggage from my shoulders before shepherding me inside. "Liss is grabbing pizza."

My lip trembles. Adam made pizza here.

"And more wine, apparently," Dakota mutters.

Inside my apartment, I sit down right on the foyer floor and pull off my boots, one, two. They thud to the hardwood, bounce and echo in my brain as Dakota deposits my bags on the kitchen table.

"Here," he says. He's holding out a glass of chilled red wine. He must have come prepared.

Wine before three in the afternoon is pushing it, even for me. Whatever. I am heartbroken and shit.

I take a sip.

"This is good," I say, before throwing back the entire glass and helping myself to another.

He snorts from his sentinel at the fridge, where he's offloading not only junk food but also green leafy vegetables and fresh eggs. "It better be, for five hundred dollars a bottle."

I nearly tip it over as I scramble to my feet. *"Five hundred dollars?"*

He shuts the fridge with his hip. "It's from Brody Boswell. A thank-you gift for all the wedding stuff Liss is doing."

I read the label more intently. "I'm in the wrong business. Do you think it's too late for me to play professional baseball?"

"Just barely," Dakota says dryly. "But maybe you could try podcasting? I have a feeling you'd be good at that."

"Wowww," I say slowly, slumping into a dining chair. I pull my knee up to my chest and rest my chin on it. These are the nice deep dining chairs where people with big thighs can do that. "Aren't you supposed to give me some super-sage life advice that has me crawling back to him with my tail between my legs?"

He laughs. "If it were me, we'd just end up staring at pictures of his triceps. I think if you want some actual advice, you're going to need to wait for Liss."

"Can I call your nana, then? She seems like a nice lady who wants to listen to all my problems. And she has the three boyfriends, after all."

Dakota looks pained. "Liss was right behind us, I swear."

The first communion I took when I was thirteen must still be in effect (probably strengthened by the wine), because as if summoned by God and all His angels, the door rattles as someone messes with the handle on the other side.

"Here! I'm here! I'm sorry!" Liss slings pizza boxes onto the table before dumping her purse and other bags on the counter Dakota just cleaned off. She pulls out a to-go box from the bakery, a child-sized loaf of French bread, and another bottle of wine. She's frazzled in the way Liss always is, blonde hair creating a wild halo around her head, and the sight of her is enough to start a fresh round of tears. I thought they all dried out on the train.

Just another thing I got astronomically wrong.

I sniffle. "You got the good bread."

Liss's rosy cheeks pull up into a sad smile. Or maybe that's a grimace. This is some *nice* wine Mr. Boswell sent. "Dakota said it was an all-carbs-on-deck situation. Is he wrong?"

"*Never*," Dakota says, affronted. "But also, no."

Liss comes around the table toward me, clutches my shoulders. "You wanna talk about it?"

I shake my head, and it's so violent a tear flies off and lands on her arm. "I just want to drink."

So we do.

As promised, they don't force me to talk about anything. We play a card game that has us all crying—happy tears this time. Dakota is surprisingly, pleasingly bad at it. He loses. We drain both bottles of wine dry and crack open a third. The pizza and bread are demolished. So are the cake and ice cream.

With all of us too wine drunk and sugar high to bother being real adults, Dakota says to leave the dishes for the morning and passes out unceremoniously on the couch.

When Liss and I eventually pull ourselves back down the hall toward my bedroom, I catch myself on the doorframe. Adam might have made the bed the morning we left, but I know we didn't change the sheets. The skin around my eyes is tight with salt water, and the fresh tears sting. "They're going to smell like him, Liss. The sheets."

Her eyes well with a lifetime of empathy. She feels my pain as much as her own. Her heart is the biggest. "Are we changing them?"

"Yes," I say, before I can think about it too greatly. "I need him gone."

So we change the sheets. The fresh ones end up with a few tearstains polka-dotting the fabric anyway. They're cold when I slide into them.

"Are you gonna be okay?" Liss's cheek is on my shoulder, the heat from her wine-flushed face doing little to warm me up.

"Yes," I say before I know if it's the truth. "I'm always okay."

"It would also be okay," she says, her mouth quirking into a frown, "if you weren't."

Fake It Like You Mean It

"Hey," I say. "Do you think when you're happily married to the man of your dreams, we can still have sleepovers like this?"

"Whoa," she says, sitting up. Her hand goes to her head. "*Whoa*," she says again. "Okay, I'm good. And, obviously. He's not the man of my dreams if there's no room for you."

Now I sit up, and my head spins in that super-bad drunk way. "Whoa."

She points at me. "Right?" We laugh together, a few easy moments between all of the hard ones of today, of life in general. "I just assumed we'll be having sleepovers until we're like, in the nursing home or whatever. Pick cemetery plots next to each other. We should maybe look into booking those, by the way? I hear they might run out of space soon."

"Yeah, well. I've been assuming a lot these days, and you know what they say about assuming." I scrub my face, throw up my hands. Fist them into the blankets so I don't cover my face and cry.

Liss reaches into the mess of duvet and grabs my hands, and my traitorous eyes water anyway. "That you probably weren't assuming anything at all, and the feelings were there, and you just got scared and ran away. Because I know you, and I saw him, and I saw the way he looked at you."

Too many feelings. Too much wine. Too little Adam.

I grab a pillow from behind us and throw it at her head. "Go to sleep. I drank too much to talk about this."

She takes the pillow from me and lies down, humming. "He looked at you the way I look at chocolate cake."

I squeeze my eyes shut, taste my heartbeat on the back of my tongue. "Good night, Liss."

* * *

She stays for two days.

We eat takeout and watch trashy reality television while she touches up my roots with ill-advised box dye. She daringly adds one single streak to the underside of her hair in solidarity. Every night she sleeps in my bed, and I wake up next to her, but I may as well be alone. This apartment is empty without him. Hollow.

I know now what Lovie meant by lonely and horny being different emotions. I don't miss Adam for the things he can do to my body; I miss him for the way he makes me feel inside it. Steady. Sure. Warm.

Angie has been filling in my role caring for Lovie. According to her, Lovie hasn't mentioned Bobby once since I've been gone. I wonder if my grandmother herself notices something different.

I keep tabs on *Forget Me Not*, post on a consistent basis from the backlog I built while in Elkhart. People still love it. I still search comments for his name.

And some days I think what we had could have even been *enough*, if there weren't other factors in our lives. We'd become confined by our circumstances, and when we found someone worth breaking the chains for, they'd already grown over and embedded in our skin.

Somewhere along the way I picked up an all-or-nothing mentality with love, the same way I've handled my podcast and my friendships and my stubbornness. I have no setting for *in between*, and that's the space Adam fits in. In between now and forever. Which is, really, nothing and nowhere at all.

CHAPTER FORTY-TWO

I'm washing dishes the week before Christmas when the call comes in.

I wasn't expecting to hear from Angie until after the holidays, when we'd know more about the options Lovie has for treatment facilities and when a spot might open for her.

She was vague on the phone, just kept requesting my presence at Lovie's house, which made me want to throw up. I couldn't ask if he was there—I'd hardly gotten used to saying his name to Liss and Dakota, and they'd witnessed my entire embarrassing descent down the Stairway to Hell (I mean, Love).

As I climb out of the Lyft now, I already know Adam isn't here. His car isn't in the driveway. The colors of the siding aren't as bright. The inside is oppressive instead of comforting.

It's louder than normal when I walk in, a telenovela playing in the living room. I slip off my shoes at the door. A habit I will never break.

Angie is at the table, a thick book of paperwork in front of her. My stomach sinks like a stone, and if I'm a little shaky, that must be ripples from the drop. I try to focus on her, but all I can stare at are the places Adam used to take up and doesn't anymore. By the stove, the doorways, where he'd do his lean-and-cross routine until my insides were the same. How long has it been since he was here? A week? Two? He wouldn't have bolted out the door—not like I did.

"Where's Lovie?" I ask.

Angie clasps her hands in front of her. "There have been some developments," she says, holding important eye contact. She's trying to say more with that than her words.

Fear seizes my chest, my limbs turning leaded. Why did I *ever* leave? I can't get enough air. "Did she—is she—"

Her eyes soften. "No, honey. Lovie's fine."

On fawn-like legs, I stumble and collapse into a chair. I grip the edge with shaking fingers.

If Angie's waiting for me to say something, she's going to be waiting a while. I still can't get enough air. I nod feebly.

She scoots a pamphlet in my direction, the edges getting caught in one of the table's grooves. "There's a place in Osceola that can take Lovie next week."

I glance at it, unseeing. "It looks really nice," I say. Colors. Text. Graphics. It all blurs together into a whirling pulse in front of my eyes. "I bet she'll love it."

At her dry, sardonic laugh, the bind around my rib cage eases a little, and I let out a slow chuckle of my own. "Okay, she'll hate it. But if it's what's best for her, then it's what she needs."

Her head tilts. "Elle."

"Yes," I say, squeezing my eyes shut. I can handle this, being back here. This was my home before it was ever his.

Another pause, and then she says, "Lovie is herself today. Lucid."

My breath hitches. "What? Where is she?"

I'm out of the chair so fast it tips backward, landing on the floor with a crash. My heart is a bass drum in my ear.

I slide the patio door open, and there she is.

The space heater's going, but there's a thick plaid blanket stretched across her lap and another draped on her shoulders. I haven't seen her eyes this bright in years.

"Oh, Ellie, there you are. Was wondering when you were going to show up. All Miss Angie in there wants to talk about is health care. Who needs to listen to that shit?" She smiles up at me, her finger marking her place in her puzzle book. "Those are cute pants. Are they new? I don't think I've seen them before."

Lovie.

My Lovie.

My eyes burn, the skin under them tight from the salt water. "I missed you," I tell her, and she reaches up, cups my face the way she did when I was younger. When *she* was younger. I sit gingerly on the bench seat beside her. She slides half the blanket over me and tucks me into her side. The moment stretches forever and is over in an instant.

"I didn't go anywhere," she says, and her mouth pinches. "But I guess that's not true, is it?"

I let my head fall to her shoulder, let my burdens fall at her feet. "You weren't exactly the same, no." Each of my words is dipped in disbelief and hesitation. "You were *mean*," I say, and a spit bubble pops the seriousness of this conversation.

We burst into laughter, clutching each other with everything we're worth, all we have. This may be the first time this has happened, but there's no guarantee it won't also be the last. I couldn't care less about the podcast right now, about saving these memories anywhere else besides in my heart.

That's where they matter most.

"I love you." I curl into her side, take in the sweet scents of comfort and home. "I love you, and I missed you, and I don't know how to—how to do this without you, Lovie." My voice breaks off on her name.

Her arms tighten around my shoulders, shielding me from wind and hurt. She's always been better at holding up my armor than I have. She hums in thought. "Don't know *how* to do this without me, or don't want to?"

Fear scrambles my gut, makes all my limbs loose. "I don't want to have to. I'm not—I'm not as good at this as you were."

"Good at what?" She laughs, kisses my freshly red hair. "*Life*? Oh, Ellie. Life isn't meant to be easy. Nobody makes it out alive."

"If anybody could," I choke out, "you'd be the first."

We have so many things to catch up on.

But she's Lovie, and like that chip in the china and all the times I broke curfew, somehow, she already knows.

She pulls back. "So. Tell me about this man. Adam, if I remember correctly?"

I groan. It hurts to hear his name, but not as badly when she says it.

"Tell me," she urges, softer, yet firmer.

"Adam is . . . intuitive, perceptive. And sarcastic. And *cross*." I smile, the emotion snagged between sadness and fondness. "He looks like Bobby."

She smiles, her chin on her shoulder. "And you look like me. Red hair and all. No wonder I was so nasty to you."

I eye her white-blonde bedhead. "What do you mean?"

"When I met Bobby," she says slowly, "when we got married, I . . . I wasn't in love with myself yet. I hated my body, thought I was too much, too loud, too front and center. I think seeing you take up so many of those characteristics now, when I'm like *this* . . . it must have gotten to me in a way I wasn't expecting. Subconsciously. We age backward near the end, remember."

The filter over my memory switches to a different color. All the times Lovie hated me, commented on my body and my too-loud mouth—it was never about me at all. It was about her this entire time. I really *was* Lovie, through her very own eyes.

"That was never part of the stories you told me."

She squeezes my knee again. Even her grip is surer today. "I really didn't give it up until about . . . twenty-seven years ago, when a little hellion with freckles lost her parents and came to live with me."

"*Oh*," I breathe.

"I *never* wanted to hear you talk about yourself the way I talked to my own reflection. I wanted you to wake up every single day thinking you were strong. Be allowed to take up space, demand more when you need it, even if the room's too crowded. And you *do*, Elle." She pulls back. Her eyes flicker between mine. The band of her wedding ring is cool against my hand, and I rub my own thumb over it, the way she does when she's nervous or needs comfort this world can't give. Water pools in the bottom of her eyes.

"You know who taught me how to do all of that?" I say. Wind whips at our hair, the blanket, but I don't feel the sting.

She gives me a wobbly, close-lipped smile. "Who?"

"You." A few tears slip free as I return her expression. It's closer to a grimace, but the intention is there.

"Well." She quirks her lips, holding back tears.

"How much do you remember?" I ask. "About the last few months."

"It's a little like a dream. Remember feelings more than specific days or things, but I think I owe you an apology. I couldn't forget that, ever."

A vigorous shake of my head has those loose tears sliding haphazardly down my chin and neck. "You don't owe me *anything*."

The silence settles between us, and like Lovie said, I try to focus on feelings of this moment rather than the memories themselves. The few birds that have held out despite the chill of winter chirp in the sycamore against the back fence. The smell of the flower beds, which are packed high with new dirt and freshly watered, because she still hasn't given up on them, even if the world has given up on her. Her hands, that should be fragile but are strong because they held this house together. For a long time, she held me together too. She's doing that now, the way her arms are around me.

And isn't the best part of any memory how it makes us feel when we remember it?

"You love him," Lovie says, splintering the quiet. "Adam."

"How'd you know?" I twist my fingers in the blanket. "If you don't remember the specifics."

The bench groans beneath us as she takes my face between her wrinkled, trembling hands. "Love is part of being human, Elle. The *best* part. It's ingrained in our skin and bones... etched onto our souls. We don't forget that easily, no matter how hard we try."

I clutch her forearms, giving her some of my strength. Taking some of hers for myself. "Is that one of Lovie's Hard Love Rules?"

"The very first," she says. "The most important."

* * *

Lovie starts to prepare for her lunchtime nap, but not before I hug her tight enough to crack her spine.

"Easy, girl," she says. "You're stronger than you think you are." I think she means it in more ways than one.

I stop at her wedding photo in the hallway. There's a fingerprint on the glass above their wedding rings, and I pull my sleeve over my hand to wipe it clean.

With Lovie moving to a new facility, what will become of this house? Selling it isn't an option, not when most of my best memories took place within these walls. It'd be nice to see more children grow up here, the way I did. Make their own

Fake It Like You Mean It

memories in the pink bathroom, run more grooves into the laminate, put bigger dents in the walls. Then again, it might not last another generation. So much life has been lived in this house. Maybe I'll turn it into a rental in the spring, when there's time and fresh air to do the updates it will need.

Steeling my spine, I push open the door to my room.

The bed is made. I told Adam during one early-morning conversation—or was it late-night?—that one of my favorite things in life is a freshly made bed, but I also really, truly, can't ever be bothered. He must have adopted the habit on my behalf.

The curtains are tied up, sunlight warming the floors and illuminating dust motes. There are still a few obvious clues we shared this space. Clothes and shoes I forgot to grab before I left are stacked neatly on the dresser, next to packages I'd guess contain the Christmas presents I started ordering. One of them, I know, is for Adam.

Extra pillows line the headboard. Two chargers are plugged in by the bed—he must have forgotten his too. And ohmyeverlovingGod, there's an open box of condoms on the nightstand, shoved back behind the miniature Christmas tree.

Someone coughs politely from the doorway. Angie. I hope she drank decaf this morning. That somehow she misses all these glaring signs, even though they're screaming at me.

My hope dies quickly. It takes two seconds to know she's seen everything. Her eyebrows are raised high on her forehead, her mouth pulled into a firm, disappointed line.

"I've got to say," she starts, turning that curious look on me. "A few more things make sense now."

"Angie, I—"

She holds up a hand. "I don't need to hear details, but I do need to know if you think this has impacted your ability to care for your grandmother."

She's never taken this tone with me. It's so jarring, I can't answer with anything but the truth. "Yes."

She nods once, her gaze weighted, like her words. Like my stomach. "And Adam? Did it affect his ability?"

I don't hesitate. "No. Adam would never"—*let me get in the way of his job*—"make that mistake."

The television still blares from the living room, and every few seconds one of Lovie's snores breaks through the stagnancy. But in here, the air is suspended. Seconds stretch to eternities in this limbo.

"Adam is, as of this morning, no longer employed with AngelCare," she says.

Something hot twists in my gut.

"You can't fire him," I choke, panic rising in my bloodstream. "He needs this. He takes care of his sister, his nieces. They're so sweet. Cora and Chloe and Claire. I usually hate matching names, but they're just . . . amazing, honestly, and I don't care if it ruins everything with insurance or ethics or what, but Angie, he *needs* this job." My breaths are raspy, uneven, and not working all that well. My head is spinning. Maybe I'm still hungover from that $500 bottle of wine. Then again, for $500 a bottle, it probably comes with a magical hangover cure. Not to mention I drank it weeks ago.

Then, Angie does something completely unexpected. She laughs. A full belly-shaking, shoulders-hunching, tears-streaming kind of laugh.

This is not the time. "You have to call him. I told him you'll keep paying him through the holidays while we transition everything. You said it'd take another week, right, to get Lovie settled? I'll leave if that's what it takes. But he has to stay."

"I'm not laughing because it's ridiculous." She lays a hand on my shoulder, the set of her eyes sharp enough to kill someone. Even as she smiles. "I'm laughing because I didn't fire Adam." Her eyes glimmer with something I can't read. If she were Adam, I'd be able to tell what she felt based on the set of her shoulders, the slope of her smile. "He quit."

CHAPTER FORTY-THREE

"He *what?*"

Angie crosses her arms. Her purple scrubs tug tight across her generous chest. "He turned in his resignation a week ago. Said it was becoming a conflict of interest."

An incredulous laugh slips from my lips, and I sink back onto the made-up bed. "What exactly does *that* mean?" I laugh again, more air than anything else. "What situations would make something a conflict of interest?"

She purses her lips. Her smile still shows through. "Any situation where he stands to gain something personal from a situation that comes up in his professional life. A vested interest beyond the regular job description."

I nod absently, watching the dust dance in front of my eyes. "Struggling to see the issue, to be honest."

"When your heart's on the line," she says simply, "you tend to get sloppy."

"His heart's not on the line." That was the entire problem.

She *hmm*s. "Okay. Sure." She sees herself out, but I'm still on the bed, staring at nothing. This doesn't make sense.

Megan Murphy

Adam is the most selfless person I know. He's the one who taught me that if you're required to give up pieces of yourself for love, it isn't love at all. *Love is supposed to make you more yourself, not less.*

That's exactly what I asked him to do, though, isn't it? I begged him to leave his carefully crafted life behind just to try to fit him into mine. I saw it as our only option, because that's how I've always operated. By myself, considering no one's feelings but my own. All or nothing. My way or no way.

I look at the Christmas tree, yet another selfless gesture he made while expecting nothing in return. From my seated position, I notice something new tucked under the lowest branches. There's a small box, wrapped in red-and-green-striped paper. I pull it out. My name is on the tag, in Adam's messy all-caps scrawl. The back reads:

ELLE,

WAS SAVING THIS FOR CHRISTMAS, BUT IT TURNS OUT WE DON'T HAVE THAT LONG. HOPEFULLY THIS ONE WON'T GIVE YOU BPA POISONING. CREAMER'S IN THE FRIDGE.

I'M SORRY.

LOVE,
ADAM

I rip the paper, the box falling into my trembling hands.

It's a butterfly mug, exactly like the one I've used since I was seven. Except this one is ceramic, kiln-fired pottery. The coloring is similar, cartoonish purple and pink. The handle is wing shaped. This was handmade, with love, care, and attention. I flip it over, looking for a brand or artist's name.

Instead, there are three little *C*s carved into the base.

Fake It Like You Mean It

Clutching it to my heart alongside Adam's note, I try not to fall apart.

It's too late for that, though. I knew I fell a while ago.

I jump up, tearing into the packages on the dresser, searching for the right one. I break two nails and slice my thumb on the cardboard. When I find what I'm looking for, I rip the Christmas tree from the nightstand, the cord dancing around my ankles as I shoot for the front door.

Lovie is standing beside it, her car keys waiting in her palm.

CHAPTER FORTY-FOUR

Adam Wheeler is a hard man to track down.

I have half a mind to drive to Goshen, start knocking on random apartment doors until I find his. There's a search for "LTAC facilities near me" in my internet history.

I roll up to a stop sign, taking a few seconds to catch my breath. The Christmas tree is buckled into Lovie's passenger seat.

Or mine, I guess. As I was walking out the door, she told me just to keep the car, that she didn't need it where she was going. Which sounded incredibly morbid for 0.2 seconds, before she and Angie started laughing and explained residents of memory care homes absolutely *do not* get cars on campus. How very college freshman of them.

"Think, Elle." My fingers are tight on the steering wheel, but not from fear.

Or maybe it is. Fear that I've ruined a good thing—the *best* thing—and that I am simply too late.

I roll out my shoulders, crank up my Queens playlist, and make my last-ditch effort.

With a small nod, he lowers the cardboard boxes to rest against his leg.

He's not the type of person who tries not to tear the wrapping, which I appreciate in my current state. He crumples it in his fist, shoving it in his coat pocket before pulling the lid off.

Adam looks at me, confused, then at the neatly folded scrubs nestled inside the tissue paper.

"You wear this color the most," I say. "I figured that meant they were your favorite, so I got you another pair." I shrug, adding halfheartedly, "I don't care where you wash them."

"Elle, I—" Something catches his eye over my shoulder, and he cuts himself off.

I turn and get a flash of three faces shoved into the window. Ruth and Cora and Chloe. The curtain flutters as they pull back.

I shiver.

"God, you're not even wearing a coat," Adam says. He's already shrugging out of his.

Because I think maybe Adam Wheeler is in love with me too. It's in the way he clutches the gift in his hand, pulls his coat closed around me and avoids touching me at the same time. The way he says my name. How he removes his scarf and twirls it around my neck.

"I'm pretty good at memorizing train schedules," I say. "But Lovie just sort of gave me her car? It's probably time I conquered my fear of driving anyway. I made an appointment for therapy about it."

His chapped lips part.

I sniffle, fight against the chill in the air. "I . . . I run away. When things get hard. I leave at the first hint of trouble, which is a problem when you find someone worth staying for."

His eyes are unreadable under his drawn-tight brows. The tip of his nose is red. Ears too. How did I ever think I wouldn't fall in love with him?

Megan Murphy

From the wind or from emotion, a tear slips down my cheek. I don't rush to wipe it away. The crisp breeze dries it onto my cheek. "I don't want to run anymore." I shrug. It stirs the scent of him around me. And I can breathe just a little easier. "It's not fair to myself. To anyone I run from. To *you*. I should have never asked you to leave like that. I'm so sorry, Adam."

One of Lovie's Hard Love Rules is to always look someone in the eye when you apologize, so I do just that as I lift a shoulder toward the house behind us. "You said those girls in there are yours. So that makes them a package deal. If you're mine, they're mine too. And if you give me time, and a hell of a lot of patience, I will love them like you do. I think I could be a really fun Auntie Elle."

I'm shivering. I lick moisture back into my lips, then bite my tongue so I don't keep talking.

I can't read him for once. I wish he'd do something familiar. Lean, quirk his eyebrow, kiss me, *something*.

But as he stays quiet, doubt worms its way through my brain. Each second of silence punches a hole in my heart. More tears break free. Which is okay. I don't have to run from emotions just because they're uncomfortable.

"Lovie was probably wrong anyway." I blink a few more tears loose, surprisingly calm. "She said she thought you—well, it doesn't matter."

"*Lovie*," Adam murmurs, brows gathering. "Lovie is *lucid*?"

"Yes? I mean, maybe not still, but she was when—"

He hugs me. So hard it almost knocks me off my feet. I kick the Christmas tree over, and the moving boxes scatter into the driveway as I enjoy being in his arms again. He pulls back, his hands on my upper arms. "I just . . . I hoped you'd get another chance to talk to her. The woman I met isn't who raised you. I know that." He snags his lower lip with his canine. "Was she okay?"

"More than okay." I suppress a smile, because there's still space for this to backfire. "She had some interesting things to say about the two of us, actually. She was under the impression that I'm in love with you."

Someone bangs the windowpane. "Speak up!"

"Be *quiet*, Ruth," Adam shouts. His eyes are on the ground, how the toes of my boots are nearly touching his. His cheeks are cherry red to match his ears.

"Tell your girlfriend to speak up, then!" Ruth shouts back. "You two are giving the girls a lesson in how to grovel."

A squeak of laughter escapes from my lips at Adam's pained expression, and I forget for a second that I am, in fact, meant to be groveling.

"She was right, you know," I say.

Adam shivers, and I unwind some of the scarf to drape it back around his neck. It is the perfect amount of stretch. The move brings us even closer, which was not strategic but is a bonus.

His mouth quirks sideways. "My sister?"

"Lovie," I say, then raise my voice so everyone can hear it, loud and clear. "I am very much in love with you, Adam Wheeler, and I think the reason you quit is because you're in love with me too. Maybe I was one of your 'once in a whiles,' but you're my 'once in a lifetime.'"

Our breaths curl and mingle in the space between us before disappearing.

If he doesn't love me—or even if he does but he's not ready for things to change—I will still be glad I came here today.

He clears his throat, his expression unreadable. "Ask me about the boxes, Elle."

My fingers are numb. My entire body. Some weather we're having. "What about the boxes, Adam?"

He pulls his phone from his pocket. His thumb flies over the screen before he hands it to me. I almost drop it from the cold, how much I'm shaking.

"I got a new place," he says. "Not in the city, but it's close. I can't quite afford Chicago. In case you haven't heard, I quit one of my jobs recently?" Adam tenses his jaw, but there's a gravity to it that makes me think he's trying not to smile.

Cold air rushes my lungs, tugs at our shared scarf. "I thought you were moving in here."

He holds up the gift box, top and bottom pieces held together in his massive hand. And then he shakes his head, lets the box drop to the frozen ground, and totes me against his body. When I gasp this time, he's there to fill my lungs. The summer-warm scent he's always had, stronger after going without.

"Why would I do that?" he says. "You're not here."

Adam, my pulse hums. *Adam. Adam. Adam.* How long has my heart been beating his name?

He licks his lips, eyes unfocused as he searches for the right words. I have no doubt he'll find the perfect ones.

"I've spent the last few weeks trying to figure out a way to make this work, us in two places." His eyes darken. "I realized a week ago that it just wasn't going to. Because you left, Elle, you ran away. But I didn't come after you. And my heart is going to be wherever you are. In Chicago or London or Timbuktu. I can keep up." He winks. "I'm a runner too."

My jaw drops.

"Do you know," Adam says, smiling in full now, "before I ever even met you, I saw your picture in Lovie's house—one of you hanging in the hall. You had scabby knees and gap teeth and these big brown eyes. A zest for life that didn't fit in the picture. I felt you right here, like an arrow." He takes my hand and holds it to his heart. "I thought if I ever got a chance to meet you, I'd fall in love with you on the spot, and it would wreck me."

Fake It Like You Mean It

I sniffle. Not because I'm crying this time, but because the wind chill is zero degrees and I'm starting to feel it, even through his divine-smelling coat. "And did you? Fall in love with me?"

Beneath my palm, his heart thuds. Steadily, but hard. The same way I love him. "Yes."

A laugh flies from my lips, and my insides turn to liquid gold. "And did I wreck you?"

"God, yes," he says, so passionately he sounds anguished.

Then his wind-chapped hands are on my face, thumbs rubbing warmth into my cheeks, and one slips to twine in my already messy hair, and he kisses me. The sound he makes when our lips connect is enough to light me on fire, in this frigid weather and without kindling. It rumbles down his chest, through my fingertips, clutching him. My lips buzz. My soul hums.

He was right. We're going to have to figure this out. I'm probably going to try to run again. But that's the thing about love. It isn't geographic; it's intrinsic. Like Lovie said, it weaves its way into our body, sometimes so fast we don't even know until it's too late. So intricately we can never come undone.

I nod, tiptoe to kiss him again. "Invite me inside?"

"With my family here?" He tsks in his throat, then bends to bite the hinge of my jaw. "You're relentless."

"To get warm," I correct, unable to stop my smile. They're all his, anyway. "We have some things to talk about."

* * *

@ElleontheL ✅*: The final episode of* Forget Me Not *is live! This week I sit down with guest Nurse Adam Wheeler (@NurseAdamIndy) about our shared experience caring for Lovie. This was the most personal, enlightening journey I've been on, and I share everything I've learned. Plus, I share the complete compiled list of Lovie's Hard Love Rules, and our final donation amount, as of Monday morning. Spoiler alert:* 🐢

Megan Murphy

@DFWMama6: *I SOBBED in carpool listening to this. What a beautiful ending.*
@Graciepowww36: *screaming crying throwing up. Mostly crying tho.*
@allthatgl!ttersxoxo: *a gut-wrenching, honest ending. starting the series again now so they can get more $$*
@thatguy3k00: *This was not the ending I was expecting, and I'm surprised to find I didn't absolutely hate it.*
    @ElleontheL ✓: *I knew I'd get you to listen one of these days 😊 so glad you enjoyed.*
    @thatguy3k00: *What do you mean? I listen every week.*

                    Show more replies

@SweetiesCakesChicago: *@CubsWifeKatija this is my friend's podcast I was telling you about at the tasting! Bring tissues.*
@DMillsBakes: *Love that you and Lovie both got some closure to your story.*

                 Show 1,540 more comments

EPILOGUE

Five Months Later

"Stop screaming," Adam grunts, red in the face. His breathing is heavy, harsh, pulls his well-defined chest taut. There's sweat dotting his brow, like I've worked him too hard.

"No!" I shout, wheezing an extra, "I won!"

"Only because I thought you tripped." He's playfully angry, with the slash of his eyebrows and downturn of his mouth. He is completely unamused by me. And completely obsessed with me.

The feeling is mutual.

Adam and I have a new sort of routine now that Lovie is safe and sound in her full-time care facility. Parts of it are the same as they were: Adam trolls my trolls on social media, puts Band-Aids on whatever injuries I give myself trying to cook dinner or tackle home improvement projects well above my skill level.

But we're different now too: I'm back in the city, and in therapy twice a month. *Forget Me Not* reached its natural conclusion when Lovie got placed in her facility, although I still pop in and give updates as necessary, for better or for worse.

Adam has a new place, an hour or so away by the hospital where he works. Exactly one hour between his family in Elkhart and me in Chicago. He has seven more months on his lease, and he already decided he won't be renewing it. I'm not sure yet whether he'll move into my apartment or if we'll find something else together. He wants an extra bedroom for when his nieces visit.

Because the beginning of our relationship was so isolated, we're taking our time getting to know each other in the real world. We spend a few nights a week with each other, at his place or mine. Go out for dinner, drinks, dancing. Not to brag, but he *did* kiss me on our first date. (He asked permission.)

And when we can, we run together, through the streets of Chicago. No matter where we start, we end up outside Liss's bakery, ready to consume all the calories we just burned off.

He rolls his eyes playfully at me now, even as he holds the door open for me.

Thirty minutes later, I'm fanning myself with the lid of an empty cake box, stuffed full of Liss's leftovers. "I don't want to look at chocolate for a month."

"I'm going to need a little bit longer than a month." Liss huffs as she licks her lips free of icing and crumbs. "Like, at least the summer." With a sigh, she drops her head to the tiny bistro-sized table in the corner of the shop. I think it's here just for our visits.

Adam's hand creeps from my lower back, down toward my ass. "Do you have a lot of business booked so far this summer?"

Dakota's eyes go alarmingly wide. "Oh, God. We're quadruple-booked almost every weekend. Which wouldn't be so bad if we had a semifunctional kitchen."

"Don't talk about the kitchen like that," Liss groans, rocking her head back and forth on her forearm. "The appliances will start an uprising."

"Complete anarchy," Adam agrees, pinching my butt.

* * *

My grandmother doesn't remember me the next day.

Even with around-the-clock care, Lovie's distant most days, unable to remember the name of the nurses who bring her breakfast every morning. I make the drive twice a week to come see her. Adam comes with me when he can, but today it's just me.

As Lovie stares absently out the window and spins her wedding ring, I tidy up her pictures, clear them of dirt and fingerprints. The one of her and Grandpa Bobby—the one that started everything—sits on her bedside table, where she can see it every night. The scrapbook of my successes sits beside it. It needs less and less tidying each time. I check her puzzle book stash, making a mental note to bring her a fresh one next week. I sit with her, tell her about my life, the podcasts.

About Adam, and how I have her to thank for him.

And when I kiss Lovie on the forehead in goodbye, she makes a little hum of acknowledgment. It doesn't reach her eyes. It still hurts, but not as much. This is the *best* place she could be. My guilt ebbs and flows at that. Today it's a stream-like trickle through my consciousness as I leave her again.

After, I head to meet Adam's sister and nieces at Lovie's house. Or their house, rather.

I decided to rent out Lovie's magical pink house after all. It was Adam's idea, of course, to see if Ruth would be interested in a safer neighborhood with a bigger yard and free maintenance.

They moved in a few months ago and have already added to the character of the place. The girls share the second bedroom, the one that used to be mine.

Megan Murphy

They greet me at the door as always. Usually, Cora is begging to live stream on my Instagram while Chloe pleads to wear my shoes, but I never let them without supervision. Turns out being the cool aunt doesn't mean giving the kids free rein. Who would've thought?

Today, though, they're searching every inch of me with observant eyes. "Where is it?" and "Can we see?" and "Did it hurt?" are given in place of normal greetings, and I slip out of my boots by the door. Old habits die hard.

"Okay, okay," I say. "Here, let's go into the living room."

The first thing to go when Ruth and the girls moved in here was that God-awful rose-patterned couch. In its place is a new kid-proof sectional, a housewarming gift from Adam and me. It sleeps *much* better than those benches in Union Station. I know, because on the off chance I end up crashing here after too much wine, it becomes my bed.

"Hey," Ruth calls from the laundry room. I showed the girls the loop a month ago, and it's their new favorite game to run it. Ruth's already used it three times to get them worn out before bedtime. "I found more of your socks behind the dryer. Still no pairs yet."

"Auntie Elle," Chloe says, tugging on my jeans. "*Show us.*"

"Ahem," Ruth yells.

"Show us *please*," Chloe amends.

Grinning at the twins, I roll up my sleeve to expose my left forearm. It's been about a week, so it's not tender anymore, but the ink is still vivid and fresh. Adam went with me, and I was proud I only cursed twice. A little bunch of forget-me-nots, four inches end to end, sits there. I decided on it the day I moved Lovie into her new facility, and it felt so right I booked the consultation before I left the parking lot.

"So pretty," Cora says, going to run a featherlight fingertip along the edges. She hesitates, her eyes full of concern, so much like Adam's. "Will I hurt you?"

"Go for it. If you rub here," I say, demonstrating, "you can feel the ink."

She and Chloe reach there at the same time. "*Whoa*," Chloe says. "I want a tattoo."

"Easy, chick," Ruth says. "Let's get you to middle school before you start getting tatted."

"It's like the flowers in Lovie's garden," Cora says absently, circling her index finger around one of the blue buds.

A chill runs up my spine. Ruth is so reasonable with the thermostat I know it can't have been a draft. "What'd you say?"

"This looks like the flowers in the garden." Cora continues running her finger over the tattoo, oblivious to the skyrocketing pulse in my wrist a few inches away. "Claire likes to play in them, but Mom won't let her because she gets so messy."

I look at Ruth. "There are flowers in the garden?"

"Uh, yeah?" Her forehead creases between her eyebrows. "Didn't you plant them?"

I head toward the patio door. Because, no. I *didn't* plant them.

This shouldn't be possible. Lovie planted those seeds in mid-October in northern Indiana, in the middle of a frost.

But yet—

I gasp when they come into view. Little forget-me-nots, exactly like the ones I have on my skin forever. The ones my grandmother spent every day tending to, watering. Looking after them, the way she's always looked after me.

"Hey," Ruth says, leaning on the still-open patio door. "Everything okay?"

I nod, gaze locked on the flowers. "I didn't think anything ever grew in this garden."

She studies me curiously but ultimately decides to leave it untouched. "Do you want a drink? I know you saw Lovie today."

Megan Murphy

I give the flowers one long, final glance. But something tells me they will still be here the next time I need them. "I wouldn't say no to some wine," I say. "I'll help with dinner."

We go inside, her wrestling away the remote from Claire before she hides it again. Adam will join us once he gets off work, and together we will head back to his place for the night. For now, the girls run the kitchen-hallway-laundry loop and show me their most recent school assignments hanging on the fridge, and Ruth and I discuss taking a family trip to a Michigan beach for the girls' summer vacation. By the time Adam comes in, fresh flowers for her table and mine, we've got it narrowed down to three cities.

I thought I knew where I belong, the people and places that keep me so well. In Elkhart, I belong. In Chicago, I belong. With Liss and Dakota, I belong. Now, with Adam, with this family, I belong too.

I don't just have happy places anymore. Now I have happy *people* too.

THE END

ACKNOWLEDGMENTS

I wrote a book. And it's been published.

Those are words that six-, ten-, fourteen-year-old Megan wouldn't believe is real life. One of those wishes you don't even know to wish for, because the dream is so outlandish it can't possibly come true.

I've spent my adult life curating my circle, surrounding myself with people who love and care for me unconditionally, and while that starts with God, it expands far beyond Him. This list is by no means exhaustive, but it is so full of adoration and heart that I cried before I ever started writing it (which, if you know me, is very on brand).

My husband, Ethan, for your unending, full-throttle support. For pulling me away from my screen to watch videos of dogs and people falling in love, ideally in the same clip. For supplying me with endless Dr Pepper and words of affirmation. There's no one else I'd rather do this life thing with.

My best friend, Michelle. There's a lot I can say and have said, but in short, this book would not exist without you. I am immeasurably thankful for your friendship, encouragement, and light. Thank you for keeping Ethan busy while I wrote this (but in a friend way and not a sex way). Let's do it again fifty more times.

My parents, Joey, Hannah, and the rest of my family. While I didn't tell most of you I wrote a book until I had an agent, you jumped in headfirst, waiting to catch me at the bottom if I fell. I flew instead, and I have you to thank. PS: I know it's a running joke, but please do not read the laundry room scene. Seriously. Don't.

The Monday night girls. I have never once skipped a meeting to write—without being totally honest about it. And to Grace, Katrina, Ashley, who read the earliest version of this book and told me it was good when it probably still sucked a whole, whole lot. Who lamented with me over querying and publishing when it was a foreign world to all of us.

Isabelle, for sliding into my DMs and demanding we be friends first and critique partners second. For rolling with the punches when I invited myself to your house on the other side of the country. For cheering me on. For lifting me up. Your turn next.

My writing friends Christine, Callie, and Georgia, for your feedback on my work, for being a sounding board when Big Pub makes me want to either throw up or throw in the towel, depending on the day. And above all for your advice, friendship, and love.

Jonlyn, my favorite bookseller, who didn't laugh when I nervously introduced myself as "actually an author" and who has refused to let me go since. And the entire team at A Novel Romance, who are the biggest cheerleaders and boots on the ground for my book. To booksellers and librarians, for fostering my joy of reading from an early age and for fighting the good fight now.

My wonderful agent, Rebeka Finch, for partnering with me in the Wild West that is publishing. For growing my TBR exponentially every time we have a meeting of the Transatlantic Book Club. For talking me off many a ledge. It's only up from here. And to the rest of the Darley Anderson Team, Georgia and Jade and Francesca and Rosanna and everyone behind the scenes, for your tireless work.

My powerhouse editor, Holly Ingraham, for loving my story enough to want the world to love it too. It's a dream to work with you. And the team at Alcove Press, thank you for handling my firstborn with care and consideration. Adam and Elle are in great hands.

The inspiration for this story: My grandfather (Norbert, if you can believe it—but how could you not, that is such a grandpa name). My grandmother, whose house was so magical I wrote a whole book about it. My great-aunt, who taught me people can be more than one thing at any given time.

The medical workers, doctors, nurses, caseworkers, and caregivers who hold lives and hearts and love in your hands every single day.

To you, reader. Adam and Elle have been mine for so, so long, and I'm tickled blue that they're finally yours too. Please keep them safe for me.

And to six-, ten-, fourteen-year-old Megan. We did it. I'm so proud of you.